THE WICKWIRE WATCH

THE WICKWIRE WATCH

THE RIVERFALL CHRONICLES
BOOK I

JACQUELYN HAGEN

MASTMARNER
BOOKS

Edited by Elizabeth Ward.

Cover design by Stuart Bache at Books Covered Ltd.

Map illustration by Luan Bittencourt.

Author photo by Brit Raley.

ISBN: 978-1-958853-00-9 (paperback)

ISBN: 978-1-958853-01-6 (ebook)

Library of Congress Control Number: 2022916387

Published by Mastmarner Books in San Angelo, TX, USA.

jacquelynhagen.com

For Mom.
We're going to have so much to talk about when I get there. I love you.

ERIARIS

THE NORTHERN SEA

Rytram

Masmather

Ban-Geren

Harroway

GULF OF ER HAEN

Vatërra

THE WEST COUNTRY

Orums River

Falls

Sp

Burgess Vall

Watcher's

Ceridwen River

Ramminburn

Camaros Falls

CIRAS

Sedgewick Glen

STALIKOS

Jaston

THE WESTERN SEA

Lockhorn Mountain

Immerton

Green Glade

Orthys

THE SOUTH

Delving

DAMIRAS

FALKIRK BAY

FENMIRE

Ulbright

Gallswell

THE HIGH
COUNTRY

Ostler's Grove

Avery

Billington

High Lake

rous Lake

NORTHCLIFF

Harburg

Anyria River

ORTH COUNTRY

THE EASTERN
SEA

Ashing Mountains

Turesia

Ashing River

Gadham

THE EAST COUNTRY

Cassria

The Blue Cliffs Sparrowhaven

N

Prison

TALAS
SEA

The Boathouse

Lower Ashing River

CALAMOR

PERENHILL

ADYEN
BAY

Westbourne

ARRAVANTIS
(KING'S ISLAND)

Varapalia

Tansey

TRY

YSIRA BAY

THE SOUTHERN
SEA

TABLE OF CONTENTS

1. Edgely Hill — 1
2. Hade Street — 4
3. A Boy Called Ink — 15
4. Sneaking — 22
5. A Most Desirable Thing — 33
6. Never Do That Again — 43
7. Explanation and Further Confusion — 50
8. On the Run Again — 64
9. Infirm in the Infirmary — 70
10. The Worst Shock Yet — 79
11. Spindler's Quandary — 94
12. Riverfall — 102
13. The Prisoners of Paradise — 116
14. The Navigator Returns — 132
15. The Great Hall — 148
16. The Commissioner and His Handkerchief — 160
17. New Friends in High Places — 173
18. Wickwire — 181
19. Drowning Before Breakfast — 189
20. Ink Is Put to Work — 199
21. Reverberations — 207
22. The Saga of Martin and Harriet Whistler — 218
23. Harvest Time — 227
24. Downright Evil — 238
25. Captain Victorious — 249
26. Something to Hope For — 257
27. How to Fall — 268
28. The Raid — 277
29. The Bloody Parade — 290
30. The Weight of the World — 302
31. Momentum — 317
32. Margaret's House — 324
33. A Girl Can't Be Too Careful — 338
34. Whirlwind — 349

35. The Hidden City   360
36. And Great Was the Fall of It   370
37. Watcher's Pass   384
38. Alliance   394
39. Name Your Enemy   412

    Thanks For Reading   423
    Acknowledgments   424
    Weather the Wind   426
    About the Author   429

CHAPTER 1

EDGELY HILL

Had Mr. Bash known this was the night he was going to die, he would have stayed at home. Instead, he found himself toiling up a winding lane with an ache in his back and both knees stiffened by the cold. His labored breaths rose in swirling wisps of vapor, and he amused himself with the idea that they were shreds of his soul stealing away to warmer climates. The wooden cart he pushed squeaked and wobbled, rattling all the half-full boxes of pens and pencils. The sound brought him some comfort for it meant business had been good—thanks mainly to all the children preparing to serve another nine-month sentence in academic imprisonment.

The last half-mile to his home atop Edgely Hill was a lovely hike. Wildflowers and ferns grew along a path which curved through thick clusters of birch and lilac. Crickets and birds chirped and whistled merrily. Blue fireflies circled the tree trunks and weaved in and out of the tall grass, their presence a telltale sign that winter would descend on the country of Eriaris in only a few short months. Mr. Bash was usually delighted with each of these small treasures. At the moment, however, he was too busy struggling to force the cart out of a deepened wheel-rut.

It was bad enough having to fight his way home in the bitter cold like this, but there was something else troubling him. It was a restlessness in the air, a kind of volatile energy, as though a great storm was threatening to unleash at any moment. He looked up into the clear night sky and shivered. Something wasn't right. He gripped the cart tighter and hobbled along at a quicker pace, trying to fill his mind with any other thoughts but these.

Not a moment later, another wave of unholy apprehension passed through him. He froze in the middle of the lane and glanced over his shoulder. The fireflies had disappeared. The birds and crickets fell silent. He hurried forward again, hunching his shoulders up around his ears and sweeping his eyes back and forth across the road until at last the cart crested the hill and a two-story flagstone house came into view. He heaved a sigh of relief.

Once inside, Mr. Bash went straight to the parlor and started a fire in the hearth. This done, he took off his hat, kicked off his boots, and padded to the kitchen where he dumped his coin purse into an old biscuit tin. He lit the stove and stood over the tea kettle as the water heated, letting the steam defrost his red nose and rheumatic fingers.

A few minutes later, he eased into his chair in front of the fire with a warm mug of tea in his hands. As his eyes fell to the numbing sight of the dancing flames, the haunting sense of disquiet and anxiety all but melted away.

It was then he recalled something peculiar. Reaching into the pocket of his waistcoat, he retrieved a small, round piece of glass no bigger than a common spectacle lens. It had given his cart some trouble when the front wheel had stopped up against it on his way into town that morning. At first he'd thought it only a piece of broken bottle half-buried in the mud and had almost tossed it aside. But a second glance had stayed his hand. The glass was a pale shade of blue, thick and warped, rippling out from the center like frozen waves on a pond. A thin line of gold rimmed its edge.

He wasn't usually one for collecting useless trinkets but he had stowed it in his pocket on impulse, quite forgetting it until now.

As he stared at the glass against the flickering firelight, the ripples appeared to move. He touched a finger to its surface.

Suddenly, a faint glow appeared in the center, spreading towards the edges and growing brighter every moment. Then, without warning, the light burst forth like a beacon with a blinding intensity that filled the room. Bash squeezed his eyes shut with a stifled cry of surprise, nearly dropping the thing into his mug. But then, as quick as it had come, the light died away.

He stared at the glass piece with eyebrows knitted together in bafflement. He'd never seen anything like it. Perhaps it was a kind of signaling device. Or maybe part of the machinery of some new invention. Whatever the case, he would put all his resources towards discovering its secrets first thing in the morning. Resolved in this course of action, he closed his fist around the object and returned his gaze to the flames.

His thoughts soon drifted into other matters, a dozen or more trivial things flitting through his head. With the heat of the small fire and the comfort of his armchair, it wasn't long before an indomitable drowsiness crept over him like a heavy fog. His shoulders slumped, his long white beard went into the mug as his head drooped, and he fell fast into a slumber deeper than any he'd ever known.

The next morning, Mr. Bash was dead.

CHAPTER 2

HADE STREET

I t was five o'clock in the morning. John Spindler snapped his pocket watch shut and started towards his corner office on Hade Street. A brief rain shower had made everything slick and gave the air a damp, metallic smell. The gas burned low in the new lanterns scattered throughout town, casting pockets of pale light across the cobblestones. In another half hour the lamplighters would be along to extinguish them, just as the rest of town would begin to wake.

When he had gone a bit farther, he noticed a constable standing on the opposite side of the street, looking his way. Spindler nodded as he approached him.

"Officer Tuppman. Good morning."

The constable raised his lamp for a better look at the man. "Ah, Mr. Spindler. What are you doing out and about before God himself's awake?"

Spindler sighed. "My paper runner fell ill yesterday. I'm picking up his shift."

The anxious frown on the constable's face melted into relief. "Oh, is that all? Couldn't you snag any other urchin to do it? There's plenty standing idle around these parts."

"Yes, but none I trust not to toss all the papers into the river and consider the job done. It's happened before." As he said this, Spindler caught sight of the constable's hand easing away from the pistol on his hip. He raised an eyebrow. "Everything all right?"

"Oh, yes. Just a bit of bother up Edgely Hill earlier on. That's all."

"Really?"

"Old Mr. Bash. Seems his heart gave out on him sometime late last night. Poor chap."

"That's a shame," Spindler replied. "The daily strolls up and down that accursed hill no doubt got the best of him. He was something close to eighty, wasn't he?"

"Something like that," Tuppman answered with a nod. "I always thought him a nice old man. Simple and quiet. Never giving no trouble."

"Nothing out of the ordinary, then?"

"Out of the ordinary? No. No, nothing at all."

Spindler shoved his hands into his pockets and looked both ways down the street. "So . . . why the need for a pistol over an old man having a heart attack?"

The constable stared at him for a moment, his expression growing uneasy. "Well . . . I did hear a thing or two. Slightly odd."

"Mm-hm," Spindler said, feigning disinterest as he scratched the back of his neck.

"Well . . . they were saying . . . and this is all talk, mind you. Nothing confirmed."

"Of course."

The constable looked up and down the street himself, then took a step closer. "Something was found in his house. I don't know what exactly. But it was something that led 'em to believe Bash might've been . . ."

Spindler frowned, watching the constable's face pale as he struggled to continue.

"That is to say, I-I heard them mention the word . . ." He faltered again and glanced away. "Oh, I can't even say it."

"Well mercy's sake, man, what was he?" Spindler said. "A serial murderer? A treasonist?"

"Worse," the constable answered in a grim tone. "Much worse."

He leaned in closer and lowered his voice.

"A Colonist."

Spindler's expression froze in astonishment, his breath catching in his throat. A hundred questions filled his mind all at once but he couldn't find the voice to speak them.

"Now, you didn't hear this from me, understand?" the constable went on. "Just rumors and things flying around, see."

Spindler could barely shake himself out of his shock to answer. "Of course."

"Well, I best get on now. Take care of yourself, Spindler."

He nodded. "Thank you, Constable. You do the same."

The constable turned and started down the pavement, returning to his patrol. Spindler stood still as his mind worked over the new revelation. A Colonist? Here? On Edgely Hill this entire time? He put a fist on his hip and smoothed down his mustache with anxious energy. If the constable could've only confirmed it, there would've been enough time to get the news to press for the morning edition. At least, he would've made the time.

"Damn," he muttered and hurried towards his office. He could feel it creeping up behind him—that insatiable itch which could only be appeased by a bit of journalistic snooping. The Colonists were one of the greatest mysteries of all time. He'd give absolutely anything to have a look through Bash's house before the law could plunder it for evidence. With another sigh, he stopped in front of his office door and fumbled with his keys.

"Ho, there!" someone called, catching his attention away.

Along the far side of the road adjacent to Hade Street, a high stone wall had been erected to fortify the base of a steep hill. One of the gas lanterns stood nearby, illuminating something strange hanging on the wall—for which Constable Tuppman was making a beeline. Curious, Spindler ventured closer and paused in the shadow of a wagon parked near the corner. The constable raised his lantern to the dark shape.

It was a man's overcoat—black and somewhat shabby—hanging by the back of its collar on a nail sticking out from between the stones. The constable leaned towards it, frowning.

"Evening, sir," came a young voice.

Spindler peered closer. From inside the depths of the coat, a boy peeked out.

"Good gracious!" the constable said, lowering his hand once more from his pistol. "And just what might you be doing?"

"Suffering humiliation with all the dignity I can muster, sir."

"And how exactly did you manage to get yourself up there?"

"As any poor victim of bullying may, sir. I was minding my own business on the way to Uncle's house when I ran into a pack of just the wrong sort, you might say."

"Have you been up there all night?"

"I have, sir."

"In the rain and all? Saints above, lad, you'll catch your death of cold. Isn't anyone out looking for you? Your uncle must be worried sick."

"Oh no, sir. He didn't know I was coming. Supposed to be a surprise visit, you see. And Mum thinks I'm staying with him tonight. She even sent me off with a gift of spirits, but they took that off me, too. Shame, that."

"Who's your mother? What's her name?"

"Oh, you wouldn't know her. We live up in Avery."

"Your uncle, then."

"Tom Starling. Just moved here two days ago. Got a job over at the mill."

The constable unhooked the boy from the wall and set him down. "Now just you be more careful about running into a pack of the wrong sort again. I don't have to tell you that even kids can get to thieving and bad mischief nowadays."

"Oh, you certainly don't, Constable. I've learned my lesson."

The boy crouched down and swept up a black top hat lying near the wall. He dusted it off, then replaced it smartly upon his head with the smallest tilt over his left eye. Spindler saw that both the coat and hat were too big for the boy, but the way he carried himself more than made up for it. He stood with all the air of a proper gentleman, allowing for a hint of swagger, and had such a charming glint in his eye one couldn't help but give him a bit of respect.

"Thank you for your kind service, sir," the boy said. "I bid you a very good morning."

He touched the curved brim of his hat and made to leave.

"What's your name, lad?" the constable asked.

The boy turned back and offered a small bow. "Inkwell Featherfield, sir. The one and only."

"Well, you take care of yourself, Mr. Featherfield."

"To the best of my ability, officer," the boy said, then whirled off into the dark street.

Spindler watched until he was out of sight, smiling at the bold scamp.

It was around three o'clock when Spindler emerged from his office later that afternoon. A nice breeze had swept through Harburg, freshening the air and lifting away the stench coming from the mill. He drew a deep breath as he stepped out onto the pavement. Many of the shops had their doors propped open, overwhelming the street with a barrage of scents—sawdust, flowers, fresh bread, and a dozen others.

As he went on, he was surprised to see the streets become increasingly crowded, the people all moving in one great swell towards the square in the center of town. A few ahead were gesturing and waving them forward, shouting something he couldn't make out. Shops were emptying. Vendors abandoned their carts. The windows looking down on the square were filling with the faces of curious spectators. He had never seen anything like it. Even Mr. Guttry, who rarely ever set foot outside his book-shop, leaned out of the second story window and craned his neck towards the head of the crowd.

When Spindler at last reached the square, he noticed Mr. Roth and Mr. Sanner of the mayor's office standing atop a raised platform and beckoning for the people to come closer. The mayor himself appeared moments later, wringing his hands as he talked with his aides.

"What's this all about, Spindler?"

Spindler turned and saw the butcher's apprentice next to him.

"Don't know," he answered. "I was just heading to the post office and got caught up."

The apprentice nodded. "Joseph Olster from across the street ran in and fetched us out. We thought there'd been an accident."

The mayor raised his hands, trying to quiet the crowd in front of him. Spindler drew a pen and notepad from his pockets.

"Gracious ladies and gentlemen!" the mayor began. "Do forgive me for interrupting your day like this. I ask only for a few minutes of your time. It will be well worth your while, I assure you." He paused for a moment and glanced at his aides. "I received some distressing news in the early hours of the morning, and I urge you to spread it to those who cannot be present to hear it now. I am very sorry to inform you that there has been a death in our community. Mr. Iophulis Bash of Edgely Hill passed away in his home late last night."

There was little if any reaction from the people, many of whom struggled to simply recall Bash's face. Spindler held his pen at the ready. Worse news was coming.

"The details are still being worked out in the investigation," the mayor continued, "but I have been allowed to relay some information . . . uh . . . surprising information that we have since learned concerning Mr. Bash. It appears . . ."

The mayor glanced at his aides again and wiped his brow with a handkerchief. The crowd had grown so quiet only the ruffle of clothing could be heard. The mayor returned his handkerchief to his pocket and attempted to continue.

"It appears that Mr. Bash is . . . or was, rather . . . to our great shock . . ."

He stalled again. Everyone seemed to have stopped breathing, hanging on his next words. The aides nodded their encouragement.

"Right," the mayor said, returning their nod and looking slightly ill. "To the purpose, then." He looked out at the crowd. "It seems that Mr. Bash was a Colonist."

The crowd's collective gasp threatened to suck all the oxygen out of the air. They glanced at one another in disbelief. Spindler's pen froze mid-sentence on his notepad. So it was true.

"Now, I-I understand how upsetting this is, believe me," the mayor continued. "To think that such a person had been living in our midst all these years. I implore you to let this proximity to danger remind you all of the importance of staying watchful and vigilant. Not only for yourselves, but for your friends and family as well. As a result of this information, my office will be collaborating closely with law enforcement officials in the undertaking of a widespread investigation effort here in town. Do not be surprised if a constable shows up at your door with a few questions. Please be as cooperative as you can, and we will all get through this with as little inconvenience as possible. I remind you that there are nearly a dozen Colonists still running free in the world. While that may seem like a small number, they have proved to be masters of chaos and destruction. Therefore, even a dozen is more than we can afford. You know their crimes. You know their punishment. I will not repeat it here."

Spindler looked up from his notepad and watched as the mayor gestured to someone standing beside the platform.

"I would now like to introduce you to someone who has come to us on very short notice from Badwell, for which we are exceedingly grateful. No doubt many of you have heard of this gentleman before. His efforts to aid in the capture of the

Colonists are renowned throughout the country, and he has graciously consented to impart some of his expertise in this area. Ladies and gentlemen, Mr. Bill Stone."

Another gasp went through the crowd, accompanied by whispers of disbelief. Spindler nearly dropped his pen. The mayor and his aides retreated to the back of the platform, making way for their formidable guest.

Bill Stone was a legend. He was responsible for single-handedly bringing more Colonists to justice than any other bounty hunter in Eriaris. A giant of a man, he was quick and sharp with a neck as thick as a tree trunk, a nose made crooked by multiple breaks, and the keenest pair of gray eyes ever to haunt the horizon. Many of those standing nearest to the platform glanced away, intimidated by his unblinking stare. But no one dared move an inch.

"The mayor here wants me to talk to you about the Colonists." Bill's great booming voice echoed throughout the square as he hooked his thumbs over his iron-studded belt. "The first thing to be done is to get your mind right about 'em. What they've done—what they're still doing—makes 'em the lowest breed of life there is. Less than human. And every last one of you has got a share in the responsibility to catch 'em."

Bill jumped down from the platform. The crowd hurried to make way for him as he strode forward.

"You must stay sharp at all times!" Bill cried. "Be alert at all times! Know where your children are! Know where your neighbor's children are! Keep your doors locked at night!" He stopped in front of a woman. "If your husband's late coming home from the office, is he just taking a sip down at the pub? Or is he face down in the river with his blood on the hands of a Colonist?" He glanced back at a constable. "If a stranger's come to town, is he here to visit family like he says? Or is he bent more on slitting throats and burning people in their beds?"

The constable, clearly horrified, made no move to answer. Bill continued towards the middle of the crowd.

"It's been done! I've seen it! There's no measure of caution too great you can take against these monsters. Sometimes the danger gets forgotten. Maybe you don't hear anything about 'em for a few years. But that's exactly what they want. To pull the covers over you and tell you to go back to sleep." He stabbed a finger into the air. "And you've let it come to your kitchen doorstep! Because of your carelessness! Your neglect! You allowed one of these fiends to live and breathe beside you for near nine years!"

He turned and jabbed his finger at Mr. Reeds, the banker, who went instantly pale.

"You. What was his day job?"

"Uh, he . . . he sold pens, I think."

"And what did he do at night?"

Mr. Reeds' gaping mouth snapped shut in answer. Bill nodded.

"That's what I thought. You got no idea what they're capable of. Merciless horrors I've seen, and all of them preventable. Know your neighbors. Know what they're doing and where they are. Never travel alone. Don't go out at night on your own. I recommend every household have at least one pistol kept loaded at all times. If you get an inkling of 'em, a sign, anything so much as a hint of a whisper, report it immediately to the authorities. Word'll get to me. And I'll get to them." He swooped around and headed back towards the platform. "If you come across one and you don't think you can take 'em on your own, don't try. Run for help. Delay 'em if you can, injure 'em, trail 'em. Whatever it takes."

With far more nimbleness than should have been allowed for a man his size, Bill hopped back up onto the platform. "They ain't easy to spot," he continued. "They've learned how to blend in with the rest of us, and there ain't much I can tell you about what gives 'em away. They might try to stir up trouble about the Entrians. Might try to bring up the past. You've just got to know the people around you. Who's familiar. Who's not. Apart from this, I have names."

Bill took a page from a stack of papers on a barrel and held it up for the crowd to see.

"Ten names! All suspected of being Colonists. All disappeared on the day of the Battle of Damiras nine years ago and not seen since. Not hard to wonder where they all ended up. Now it's not a complete list. We know they number more than ten, but it's the best we got. Some of you might recognize a few names. Maybe you knew 'em. I say that's all the more reason to lend a hand bringing justice to those who betrayed their own neighbors!"

The next moment, half a dozen constables rounded the front of the platform carrying similar stacks of paper.

"Take 'em," Bill continued. "They're for you. Learn the names. Protect yourselves. If you truly want to show your love for kin and country, do as I did. Become a Colonist-hunter. Help us root out these devils on earth. All it takes is a bit of signed paper from the Assembly and you're granted the authority to bring peace and justice to our lands again. No calling will give you greater satisfaction in this life. In the meantime, you must never let your guard down again. Just because things go quiet don't mean they don't exist no more. Just because you don't hear the wolves howling outside don't mean it's all right to leave your house. Don't for a moment think you're safe. Not 'til we've sent the last one of 'em back to Hell."

With that, Bill turned and walked off the platform.

The papers spread through the crowd like wildfire. No one wanted to be caught dead with an empty hand. Spindler grabbed one as soon as he could and skimmed through it. During the first three years the Colonists had been on the run, the Assembly had required every newspaper in the country to print the warrant list on the front page of every edition. That requirement had faded over time, along with public interest, as news of the fugitives became ever scarcer. Spindler still kept to the policy somewhat, printing the list on the back page of his paper, though he knew no one usually paid it any attention. That would change now. Everyone was nervous, if not terrified. There was nothing like a dead Colonist and dose of Bill Stone to shake the world out of apathy.

The mayor retreated to his office with Bill at his side and his aides in tow. The people began to disperse. Spindler looked around, hoping to spy out a constable who might know more about the situation than Tuppman had that morning.

Then, from out of the corner of his eye, a familiar hat caught his attention, bobbing and weaving in and out of the crowd. It was heading for the Hade Street Café. The gears in Spindler's mind began to turn. With a twitch of his mustache, he folded up the warrant list, tucked it inside his coat, and made for the café.

CHAPTER 3

A BOY CALLED INK

As Spindler pushed open the café door, Mr. Cordon and his wife looked up from behind the counter and greeted him. The smell of coffee was strong, along with the scent of a bushel of green apples with which they were preparing to make preserves. There were no more than half a dozen customers inside, all of whom were talking about Bill Stone and the Colonists with hushed voices and worried expressions.

The black top hat he'd followed into the place now lay on a table in the corner of the room, far from all the other patrons. Spindler sauntered around the counter and spied its owner. Yes, that was him—the same boy who'd been hanging off a wall earlier that morning, now face-deep in a plate of blueberry pastries and oblivious to the world around him. Spindler strode forward and took the chair behind the boy, then waited for the Cordons to finish up with their last customer. Once they retreated into the kitchen, he leaned back and turned his head towards the seat behind him.

"You're to be commended."

The sound of messy devouring stopped for a moment. "For what?"

"Your cleverness. Your ingenuity. Your ability to eat that way without losing whole fingers."

Another short silence. Spindler knew the boy was sizing him up.

"You a cop?"

"No. Why? Are you on the lookout for the law?"

The noise of ravenous smacking continued, and the boy's answer was muffled in blueberries. "Most of the time it's only cops who cheap talk that way with people. Usually before picking 'em up."

"Ah," Spindler said. "Well, I wasn't cheap talking."

"That's refreshing," the boy replied. "Most people who bother to strike up a chat usually want something. Now if you'd be so kind, I'd rather eat than talk just now."

Spindler hesitated. He glanced around the room again, then moved to the boy's table and sat across from him. The boy glared at him with dark eyes and a blueberry-stained scowl. The newspaperman tried to ease the tension with a smile.

"You must have awfully nice parents to let you fill yourself up with sweets before supper."

The boy let his pastry drop down onto the plate and brushed the crumbs from his hands. "And you must be a cop to be asking such stupid questions."

"I didn't ask a question."

"Look, don't play dumb with me," the boy shot back. "You're all alike. One thing out of the ordinary, one dog without a leash, and it upsets the whole balance of your lives!"

"There's no need to get upset."

"There's plenty of need! You've spoiled my nice meal and lied to me at the same time. Now what have you got to say for yourself?"

Spindler sat back in his chair. He'd never met such a brash and brazen kid. He almost felt belittled, reduced by a few inches. He removed his hat and set it on the table. "Look, I'm sorry. I didn't mean to get off on the wrong foot like this. Let me start again.

My name is Spindler. I run a newspaper here in town and I thought you might be interested in doing a little job for me."

"Wait," the boy said. "Give me a moment to get over my shock." He put a hand to his stomach and belched. "There. Now I'm over it."

"You were in the square. You heard what the mayor said about the Colonists."

"So?"

"So what do you know about them?"

"I dunno. Not much. Just another pack of starving dogs doing what they can to get by."

Spindler raised an eyebrow. "Is that all? What about the killings?"

The boy shrugged. "Some dogs play rough."

Spindler wondered at him again with an inquisitive frown. He saw the boy's hair had been neither cut nor combed in a while. The shirt beneath his oversized coat was dirty and bedraggled, hanging loosely from his thin shoulders. He may have been as young as twelve or as old as fifteen, but it was hard to know for certain. Spindler glanced around the café again. It was still quiet. He ducked his head down and leaned in closer.

"All right, listen," he said, "I've been after the Colonists' story for nine years. They've managed to hold the world in terror all this time and no one knows hardly anything about them. I want some insight into the minds of these people. I want to uncover some of their secrets. Where do they hide? How do they live? How do they justify the lives they've taken? It's about time we had some fresh information on them."

The boy frowned. "You called 'em 'people'. Didn't that Bill Stone bloke say they were less than human?"

"Yes, yes," Spindler replied, waving a hand. "Bill said a lot of things to paint the picture he wants the public to see, but I for one think there's more to them than we're being told. I want to find out what that is, and I think you can help."

"Me?"

"Yes. There's a big hill outside town, right by Corvus Lake to the northwest. It's where old man Bash lived, the one they say was a Colonist. The law usually won't ransack a place until they get permission from the next-of-kin, but they'll go in after twenty-four hours if they can't find anyone to contact. That leaves you a good twelve hours or so before anyone shows up."

"You want me to break into his house?"

"It's just a bit of sneaking around. No harm in sneaking, is there?"

The boy scoffed. "No more than a mouse creepin' into a sleeping wolf's den. But what if the wolf wakes up?"

"I'm willing to pay quite handsomely for it. At least three times the amount you just spent on pastries."

"Well three times ain't nearly enough."

"We can haggle price later," Spindler said. "Just be as quick as you can and try to find anything you think might be of interest to me. They found something in his house this morning. Something that betrayed his secret. I don't know what it was, but if there's more to be found it's going to be put under lock and key once the law gets their hands on it. Then they get to tell whatever story they want. But we deserve to see what's going on. We deserve the truth, even though it might be hard to come by. I'd do the job myself but it could mean a great deal of trouble for me if I were to get caught, especially now that the matter will be under the jurisdiction of the Assembly."

The boy rolled his eyes and stuffed the last pastry into his mouth. "The Assembly? That ain't a wolf, that's a lion! That's a whole gang of lions!"

"Leave that part to me. Just get whatever you can. Any sort of records you can find, any papers or books. Maybe a journal or a diary of some kind. Anything."

"Why don't you just become one of them hunters?" the boy said. "Go out there and find these Colonist people yourself. Then you can sit down and have a nice chat over tea."

Spindler sighed. "Listen, I'm sure a lot of people found Bill's little recruitment speech very inspirational, but you can't just take up a rifle and go off into the woods."

"Look, I know what this is," the boy said. "Things get slow, crime goes down, you need something to sell a few papers, you try to mix up a little trouble, right? I get it. So why don't you just make it all up? Ain't that what you newspaper folk do anyway?"

"That is an incredibly unfair thing to say . . . and besides, I don't want to make it up. I want the truth."

"Then why me? Ain't there anyone else to do your dirty work for you?"

Spindler's mouth twitched in agitation as he debated how to answer. "I do have a small network of dependable contacts, yes. But the fact of the matter is . . . when it comes to the Colonists . . ."

The boy raised an eyebrow. "Oh, I see. That's too much dirt."

Spindler nodded. "So to speak."

"All right, so what if I can't find anything? What then?"

"You'll still be paid, I promise. And I'd be grateful if you didn't let my name slip in any future conversation with anyone. I prefer my intentions remain unknown for the time being."

"Huh," the boy said, wiping his mouth on his sleeve. "Now that's interesting."

"What?"

"Well, I could risk my neck going to a dead man's house to poke about for some old papers. Or . . . I could collect on your generosity right now by keeping my mouth shut about your *intentions*."

Spindler leaned back in his chair and fixed him with a glare.

The boy raised a smug eyebrow. "And I bet I could even catch that Bill Stone chap before he hitches out of town. I'm sure he'd be very interested to hear about your little project. He'd be on your tail faster than a fox on a hen."

Spindler crossed his arms. "You could do that. Or I could take you over to the chief constable's office and expose the fact that this morning proved your third successful theft from an officer in the course of two days."

A wild glint flared up in the boy's eye. "You been watching me?"

"It's my job to pay attention to everything that goes on in this town. I don't miss a detail. Not even one as small as you, Inkwell. It is 'Inkwell', isn't it? Did I hear that right this morning?"

The boy clutched the edge of the table. "I'll slip through your fingers if you try to lay a hand on me! You'll never see my face again! I never set foot in the same town twice and no one's ever been able to track me down! Least of all a cut-rate hawker like you." He swept his hat up from the table and stood.

"Wait!" Spindler said. He pulled a small card from his pocket and held it out to the boy. "If you change your mind, take this so you'll know where to find me. It takes guts to try and outfox the law, and I'll wager you won't have much more trouble with the wolves and lions at the rate you're going. And I know you must need the money. So just think it over. Please."

After moment of icy silence, the boy took the card and glanced at it. When he looked up again the fierceness in his eyes had softened. The defiance remained.

Spindler held his gaze. "It's just an empty house."

The boy shoved the card into his pocket. "Not Inkwell. Just Ink."

He donned his top hat, then strode across the café and out into the street. Spindler stood and looked out the window, watching the hat bob away until he was quite assured young Ink was not heading for the mayor's office or any other such troublesome place.

Once it was out of sight, Spindler rose and approached the counter. Mrs. Cordon emerged from the kitchen, wiping her hands on her apron.

"What can I get you, Mr. Spindler?"

"Just a couple blueberry pastries, ma'am."

As she went to retrieve his order, he reached into his back pocket . . . then smiled.

His wallet was gone.

Inkwell Featherfield stopped in an alleyway to count the contents of Spindler's property, congratulating himself on his fourth successful pinch in two days. After stuffing the bills into a leather pouch he wore around his neck, he went to the far end of the alley and tossed the wallet into a water trough. Then he washed his face and hands clean of the blueberry and dirt smudges and dried himself on a skirt hanging from a clothesline.

This done, he set off into the middle of the street with his thumbs hooked over his belt and strutted through town with all the self-possession of a king. When he approached a group of ladies gathered outside a tea shop, they giggled at him from behind their handkerchiefs. Ink strode up to them and touched the brim of his hat.

"Morning, ladies," he said. "Might I be so bold as to inquire after directions to the infirmary? I mean to visit my sick grand-mother, you see."

Only one of the ladies managed to turn her snickering into a good-natured smile.

"You poor darling, how nice of you," she said. "It's just a few blocks away down Cherton Street. Left at the post office."

Ink put on his most gracious smile. "My deepest thanks. A good day to you fine ladies."

He bowed, tipped his hat to them again, and moved off down the street.

CHAPTER 4

SNEAKING

I nk pushed through the infirmary door, then wrinkled his nose as a pungent wave of camphor slapped him in the face. Behind the front desk a woman sat fanning herself and sipping a cup of tea. She smiled as he approached.

"Can I help you, child?"

Ink frowned at the insulting term but did his best to let it pass. "Good day, ma'am. I've come to inquire as to whether you got any patients here by the name of Revore."

The woman set down her cup and leafed through a few papers on her desk. Ink clenched and unclenched his fists, trying to calm his nerves.

"Hmm . . . no Revore," she said at last. "But we had some late-comers last night and the patient roster hasn't been updated. Miss Bruck will have that list. If you'd like to wait a moment."

Before Ink could answer, the doors behind him swung open. He decided against glancing over his shoulder but counted the steps taken across the wooden floor. A group of four had entered. He saw the receptionist's eyes widen as she looked at them.

"Good morning, Mrs. Hampton," one of the men said, his voice thin and nervous. "We need to speak with the coroner. Is he in?"

"Uh, yes," she answered, her face still frozen in wonderment. "Yes, I believe he's just returned, Constable."

Ink tensed. Damn. A constable. And probably more than one. It was a good time to begin moving away from the desk. He started with short, unassuming steps, sidling towards the dimly-lit hall to his left.

"Thank you, Mrs. Hampton," the constable said. "We'll let ourselves in. It's just down the hall this way, sir."

Another voice cut through the air like a steel blade.

"Your help is appreciated, Constable, but all further information regarding this case is now privileged. I will go alone."

The constables stepped aside to make way for the man. Ink had just managed to reach the narrow hall when the owner of the strange voice swept past him like a gust of wind. Ink froze as he caught sight of the back of him. This was no constable. His clothing was finer than any he'd ever seen. Jeweled cufflinks and gold embroidery glittered in the pale light, like the dress of some prince or noble, and his boots were so shiny they might have been made only yesterday.

"Blimey," Ink muttered under his breath. Who was this man?

Though Ink was caught off guard for only a few seconds, it was enough to get him into trouble. The receptionist had noticed him and now called out, obliterating his plan of a gradual, inconspicuous escape.

"Oh, wait just a moment, young man! I can get that night roster for you now."

She rounded her desk and took off down the hall. Ink, meanwhile, tried to melt into the shadows, keeping his face turned towards the pale green wallpaper in front of him. The dim hall grew even darker as three shadows suddenly closed in around him.

"I know that hat and coat," a voice said.

Two big hands spun him around by the shoulders, hoisted him off his feet, and slammed him against the wall into which he had been trying to disappear. Ink found himself staring into the faces of three angry constables—all of whom needed a shave and a decent night's sleep.

"Ah," Ink said with a grimace. "You all know each other. How nice."

The tallest of them, who had Ink in his grasp, glowered down through bloodshot eyes. "Well, Mr. Featherfield. What a surprise to bump into you again. You know, you really oughtn't wear such a distinguishing get-up if you don't want to be recognized."

"I realize that, sir," Ink replied. "It's just so comfortable I can't bear to part with it."

The officer shook him roughly. "Check him, lads."

It took six seconds for them to find the purse around his neck and snap the cord.

"It's at least two hundred, Sergeant," said one of the constables after he had inspected it.

"My, my," the tall one said, "you made quite a nice pot there. And lifted it off three lawmen at least. Incredible."

Ink met the officer's gaze of scorn. "Well, I guess I don't have to tell you, Constable. Even kids can get to thieving and bad mischief nowadays."

With a jerk, the constable pitched Ink from the wall and into the clutches of his fellow officers. "Take him to the jailhouse. And be sure to cuff those fast hands of his before you put him in the coach."

Ink struggled as the officers carried him out of the infirmary. He managed at one point to clamp his teeth onto one of their wrists, but a sharp slap to the ear brought an end to that, and he was thrown into the back of a jail coach. Before he could pick himself up, one of them climbed in and handcuffed his wrists behind his back. Ink continued to thrash about in resistance all the while but without result. When the constable finished, he got out, locked the rear door, and joined his partner at the front of the coach.

"Bleedin' uncle," the constable said, rubbing his wrist. "Like a wildcat, that one. Might as well have fur and claws!"

"Aw, don't get dramatic. He's just a kid."

"He didn't bite *you*!"

Ink heard the reins crack, then fell backwards as the coach surged forward across the cobblestone lane. His ear was still ringing from the slap, and he tried to rub it by hunching up his shoulder. He heard one of the officers in the front chuckle.

"Never seen Sergeant lose his color like that before. Did you see his face when that Entrian fellow told him off?"

"I don't like it," the other replied. "Ordering us around, high and mighty as you please. Where do they get off behavin' like that? Just 'cause they've got a few tricks up their sleeves?"

"It's a lot more than tricks, mate," the other one answered. "And I'd be careful of talking about the Entrians like that. They're likely to blow your head off with a snap of their fingers."

"Aw, they can't do anything like that. It's all a bunch of illusions and rubbish. And these ones *flaunting* it right in the middle of the street? That ain't right. It's best they stay put out west, out of the way, like they have been."

Ten minutes later, the coach pulled up to the jailhouse. After tying off the reins, the first constable went to the back and arrived in time to hear the second swear and see him whirl back towards the road, his eyes darting in every direction. The first constable sighed and rubbed the back of his neck while his partner began a frantic search through his pockets.

"How'd he get the keys off me?"

"Probably the same way he lifted your wallet the first time. He's a smart kid."

"We've got to go after him!"

"Well, you can try," the first constable replied as he shut the coach door, "but he probably jumped down the first rabbit hole he came to."

"We'll send the dogs after him, then!"

"Ain't worth the bother. Besides, when have you ever seen a dog catch a wildcat?"

∿

Ink had long since fled the scene by the time the constables discovered his escape. Though he was small he had the advantage of long arms, which had made his liberation from the handcuffs a great deal easier. Almost easier than picking a constable's pocket.

He avoided the main streets of the city, taking farm roads and crossing fields whenever possible. Snatches of clouds floated in from the west, wisps at first but growing broader and darker over time. He turned up the collar of his coat around his ears and tugged down his hat more snugly. The pastries he'd eaten would likely carry him through the rest of the day. If not, there wasn't time to consider it a problem until he was out of town. The jailhouse wasn't yet as far away as he wanted, and it was entirely possible the coach could come thundering up the road at any moment. He turned northward and made his way through a line of trees.

An hour passed, the shadows grew long, and all that time Ink was haunted by a single galling thought: no money. Everything he'd rightfully earned in the past three weeks had been in that pouch. For a while, he'd been living comfortably under the pretense of visiting distant relatives, sleeping on soft inn beds and having at least one hot meal a day. It would be a hard job making up the loss. If only he hadn't been distracted by that strange man in the infirmary.

"Curse the poncy prat," Ink grumbled, kicking at a stone.

The next town on his route was Ostler's Grove, almost twenty miles to the north. It was a laborious hike even for someone fully fed and rested. For a moment he considered returning to Harburg to hitch a ride on the back of a wagon or carriage. But he wasn't about to risk being caught again. There was too much at stake. He'd just have to go it on determination alone. With a shake of his head, he stuck his hands into his pockets and marched on.

But wait. What was this? Ink drew a piece of paper from his pocket—and felt his heart leap at the sight of it. Spindler's card! That sorry git had offered him money for doing his dirty work, and what he'd intended to ignore might now be the ticket to saving him several days of hardship on an empty stomach. Ink looked around. His target wasn't hard to spot. There in the far distance, beyond the field to the northwest, was a massive, tree-filled rise that towered high above the surrounding area. It had to be the hill where that Colonist had lived. It even appeared possible to get to it without taking any roads or going near any houses. Ink squinted, trying to judge the distance. He hated to delay his personal business, but circumstances were forcing his hand. A few hours' detour would do no harm. He shoved the card back into his pocket and started off with renewed vigor.

Ink cursed when he finally reached the base of the hill—an hour later than planned and with the sun already touching the horizon. Not only had he underestimated the travel time, he hadn't considered how long it might take to climb the thing and even felt a twinge in his neck just attempting to glimpse the summit. With a frustrated sigh he began to circle the base of the hill, hoping to discover a path leading up to the house. A quarter of the way around, he spied the remnants of an old fence rotting under the brush. Beyond it was a kind of lane, distinguishable by nothing more than two deep wheel-ruts worn into the ground.

As he began the long climb, his thoughts turned again to the mysterious man in the infirmary. The constables had called him an Entrian, and though it seemed impossible that such a person would ever set foot in the North Country, Ink knew it had to be true. Everything about him—his voice, his clothing, his walk—had seemed to lend itself to another age. Perhaps even another world.

Entrians had once covered the length and breadth of the land, ruling Eriaris by virtue of their supernatural powers. Some said it was little better than trickery or pagan ritual, but others thought it more akin to holy miracles. All life had flourished under their care, every person prosperous and fulfilled. But something had happened. Some shift which had led to the downfall of their sovereignty. Everyone had their own theory as to the cause, but Ink himself had never bothered to speculate. All he knew for certain was that they now lived apart from the rest of the world, keeping to their lands in the West Country. Before today, Ink had only seen one other such person—a cool, regal figure sitting in the most expensive box seat of a theatre house. Ink had thought the man a king, until his granddad pointed out there had been no monarchy in Eriaris for over two thousand years.

Ink shuddered. There were entire cities in the west filled with those people, a whole nation of gods and goddesses. And what a dirty, common people filled the rest of the world, his own self included. "Cassrians" they were called. Legend said their ancestors had first landed in the small village of Cassria after a decades-long sea voyage from a far distant country. From the eastern shores of Eriaris they had spread, thriving, despite having no extraordinary powers of their own. As far as Ink knew, both nations were now content to largely avoid one another. The matter of a dead Colonist, however, would make a definite exception to that rule.

Ink felt a wave of anxiety rush through him. *Colonists.* He'd described them to Spindler as nothing more than a pack of starving dogs, but in truth he feared them much more. Though they were Cassrians, there were rumors they had gained twisted powers through dark.rituals. It was said they drank the blood of their victims before putting them into trances, making them see strange things until they went mad and took their own lives.

There were accusations of cannibalism, demon possession, and some even declared they were led by the Devil himself. The insidious cult had fixed their malice and bloodlust squarely on the Entrian people, culminating in a vicious battle nine years ago which had cost thousands of Entrian lives.

Ink felt sick to his stomach. And now he was on his way to a Colonist's house?

Several minutes later, he rounded a clump of bushes and froze. The house had come into view. He stepped behind a tree and pushed back the brim of his hat, rubbing at the mark impressed upon his brow. Was he really going to do this? He was no stranger to a bit of risk or daring, but this was an entirely different game. He craned his neck around the tree and glanced at his destination again. Under any other circumstances he wouldn't have thought twice. It appeared to be a simple, well-kept residence. There were cheery rosebushes beneath the windows and a few bird feeders on a maple tree. But his chief concern was what might be hiding inside. Would there be corpses rotting in the attic? Unholy shrines slicked with blood in the bedchambers?

Before his thoughts could trip towards even worse ideas, he shook himself out of it and stepped around the tree.

"Here now," he said, straightening his hat as he moved forward. "It's just an empty house. And you've got to eat sometime within the next week, so best get it over with. It's just a house."

He walked to the front door, thumped his chest to scold his nervous heart, and put his hand on the doorknob. It was locked. With the aid of a pick from inside his boot, he swung the door open in a matter of seconds. He glanced around, took a deep breath, and stepped inside.

He stood still for a moment, letting his eyes adjust to the darkness. A half-used candle lay slumped in a brass holder on a table by the door. Ink took hold of it, swiped a match from a nearby box, and lit the wick. A flight of narrow stairs in front of him divided the house from kitchen, dining room, and parlor. He began his search of the first floor with slow, deliberate steps, taking note of everything around him. It was, by all accounts, the home of a simple and quiet bachelor. Ink knew he would have to dig deeper.

Once the initial patrol was complete, Ink took to every drawer he could see. Most were full of pencils and ink bottles. The desk drawers in the parlor were crammed with papers and notebooks, all blank. Another revealed a large number of pens. He picked one up and looked it over. It was a finely-crafted thing, tipped with silver at both ends. Ink took a second from the drawer and pocketed them both. Then he returned to the kitchen and opened the cupboards, helping himself to all that was left of a small wedge of cheese, the remaining two pieces of a half-stale apple pie, and more than one swig from a dark bottle behind a tall package of oat flour. He left the kitchen gnawing on an apple and headed for the staircase.

He stood at the bottom and gazed up. The fact that he had found nothing of interest on the first floor did not bode well for the merits of the second. And though he was not afraid of the dark, he still felt an apprehension he couldn't shake. With a deep breath, he stuffed the half-eaten apple into his pocket, shuffled the candle to his other hand, and climbed the stairs.

The upper hall was short and wide with a door on either side. Ink pushed through the left one and found himself in a bedchamber. It was a small room with a neatly-made bed set against the far wall. There were two narrow wardrobes, a side table with a wash basin on top, and a little framed mirror. Ink opened the nearest wardrobe, taking care to stand well away in case something jumped out. A handful of shirts and trousers hung inside, some faded, a few fraying at the hems but otherwise clean and ironed. Two pairs of black boots sat at the bottom.

The second wardrobe was empty.

Ink shook his head as he returned to the hall. He'd been expecting to find a decrepit place full of unspeakable horrors, but there wasn't so much as a cockroach. Then again, there was still one more room to visit. The second door swung open on silent hinges, and it struck him as odd that the place had never once let out a groan or a creak like an old house usually did.

As he entered the room, he tripped over the reason. The candlelight revealed a small oil can on the floor, covered with a soiled cloth. Looking around, Ink guessed he was in Bash's workplace. There were three tables all stained with the drippings of different colored inks, chipped and gouged on the surfaces, no doubt from the instruments of Bash's trade which he had left strewn about the place. Wood and metal shavings littered the room, along with more bottles of ink and empty pen cases. Reams of paper and a large stock of pencil lead lay in boxes stacked against the wall. There was also a strong smell of oil and sawdust, especially near the hand-cranked drilling machine by the door. Ink reached into his pocket for the rest of the apple and let the candle follow along the wall.

There was nothing here. It appeared this terrible monster of a man had lived the single most boring and uninvolved life of anyone in Eriaris. He had apparently fostered no interests—save for his dull trade—had no friendly relations, read no books, wrote no letters or journals, and only entertained himself by making sure all the hinges in the house were well-oiled and the floorboards didn't squeak.

"Well, Mr. Spindler," Ink said aloud, "it looks like you're going to lose a pretty sum for a whole lot of nothing. What a shame. If only I felt worse about it."

He finished the last of the apple and tossed the core into a corner of the room. As he did so, his gaze fell on a strange black shape. Curious, he went to the spot and held the candle down towards it. Leaning against the wall was a broad piece of thick stone, shaped like a grave marker and with a long inscription etched into the surface:

Heed not the love of Mortals
In truth, Betrayers all
Cast down the bonds of Brotherhood
Forsake the Woman's call
Deceit is dealt to goodly hands
And Harm with bloody fall
Sentenced hence to death in Life
A cold and lightless hall

This was something. The verses made little sense as a whole, but contained in them was an unmistakable feeling of anger and bitterness. Ink knew the stone would be far too heavy to carry all the way back to Spindler's flat, so he grabbed a sheet of paper from a nearby pile and took one of Bash's pens from his pocket.

He had nearly finished copying down the last sentence when a noise of horses and wagon wheels threw all his senses into high alert. He pocketed the pen and blew out the candle, then dropped to all fours in the utter darkness. Crawling to the window, he raised himself to his knees and used a finger to draw aside the curtain half an inch.

There were men below, just short of a dozen, all bearing lanterns and climbing down from mule-drawn wagons. Another man, clothed in very elegant dress, was just shutting the door of an equally fine carriage.

Ink abandoned the window and shot to his feet. He didn't need to see any more. It was the search party, come early, and it was now or never to get out.

CHAPTER 5

A MOST DESIRABLE THING

I nk flew out of the room and down the stairs, keeping a sharp
eye on the front door as he neared it. The window glimmered
as a lantern approached. He swung around the banister and
sprinted to the back kitchen door, taking care to close it quietly
behind him. Moonless night had descended. Ink knew what a
stroke of luck it was, for there was no shadow to expose his
fleeting form as he plunged into the thick barricade of shrubbery
a few yards beyond the house.

He was well-hidden for now, but total escape looked unlikely.
The hill cut away at a steep angle from where he stood and there
was no gentler slope nearby. Sneaking around the foliage to the
winding path would be tricky work as well, especially where the
bushes grew thin in several places along the way. But there was no
alternative. He would just have to try for it as soon as the new
arrivals went inside. He crouched and peered at them through the
leaves.

A constable stood at the front door, twisting the knob with a
baffled frown upon finding it unlocked. To Ink's relief, the
constable only muttered a vague curse against incompetence and
declined to alert anyone else to the slip-up in security.

Standing apart from the rest was the richly-clothed man he'd seen departing the carriage. Yes, it was him—the Entrian from the infirmary—standing tall and rigid like a god of old. His long, dark coat fell to the knee, the cuffs and hems embroidered with thin gold threading which spread upwards in a curious pattern. The cloth appeared black at first glance but changed with any slight movement, shifting almost imperceptibly in the lantern light between half a dozen different colors, all of which were so dark Ink wondered if his eyes were working properly. His waist-coat was silver silk, and tucked beneath his upturned collar was a splendid blue cravat. Ink had never seen such fine dress in all his life.

The constable pushed the front door open and glanced into the darkened house. He cleared his throat—with apprehension, Ink thought—and turned to the group of men behind him.

"Well, boys . . ." he began.

"We will wait," the Entrian said.

The others stared at him, puzzled.

"Wait?" the constable repeated. "I'm sorry . . . for what, sir?"

But the Entrian would say no more. The wind picked up from the west and sent the treetops swaying. A few of the men shivered and tightened their hats down around their heads. The constable looked around uneasily.

Half a minute later, they heard a shout from the path on the far side of the hill. A second carriage came into view, drawn by two black horses whose driver guided them forward by neither whip nor reins. "Up you go! Ho!" he cried. The horses drew around in a half circle until the carriage door faced the house, then came to a stop. The Entrian man turned and fixed his gaze on it as the driver descended to open the door. Ink dared another step to his left for a better view.

The constable and his men exchanged anxious glances as a second Entrian stepped down from the carriage. He looked for all the world like a member of royalty, with an air about him that was at once foreign and ancient. Ink noticed a ruby hanging from a short gold chain upon his own silk cravat. The first Entrian greeted his colleague with a nod.

"Lord Pallaton," he said. "Night came swiftly enough."

"Indeed, Drystan. Eager for things to proceed, no doubt."

He glanced over at the company standing near the house. There was something in his face that betrayed a harder edge than the other, a leaner quality of attitude in his bearing. Even at such a distance, Ink could tell he was sneering.

"Get them into some kind of order," he said.

Needing no further urging, the constable set at once to arranging them into two lines in front of the house while Pallaton returned to the carriage door and held out his hand. Drystan raised his head and checked his posture. Ink strained to see what was happening.

A gloved hand rested for a moment in Pallaton's palm. Then, a woman stepped out of the carriage; one Ink had never seen the like of before. Her dark hair cascaded down her shoulders, untamed by hat or ribbon. The long cloak she wore flowed around her in the breeze and glittered silver in the folds. A sapphire jewel on her breast sparkled even in the gloom. Ink was utterly transfixed. He knew, without a doubt, that for the first time in his life he was looking at an Entress—a living, breathing goddess.

She moved forward and greeted Drystan, who responded in kind. When Ink failed to catch her name, he took another step closer, desperate to hear her voice. He was distracted for a moment by the addition of a third person to the party, and tensed at the sight of Bill Stone stepping down from the carriage. A hint of envy flickered in Ink's heart. This man must have been the only Cassrian in the world to have ever gained such high favor with the Entrians.

Pallaton muttered a word to the lady and she turned her arresting gaze on the constable and his men. Ink watched in amazement as they all proceeded to remove their hats and bow to varying degrees. Some didn't even dare right themselves all the way up again.

"Well?" Pallaton barked at them. "You have your orders. Waste no time."

The constable ushered the others into the house, then followed the last of them and disappeared inside. Thunder rumbled overhead. Bill shifted his weight from one leg to the other and glanced between the three faces in front of him.

"You do know, of course, they ain't gonna find anything," he said. "A Colonist who managed to hide all this time won't have slipped up by leaving any other damning traces behind. That crest jewel in the drawer was a lucky find."

"That is precisely why *we* are here, Mr. Stone," Pallaton replied. "There will be nothing for the eyes of the blind to discover, but for those who see, there may be much to reap."

Bill nodded towards the house. "You always send the blind in first?"

Pallaton sighed. "Your Assembly requires an investigation of joint cooperation. The constable and his band of oafs are for show."

"I see," Stone replied. "What gracious obliging."

Pallaton turned his attention to Drystan. "What's been done with the body?"

"Locked away in the infirmary. They're quite unwilling to handle it any further, especially after the results of the autopsy."

Bill grunted. "Don't blame 'em. Had to sit down myself after hearing it. Not a mark to be found on his body, but all his innards torn to shreds and mixed around 'til pieces of his brain were in his stomach. Like someone took a meat grinder to him from the inside."

At this, Ink felt the blood drain from his face. He looked to the woman for her reaction, but she only stood quietly by, gazing at the house.

"Do we know how it happened?" Bill asked.

Pallaton hesitated. He glanced at the lady for a moment, as if wanting direction on how to answer, but received no response.

36

"There is much yet to examine," he replied. "But we will inform you of our conclusions the moment we see fit."

"Be sure you do," Bill said. "I'm certain you don't need reminding that I'm your best chance of tracking the Colonists down. Leave me out of anything and you miss a hundred chances to chop another neck."

"We're quite aware of your qualifications," Pallaton replied. "See that you don't forget who truly has the right to those necks."

"Oh, I'm sorry," Bill answered, ruffled. "I thought it was you who came to us for aid. After all your spells and magic tricks failed to get you results."

"You are merely one of many tools in our employ, Stone. A blunted chisel that seems to fancy itself a divine sword."

"My lady," Drystan interrupted, causing the duelists to break up their spar and turn their attention to her. "You are quiet tonight. Is everything well with you?"

The woman broke from her trance and answered. "Well enough, Drystan. Thank you."

She stepped towards the house and held a small object up to the light of a lantern hanging by the door. The sparkle of amethyst gleamed in her hand.

"An extraordinary find," she said. "And so far from its home."

Pallaton nodded. "A most desirable thing indeed for a Colonist wanting a trophy. Not two days ago I was alerted by a dependable contact to hold Bash in suspicion of being what he was. I had not even the time to inform the proper offices before news of his death reached me."

"I recognize the crest," Drystan said, peering at the gold symbol engraved into the jewel. "A mark of the house of the murdered Artavious family."

The woman closed her fist around the jewel and let it fall to her side. "It has been more than two years since we captured our last Colonist. And while we continue to appreciate the efforts of fellow colleagues like yourself, Mr. Stone, I can't help but feel we've done too little too late. The people were outraged when the treachery on Damiras occurred that day nine years ago, but outrage turned into frustration, which I now fear is passing into indifference. We cannot claim a full victory here in that knowledge."

Another roll of thunder sounded above. Ink blinked and realized he'd been holding his breath as the woman spoke.

"Lord Pallaton," she said, "do you remember our last success? A young man by the name of Pitman?"

Pallaton frowned and glanced at the ground for a moment. "Pitman . . . yes. Caught trying to break into a granary. Confessed almost immediately to being a Colonist."

"He did," she said. "And we set the axe to his neck readily enough. But he looked at me with all the startled fear of a child, and I felt a sickening inside me the moment we took his life. It was a thing of such diabolical cunning for a condemned murderer to maintain a bearing of total innocence even to the end. And I knew then as I do now—we are underestimating them. It is by this same cunning that Iophulis Bash managed to hide in plain sight all these years. It is by this guile that the Colonists' numbers may even be growing. So what are we overlooking? Why have we made so few gains?"

"The trail's gone cold," Bill answered.

"A mutilated corpse was taken from this house today, Mr. Stone," she replied. "Someone out there would not agree with you."

"Well, I'm doing all I can with what I'm given. Besides, Bash may have been murdered whether or not anybody knew he was a Colonist."

"And for what reason, Mr. Stone?" Drystan asked. "He was not wealthy. Not well-connected. Not disliked."

"Maybe reason's got nothing to do with it," Bill answered. "Sane people aren't the only ones who commit crimes. Especially ones where the victim gets his guts ripped to shreds."

The clouds opened, and Ink shuddered as cold raindrops began to soak into his clothes. The woman raised her hand into

38

the air and made a swift motion as if drawing a curtain, leaving a faint trail of blue light. As soon as she had done so, Bill removed his hat and shook the water from it. Ink looked on, astonished. The rain no longer touched them.

"We must double our efforts," the lady continued, raising her voice above the sound of the rain. "I don't want to see another Colonist murdered in this fashion, or subjected to anything else which might rob us of our chance to question them. We will work to double, triple if we may, the number of Colonist-hunters in this country. We will have the warrant lists printed up and distributed on every corner. Accounts of the Battle of Damiras printed in every paper. We must make it as though it has happened all over again."

"The Mourning Processions will commence within the month," Drystan said. "What if the Entrians were to parade through the Cassrians' streets? Let them hear the sound of weeping voices rising up to Heaven as they did that day."

Bill nodded. "That'd be an effective tactic for recruiting more hunters, at the very least."

"Do the Cassrian schools still teach what happened?" the woman asked.

"A brief lesson, but yes," Bill answered.

"We will make a request to the Assembly that it play a more prominent role in their curriculum."

Pallaton tugged on the lapels of his jacket as he glanced at the ground in thought. "There is yet another course of action we may take." He lifted his gaze and looked at the woman with a tentative expression. "There is Darian."

An uncomfortable moment of silence followed. Drystan and Bill both glanced at the lady, whose face had gone deadly solemn.

"What of him?" she asked.

"He was regarded by many as a prophet," Pallaton said. "And many today still hold him highly in that esteem. There is even a statue of him in a temple on Perenhill. Of course, it is also true that some considered him—and you will forgive the term—a madman. But he was our first martyr that day. And perhaps a greater understanding of who he was and what he worked for would do well to advance our cause, inspire even greater sympathy."

The woman remained silent.

"At any rate, it is a method we haven't yet approached, and I believe it would serve us well in the interest of progress." Pallaton let his hands drop from his jacket and made the slightest of bows. "If it would not, in any way, grieve you or your memory of him."

The face of the Entress was unreadable, but there were fires of great emotion churning in the depths of her eyes. "Of course," she said at last. "Of course we must try it."

Pallaton nodded.

"I myself will inform Commissioner Marlas of these preparations," she continued. "We must suffer no more delay, gentlemen. Thousands of souls are waiting to be avenged. Our own be damned if we fail them in the end."

Another peal of thunder rolled overhead, and the rain worsened. Ink cursed. The leg he'd been kneeling on had fallen asleep. He looked up again and saw the small party had drawn closer together to better hear one another over the storm. Ink himself could make out nothing now, and so dared to do something he knew was downright idiotic. But he was not to be deterred. Bill had shifted over a step and was now blocking his view of her. Slowly, and against the cover of a beech tree, Ink rose to his feet.

But owing to his numb leg, it was hard to do with any gracefulness, and he slipped on the wet leaves and fell to a knee. He bit his lip and froze, daring to move nothing but his eyes.

To his horror, he found himself no longer looking at the back of Bill Stone, but at his full and terrifying front. The Entrians were also looking in his direction, each with an expression so fierce that Ink was sure they could've seen him even had he been invisible. Bill moved forward on the hunt, sniffing the air and turning his head this way and that, all the while moving straight towards the beech tree. Without a second thought, Ink turned and plunged into the dark undergrowth behind him.

For the second time that day, he'd been stupid and careless in ways he'd never been before. The first time had only resulted in being clapped up in a jail coach for a short while; but now the fearsome Bill Stone was coming for him, and there would be no key to steal or lock to pick. His sole escape route was down the steep, slippery incline of Edgely Hill—which Ink now discovered was not so much a hill as it was a cliff.

Down he went, hurtling forward at an alarmingly increasing rate, half-running, half-slipping, half-falling, his hands raised to avoid hitting tree trunks or branches. At one point the ground beneath him dropped away completely, and he stifled a cry as he fell and landed dangerously close to a mass of sharp rocks. He picked himself up and continued down the hill, wondering all the while whether or not Bill was following fast behind. He didn't dare look.

At the bottom of the hill, with a scraped knee and badly scratched hands, Ink continued to run through the woods until he stumbled upon a small, run-down shack. There were no other dwellings nearby, and the woods only seemed to thicken farther on. Ink circled around the hut searching for signs of recent activity. It looked as though it had been standing there for a hundred years. Even the lock on the door had long since rotted off. Once he was convinced it had been abandoned, he wasted no time dashing inside.

A quick glance around the room revealed nothing more than a few rusted tools on a narrow table and a threadbare canvas tarp. Ink sat down and tried to catch his breath, but soon began to entertain horrible thoughts of Bill tearing through the walls or lifting the whole shack right up off the ground. He shook for fear, every muscle tensed. He strained his ears but heard nothing apart from the rain.

After a long time of listening and trying not to breathe too loudly, he began to relax. No one had followed him. They must have thought him an animal or a fallen branch. So what now? He was tired, wet, and freezing, but he knew his rattled nerves would never let him venture out again. For tonight, he would just have to make the best of his surroundings. He crept to where the tarp was heaped up in a corner. Its condition was poor, but it was large enough to cover him from head to toe. He crawled under it, put an arm beneath his head, and cradled his hat to his chest with his other arm. This would do.

At once, he began to wonder over the baffling things he'd seen and heard. Bill Stone mouthing off to an Entrian. The strange jewel found in the house. The invisible shield from the rain. Bash's horrifying fate. But most overwhelming of all—the thing which banished every trace of physical pain and discomfort from the realm of his thought and care—was the woman. He'd seen an Entress at last. And *such* an Entress! Oh, if only he'd caught her name. Spindler might be of help there. Yes, he was sure to know. He would ask him tomorrow.

Provided his madly-pounding, terror-stricken heart would let him live that long.

CHAPTER 6

NEVER DO THAT AGAIN

I nk felt a rush of anxiety as he opened his eyes the next morning. The events of the previous night came flooding back in a great swell of fear and confusion, and he held his breath as he lay still under the tarp. Would Bill be waiting outside the shed door? Would he be peering in through the window? Ink squeezed his eyes shut and listened. Only the faint creak of swaying tree boughs sounded in the distance.

After a long while, he pushed the tarp away and sat up, rubbing his stiff shoulder. Hazy daylight filtered in through the dirt-encrusted window above. He grabbed his hat and stood, brushing the dust and bits of twig from his coat. Though the world had lightened, there was little else to see of his surroundings. Besides the tarp and table beneath the window, there were only a few empty leather pouches and a rotting grain barrel. A mallet, chisel, and crowbar lay on the table's surface, all rust-covered and cobwebbed. Ink pushed them aside and climbed onto the table for a look out the window. A thick maze of trees greeted his view. Ink wiped his nose on his sleeve and cautiously ventured outside.

The morning air was still chill with the fresh memory of the storm. In proper light, he could now see that the shed in which he'd been hiding was so weather-beaten and dilapidated he was surprised it had held through the night. He wandered around to the back and saw a rusty axe stuck fast in a tree stump, as well as a few grimy cords of rope hanging from the moldy timber of the wall.

He paused and swung his gaze around again, watching for the slightest movement among the trees. All was still and silent. He heaved a sigh of relief and rubbed a hand across his eyes. Good. They hadn't followed him. He could make his way back to Harburg now, collect what he was owed from Spindler, and be on his way again before midday. He put a hand to his stomach and glanced back at the shed. There was probably no hope of finding anything to eat nearby, nor anything useful that he might pocket.

But the moment he turned to walk away, something caught his eye—an odd, dark shape mostly-hidden inside a great tuft of overgrown grass. He went to the back wall of the shed, crouched down, and dragged it out. It was a small metal trunk, as tarnished and battered as everything else. The lock was so badly corroded by rust that Ink's trusty lockpick had no effect.

Undeterred, he returned to the shed and retrieved the tools from the table. The stubborn lid yielded at last to the third hit of the mallet on the chisel, popping open with a rusty squeak. Inside lay only two items: an old flask and a leather pouch.

Ink grabbed the flask at once, unscrewed the cap, and put it to his lips. Dry.

"Of course," he muttered, then pitched it back into the trunk.

He reached next for the pouch . . . and frowned. Whatever it contained was heavy. Damned heavy. Even more so than the metal mallet he'd just used. He set the pouch on the ground, opened the top, and reached inside. It was something cold and metallic. As he drew it out, his face brightened with delight.

A silver pocket watch. Well, well. Perhaps his excursion to Edgely Hill had not been such a complete disaster after all.

He brought it closer to his face, examining the ornate patterns etched across its surface. As he did so, he discovered that when he tilted the watch towards him, the silver changed color. One way, it suddenly darkened and looked almost black. Another way, it changed to gold—or at least what looked like gold. Intrigued, he grasped the silver chain and held it up in front of him, watching the case slowly spin. One moment, it looked to be a large emerald, the next it became a sapphire, and then a ruby. He twisted the chain to make it spin faster. It sparkled like a diamond, an array of fantastic colors changing more quickly than he could blink. It was beautiful. It was incredible. Probably of Entrian make and design. Definitely worth more than he could begin to imagine.

Eager to see the inside, he pressed his thumb against the winding crown to open it. Nothing happened. He held it to his ear as he turned the mechanism between his fingers. There were no sounds of moving gears or ticking hands. Nothing at all. He then tried to pry it open at the seam, but still it wouldn't budge. He reached again for the mallet, intent on making a few gentle taps to help it along.

Before he could do so, however, a dreadful scream cut through the air.

Ink froze, feeling the hairs rise on the back of his neck. The sound was close. Perhaps within a hundred yards. He stood and glanced around, straining his ears. His first instinct was to flee in the opposite direction. But his legs wouldn't move.

"Come on, Ink," he said to himself. "You can't do any good. You'll only make things worse."

He shook his head, willing himself to turn and run. But a force stronger than fear was working its power over him. As much as he clung to the principles of disinterest and indifference, the sound of suffering struck a deep chord inside of him.

The scream came again, even more desperate, followed soon after by a sound of splashing. Ink clenched his fist around the watch. For all he knew, he was the only other human soul around for miles.

"Oh, you bleeding heart!" he cursed, then took off as fast as he could through the forest.

Fifty yards later, he broke through the tree line and came to the shore of a lake. Early-morning mist hung low over the surface of the dark water, obscuring the far side. Ink halted at the edge of the bank and swept his gaze across the water as far as he could see. Nothing but a few ripples floated towards him.

"H-hello!" he called out. "Is someone out there?"

The scream came a third time. Ink took off again, realizing it was coming from farther down the shoreline. He soon found himself in a place where the mist thickened and swirled so heavily he could barely see the ground beneath his feet. He stopped again and cried out.

"Hello! Is someone there? Curse my eyes, what am I doing here?"

He peered through the fog and took a few steps forward. The mist parted before him, enough to bring the lake's surface into view again. The ripples in the water had strengthened, pushing towards him with foreboding energy.

And then he saw something. Thirty feet off or so, a dark shadow moved beneath the water. The shape gave no hint of distress or panic, but flowed about with haphazard purpose and no intent toward any particular direction. Ink stepped to the edge of the shore and leaned closer.

Suddenly, the shadow changed course and began sliding towards him. He crouched down as it floated nearer, mesmerized. Of course it couldn't be anything but an animal. He even recalled that foxes had the ability to make shrieking noises, though he'd never heard it for himself. If it was a fox—particularly a small one—he might be able to catch it and get a good bag of coin for the fur. Then again, he wasn't sure he'd ever heard of one swimming underwater. He reached out a hand.

"Come on. Just a bit closer. That's it. I ain't nothing to be scared of."

The shadow quivered as it came to a stop near the edge of the bank. It appeared to be just a few inches below the surface. Something silver glinted in the pale light.

"Come on, come on," Ink said, his fingers a hair's breadth from the surface. "Show us your pretty face."

In one swift and terrible motion, a massive pair of gaping jaws suddenly broke through the surface and rushed towards him, revealing two hideous rows of silver teeth. The scream rang out again, a mixture of a howl and a shriek which stole through Ink like an icy dagger, turning his legs to stone. He squeezed his eyes shut, certain he was about to die.

A shout tore from his lips as he was suddenly hauled into the air and thrown backwards. The pocket watch flew out of his hand. The piercing scream rang in his ears as he hit the ground. He recovered himself quickly and glanced back towards the shoreline. His eyes went wide.

A man stood between him and the lake, clad in a dark coat and a wide-brimmed hat, holding his left hand out towards the water with his fingers splayed apart. The shadow began to hiss and sway under angry swells, coiling and writhing as if in pain. The man remained silent but forcefully reaffirmed his strange gesture. The ghastly hisses became low, guttural sounds, intimations of what seemed to be both intelligent and malevolent thought.

At last, the shadow began to back away from the shore, wailing and shuddering all the while. The man did not move but held his position until the creature was finally gone from sight. The mist returned and settled heavily around them, as if to muddle a dream.

Ink glanced down and saw the silver watch lying nearby. He grabbed it and shoved it into his pocket. The next moment, the man spun around and swooped forward, seizing him by the lapels of his coat. Ink caught only a glimpse of his dark, flashing eyes beneath the brim of his hat as he growled in a low voice.

"Never do that again."

Ink could do no more than squeak out a bewildered reply.

"All right."

The man stood, dragging the boy to his feet.

"Tell no one what you've seen," he said, "neither of me, nor our dark friend in the water."

Ink shoved the man's hands away from his coat. "What was that thing?"

"Go home," the man said, then turned and stepped back towards the lake.

"Go home?" Ink echoed with a rising voice. "Go home? After all that? After I've had my guts turned to gravy? Not bloody likely! Who are you? And why did—"

The man spun around again and shoved him back. Ink stumbled, barely keeping his footing.

"Get out of here! Run!" the man roared. "The danger isn't over!"

He turned his back, removed his coat and hat, and cast them to the ground. Then, without another word or moment's hesitation, he dove into the lake.

Stunned, Ink rushed forward in time to see the soles of the man's boots disappear into the murky depths. He crouched down for a better look but soon shot up again and backed away, remembering his final warning. He waited breathlessly with his mouth agape, his heart pounding in his chest. There was no shadowy form below, nor any sounds of splashing or stirring. By and by, the surface returned to utter stillness. He glanced at the hat and coat crumpled on the bank.

"Is this some kind of joke?" he said aloud.

Another minute passed. The mist drifted away, slinking off into the dark woods on the far shore. Ink scanned the bank, hoping to see the man re-emerge there. But there was no hint of movement. Not even a ripple in the water.

"What's he done?" Ink said, panic rising in his chest. "The stupid clot. What's he done?"

He glanced back through the trees. Should he go for help? He couldn't swim himself, but even if he could, there was no chance of him pulling a full-grown man to safety. Ink let another minute go by, scanning every inch of the lake in sight, wishing with all his might for a sign of life, and all the while becoming more and more frightened.

Then another scream came, this time from a great depth beneath the water—a furious, violent shriek which put a poisoned chill into the air and made Ink's blood run cold. A sound to remain in the darkest corners of his memory for the rest of his life.

It was too late. No one could help the man now. With a curse, Ink turned and fled back through the trees with all the speed he could summon.

CHAPTER 7

EXPLANATION AND FURTHER CONFUSION

Mr. Spindler pulled open the police station door, careful not to hit anyone in the crowd standing outside the place. He heard someone mutter his name but met no friendly eye, only glances of suspicion and mistrust.

Inside the building, constables rushed about in a flurry of busy activity. Only Constable Burke was still, manning the main desk. He glanced up as Spindler approached.

"Mr. Spindler. To what do we owe the pleasure?"

"Hello, Burke. Just here for the crime report."

"Where's young Swipson? Don't you usually send him out on the small jobs?"

"He's been ill," Spindler replied, then jerked a thumb towards the front door. "Has it been like this all day?"

"Since yesterday." Burke reached for a stack of papers and pushed them forward. "Here you are. Seventeen pages."

Spindler scooped up the report with an incredulous frown. "Seventeen?"

"That's right. Nothing but dubious activities and suspicious sightings. All of which have suddenly multiplied since Mr. Stone's visit. As if we didn't have enough problems to deal with—ah, hold on . . ."

A frazzled-looking woman with splatters of ink on her fingers passed by the desk, threw another page at Burke, and moved on down the hall. Burke's sullen "thank you" was answered with a "humph." He looked over the sheet, then handed it to Spindler.

"Eighteen."

Spindler added it the rest. "This is incredible!"

"Well, that ain't the adjective *I'd* use," the constable retorted.

As Spindler glanced up again, a gust of wind came through an open window behind the desk and sent several papers fluttering on the wall. One of them caught his eye. He furrowed his brow as he moved towards it. "What's this? A new advisory?"

The constable barely looked up. "Yeah. Just in today."

Spindler's curious stare intensified as he read through the notice.

ADVISORY TO THE PUBLIC

SUBJECT: RUNAWAY FROM KINSINGTON ORPHANAGE, DELVING
DESCRIPTION: MALE, BROWN HAIR, BROWN EYES, AGE APPROX.
12-15 YEARS, HEIGHT APPROX. 5'7"
GIVEN NAME: ANTHONY REVORE
PLEASE CONTACT MR. IVAN MEWES WITH ANY INFORMATION
REGARDING THIS CASE.

"Constable Burke," Spindler said, "does this go 'round to all the stations?"

Burke nodded. "Every government-run place in the country. Those runaway notices come in about every other month. Always manage to catch 'em after a week or two. Though I will say that's a rather vague description. And it's a bit strange they don't even know his proper age."

"May I take this?" Spindler asked.

"You seen him?"

"Don't think so. Just thought I might print it in the paper. Give it a little more exposure."

"Oh. Sure. Good idea."

By the time Spindler left the station, the queue outside had almost doubled in length. He quickened his pace, avoiding eye contact. No one wanted to be accused of hindering efforts to capture the Colonists, but he knew Bill Stone's fear-mongering would only do more harm than good. He rounded the corner towards Hade Street and scanned the advisory once more.

"Coming down!" a voice shouted from somewhere above.

The next moment, Spindler found himself being showered with two and a half gallons of cold, gray water. Or what he desperately hoped was water. He looked down at his suit and trousers, soaked through. A woman stuck her head out of a window two floors above.

"Oh," she said. "Did it getcha?"

He shot the woman a fiery glare. She shrugged.

"Plumbing's broken."

Once in his flat, Spindler threw the crime report onto a counter and heaved open the stubborn window over the tiny kitchen sink. He laid his hat on the windowsill to dry, then undid his tie and took off his jacket, inspecting the extent of the damage. Muttering a curse, he walked into the bedroom. It was a small, dim area with just enough room for a narrow bed, a wobbly washstand, and a small bathtub in which a grown person had to draw up their knees to fit. He draped the tie and jacket over the edge of the tub and returned to the sink to wash his hands.

Spindler's flat wasn't spacious, nor particularly nice, but he kept it neat enough so that if anything was out of order he was soon able to spot it. This was the main reason it came as such a great shock to him that until that moment, drying his hands on a towel in the kitchen, he hadn't seen the person sitting at his breakfast table at the back corner of the room. He froze, staring at the intruder in disbelief.

"Afternoon," Ink said, then stuffed a cream roll into his mouth.

"You . . . you broke into my flat?"

"I was sneaking," Ink replied. "Ain't no harm in sneaking, is there?"

Spindler walked over to the table. There he saw not only cream rolls but a large assortment of food from his cupboards, as well as a small bottle of gin the boy had already drained by a fourth. Spindler shook his head. "I honestly didn't think I'd ever see you again."

Ink pulled a piece of paper from his coat pocket and tossed it across the table. "Here."

"What's this?"

"The only interesting thing I found in his house. The rest was mostly just pencils and pens. Here, I got you one of them, too. They're quite nice." Ink took one of Mr. Bash's pens from his pocket and lobbed it across the table.

Spindler's brow furrowed in confusion as he read the paper. "Sentenced hence to death in Life, a cold and lightless . . . ha?"

"Hall," Ink corrected. "I was a bit pressed for time when I wrote it. Copied it from some kind of sign he had. Probably don't mean anything special." He picked up another cream roll.

"Hey, my landlady made those for me," Spindler said.

"And they're very good," Ink replied with his mouth full, spewing flecks of cream. "My compliments to her."

Spindler sat down at the other end of the table and looked over the paper a second time. "So this was it? A few lines on a piece of paper, a pen you stole—from a dead man, by the way—and that gives you the right to be eating all my food?"

"And drinking all your gin." Ink grabbed the bottle and took a sharp swig. Spindler leapt across the table and pulled it back, then set it on the floor out of sight. The boy smirked and slapped the table. "No, my good man, I get the rights to all this and *more* after what you put me through."

"What *I* put you through?"

"Yeah. 'Cause that little job wasn't half so nice and easy as you made it out to be. You said there wouldn't be no cops for at least another twelve hours, and who shows up on the doorstep not fifteen minutes after I get there? Not only cops, but Bill Stone himself. And not only Bill Stone, but something else. Something worse."

"And what was that?"

"Entrians."

Spindler shot up from the table, rushed back into the kitchen, threw his wet hat to the floor, and slammed the window shut. He whirled back to the boy and jabbed a finger at him. "You're not lying to me, are you?"

Ink narrowed his eyes. "I wouldn't have risked my neck coming back into town just to tell you lies. 'Specially not after what I've seen."

"And what have you seen?"

"First, I want what I'm owed. You said I'd be paid whether I found anything or not."

Spindler looked hard at the boy. After a moment, he picked up the advisory notice from the counter, returned to the table, and laid it down in front of him. Then he waited with a self-satisfied smirk as Ink read it over. When he finished, the boy flicked a bored glance up at the newspaperman.

"What's this?"

Spindler was caught off guard for a moment. "Well . . . it's you, isn't it? You're famous now. All over the country."

"Who says this is me?"

"The description . . . and—"

"Do I look like I'm five feet seven inches?"

"Well, no. But I'm sure that's just a typographical . . . uh . . ." Spindler grabbed up the sheet and re-scanned the print.

Ink scoffed. "And they don't even know the kid's age? That's a lousy orphanage."

"So . . . this isn't you?"

"Look," the boy said, "I'll save you the trouble, all right? I ain't never been to Delving. I don't even know where that is. I'm not even *close* to five feet seven inches, and as for the name, I've already told you that, and it certainly ain't that rubbish printed there."

"You could be lying about your name."

Ink nodded his head curtly. "I could be. I could be lying about a lot of things."

"Well, maybe you are!" Spindler said, raising the paper in the air.

Ink stood from his chair with so much force that Spindler almost took a step back.

"If you want to believe something then believe this!" the boy cried with an air of menace. "I ain't an orphan and I never have been! That kid on that paper ain't me! And if you like, I'll cut my wrist open right here and swear a blood oath to prove it!"

Spindler didn't doubt the boy's threat for a second and even glanced across the table to make sure there was no instrument within reach to do the job. Ink's eyes blazed, and every breath seemed a puff of smoke from a furnace boiling somewhere deep beneath his oversized coat.

"All right," Spindler said. "All right, I believe you. Just . . . calm down. I won't turn you in. That was never my intention. I just like to know a bit about who I employ."

"Forget it," Ink said. "I don't trust you. And besides that, I still don't see any payment in front of me."

Spindler sat back down in his chair and crossed his arms. "Well, you're out of luck there, Mr. Featherfield, because that payment consisted of the contents of my former wallet, to which you privileged yourself. You want to keep talking about trust now?"

"Pinchin' your wallet was a professional obligation," Ink said, taking his own seat again with an air of swagger. "You of all people oughta know better than to be so careless. I taught you a jolly good lesson and your cash was the cost of learning it. Now do you want the information or not?"

Once again, Spindler was forced to choke down his temper. He might even have laughed under different circumstances. The boy had him beat. With an irritated twitch of his mustache he got up and went over to his bedroom door, pausing to glare at Ink once more. "Entrians?"

Ink held up his fingers. "Three of 'em."

Spindler sighed and ducked into the bedroom. After a minute, he returned with a small roll of bills and set them on the table. The boy reached out and thumbed through the banknotes with one hand, then took the topmost one from the stack and held it up to the light.

Spindler rolled his eyes. "They're real."

"Just checking. Standard procedure." Satisfied, Ink scooped up the rest of the bills and tucked them into his pocket.

At last, he began his story. Spindler listened intently at first, analyzing the boy's face for any hint of falsehood—from the long climb up Edgely Hill, to the search through the house, to the arrival of the unexpected visitors. But by the time Ink's tale came to the appearance of the second carriage, his arms had come uncrossed, and the lie detection efforts dropped altogether. At the mention of the mysterious dark-eyed Entress, Spindler sat back in his chair and rubbed a hand over his chin in thought.

"Do you know her?" Ink asked.

"I'm not sure. But I remember that the Entrians appointed a woman to lead the search for the Colonists after what happened. The daughter of an Elder, I believe. From what you tell me, this may very well have been her."

"What's an Elder?"

"A sort of politician. The Entrians have a group of Elders governing them called the High Council, much like our Assembly."

"So you know her name?"

"I'm sure I must, but I can't recall it now. It's been a long time since we printed any news to do with the Entrians. But old Mr. Bash must have been the real thing if she showed up."

"About this woman," Ink said, shifting in his chair, "after it started raining last night she did some strange wavy motion in the air, and then the rain didn't touch 'em. I know people say they can do magic, but until last night I always thought it was a lot of rot and nonsense."

"It is neither rot nor nonsense," Spindler answered. "I've been once or twice to an Entrian city myself. Saw some incredible things. And they don't call it magic. It's natural to them, the things they can do. Just as you or I might think nothing of lighting a fire with flint and stone. Only they can do it with their hands."

Ink frowned. "With that kind of power you'd think they'd be running everything."

The newspaperman shrugged. "They had their chance. Didn't quite work out. Now back to these Entrians. Did they find anything else in the house? Apart from the crest jewel?"

"I didn't stick around long enough to find out. But I did hear something awful strange about this Bash bloke. They had a closer look at him and came to find out all his insides had been ground to a pulp. Not a single mark on the outside."

Spindler stared at him with a look of horror. "What do you mean 'ground to a pulp'?"

"Exactly how it sounds," Ink answered. "Bill asked 'em how it happened. He didn't get a straight answer, but I got a feeling those Entrian folk knew more than they were telling."

"Ground to a pulp . . ." Spindler repeated, bringing a hand to his brow.

"Rough way to go," Ink said. "Hey, you got any more of them cream rolls?"

"Forget the cream rolls. What else did you hear?"

"Not much else. Bill started to catch my scent so I had to

hitch it out of there fast. The lady did mention something about going to see some commissioner."

"Hm. That would be Marlas."

"Who's that?"

"The man leading the effort on our side—the Cassrians' side—to find the Colonists. He actually claims to have been one of them. Says he was tricked into getting involved in the whole business on Damiras."

Ink clasped his hands together on the table, suddenly looking uncomfortable. "Talking of which . . . I've been wondering 'bout that. I mean . . . that terrible thing the Colonists did. That massacre they all talk about. What happened exactly?"

Spindler stared at him, his face falling into a look of incredulity. "Oh, don't tell me. *Please* do not tell me you've never heard the story. No kid's supposed to get past their fifth year in school without hearing the story!"

Ink flushed as he threw up his hands. "Do I look like someone who'd waste time on something as useless as school? I learned my letters then put that place behind me as fast as I could. I ain't stupid, you know."

"I told him. I told him this would happen," Spindler grumbled, pinching the bridge of his nose. "That infernal mayor asked me to stop printing the story. Said it was making the news even more depressing. And this is what comes of it. Blatant ignorance."

"Hey," Ink said, "there's plenty of other places I could go to be insulted. Much nicer places, might I add."

"I'm sorry," Spindler said. "All right, listen. It used to be that the Entrians were broken up into feuding clans, at each other's throats for generations. It grew so bad that fights would break out in the middle of markets and crowded streets. Innocent people were often caught in the middle, even Cassrians were killed, and the entire country threatened to erupt into war because of it. It's no secret that we Cassrians have compensated for our lack of supernatural abilities with other things—great advancements in industry and invention. Because of this, the Elders began to consider they might lose a war between us, at which point they decided the only way to save their people was to leave. Withdraw to their cities and villages in the west. The Elders couldn't agree on a plan to end the feuds among their own people, but they implemented a decree of complete separation to avoid doing any more harm to us. Worked a bit too well in my opinion."

"I never even saw an Entrian close up 'til yesterday," Ink said.

"Exactly," Spindler replied. "The decision to separate their people from ours made our country even more divided, good intentions aside. But it wasn't until years later that an Entrian named Darian decided to do something about it."

Ink sat up straighter. "I heard that name last night."

"I'm not surprised. He was one of the first Entrians to speak out against the Separation Decree. He started traveling across the country, calling for unity between us and peace among the clans. Within a few months he'd gathered a large following of supporters who agreed with his message. He became very influential. Very powerful. Some even began to regard him as a prophet. But he also put a lot of people off. People who liked the way things had become. Then one day, he went to the Elders with an idea. A mass gathering of representatives from every Entrian family, every clan —a great council of sorts—to put an end to their feuds. Heal wounds and forgive wrongs. And contrary to expectation, the Elders actually agreed it was worth trying. They started setting up camps weeks ahead of time on the island of Damiras. Weapons were strictly forbidden. Priests walked the grounds. Everything was meticulously planned. And perhaps it would've worked. But when the day finally came, the Colonists didn't even let the talks begin."

"I don't understand that," Ink said. "I mean . . . the Colonists —they're Cassrians, right? Don't got no magic powers or anything. So how'd they get on that island without being noticed?"

"It's believed they found an Entrian willing to turn traitor for a bribe, who helped disguise them and get them access to the island. They stood among the clans as they gathered around a platform where the Elders would be speaking. After a few priests said prayers over the crowd, Darian got up to give a speech of encouragement."

He paused, hesitating. Ink raised an eyebrow impatiently. "And?"

"And . . . he wasn't halfway finished before one of the Colonists shot him through the heart."

Ink sat back in his chair.

"It was utter chaos after that," Spindler went on. "More shots were fired. Everyone started to run. There was so much confusion it was all too easy for the Colonists to take down so many. No one was safe. And once they ran out of bullets they started using axes and knives . . ."

He shook his head and stopped, deciding to skip ahead in the story. The boy let him.

"Eventually they set the entire island on fire," he continued, "so that the land itself became a mass grave. And once the dust cleared, they discovered that nearly half of all the Entrians who had come to Damiras had been massacred."

Ink's eyes widened in shock. *"Half?"*

Spindler nodded. "To this day no one knows how they managed to kill so many so quickly. The Colonists are thought to have numbered only thirty or so at the time. Afterwards, the Entrians took stock of their shattered society and finally realized they were stronger as a whole, no matter their differences. Now the clans are no more. It was the one bright spot in the wake of the tragedy, as well as the tension easing between us and them. Even those Cassrians who didn't particularly care for the Entrians found it hard not to be sympathetic."

"And the Colonists?" Ink said, frowning. "They just vanished off the face of the earth?"

"At first, finding them was easy. They made the mistake of splitting up afterwards and were easily caught—individually—as they tried to return to their homes. When they realized nowhere was safe for them anymore, they re-grouped and learned to live away from civilization. Where that is, of course, is one of the biggest mysteries of all."

"So what about Bash, then?"

"I don't know," Spindler said. "Maybe he left them. Maybe he was cast out. Maybe he stayed in town to serve as a supply runner."

"And what about that name of theirs? The Colonists. Why are they called that?"

"A moment before Darian was shot, somebody shouted 'Colonists, arise!' from the middle of the crowd. No one knows what it means. Maybe they're implying the Cassrians have the only right to colonize Eriaris. Maybe not. It's just another mystery to add to all the rest."

The two of them were quiet for a long time after that. Spindler stared at the table and tried to organize all the new information in his mind. After a while he raised his eyes and studied the boy across from him. Ink's spirited energy had lapsed into a solemn stillness. He was clearly disturbed. That, or feeling sick from all the gin and cream puffs.

"Well," Spindler said, breaking the silence. "Strange words on a stone . . . Entrians on Edgely Hill . . . a Colonist who most definitely did not die of a heart attack. You had quite the adventure. Is that the end of it?"

Ink leaned back in his chair and crossed his arms. "I'll be needin' another fifty for the end."

Spindler spewed out a half-snort, half-chuckle. "What?"

"I've been good for the money so far, haven't I?"

"So?"

"So I ain't even got to the best part yet."

Spindler glared hard at the boy. This Inkwell knew how to play his hand. He knew any respectable newspaperman would never be able to let a tantalizing phrase like that go unexplained. With a shake of his head, he reached into his back pocket for the rest of the banknotes and tossed them across the table. Ink swept them up, stuffed them into his pocket, then began the tale of the screaming shadow in the water and the mysterious man who had intervened.

When the story was finished, Spindler rose from his chair and began to pace the room, smoothing down his mustache. "That's a bloody odd thing to happen so close to Bash's place, so soon after his death. I wonder if the events are connected somehow. Do you think you could take me back to the spot where it happened?"

"Oooh," Ink replied, getting up from the table. "Tempting. Quite tempting. But I think I've had my share of terror and panic today, thank you very much."

He donned his hat and moved around the table towards the door. Spindler stopped him. "You'd get more money. I'll give you another twenty once we get there."

"Not a chance."

"Twenty-five."

"No."

"Thirty! That's all I can spare and still afford to eat for the rest of the week."

"Eat all you like 'cause I ain't doing one more blasted thing for you," Ink said. "You nearly got me mixed up in some very dark stuff and I don't like a bit of it."

"I think you're already mixed up in it, Mr. Featherfield," Spindler replied. "You know it, too. I can see it in your eyes. You've been affected. I think it's a bit late for backing out now."

"I've been startled. That's all," Ink shot back. "And I've had enough of you and this stinking town. I've done your little errand. Now I'm off! I've had enough of cops, and magic people, and ground-up corpses, and men who drown themselves in lakes—"

"But don't you care?"

"Care?"

"Yes, *care*! Be bothered with! Have concern for! Damiras didn't end nine years ago, you know! That battle is still being fought! The Colonists keep killing! And you may regard it all as bothersome noise but you can't live your whole life keeping out of the way!"

"Watch me!" Ink cried. "Just you watch me! And when you're old and feeble I'll come back here and tell you all about it! Then you can write a book about *me*! Inkwell Featherfield . . . The Man Who Kept Out of the Way!"

Thud.

Something bumped against the front door. Ink turned his head, then let out a small gasp of shock, feeling a brief sensation of pain. He put his hand to his right cheek and felt something wet. His fingers came away with a thin streak of blood. Spindler frowned at the sight of it.

Before either could say a word, the *thud* came again. Dumb-founded, they watched as a huge crack appeared in the door. It split the wood from frame to floor right through the center, then branched out in a series of smaller fractures. The sound was like ice breaking on a frozen pond. The cracks grew, widening and lengthening until at last the entire door burst into pieces. Spindler shouted in alarm and raised his arms as splinters of wood flew in every direction. Ink didn't move, but stood staring at the three people who had rushed into the room.

CHAPTER 8

ON THE RUN AGAIN

One of the strangers was a tall, light-haired man who glanced around the room with a fierce gaze. The second was a lanky young man sporting a shock of tousled red hair and a scraggly patch of beard. He raised a lantern to his eye and stared into the high flame flickering inside the glass. The third person was a golden-haired woman who appeared to be no more than a year or two past twenty, barely out of the frocks and ribbons of girlhood. She beckoned to them with an urgent panic.

"Hurry!"

"Hurry?" Spindler echoed. "Hurry where? You've broken my door!"

"There's no time for explanation!" said the older man, waving towards the hall. "We have to move!"

The red-head lowered the lantern and glanced at Ink with a look of dread. "You're gonna get a lot more than a scratch if you wait any longer! Let's *go*!"

He sprang forward, grabbed Ink by the arm, and pulled him out of the flat. The woman did the same to Spindler, who was too bewildered to protest. The light-haired stranger led the way through the hall and down a flight of stairs.

"As soon as we're out, run as fast as you can!" he called back. "We'll explain later, but you've got to trust us!"

Neither Spindler nor Ink bothered to argue, for just as the group approached the front door of the building, they heard a horrifying scream from the floor above. Spindler halted and glanced back, feeling as though his heart might stop for fear.

"Go!" the woman cried, pushing him forward.

They took off down the street, dodging people left and right. Spindler bumped into a man carrying an armload of parcels and yelled out an apology as he ran by. Ink held onto his hat as they turned a sharp corner into a narrow alleyway. They hung a quick right soon after and sprinted past a baffled gaggle of school-children and an alarmed priest.

"Where are we going?" Ink shouted.

"Away from here!" the woman answered. "Out of the town!"

The light-haired man at the head of their party swerved off the path and cut across a field, leading them down a hill. Ink seemed to have no trouble keeping up, having no doubt relied on his legs for quick getaways many times before. Spindler, however, was not accustomed to long-distance sprinting and held a hand to his aching side.

A minute later they broke through a line of trees bordering a farm, then made straight for a large barn a few hundred feet away. As soon they came to a stop behind it, Spindler stooped over with his hands on his knees, breathing hard.

"Take a look, Evering," the older man said to the red-haired one.

Evering rushed to the edge of the barn and peered around the corner. The others watched as he raised the flame once more to his eye and surveyed the terrain.

"Nothing," he said at last. "I think we've got clear of it."

"Thank God we were just in time," the woman said, brushing her hair from her face.

"In time for what?" Spindler asked. "What do you mean by all this? Who are you?"

The older man knelt in front of Ink and gently took his chin in his hand, looking over the wound on his cheek. "Lucky. Very lucky. And that's saying something, considering I don't even believe in luck." He withdrew a small vial of liquid from his pocket and poured a few drops onto a handkerchief. "Here. Hold this to the wound."

Ink frowned at the handkerchief in suspicion.

"It's just something to help it heal a bit quicker," the man assured him.

Ink took it and pressed it against his jaw. "What happened? What did this to me?"

"Simon," the woman said, "maybe you shouldn't frighten him. He's just a boy."

Ink bristled, then glared hard at the man in front of him. "Frighten me."

Simon glanced at the young man called Evering, who nodded. After a moment's hesitation, he met Ink's eyes again. "It's difficult to explain," he began, "and twice as hard to understand. But you were attacked by something called a Spektor."

"A what?" Spindler said.

"They're nearly impossible to see, unless they want to be seen," Simon continued. "But no less real in this world than in the one to which they truly belong."

Spindler scoffed. "A ghost? You're talking to us about ghosts? Are you serious?"

"Far worse than ghosts," Evering replied. "Spektors are the souls of the dead allowed back to this side of things. They can get inside you. Inside your head—"

"But it's very rare for them to physically attack anyone," Simon said, his steady gaze still on Ink. "Which is why you're such a great wonder. In all of history, Spektors have never set upon someone so young as you."

"Wait a minute," Spindler interrupted. "You're saying an evil spirit is after him? You actually expect us to believe that?"

"We never expect anyone to believe it," the woman answered. "But that doesn't make it any less true."

"Who are you?" Spindler asked. "Some kind of . . . evil spirit rescue patrol?"

"Just ordinary folk who spotted someone in trouble," Simon answered. He looked back at Ink. "But we don't have a lot of time to stay here talking. For some reason the Spektors are following you. Seeking you out. And if the one back in that room doesn't find you again, another will. It's only a matter of time."

"Then I'll just keep running," Ink said. "I'm always on the move. If what you're saying is true, I won't let 'em get close to me again!"

"Running won't be enough," Evering replied. "No matter where you go, they'll follow. If you escape down one road, there'll be three more waiting for you at the other end. That's why you have to come with us."

Ink frowned. "What?"

"There's only one place in this world where no Spektor will dare go," Simon answered. "And we can take you there. You'll be safe. But we have to leave now."

"Where is this place?" Spindler asked.

"I'm afraid we can't tell you that."

Spindler scoffed, sneering with a mixture of anger and disgust. "What are you trying to do? Take advantage of this boy by frightening him out of his wits? Get him to trust you before you kidnap him? Is that the trick?"

"We're not kidnapping you," Simon said to Ink, rising to his feet. "We won't force you to go with us. It must be your choice. But you'd do well to go on a little faith after what you saw at the lake earlier this morning."

A look of wonder crossed Ink's face.

"How do you know about that?" Spindler demanded.

"There's no time to explain everything!" Evering said.

Spindler wheeled on him. "Look, kid, if you don't start playing straight I'll knock the red right out of that hair! You're already in the wrong for breaking into my flat, but to feed us this ridiculous drivel about spirits and secret safe havens? Come on, Ink. We've got a police report to write up. And you lot had better clear off while you still can!"

"I don't need you to save me, Spindler!"

Spindler stared at the boy, stunned. Ink straightened his hat and glanced at the strangers.

"Now I don't know if what these people are saying is all on the level, but I aim to find out. If they *are* right, I don't fancy being a target for something I can't see. I can afford a few days to hang around in this safe place of theirs. And if they're liars, I'll slip through their fingers easy as ice. I've done it before. Been taking care of myself for a long time now. So don't trouble yourself, all right? Just go back to your cozy little life and forget all about me. Should be easy enough."

Spindler didn't answer. It was all happening too fast.

Simon stepped towards him. "I know it's hard, but try to put your mind at ease. We'll take good care of him. As for you, don't return to the flat for another few days. We're sure it wasn't after you but that doesn't mean . . ." He paused, then clapped him on the shoulder. "Just take a little holiday." He looked back at the others. "Let's go."

He turned and headed back towards the tree line, sweeping his gaze in every direction as he went. The woman followed quickly behind, while Evering kept pace beside Ink. Spindler watched as they walked away, confounded. Ink wasn't his son, not his nephew or his neighbor. They weren't even friends, really. He had no influence or powers of persuasion to talk him out of this. Besides, it was three against one, so there was no hope of taking the boy back by force. All in all, there was nothing more he could do.

"Oh, by the way!" Ink cried out, looking back over his shoulder. "Don't keep your money under that squeaky floorboard in your bedroom. Way too obvious."

"How did you know . . ." Spindler began, but dropped it.

One by one, they disappeared into the woods. The moment the boy's coattails melted into the shadows, Spindler woke from his stupor and cried out.

"Hey! Hey, wait!"

Without a second thought, he dashed across the field and hurtled into the woods not fifteen seconds after them. He slowed to a stop, glancing around in bewilderment. All was still and silent, the adjoining field clearly visible only a dozen feet away.

They were nowhere to be seen.

CHAPTER 9

INFIRM IN THE INFIRMARY

"I shy aw iet?"

The first sound Ink heard upon stirring awake were the words of a strange language.

"A henk ees omin oud ow."

He couldn't open his eyes, nor move his limbs. He was also so groggy and nauseous he didn't even have the urge to panic over having lost consciousness. With every second that passed the strange speech began to morph into another language, the voices sharper and clearer.

"He's all right," a man's voice said. "Let's get to the infirmary. Grab his hat, Evering."

Ink felt himself being lifted up and carried. Wherever they were, it was windy. The air rustled through his hair and clothes. Hollow moaning noises sounded in the distance, like the rush of wind in a cave. The footsteps around him suggested the ground below was wooden but it was a thinner, echoing noise, as though they walked on a seaside dock. Dripping water and the soft hiss of steam resounded nearby. He tried again to lift his eyelids but couldn't.

After going up a long flight of stairs, a door creaked open, and the darkness around him lightened. They were outdoors. The trickle of water was far off, as was the sound of leaves fluttering in the breeze. They traveled a good while, each step now sounding as though cobblestone lay underfoot.

"I'll get the door," a woman's voice said.

There was a pause in momentum, followed by a heavy door groaning open. Then it was three steps upward and he was under a roof again. The door closed behind.

"Riva, clear that stuff off the cot, will you?" the man said.

Ink heard a great deal of noise—papers being gathered, books clapping shut, chairs scraping along the floor—before he was set down on a soft surface. He felt a thin layer of linen beneath his fingertips.

"Bring some water," the man's voice came again. "And my smelling salts from the cupboard above the wash basin."

Ink tried to speak, putting all his energy to the task. "Dun ned sim sets."

"What's he's saying?" a younger man's voice asked.

Ink felt fingers go around his wrist, pressing gently into the pulsing artery.

"Dun ned simlin sats," he tried again, sounding stone drunk.

"Take it easy, now. Take deep breaths," the man said.

Ink took the advice. After a while the pressure on his chest began to lift, and his head began to clear. A set of footsteps neared the bed.

"Eastern Calamor Spice?" the woman said. "That's a new one. Where'd you get it?"

"Some apothecary shop near Yelton. Delia brought it up for me last spring."

Ink clamped his hand down on the man's arm and forced his eyes to open at last.

"Don't . . . need . . . smelling salts."

Simon handed the bottle back to the woman. After a few moments, Ink decided he was able to move, though upon being helped to a sitting position he felt a sudden sourness in his stomach which threatened to rise.

"Go slowly," Simon said. "Don't force yourself to recover faster than you can."

The young man shook his head. "I didn't think he'd be so affected as that."

Ink fought the urge to collapse back onto the cot. More deep breaths and a few sips of water helped a little. "Where'm I?"

"You're safe," the woman answered. "There's nothing to worry about now."

"Wha . . . happ'n t'me?"

"You just need a bit of time to adjust," Simon answered. "Sit here for another few minutes. Take some more water."

Ink wasn't sure why there should be a need to "adjust," but his head wasn't yet working properly. He concentrated on getting his eyes to fully open as he looked at his surroundings. He was in a large room shaped in a curious half-circle, with one straight wall on the far side where the door stood. He could just make out the shape of a narrow staircase in the dim hall beyond.

"Shall we go and tell the others?" he heard the woman ask.

Before anyone could answer, a flood of daylight suddenly poured into the hall, followed by a loud bang. Ink squinted as a stout, burly man with formidable muttonchop sideburns came tromping into the room. His sleeves were pushed up over his elbows and a streak of dark grease ran along his hairy right arm.

"Hey, Dad," Evering said.

"Evering!" the man barked. "What the blazes were you doing down there? I heard it just now from Martin. Why didn't you tell me you were going? And Riva, you went too?"

"Well, yes," the young woman answered, "but—"

"For goodness sake, Simon!" the man said. "They're just kids! Kids!"

Evering frowned. "Uh, Dad, I'm twenty-four."

"You shut your trap," the man said, then turned back to Simon. "You should've fetched *me*. Or Delia. Or Jeremy. That's dangerous work, man! Too dangerous for them!"

"I'm sorry, Abner," Simon answered, "but the situation came

up suddenly and they were nearest by. I think you would've been proud to see how they handled things."

"It's not Simon's fault, Dad," Evering said, then turned towards Ink. "And it's him who should get the worrying. He's the one it was after."

It was only then Abner realized there was another person in the room. He looked at the boy on the cot and blinked with a furrowed brow, the fury of his temper all but evaporating.

"You? A Spektor went after you?"

Ink shrugged. He wasn't sure he could have managed much more of an answer.

Abner took a step closer and peered at him in wonder. "Gracious me. You can't be much more past a decade. How old are you?"

Ink raised an eyebrow. "Younger'n ma father. I think."

"He's a bit addled right now," Simon said. "The trip didn't go so easy with him. But while he recovers we need to start rounding everyone up for a meeting."

"Of course," Abner said, still staring at Ink in bafflement. "I'll help you to that."

Simon turned to Ink. "I want you to rest here and keep on drinking the water. There's a small plate of apple pieces here as well. Eat what you can but not too quickly." He looked over the wound on the boy's cheek once more. "Already beginning to heal. Good. How do you feel? Sick to your stomach?"

"Jus'a bit."

"Evering, Riva, I want you two to keep an eye on him. Get him anything he needs and see that he doesn't wander."

The young people nodded at him. As Simon and Abner moved for the hall, Ink noticed—with some relief—that his hat was hanging on a peg near the door.

"Hold on!" Evering called out after them. "What about Caradoc?"

"We can't wait for him," Simon replied. "And anyway he asked for a meeting to be called whether he was here or not."

"Then let's not waste time," Abner answered.

"Back in a bit," Simon said to the others. "And don't ask him too many questions."

Once they had gone from the room, Evering dragged two chairs nearer to the cot, then sat down and hunched forward with his bony elbows on his knees. Riva took her chair with a quiet sigh and stared towards the hall.

It took only a few moments for their eyes to turn back to the newcomer. Their attempt was discreet at first, but their curiosity was such that they were soon staring at him as though he might burst into flame. Ink fidgeted under their gaze, indignant at having been placed under guard. He grabbed the plate of apple pieces and dusted it off within seconds. It wasn't much, but it steadied his roiling stomach and eased his lightheadedness.

With his senses restored and the dizziness gone, he began another survey of the room. The cot on which he sat was one of three set against the curving wall. Heavy curtains were drawn across three huge windows. The walls were made of white stone and the floor set with burnished tile. The ceiling was dark timber. To the far left were a series of tables and counters which looked like a makeshift workstation. Two large cupboards hung over a wash basin, and next to these was a collection of instruments consisting of a saw, hammer, clamp, a large pair of scissors, and a row of assorted knives. A pile of rolled bandages was heaped on a corner table. Everything was clean and tidy—far nicer than any other infirmary he'd seen. There were no peculiar smells of chemicals, nor was the room stuffy or overheated. The place had a sense of calm to it, which put Ink more at ease than he would have thought possible under the circumstances. He glanced back at the two sitting in front of him and set his water glass down, unable to continue ignoring the two sets of eyes burning holes through him.

"All right, look," he said, "if you're waiting for me to do a trick, the only one I know involves a hot iron and a cat."

Evering dropped his gaze for a moment. "Sorry. We've just never had anyone new here."

"You never had anyone here in hospital before?"

"Oh, yes," the woman answered. "Just no one new."

Ink frowned. Her answer made his head start to swim again.

"What's your name?" she asked.

"Inkwell," he said. "'Ink' for short, if you like."

"Ink?" the red-head said, grinning in amusement. "You mean like pen and ink?"

"Boy, you catch on quick. You're called Evering, yeah?"

"That's right," he said. "And this is Riva."

The woman smiled. "Rivalia for the long way, but I prefer 'Riva'."

"And the blonde-haired chap?" Ink said. "You called him 'Simon'?"

Evering answered with a nod. "And the other was my dad, Abner."

They fell quiet again. Ink took the time to study his rescuers —if they even had the right to be called as such. Evering, he thought, had a stupid face which conveyed an almost perpetual expression of both surprise and confusion. He was a reedy lad, and pale as the colorless walls around him but for the fiery red of his shaggy hair. The weak patch of beard on his face seemed to be struggling to remain in existence. The younger woman, Riva, smiled readily with a cheery sparkle in her eyes. Her wavy gold hair fell to the middle of her back, curling at the ends.

"So how'd you do it?" Evering asked.

"Do what?" Ink said.

"Get on the wrong side of the Spektors."

Ink shrugged. "Hanged if I could say. I didn't even know they existed 'til a few minutes ago, if they do at all. I know I saw something strange. Dangerous, even. But I ain't one to go believing in spirits and all that kind of rubbish. There's got to be some other explanation."

"What about that scratch on your face?" Evering said. "What do you suppose did that?"

Ink put a hand to his cheek. "Dunno. Maybe I did it to myself and just didn't notice. Can you explain all the little nicks and bruises you've got?"

Evering turned and nodded at Riva. "He must be one of them *logicals*."

"Why'd I faint when you brought me here?" Ink asked. "That Simon said something about needing to 'adjust'. What'd he mean by that?"

"Adjusting to all the excitement," Evering said hurriedly. "Your blood pressure must've gone up and . . . or your heart rate, you know . . ."

"That don't make sense," Ink said, frowning.

"Doesn't it?" Evering said, looking to Riva.

"What about that man you were with?" Riva said, changing the subject. "Is he your father?"

Ink scoffed. "No."

"Uncle?" Evering offered.

"No relation."

"He certainly seemed to care about you," Riva said.

"He had me running a few errands for him. That's all," Ink replied. "I ain't nothing more than a business concern to him. But what about that trick you pulled with his door? Blowing it to bits like that. Did you use an explosive?"

The two in front of him exchanged a furtive glance.

"You might say that," Riva replied.

"I *might*?" Ink said. "Would I be right if I *did*?"

Evering considered this for a moment, then nodded with enthusiasm. "You might just perhaps be in the realm of possibility!"

Ink put a hand to his head. They were talking circles around him—clumsily—but enough to addle his thoughts. He would have to let them get away with it for now.

"All right," he said. "At least tell me where I am. What kind of place is this? It don't really have the look of any common infirmary."

Evering shrugged. "Well, we do our best with what we get."

"And what have you got?" Ink asked with raised eyebrows, still waiting for a real answer.

"You'll see it all for yourself soon enough," Riva answered. "All you need know for now is that you're in the safest place in the world. You can put your mind at ease about that."

"What makes it so safe? You said it keeps these Spektor things away. But how?"

"Well," Evering began, "it's not really so much a matter of *what* or *where* as *who*."

"All right," Ink said, rolling his eyes, "then *who* makes it safe? And how'd you know about that Spektor coming after me in the lake? Were you watching me?"

Riva smiled again. "I don't think we're the best ones to answer the sorts of questions you have, Ink. But others will. All in good time."

Ink heaved a quiet sigh. They were keeping a lot of secrets here. Too many for his liking. Under any other circumstances, he would have cut loose and rushed off on his own again. But then he recalled the sound of the scream piercing through the thick fog, and the sight of gaping jaws of silver teeth charging towards him. He clutched at the edge of the cot. He had no reason to trust these people, but he had to know if they were right. If their claims were true. He would live in constant fear otherwise. Besides, there were no warning feelings in his gut about them. No one he'd met so far came off as the violent or dangerous type. Granted, he would keep his guard up, but he would stick it out and see what they had to say—if only for a bit longer.

He put his hands on the cot behind him and leaned back, passing his gaze around the room again. "Have you all been here very long?"

Evering nodded. "A fair few years. Why?"

"I was just wondering if you ever had anyone here by the name of Revore."

"Can't say I've ever heard that name before," Evering said.

"Nor I," Riva replied. "But it looks like you're getting your color back. You must be feeling better. Does your cheek still hurt?"

"Nah."

"You're lucky it wasn't deep," Evering said. "You won't have a scar to show for it."

Ink touched his cheek again and smirked. "Shame that. Always fancied myself a few scars. Makes you look a bit fiercer. Like you seen a thing or two, you know?"

Evering dropped his gaze to the floor. The light in Riva's eyes dimmed as an expression of melancholy passed across her face for a moment. The front door opened again. Simon stepped into the room and beckoned to them.

"All right. Everyone's been called. Let's go."

Riva helped Ink to stand, making sure he was steady on his feet. Evering grinned as he led the way to the outer hall.

"Hey, Simon! His name is *Inkwell*. Ink for short. Ain't that a laugh?"

Ink scowled as he swiped his hat from the peg near the door.

CHAPTER 10

THE WORST SHOCK YET

T he first thing Ink noticed upon leaving the room was the scent of the air. It was fresh cut grass, apple orchards, tilled earth, a crisp hint of coming snow, and the enlivening fragrance of a wood-burning fire. He took a deep breath and felt all traces of sickness instantly vanish.

He had not emerged from any common hospital building on any common dirty street, as he'd expected, but in a curious place unlike any he had ever seen. It was a small village of round houses set in a large circle, and the stone path on which he now stood connected the front steps of each to all the others. As Ink followed his hosts down the curving path, he noticed that the second story of every house consisted of a domed room made of glass. Ink frowned at the sight. Why would anyone want a glass room? It seemed a great way to attract meddlesome neighbors.

Inside the circular path was a dense forest of trees and shrubbery. Mid-autumn had caught them in a costume change. Fiery reds, deep oranges and yellows dotted the inner reaches of the grove, which was so expansive it was impossible to tell just how many houses lay along the path. Wildflowers dotted the grass everywhere he looked. As they walked on, they came to a place where the stone path swelled up into a footbridge. A clear stream drifted underneath, nearly ten feet wide, running between two of the houses and disappearing into the dense grove.

Ink started to lag behind, intrigued by the odd surroundings and eager to take in whatever details he could spot. He had made it a practice to mark the particulars of any new place in which he found himself, noting escape routes and hiding places that might come in handy later. His eyes lingered longest on the most eye-catching feature of the village—a massive stone tower set in the middle of the garden grove, rising high above the rest of the village. Windows were set around the second and third levels. The fourth was made of glass, mirroring the construction of the houses below. Ink tilted his head back to look at it. At sea, he would have guessed it to be a lighthouse. On land, it looked like a guard tower.

"What is this place?" he asked aloud.

Riva glanced back at him, slowing her pace. "I'm sorry?"

"I ain't never seen a village like this before. Where are we?"

"We're here," Evering replied from ahead. "You can ask questions later. Let's just get this meeting over with first."

As Simon went up to one of the houses and pushed through the front door, Ink's pace faltered. "And who exactly are we supposed to be meeting? No cops or judges or anyone of that sort?"

"Nothing like that," Riva said, patting his arm. "Come on. There's no need to worry."

Ink frowned as she and Evering followed Simon through the door.

"Of course not," he muttered.

Inside, the house appeared identical to the infirmary. There was a narrow staircase in a dimly-lit hall and two doors on either side, both shut. As the group made their way upstairs, Ink trailed them while taking note of the back door at the far end of the hall. Another escape route.

He soon found himself in the domed glass room of the second story, which seemed to be a sort of music chamber. An old piano sat nearby, as well as a large harp half-covered with a linen sheet. There were stringed instruments, goatskin drums, and a collection of whistles and pipes in wooden boxes. On the far side, a man was sweeping back a heap of sheet music which had tumbled over itself. He stood and returned to a circle of chairs in the center of the room.

Ink froze mid-step when he saw the chairs were all occupied. His eyes darted to every face as they turned to look at him. He counted eleven altogether, and noted Abner nearby stroking his chin and leaving traces of dark soot. Once Riva and Evering were seated, Simon stood beside Ink and put a hand on his shoulder.

"Everyone, this is Inkwell. Ink, for short, as I understand it."

Ink stared in disdain at the hand on his shoulder. Simon withdrew it before continuing.

"Early this morning, Ink had an encounter with a Spektor who sought to do him harm. This, of course, alerted Caradoc into action, which is why he isn't here with us now. We had a brief discussion before he left and agreed that I should take a small party down to seek the boy out. We found him mere moments after another Spektor did. Ink came away with a small scratch on his face and a terrible scare, I daresay, but thankfully we were able to get him away in time and bring him here to safety."

Ink had assumed an expression of cool indifference, but he was more worried than ever. They must have been watching him at the lake. How else could they know what had happened?

"You think that was a wise decision?"

The question came from a man sitting a few seats to the left. He appeared to be the same age as Simon but stood in stark contrast to him, bearing a proud cleft chin and an entirely humorless expression.

"For goodness sake, Martin, look at him," said an older woman four seats down. "He's only a child. What business could a Spektor possibly have with a child? This is a strange case."

A woman next to Evering leaned forward and clasped her gloved hands together in earnest. She was almost as plump and round as the cushion against which she sat. "Perhaps if you told us what you've done today," she said to Ink, "we could figure it out. See what you did wrong."

"You don't have to do anything wrong to call on a Spektor, Jo," the woman beside her replied. She resembled the other so closely in face and form, Ink figured they had to be sisters.

Simon gestured for Ink to sit, and he did so. Simon took a seat beside him.

"Ink," he said, "can you remember doing or seeing anything odd before you met the first Spektor this morning? Or perhaps the night before?"

Ink thought it over. There were the thefts of the constables. His arrest and escape. Breaking into the dead man's house. The strange words on the stone. The goddess in the rain. His business with Spindler. But he was a fool if he was going to tell them anything. For all he knew, the moment they found out he was both a thief *and* a spy they would turn him over to the nearest constable or judge. Better to deny everything than to see that happen.

He shook his head. "No. Nothing odd at all."

"Nothing?" Abner echoed. "Everything was completely business as usual? You're sure?"

"Yeah, I'm sure."

"Was he alone when you found him?" said the darker-haired of the two large ladies. "Perhaps the Spektor was after someone else."

"There was another man with him when the second Spektor came," Riva said, "but we don't think he was a target. And he wasn't harmed."

"Twice now they've been on the hunt specifically for Ink. The first time he was completely alone," Simon added.

"Well, we'll never get anywhere if we don't find out more specifics," the stern man called Martin replied. "Who are your parents, boy? What do they do?"

"They got nothing to do with this," Ink snapped.

"How do you know?" Martin shot back, uncrossing his arms and putting a hand on his thigh. He was missing half his left arm at the elbow.

"I just know," Ink said. "And anyway, why should I tell you? Why should I tell any of you anything?"

"Oh, dear," said the first plump woman. "He doesn't believe yet, does he?"

"Well, why should he?" another man replied. "All he's got to show for it is a scratch."

Ink glanced at his sympathizer. He looked like an actor or a smarmy salesman, sporting a pointed beard, a finely-trimmed mustache, and his hair slicked down with so much grease the sun reflected off it. There was a touch of gray at his temples and in his whiskers. He sat slouched in his chair with his hands clasped over his prominent belly. A cigar in the front pocket of his shirt slumped to one side.

"He probably thinks he did it to himself somehow," the man continued. "Passed too close to a branch or something. Half of us didn't believe this Spektor business 'til we saw with our own eyes. More than likely, that's just what it'll take for him."

"Well, we can't send him off on a Spektor hunt," Abner said. "For now he'll just have to take our word for it."

"Help us, Ink," Riva said. "Give us something to work with."

Ink sighed. "I've already told you. I slept, ate, and walked around town. Nothing else."

"He's not telling the truth," Martin said.

"Look, Stumpy," Ink snapped again, "I couldn't care less if you don't want to believe me. My time's being wasted here just as much as yours."

Martin's mouth fell into an ugly scowl. He jabbed a finger at

Ink from the hand he did have. "You can be *hanged* if you don't want our help, you little ingrate."

"Martin!" chided the woman sitting next to him. Ink guessed she was his wife, younger by a few years, mid or late thirties perhaps. She was a gentle-looking lady. Her soft eyes held kindness and warmth yet were also tinged with a hint of sadness. A cane lay against her chair.

The man brushed off her admonition. "If he won't tell us anything, I say we turn him loose. I don't see how this affects any of us in the long run anyway."

"You cold-hearted brute, can't you see he's frightened?" the older lady rebuked.

"Spare me, Delia. Need I remind you that even children are not above suspicion here?"

"That was different." Delia shot a hesitant glance at Ink before continuing. "That was one isolated incident. This boy doesn't know what's going on. He's in the middle of a group of strangers in a strange place. We can't expect him to open up his whole life to us here and now."

"Then he'll have to stay here until he does," Evering said.

Silence fell over the room as all eyes turned his way. Evering shrank in his seat at the sudden attention.

"That's impossible," Martin replied, still sulking from Ink's backhanded insult. "If he stays here even an hour longer, we can't let him back down again. Not even if we keep him confined to a room."

Ink's heart began to beat faster in his chest. What had he gotten himself into?

"We all know to be . . . prudent," Simon answered. "As long as Ink remains on the immediate grounds there shouldn't be a problem."

Martin scoffed loudly and shook his head.

"Well we're not feeding him to the wolves, Martin, so you can just let up on that point," Simon said. "Evering's right. He'll stay. At least until Caradoc gets here. Then we'll decide what's to be done. Which rooms do we have open?"

Abner stroked his chin and stared at the ground in thought. "The only empty house we've got now is this one. Ackland and Bash shared it last, I think."

"No, it was the Pitmans," Riva said.

"Oh, that's right."

Ink's ears perked up. "Bash?"

Everyone turned to look at him.

"You know that name?" Simon asked.

Ink hesitated under the stare of eleven pairs of eyes. For a moment he felt like melting away into the shadows, but instead he sat up straighter and tipped his hat back from his face. "Sure I know him. Everyone in town knows him. Or at least they do now if they didn't before."

The others exchanged nervous glances.

"And why is that?" the pointy-bearded man asked. "What's to know?"

Ink glanced around, confused by the mysterious mass reaction. "Well . . . he's dead."

The mood in the room immediately darkened. The gentle-looking woman put a hand to her mouth. The sisters gasped and exchanged wide-eyed glances. The one-armed man sighed and sat back, smoothing his hair. Both Riva and Delia looked as though they would be ill. Evering gripped the edges of his chair until his knuckles whitened.

"What happened?" he said. "Was he killed?"

"He was . . ." Ink began, but stopped. "Hang on. Why would you think straightaway he was killed? And whatcha mean 'Bash shared the room last'? Was he here once?"

"Only very briefly," the pointy-bearded man said hurriedly as he sat up straight. "Passed through on his way to another village."

"The room is very nice," Abner said, standing. "I can show it to you now."

"I'll bring you some fresh linens as well," Delia offered.

"I I-have you had something to eat?" the kind-eyed woman

asked, picking up her cane. "I'd be happy to make you something now, if you like."

Ink also rose from his chair, not about to be thrown off the disturbing scent he had picked up. A growing panic brought fear and anger into his voice.

"All right, just stop it," he said. "Where am I? Where'd you take me? Why's this place so secret that you can't tell me? And why should you think Bash was killed? And why, if this place lodges passersby, would you all be staring at me like I was the first person to set foot here in a hundred years?"

"Stay calm, Ink," Simon began. "There's no use getting—"

"And why'd I black out on the way here? Did you crack me on the head?"

"Of course not!"

"Son, there's no reason to get upset," Abner said.

"There's plenty of reason! And don't call me 'son'!"

"Can't you understand we want to help you?" Riva said.

"No! No, I can't!" Ink cried. "Why would you want to help me? You don't know me! And I don't know you! So why should I trust you? I shouldn't have let you talk me into this. This was a mistake."

Martin rose from his seat with a rising temper. "Turn him loose, Simon. I haven't waited nine years just to have everything blown to the wind by a kid in a circus costume."

At that moment, everything came together. Bash. Secret location. No visitors. Nine years. Ink felt his knees weaken as the terrible revelation hit him like a blow from a cannon. He stood silent for a long moment, then whispered a word on the hint of a breath.

"Colonists."

By the looks on their faces, he knew he'd hit on the truth. He needed no better proof. In a flash, he turned on his heel and fled as fast as he could across the room. An outcry of protest flared up behind him.

Ink didn't falter for a moment. He flew down the stairs, out the back door, and into the meadow beyond. Everything he had ever heard about the Colonists rushed to his mind. What they had done—and what they might yet do—was enough to convince him that he was not only running for his liberty but for his life as well.

Voices shouted out from behind. They were following. He pumped his arms harder and lengthened his stride, making for the towering tree line at the far side of the meadow. He had a clean track record of successful getaways throughout his short career and this was no time to put a mark against it. When the two men following him saw where he was heading, their cries grew to a frantic pitch.

"No! Not that way! Stop!"

"Ink! Come back! We're not going to—"

Ink plunged into the thick green darkness. Branches whipped him in the face. Brambles caught at his coat. He took a twisting route around the trees, doubling back to the west, then to the south to befuddle his hunters. But the men knew these woods well and fell back by no more than a few seconds.

"There! He's right there! Grab him!"

Ink felt a hand tug at the edge of his coat. He surged forward and turned eastward again, pulling back a thick tangle of branches as he went, then releasing them. The curse that followed told him he'd hit his target.

The trees began to thin out soon after, and Ink realized he was approaching the far side of the wood. He wondered if another open field lay beyond, and whether it might be best to stay in the trees under better cover. Again, a voice cried out from behind.

"Ink! Stop! For your own sake, stop!"

The edge of the wood came into view, but the strong sunlight dazzled his eyes and kept him from seeing much more beyond. He heard footfalls closing in on him, and with a great leap he broke out of the trees.

It was then he saw the ground suddenly dropping away only a few steps farther. With a cry of terror he dug in his heels and tried to skid to a halt. Instead he sprawled forward and pitched down onto his stomach with his head sticking out over the edge of the drop-off. As he looked down, the remaining breath in his lungs left him.

The town of Harburg lay below, curtained by a river that flowed out to a range of green hills in the distance. Tiny specks of people moved along the streets. Carriages and wagons appeared no bigger than pumpkin seeds. Raising his eyes, he caught sight of three more cities in the distance, like tiny islands in a sea of green. An entire valley lay before him.

And it was moving.

Two pairs of strong hands pulled him from the edge. It was Simon and Abner. They held his arms to his sides as he struggled half-heartedly, most of his energy stolen away by shock.

"You're thirteen hundred feet above the ground," Abner said in his ear. "You can't get down by yourself. Not alive, anyway."

Ink felt his blood run cold. "What is this?"

"You're on a floating piece of land," Simon replied. "Moving slowly but perfectly safe."

"*Safe?*"

"Come back with us," Abner said. "Everything will be explained."

"Give us a chance, Ink. Please," Simon added. "I promised we wouldn't harm you."

Ink began anew his struggle to break free of Abner's hold. "You're murderers! Butchers! Cannibals! Cursed even by the Devil!"

"That's rubbish!" Abner replied. "That's all rubbish. We're none of those things. Now if you keep fighting us like this we're gonna have to tie your hands."

Ink's struggle lasted another half minute before his limbs and nerves both gave out. He lay in Abner's arms like a limp fish, shuddering and gasping for breath. His heart was in his throat and a pain in his ribcage seemed to be squeezing his lungs.

For the second time that day, Ink found himself being carried away.

~

They brought him back to the music chamber with considerable effort. Ink managed a fast recovery from his shock and put up the best fight he could, once even knocking Simon in the jaw with his elbow. He stopped flailing only when they dropped him into the middle of the circle of chairs. The others stood around him, blocking his paths of escape.

"There's nothing for it now," Martin said, standing over him with a bitter glare. "He'll have to stay. Lock him up in the Pipeworks House, I say."

"Oh, not there," his wife replied. "The infirmary's the best place."

"Or Bash's room," the pointy-bearded man said. "Riva can even reinforce the windows."

Ink remained on his knees like a cornered animal, looking wildly around at the ring of faces staring down at him. They were deciding his fate. Choosing the best cage for him. It was his worst nightmare come true. With one swift movement, he reached down into his right boot and pulled out a small pistol.

"Get back!" he shouted, rising and swinging the weapon in every direction. *"Back!"*

Everyone but Simon retreated several steps.

"Take me down! Right now!"

"We can't do that, Ink," Simon replied.

Ink cocked the pistol and aimed it at his head. "Oh yes you can, Blondie! You can and you will! I've got important things to do! I can't be delayed! I wasn't supposed to get mixed up in any of this!" He blinked, feeling beads of cold sweat on his brow. "Curse that Spindler. *Curse* him!"

"Listen to me," Simon said. "Everything you've ever heard

about the Colonists is a lie. We were there on Damiras that day, but we went to prevent a massacre. Not cause one."

"Of course that's what you'd say!" Ink retorted.

"Believe us or not, but you will be in mortal danger if you set foot down below again. We will not hurt you. I promise this. I swear it. I know you're frightened, and you came about all this in a very bad way, but you need not fear us. We've had plenty of chances to hurt you by now if that was our aim."

"I want answers," Ink said. "Answers and explanations for every question I've got, or . . . or ever had or will have!"

"You'll get them. I promise. But understand it's going to take a bit of time. If we work together, if you let us help you, we'll do our best to get you back down to the world again, free and clear of danger."

Ink lowered the pistol slightly. Simon ventured a step closer and bent down on a knee.

"Mr. Bash . . . he *was* killed, wasn't he?"

Ink looked at him for a moment, then nodded. "His insides were all tore up. Not a scratch on the outside."

Simon's gaze of concern melted into one of astonishment. He glanced at the others, who were all wearing similar expressions of horror.

"That can't be right," Abner said, his mouth agape. "It can't be."

"Jeremy," Simon called out. "Let me see your luck charm for a minute."

A man came forward whom Ink hadn't noticed before. He was meek-looking and small in stature with hunched shoulders. A chain hung around his neck bearing a shiny object at the end. Without a word he lifted it over his head and handed it to Simon, who then put the charm in his palm and held it out towards Ink. It was small and silver, a kind of misshapen heart with a pointed end, enclosed in a tiny case of glass.

"I think you may have seen this before. This morning at the lake."

Ink recalled the sight of the shadow's wide jaws rushing towards him from beneath the surface. Something had glinted under the murky darkness, like stars on the wrong side of the sky.

"I remember," Ink said. "Silver in the shadow."

Simon opened the case and withdrew the item from the glass. He brought the tip of the charm to the ground, and with hardly an ounce of effort, cut a long slit into the stone floor as though it were made of butter. "Sharper than a cut diamond edge. Small as a seed. Nothing like it in this world."

Ink frowned and let the pistol drop to his side. "What is it?"

Simon held it up again. "A Spektor tooth. It's what gave you that cut on your cheek, which is why, you'll remember, I said you were very lucky. And—from what you tell us—it might also be what killed Mr. Bash."

Ink looked up at Simon's face, which held no hint of deceit or mockery. He touched the scratch on his cheek, feeling the blood drain from his face.

"No one is kept here against their will," Simon continued, "but now that the Spektors have revealed themselves to you, they're not likely to leave you alone—which means you wouldn't survive another day on your own. Do you understand that now?"

Ink shook his head, and when he spoke again his voice quivered. "You mean . . . you really think . . . they're trying to kill me?"

Simon drew his eyebrows together but didn't answer. Alarmed, Ink looked up at the other faces around him. Each one was solemn and full of dread. Most were even worried. Ink's breaths came shorter and quicker, panic rising in his chest. He looked away from the charm and tried his best not to throw up then and there all over Simon's shoes.

"But why?" he said. "What do they want from me? What did I ever do to them?"

"We don't know," Simon replied. "As I told you, it's extremely rare for a Spektor to be allowed to kill. They usually don't even cause injury unless made desperate. I suppose it's possible they meant no more than this, but . . . the way that Spektor in the lake charged towards you . . ." He paused to cast another worried glance at the others behind him, then returned his gaze to Ink again. "Whatever the case, it'll take time to find answers. Nothing like this has ever happened before. That means we'll need your patience as much as your trust. And in the meantime, I must ask you to hand over your pistol."

Ink's desire for a fight had long since passed, and though he hated parting with his only weapon, he needed no further convincing. He had no choice but to stay a bit longer, whether he liked it or not. He uncocked the hammer and put the pistol into Simon's hand. The company behind him breathed a collective sigh of relief.

Simon nodded in gratitude, then rose to his feet. "We won't badger you anymore today. You've got a lot to think about. We'll let it rest 'til tomorrow."

"And you can stay with Evering," Abner offered. "That way if you need anything, he'll be right there to help you."

"Yes," the elder lady agreed. "And we'll have you properly fed and fitting into those clothes in no time."

Abner nodded. "Come on. This way."

He put a hand on Ink's shoulder and steered him towards the stairs. Ink let him, feeling himself in a trance of bewilderment and far too exhausted to argue.

As soon as they were gone, Martin cast a sidelong glance at Simon. "You told him we'd let him back down after the danger was passed. Another new policy you and Caradoc have unilaterally decided on today?"

Simon's face darkened. "I had to tell him something."

"You did right, Simon," Delia replied.

"This'll come to nothing but trouble," Martin said, glaring up at the sky through the domed glass roof. "Nothing but trouble for us all. And Bash done in by a Spektor? That bodes more evil than we can possibly imagine."

"We'll discuss it when Caradoc gets back," Simon replied. He handed the silver tooth back to Jeremy. "In the meantime that boy will need all the care and guidance we can give him."

"He *is* such a young thing," said the woman with the cane.

"And an undertaking, too, I'll wager," the pointy-bearded man replied. "He threatened us not only with a pistol but with questions. This ain't no empty-headed kid we're dealing with. And how much are we to tell him?"

"If he's here for good, isn't it only right we tell him the whole truth?" Riva asked.

"Don't know that he'd believe us even if we did," the darker-haired sister replied.

"We all know what needs to be kept under lock and key," Simon said. "And besides, Evering's going to be there to watch him."

Evering reacted to this with a pained grimace.

"You don't mind, do you?" Delia asked.

The young man scratched his chin. "No, not exactly. It's just . . . well, I would've liked to have checked his other boot before sending him to *my* room!"

CHAPTER 11

SPINDLER'S QUANDARY

For the third night in a row, a cold rain swept across the streets of Harburg. Spindler stared at it through the window beside his table in the pub. The sickly light of the nearest lamp post showed small rivers of water had begun to flow down the street on either side. The sound of it pounding on the cobblestones was so thunderous he was sure it would mask all other sounds of motion outside, had there been any.

Just then, the last light in the row of houses opposite the pub finally winked out. Spindler glanced nervously at the clock on the mantle. Eleven thirty. He picked up his pint of beer, swirled it absentmindedly, then set it down again and looked around. Nick was standing behind the bar, resting his head against his hand and doing sums to tally up his takings for the day. The only other person in the place was old Mrs. Purkis who was fast asleep in the corner booth. Nick would wake her in about fifteen minutes, then nod at Spindler with a tired but polite reminder to take himself home as well.

Just where he couldn't go. For the past five hours he'd been arguing with himself over every little detail of the incident with Ink and the three strangers. Had it been a hoax from the beginning? Some elaborate plot to get a good deal of his cash—which the boy had indeed walked away with. He was already a thief and a trickster; of course his entire story about Bash's house and the excitement at the lake must have been nothing but lies.

But there were three points he couldn't explain so easily away. The first was the fate of his door. How it had cracked to pieces and fallen to bits. The second was the supposed 'plot' itself. If Ink really had been working with the three strangers to cheat him out of his cash, why come up with such an elaborate hoax to do it? Why would the boy not simply lead him out to an unassuming spot, have the others knock him on the head, then take what they wanted and run? Why all the nonsense about evil spirits and a place to keep the boy safe?

The third point was the scream—that raw, piercing, guttural noise he'd heard as they'd fled the flat and raced out into the street. It had made his blood turn to ice then, and every time he thought about it since. It had not been human, not by any stretch of the imagination.

And so, as the blonde stranger had suggested, he would not go back to his flat. Not for a few days, anyway. When Nick would come to nudge and prod him along, he'd simply have to return to his printing office and make himself comfortable on the couch in the front room. He'd spent the better part of the day there already, trying desperately to keep his worst anxieties at bay by throwing himself into his work. When night fell, however, he had suddenly found himself in desperate need to be around other people. He'd also briefly considered paying a visit to his landlady to explain why his door lay in ruins in the hallway, but when he remembered her tendency to be excitable and overly-talkative, he came to the conclusion that it would be too much for his already-fragile nerves. Besides that, he had yet to come up with a convincing explanation that would not send her straight to the infirmary with a panic attack.

That led to the next difficulty. If it had not been a hoax, if there really was a sinister creature in his room, and the boy had actually been taken off by three complete strangers, who could he tell about it? The chief constable? The mayor? A priest? He wasn't sure. No one person was likely to believe all of it *and* have the means to take appropriate action in response. There was also the current atmosphere to consider. It was the Colonists everyone was worried about now, a very real threat made of flesh and blood. No one had time for ghost stories.

No. This went beyond the local authorities. Beyond Harburg. This was the province of those were used to dealing with unusual crises. Were he to decide once and for all that this was a real danger—and God only knew if he ever could—he would need someone bigger who could properly deal with it. Someone much more powerful.

The door to the pub swung open. Nick glanced up from the bar.

"Sorry, sir, we're closing in . . ." He stifled the rest of his sentence and stood upright with a look of amazement. "Mr. Stone, sir! What can I get for you?"

Spindler gripped the handle of his pint glass tighter as the hulking customer lumbered in and up to the bar. He was soaked with rain and shook his hat out onto the floor, scoping out the room as he did so. Spindler quickly averted his gaze. Bill Stone. Hm. Ink had said he'd been at Bash's house with the three Entrians, discussing the old man's cause of death. Perhaps he would have some useful advice regarding how to handle a situation which wasn't likely to be believed by many others. But Spindler knew he could never ask him directly, not without admitting the great hunter had been spied upon by a boy he'd paid to scope out the dead man's abode.

His thoughts were interrupted when another pint glass was plunked down opposite his own. Without waiting for an invitation, Bill took the seat across from him and regarded him with a cursory nod.

"Spindler, right?"

Even sitting down, the massive bounty hunter towered over him. Spindler stiffened and managed a nod. "That's right."

"You run the newspaper in town?"

"I do."

Bill took a swallow of beer and squinted at him from over the rim of the glass. Spindler felt his heart quail. He knew those gray eyes were searching for whatever information his expression might tell. Bill would perceive he was nervous. Even jittery. Spindler could only hope that such a reaction was customary for those finding themselves in conversation with Mr. Stone, and that the sharp-eyed bloke had come to expect it by now.

"Is there something I can do for you?" Spindler asked, eager to show himself cooperative.

Bill set his glass down with a *thunk*. "I always like to chat with folk like you when there's been Colonists about. You know things most people don't. Hear things."

Spindler nodded. "That's quite often true. But if you're wondering if I knew anything about Bash, I have to admit I was just as stunned as everyone else."

Bill glanced out the window. "People always are. Those sneaky devils have gotten so clever after all these years, they could parade themselves right through the Great Hall and nobody would notice."

Rain spattered the window with a gust of wind, like a handful of pebbles being thrown against the glass. Nick went to the hearth and put another few sticks on the fire. Apparently, he was all too happy to keep the place cozy for as long as Bill Stone made use of it.

"I'm surprised to see you out so late on a night like this," Spindler said. "I can't imagine there's any investigation business to be done at such an hour."

"The investigation's been closed," Bill said. "At least so far as it can be. Whenever there's Colonist mischief, I always do night patrols for at least a week afterward. They have a history of retaliating when one of their own is taken out."

Spindler frowned. "What kind of retaliating?"

Bill grunted before answering. "A body for a body. Usually cut to ribbons and usually with a note pinned on the poor sod with their old catchphrase. 'Colonists, arise.'"

Spindler reacted with a worried frown, then sat back in his chair and shook his head. "You say the investigation's been closed. That's the first I've heard of it. What were the results?"

"Confidential," Bill said, then took another huge swig of beer.

Spindler nodded, but inside himself another round of fresh panic had begun. Colonist investigations were not usually confidential. The details were typically spread far and wide to warn as many people as possible and to prevent the same from happening anywhere else. Beyond that, it made for great publicity to the cause, and was a boon to both the Cassrian and Entrian governments who could show themselves to be taking action against the the threat. But confidential? That could only mean something had gone more wrong than usual. Something they didn't want known. Perhaps the fact that Bash had not died of a heart attack after all.

Spindler put a hand over his face in exasperation. Every moment, Ink's story was seeming more and more like the truth. He ought to have been grilling Bill about the investigation, trying to ferret out what he could as the professional newspaperman he was. But he dreaded what answers might be given. He feared to hear the truth confirmed.

"I, uh, heard there was an Entrian in town today," Spindler said after clearing his throat. "I don't suppose he's still around?"

"No, he ain't. And wouldn't likely talk to you even if he was." Bill shook his head with a noise of disgust. "They could hardly lower themselves to talk to me and the mayor. Like it was the greatest inconvenience to their time. As if I wasn't risking my neck day after day for their sakes."

"Yet still you do," Spindler replied.

There came into Bill's eye a sudden gleam, whether of pride or anger—or a combination—Spindler wasn't certain.

"Yes. But only because I was *born* to do such work."

Spindler smoothed a hand over his mustache, deep in contemplation again and only stirring himself out of it to question Bill further. "You don't trust them, then?"

Bill glanced around the pub. Nick was wiping out a row of already-clean glasses. Mrs. Purkis had begun to snore.

"I don't have anything against 'em as a whole," the hunter replied. "I got a fair bit of admiration for the great nation they were. And for what they might be again. But these ones today aren't making things easy on anyone. Far too self-important for their own good, and that's besides the vast majority of 'em not having anything good to say about us lowly Cassrians."

Spindler nodded with a troubled frown. He had just begun to wonder if the Entrians weren't the very people he needed to seek out. They believed in the supernatural. They wouldn't throw him out into the street for telling such tales. But for being a Cassrian, they might not even let him through the gates to tell it.

That left him only one place; the Assembly. The highest seat of Cassrian government. Spindler felt his stomach churn at the very thought.

"So what's got you up so late?" Bill asked. "Papers go out early, don't they? A man in your line of work can't afford to be kept up all night by whatever else is worrying you."

There was a knowing look on his eye, verging on self-satisfaction. Spindler felt more cornered than ever, which would have angered him had he not been expecting such an inquiry. He shook his head dismissively.

"Just some business with a boy I sent to pick something up for me. Hasn't come back yet. I was starting to worry."

Bill frowned. "About an errand boy?"

"Yes. I suppose it's high time I went to the station and reported it but—"

"Listen," the hunter interrupted. "Let me give you a piece of advice."

Spindler looked at him with raised eyebrows, surprised to hear the very words he'd been hoping all along to hear. Bill lowered his broad, weather-beaten brow and locked eyes with him.

"People," he said, "are animals. You. Me. Him behind the bar. Her in the corner. The cobblers, the lamplighters, the saps working in the mills. Even the mighty Entrians in their shining cities. All of us. Every last one. Now you want to gray your head and shorten your life by wearin' your nerves out over 'em, you go right ahead." He tapped a massive finger against his temple. "But better to think like a hunter. Understand what's really worth being troubled about. The bears. The wolves. Those coming after *you*. Then your one and only worry becomes stayin' at the top of the food chain. That's the only fight there really is. The only one *worth* fightin'. You see? This lost boy of yours ain't really nothing more than a dumb rabbit who's run off into the brush. You don't waste your time fretting over something like that."

"Never?" Spindler asked. "Even if it's gone and got itself injured? Stuck in a trap?"

"Even then. Especially then. Shoulda kept his eyes open. Been smarter about things. Now he's just someone else's dinner."

Spindler felt his stomach churn. He almost put a hand to his mouth but stopped himself and rubbed his brow instead.

"I know that's a hard thing for most folks to hear," Bill continued. "But once you see it's true, the world gets a whole lot simpler, and you'll be happier for it. Trust me."

"So that's why you do what you do?" Spindler said. "Because going after all those wolves and bears gets you to the top?"

Bill cocked his head with a grin of pleasure. "There ain't no greater sport on this side of life. No greater thrill. And the Colonists? They're the biggest beasts of all."

Spindler remained silent, feeling the terrible depth of his disappointment. This was not a man to bother with ghosts or evil spirits. He wasn't even interested in humanity. The solemn commission to hunt down the desecrators of Damiras was nothing more than a big game for him. A match of wits to be won. A contest of strength. He wasn't interested in saving anyone or serving a need with self-sacrifice. It was all about power.

Success. Personal glory. In the end, the great Bill Stone was nothing more than a common mercenary.

"You got a pistol?"

Spindler looked up again with a bewildered frown. "What?"

Bill nodded towards the window. "Dangerous times to be walking home alone and unarmed."

"Oh. Right. Well, no. I'm afraid I don't."

"That's what I thought." Bill reached into the depths of his huge coat, withdrew just such a weapon, then placed it on the table in front of Spindler. "Take that. Walk the old woman home first. See she gets there safe. Keep your eyes and ears open. *Assume* you're being watched. I don't want to find you tomorrow with your throat slashed and a note pinned to your chest."

He rose from the table and took a final gulp of beer. Spindler meant to thank him, but he was too taken aback to let the words through. Bill went to set the empty glass on the bar, exchanged a nod with Nick, then donned his damp hat and went out again into the pouring rain.

Spindler sat looking at the pistol for a long moment, thinking about everything Bill had said. Then, the memory of the horrifying scream returned to him again, and he snatched up the weapon and opened the chamber. It was full. Six bullets. That was plenty to defend himself in close action, if it came down to it.

And absolutely bloody useless against shrieking evil spirits.

CHAPTER 12

RIVERFALL

By the next morning, Ink had forgotten where he was. He stared at the wall in front of him, painted pale pink by the light filtering through the scarlet drapes, shadows of branches moving over his head. He shivered under the bedclothes and pulled the blanket tighter. It was much colder than usual. Too cold for October. Perhaps a storm had passed in the night. That, or he had gone to sleep high on a mountain. No. No, that wasn't it.

Colonists. He clutched his arms to his chest as a chill ran through him. He was with the Colonists. After being shown to the room he would share with Evering, Ink had locked himself inside—and they'd let him, not begrudging him his fears. For a long time he'd stood at the front window, peeking through the curtains and watching the others go to and fro with questions multiplying in his head by the minute. How many Entrians had each one slaughtered? How had Martin lost half his arm? Which one had fired the pistol that had killed the Entrian prophet?

Twice, a knock had come at the door, once for his dinner, delivered by Riva, and once to let Evering go to bed. Ink glanced over his shoulder and saw the young man was still asleep with his mouth half open. How long had Ink fought against closing his own eyes last night? How long had he thought about squeezing his hands around Spindler's throat for leading him into this mess? Two days ago he'd been in a jail coach on his way to some bare, dirty cell on solid ground.

Oh, what he wouldn't give to trade prisons now.

A soft creaking noise interrupted his thoughts. He sat upright. Little by little, the door was opening. With his heart pounding in his chest, he glanced around for something he might use as a weapon. Only his top hat was in reach.

"Oswald!"

The hoarse, high-pitched whisper of a woman's voice floated into the room.

"Oswald! Get back here!"

A large gray cat wandered in through the door, swishing its tail lazily through the air. It saw Ink a moment later and froze, arching its back and staring at him with a large yellow eye. The other was covered in a milky white film.

The door opened wider. A woman stepped quickly into the room, then swept the cat up into her arms. "Silly old thing, you *never* listen to me!" She caught Ink's gaze and froze, much as the cat had done. "Oh. Sorry we woke you."

Ink remembered her as the lighter-haired sister from the previous day. This morning she was dressed in a pink velvet coat with a ruffled cravat at the collar, as well as a white hat with a large plume of red feathers. Ink had to look close to assure himself that it was not, in fact, a sleeping rooster on her head.

She moved towards him, holding the cat like a sack of potatoes in both arms. "I've given everyone warning to close their doors properly but sometimes they forget. I'm afraid he's prone to wandering at will, the little sneak." She gave the cat a light shake. He uttered a peevish growl and flattened his ears. The woman let out a squeaky chuckle and stuck her hand out towards Ink, letting the cat's bottom hang loose for a moment. "I'm Josephina Plumsley. It's so nice to finally have a new face here!"

"Nothing against you," Ink said, his first three words to the lady a complete lie, "but I don't shake hands. Matter of principle."

"Oh," she replied, returning her hand to support the cat again. "Well . . . nice to see a young man sticking to his principles. And now that you *are* awake, I suppose you ought to head over to the Dining House before you miss breakfast." She moved around the bed towards Evering and patted the top of his head. "Evering! Time to wake up. Come on."

"Wha?" he groaned, then looked up at the woman and gave a cry of alarm.

"Ahh! Get it back! Get it back!" he cried, scrambling out of bed and backwards along the wall. "Why do you do that to me, Jo? *Why?*"

"He's not going to hurt you, Evering! If only you'd let him get close enough—"

"I don't want him getting close! That cat is evil!"

"Oh, shush, now! Don't let him hear you talk that way!"

Evering swung around a desk near the foot of the bed. "He's always prowling around, looking at me with that big creepy eye. He never blinks, you know. Never!"

"For heaven's sake, of course he does!" Josephina replied. "Now get washed up, the both of you, and hurry! You've nearly slept through breakfast. They're about to start clearing the things away."

Evering went for the wash basin between the two beds, all the while making sure his back was never fully turned towards the cat.

Ink hesitated. He was reluctant to leave the room. There was no telling what might be waiting outside. Or who. Maybe these Colonists had changed their minds and decided he wasn't worth saving from the Spektors. Or maybe it was all a load of rubbish to begin with—all part of that brainwashing witchery people said they were capable of doing.

But then he remembered the scratch on his cheek. The silver tooth cutting through stone. The unnatural scream in Spindler's flat and the lakeside before it. No. As much as he hated to admit, it wasn't rubbish. And what was more, he hadn't eaten a great deal of his dinner the night before and was now properly starving. He thought for a moment about demanding that his meals continue to be delivered, but such a course of action would only serve to make himself more a prisoner than the Colonists themselves intended.

Besides that, much of his immediate fear over the situation had now been replaced with curiosity. He was with a group of fugitives in their secret hideout *and* being allowed to walk freely. Already he'd learned secrets that would earn him a hundred times what Spindler had paid. So he would leave the room. He would go to breakfast. He would keep a sharp eye on his surroundings as he usually did. All things considered, it simply made good financial sense.

This decided upon, he went to retrieve his hat and coat from the bedpost.

"Oh, dear," Josephina said with a chuckle. "Look at the state of your things. I can fetch you some nicer fitting clothes if you like. I've got a wonderful green satin jacket you could wear to breakfast."

Ink shook his head. "These'll do me fine."

"Are you sure? It's no bother."

"It would be for me."

And that was the end of the matter.

As they stepped outside and onto the curving stone path, Ink marveled once again at the charming little village. Morning light filtered through the treetops. A layer of mist seeped out from the center garden, casting a dreamlike haze over everything. The dew was thick in the grass around them, and the cool dampness felt so good in his lungs he could almost believe he was breathing in the air of a world newly created.

"Ah!" Josephina said, sighing as she smoothed down her velvet coat. "And so comes my least favorite part of the day. How I do hate having to change for work. Why must it be impossible to look splendid while engaging in physical labor? If only the gardens didn't have so much dirt."

"You could save yourself some heartache if you started out the day wearing your work clothes," Evering replied.

"Oh, no no no no. That would never do. A proper lady always dresses for breakfast. She is always prepared to meet the first hours of the day looking her absolute best."

"None of the other ladies bother about it as you do."

Josephina answered with a wave of her hand. "Alas, that is their own unfortunate choice. Speaking of which, Evering, darling, about that beard you're trying to grow . . . that is on purpose, is it not?"

Evering's cheeks flushed as his hand went up to his chin. Josephina continued.

"You may want to speak to Chester about some liniment he uses to stimulate follicle growth. I'm sure it would do you some good. Anyway, I must be off. You boys enjoy the day!"

With a small fluttering wave, she turned on her heel and went down the path in the opposite direction. The cat followed, flicking a final wary glance at Ink.

"Good 'ol Jo," Evering said. "She means well. At least her sister ain't half so ridiculous."

"Oh, so they are related," Ink replied.

"Yeah. The other is Wendolen. They used to be famous opera singers down below. Sometimes it's hard to tell 'em apart when they dress the same, but Jo's voice is a bit higher. She says it got that way after knocking her head on a tree branch when she was a girl. Which explains a few things, actually." He nodded toward a house farther down the path. "That's the Dining House up ahead. Two to the left of our place."

Ink followed as Evering headed towards it. The house appeared a bit larger than the others and had a second story built of stone instead of glass.

"We take all our meals there," Evering continued. "It's the biggest house in the village, at the northernmost point of the path. We call it the northern side even if we aren't necessarily true to compass bearings. See, the sun's coming over the trees to the west now, so we're all turned around but we still—ooohhh! Hold on! I think they've made pancakes!"

He rushed forward, bounded up the steps of the Dining House, and flew through the door. Ink paused at the threshold, noticing the brief flash of sunlight on metal. Upon the door, an iron circle lay imprinted into the wood. Within it was the image of a wine goblet.

The front door opened into a large room. A staircase sat to the far left, while the rest of the space was taken up by the biggest table Ink had ever seen—solid dark wood and polished so well it gleamed like the surface of a frozen pond. Underneath lay a magnificent green and silver rug, patterned after trees and winding ivy. Definitely expensive. To the far right, a straight wall cut across the cavernous chamber, and the sounds of clanking dishes and running water issued through a door in the center. A woman in an apron stood at the table clearing away dishes.

"Oh, hang it all to pieces!" Evering groaned, deflating at the sight of the empty plates.

"You're late," she replied.

"Wasn't my fault. Dad didn't wake me this morning." He grabbed a lone rasher of bacon from one of the plates before she swerved it out of his reach.

"Now don't make any more mess in here, Evering. Go into the kitchen and see if Martin's left you anything."

"Are there more pancakes?"

"I don't know. Go ask *Martin*."

Ink recognized her as the gentle-looking woman from the day before. There was no sign of her cane this time, though she did lean a bit heavier on her left leg. She paused when she noticed Ink and tried to smile but couldn't quite hide her nervousness.

"Oh. Good morning."

"Ink, this is Harriet Whistler," Evering said. "She and her husband work in the kitchen. She's the best cook I've known since my own mother and she'll make you anything you like. Just don't bother asking *Mr.* Whistler for anything. He'll have you scouring pots for it in return."

"Which is reason enough to be on your best behavior if you're wanting pancakes," Harriet said as she gathered the last few plates. "He's already in a bad enough mood."

Ink fidgeted and glanced back at the door. He wasn't keen on meeting a Colonist in a decent mood, much less a bad one. But it wouldn't do any good to go fainting from hunger. He followed Evering and Harriet into the kitchen. Inside, a man was a flurry of motion, pumping water into a large set of sinks, scraping dishes, washing, drying, and replacing them in their cupboards like a well-rehearsed dance.

Harriet set the last of the breakfast dishes on the counter beside him. "Martin, these boys are looking for something to eat. Is there anything left?"

The man paused, agitated with the interruption, and turned from the sink. Ink stiffened, recognizing the stern face that had glowered down at him throughout yesterday's meeting. It was hard not to feel bitter towards the man who'd wanted to drop him back down below, but Ink couldn't deny a twinge of awe upon realizing how fast he worked with only an arm and a half.

"Breakfast is over at eight," he said coldly, wiping his hand on his apron.

Evering shot Ink a knowing look.

Harriet brushed a stray hair from her face. "The clock's not yet struck eight. We've plenty to—"

Just then, she was interrupted by the long, doleful chimes of a large clock somewhere outside. Harriet looked helplessly between her husband and the boys beside her. Martin remained stone-faced, staring straight at Ink all the while. When the eighth toll had rung, he spoke again.

"Breakfast is over at eight."

As he turned back to the sink, Harriet nodded at the boys. "I'll whip up something quick for you two. It'll just be a minute."

"Harriet!" the man said, jabbing a soapy finger at her. "Don't you dare! We're just about done with the cleaning up and I won't be put to more work by these idlers."

"I can take care of their plates afterward."

"No, you won't. Evering knows the rules. He knows better than to sleep in so late."

"Martin, they've got to eat."

"There's apples in the pantry. One for each and not a scrap more."

He turned his back on them and continued washing dishes. His wife suppressed a defeated sigh and glanced at the boys with apologetic eyes before disappearing through the pantry door. As soon as she had gone, Martin turned from the sink again and glared at Evering.

"You're off to a great start hosting our distinguished guest. Planning to be late for lunch and dinner as well? I've got to prepare, you know. Two less mouths to feed means less work for me."

Evering's ears went red. Martin took a step towards Ink. The boy did his best to assume a hard look, but the man stared down with such a nasty glare Ink feared he'd be struck.

"Hats off in my kitchen," he said in a low growl.

Ink was so relieved he pulled off his hat before even thinking to defy, as was his customary reaction to orders and commands.

"Hot in here anyway," he replied, trying to maintain a foothold in the contest of wills.

Martin turned away and gathered the last of the dishes his wife had brought. "Breakfast is seven to eight. Lunch is twelve to one. Dinner is six to seven. You miss a meal again, you go beg Jeremy for a carrot stick from the garden. Understood?"

Evering glanced at Ink and decided to answer for both of them. "Understood."

Harriet returned from the pantry and handed Evering and Ink

an apple, then moved behind them and slipped something into each of their pockets.

"Off you go now, boys," she said, guiding them out of the kitchen. "Try not to be late again."

"Thanks, Harriet," Evering said. "You're a good apple."

"Get out, you pest," she replied. Ink saw her smile before closing the door behind them.

The treasure in their pockets turned out to be a large, rolled up pancake. Cold, but enough to tide them over. They ate them as they stood on the path outside the house.

"That Stumpy's a mad bull," Ink said between bites. "I thought he was going to burn right through me with his eyes. And what happened to his arm?"

Evering considered carefully before answering. "Had to be cut . . . to save his life."

"What, like he had an infection?"

Evering tilted his head. "Something like that."

Ink started on the apple as he glanced around. "So . . . did you lot build all this?"

"Not really. Most of it was already here. We just happened to stumble upon it while we were looking for a place to camp."

Ink frowned. "How do you stumble on a village floating thirteen hundred feet in the air?"

"It wasn't in the air then. That came later."

Ink's frown deepened. "Then how—"

"I'm really not the best one to answer that," Evering said with a smirk.

"You mean you can't tell me," Ink replied crossly.

The young man's smirk widened into a grin. "Knew you'd catch on quick. Come on. I know where to get more food."

Ink followed Evering down the eastern arc of the path, over another stone footbridge and past the infirmary. A little farther on, new features of the village came into view. The dense copse of trees in the center gave way to a small field of golden corn. Next to this was a vegetable garden so expansive it ran out of sight towards the southern end of the path. There were also several small fountains. Two flanked the cornfield. Others were scattered throughout the vegetable garden. Water trickled over the edge of the basins and down to the ground, running in rivulets through the tilled rows of earth.

Ink shook his head in wonder. "Bless my eyes. Look at this place. Plenty of food, shelter, water. No wonder they couldn't find you. You don't need to set foot on solid ground ever again!"

"Oh, there's need," Evering answered. "Every so often there'll be a supply we can't replace ourselves. Or something we need specially made, like medicine."

"I thought your man Simon was a doctor."

"Simon? No, he ain't a doctor. Teaching's his proper profession. But it got too dangerous for us to get help whenever we got sick or injured, so Simon picked up a few books and taught himself the basics. He's done a lot of good since we came to Riverfall. Saved me from a nasty case of bronchitis a few years back."

"Riverfall?"

"Oh, that's what we call the village."

A few moments later they came to a house ringed with rose-bushes. The front door had been propped open to let the morning breeze into the rooms. Evering knocked twice on the doorframe and stepped inside, wiping his feet on a grass-weave mat.

"Morning, Delia!" he called out.

"In the work room!" a voice answered back.

Evering led the way into a room which turned out to be the Colonists' dairy. Narrow cupboards were filled with pots of cream and blocks of cheeses. Slotted spoons and knives hung on the walls. Cheesecloths lay heaped in piles. The woman within was using a screener to remove the curds from a copper cauldron full of milk.

"Morning, boys," she said as they passed through the door.

"Morning," Evering returned. "Ink, this is Delia Ingleby."

Ink remembered her as the older lady who had defended him against Martin's less-than-charitable ideas. She greeted Ink with a cordial nod.

"Mr. Featherfield. I can't imagine you slept very well last night, but I do hope you were comfortable at the least."

Ink answered with a small nod of his own.

"Sorry for the bother, Delia," Evering said, "but we seem to find ourselves on the late side of breakfast and . . . well, we were wondering if—"

Delia put up a hand. "Say no more."

Evering smirked at Ink as she went to retrieve two glasses and a pitcher of milk from a nearby cupboard. Ink gazed at the women with curiosity. He guessed she was in her fifties or sixties by the wrinkles on her face and the faded color of her hair. She looked like someone's elderly aunt. Not a fugitive from the law.

"This was made fresh this morning," she said, filling the glasses to the brim. "Don't be afraid to ask for seconds or thirds. Or fourths in Evering's case."

"Pay attention, Ink," Evering said. "Those are words Martin will never say as long as he lives."

"You shouldn't talk like that," Delia said, handing them the glasses.

"Why not? Even Caradoc would say so, and he's about the only friend Martin's got."

"Just hold your tongue and drink your milk."

The boys tipped up their glasses. It was the best milk Ink had ever tasted. Not watery and thin like the milk sold in most shops, but creamy and cool, with a thin layer of froth that stuck to his upper lip. He drained his glass before Evering was even halfway through, then wiped his mouth with the back of his hand and felt that if he never drank anything else for the rest of his life he would be perfectly content.

He set the glass back on the counter with a thoughtful frown. "Caradoc. I've heard that name a few times since I got here. Is he your leader or something?"

"We don't have a leader," Delia answered. "Not exactly. No one necessarily has to answer to anyone else." She went to a cupboard and picked out a block of cheese wrapped in paper.

"But this Caradoc person," Ink continued, "he's the one who got between me and that Spektor thing down at the lake, wasn't he?"

"Yes, that was him."

"But he's still down there, right? Down below? Ain't you all afraid he'll be caught?"

Delia set the cheese onto the counter and nodded with a grim look. "Every time."

"Then what is he—"

"It's not really my place to answer any questions about him," she said, cutting chunks from the block of cheese. "If there's anything you ever want to know about someone, it's always best to go to that someone themselves. Otherwise things get twisted around upside down and backwards."

She handed them two generous portions of cheese and poured a second glass of milk for each. Ink had just taken his first bite when a low, mournful bellow came floating in through the open window.

"Nyssa's been talkative lately," Delia said. "Must feel a change coming in the weather."

"Poor thing's still mourning her calf," Evering replied, then headed for the back door.

Ink followed him outside. A large chicken coop stood a few yards away. Nearby was a fenced area containing feed sacks, a water trough, and a covered stall filled with straw. Chickens roamed the meadow, and some wandered into the pen where a black cow stood chewing her cud and whipping her tail around her hindquarters. Evering jumped the fence and went to the mournful-looking creature. She turned her head towards him as he reached out a hand and stroked her between the eyes.

"Ink?" Delia called.

Ink turned as she emerged from the house carrying two bags of grain in both arms.

"Grab one of these for me, will you?"

They carried them to the backside of the chicken coop where barrels and crates were stacked along the wall. Delia cut the bags open and began pouring grain into a barrel.

It was then Ink noticed a blood-stained apron hanging on a nail. He felt a heavy lump form in the pit of his stomach and turned from the sight. And there, farther off in the meadow, was an axe stuck fast in a tree stump slicked with dried blood. Feathers littered the ground around it. As Delia replaced the top of the barrel, she noticed Ink staring at the stump.

"Not the prettiest spot on Riverfall," she said, putting a hand on her hip and trying to lighten the moment with a smile. "But certainly one to be thankful for when suppertime comes around."

"You got a nice set-up here. No arguing that." Ink turned away from the unsettling view. "A paradise to make any criminal on the run green in the face."

Delia's smile dropped away. "You'll see in time. Criminals aren't the only ones in need of a refuge now and then."

She turned and headed towards the cow pen. Ink followed.

"When do I get my answers? And don't keep saying 'all in good time'. I've heard just about enough of that."

"Then you'd better go and talk to Simon."

"Do you know where he is?" Evering asked.

"I haven't seen him this morning. He's likely either in the garden grove or the pipeworks. But remember, Ink," she said, turning back to the boy, "questions are dangerous. Questions have gotten us killed in the past. I know you're frustrated, but until we think you can be trusted with things, you'd better start asking the right kinds of questions. Just think on it a little first."

Evering clambered back over the fence and nodded at her. "Thanks for breakfast, Delia."

"You're welcome. And try to enjoy the day while you're out and about. Not much longer before our little paradise here will be covered in frost."

Ink barely heard her. He was already heading back towards the stone path.

CHAPTER 13

THE PRISONERS OF PARADISE

Evering figured they would find Simon in the orchards, so they cut across the path and made their way into the shadowy grove. Ink had never seen so much fruit. There were clusters of pear and plum trees, apricot and cherry, bushes chock full of blackberries and raspberries. The apple orchard covered the most ground and was just about ready to harvest. Ink had learned to tell such things by swiping many a piece of fruit while passing through fields and farms.

"I just can't believe this place," Ink said as he gazed up at the trees. "It's perfect. And not only that but you're free up here! Free to go wherever you want whenever you like!"

"No one's free who has a price on their head," Evering replied grimly. "We're really no better than prisoners—cut off from the rest of the world, never to be with friends or family. Delia's got five children and eight grandchildren she can't see again. All my schoolmates have gone on with their lives, starting families of their own . . ."

"Well, you did bring it on yourselves," Ink retorted.

Evering fixed him with a glare. "You get a soft bed and pancakes for breakfast and we're still cold-blooded murderers? You don't know the whole truth of it, all right?"

"I will. Just as soon as we find Simon."

A minute later they entered a grove of cherry trees. A man stood on a stool plucking the fruit from the lowest branches. Ink recognized him as the quiet owner of the Spektor tooth pendant. He appeared to be in his late forties, but stooped his shoulders like a man twice that age. The bottoms of his boots were mucked with mud and fruit skins.

"Morning, Jeremy," Evering said.

The man dipped his head with a smile as he stepped down from the stool. "Morning."

"We're just out looking for Simon. Have you seen him around?"

Jeremy rubbed the back of his neck. "No, I haven't. I'm sorry."

He had the softest, mildest voice Ink had ever heard from a grown man, and he seemed genuinely sorry, as though he had an actual reason to apologize. An awkward silence followed.

"So," Evering said at last, "picking cherries today?"

Jeremy nodded. "Harriet's making a special dessert for tonight." He held out his half-filled basket towards them. "Try a few . . . if you want."

Both Ink and Evering obliged him.

Jeremy's simple smile faded as he looked at the boy, and his brow wrinkled in concern. "I'm . . . I'm very sorry for your troubles. I know it's . . . it's a frightening thing, having a Spektor on your heels." He reached into his shirt and pulled out the Spektor tooth. "But . . . it helps to have a remembrance. Something to look at every now and then so you can't forget. Because once you forget, they've won. And once they've won, it's all been for nothing."

Ink stared at the tooth and felt another wave of unsettled dread, like a dark cloud passing over the sun. Here, in this peaceful village of lush gardens and simple living, it was easy to see himself forgetting all about his earthly troubles. Jeremy summoned another gentle smile and dropped the tooth back under his shirt.

"Plums are ripe on the south side," he said. "You can take as many as you like."

"Thank you, Jeremy," Evering replied. "Always so generous."

Jeremy dipped his head, picked up the stool, and shuffled away through the grove. Evering glanced back at Ink with a raised eyebrow.

"There now. Is that a cold-blooded murderer?"

"Well, I couldn't know for sure, could I?" Ink replied. "He might be putting on an act."

"An act?" Evering said. "You think that was an act? That man lost both his brothers after all three of them joined us, then afterward started drinking liquor like it was gonna bring 'em back to life. I can remember whole days he was never dry. It got so bad we had to forbid him to go anywhere near a bottle again, but he's not been able to get on very well without it. Sometimes you can hear him crying out here in the orchards, or in his room at night. So don't you dare shame him further by calling it all an act. You got me?"

"Fine," Ink said. "But don't blame me for being suspicious. This ain't exactly my first run around the mill. I learned plenty of hard lessons about not being so quick to take people at their word, and I don't intend on unlearning 'em now. I got a right to make up my own mind about things. About people."

Before Evering could answer a strange noise cut through the air—a kind of warbling wail, like the mating call of a large bird.

"Come on," Evering said, moving off again. "That's our next stop."

∾

Farther into the grove the fruit trees gave way to grapevines, growing on rows of wooden staves fixed together with twine. Ink couldn't believe his eyes. They even had a vineyard.

Soon the warbling noise changed, and Ink realized there were words in the sound. A pair of beautiful voices were lifting in song, floating through the leaves like rays of sunshine. Ink and Evering strolled into the last row of the vineyard and came upon Josephina and her sister perched on stepladders. Each wielded a pair of shears and worked to cut away dead vines and leaves. The sunhats they wore had such wide brims Ink wondered how they kept their balance. After a few seconds, the song came to an abrupt halt.

"No, Josephina, no. It's *white*, not *light*. 'O'er the hills of lingering *white*.'"

The fair-haired sister let her shears rest for a moment. She wiped a hand across her brow and frowned as she repeated the line in its entirety. "'The sunlight beckons to you far away, o'er the hills of lingering light.' It's *light*. I've always sung it as light."

"Then you've always sung it wrong," Wendolen said. "The song is called 'Merry in the Springtime.' It's referring to the winter snow lingering into spring."

"I always thought the light was lingering because the sun was setting. Not once have I ever heard *white*."

"Well you should have."

"How do you know it's 'white'? Did you write the song?"

"Of course I didn't write the song! I just know how to sing it *correctly*!"

Evering cleared his throat to put an end to the argument. "Good morning, ladies!"

"Ah! Good morning, gentlemen," the dark-haired sister said.

"Ink, I don't believe you've been formally introduced to my sister, Wendolen," Josephina said. "Apparently suffering from hearing loss for God knows how many years."

"We're on the hunt for Simon," Evering said, rushing his words together to prevent another argument. "Have you ladies seen him anywhere?"

Wendolen leaned on one of the wooden staves. "Afraid not. But you could ask Chester."

Josephina giggled like a girl a quarter of her age. "Who's probably sitting outside his house sampling the fruits of his labor again."

"Dear, darling Chester," Wendolen sighed, looking at Ink. "He can be such a wickedly rakish man, but we do love him dearly and try our best to keep him out of trouble."

Ink cocked his head. "Was he the chap with the hair cream you could smell from across the room?"

"Across the room?" Evering said. "When the wind's in the right direction I can smell it clear across the village."

"I've just been thinking about what an inspired name you have, Ink," Josephina said. She waved her arm as though conducting an orchestra. "The very sound of it rouses the senses. *Inkwell!* What is your surname?"

"Featherfield."

"Oh, it does possess a quality of the arts about it!" Wendolen said.

"Perhaps he's destined to become a composer or playwright," Josephina replied.

"The next Drester or Alfred Melmordian!"

"Do you write, young man? Any poetry? Plays? Orchestral compositions?"

"Uh . . . no."

"Hm. We'll have to work on that. Won't we, Jo?" Wendolen said.

"Oh, undoubtedly," her sister answered. "We can't let such a great name go to waste! It must be earned, young man! But don't despair. We will have you up to par in no time. Why we were filling concert halls by the time we were eighteen, weren't we, Wen?"

"Indeed we were!" Wendolen answered. "And how old are you, Inkwell?"

Ink tipped his hat back and tucked his hands into his pockets. "Well, I ain't quite sure. See, the nurse who recorded my birth date forgot her glasses that day and marked me down for ninety years old straight off."

"Ninety, you say?" Josephina said, putting a hand to her heart. "Why that's terrible!"

Wendolen rolled her eyes at her gullible sister.

"It is indeed," Ink said. "I once had to tell a magistrate my true age. He fainted dead away, right in the middle of court. His wig flew off and everything!"

Evering coughed, stifling a laugh as he gripped Ink by the shoulder and steered him away from the vineyard. "Well, thank you, ladies. We have to be moving on."

"Fare thee well, gentlemen!" Josephina called out.

"We'll be keeping our eye on you, Inkwell!" Wendolen cried. She let out a sigh and glanced at her sister. "Now then. Shall we call a truce and move on to 'Softly Doth the Blossoms Fall'?"

"An excellent choice," Josephina agreed.

As soon as they were out of the vineyard, Ink smacked Evering's hand away from his shoulder and straightened his hat.

"So what's all that about?" the young man asked. "Why do you keep your age a secret? Ain't the first time you've done it."

"People look down on you for your age," Ink answered. "And why should it matter what number I give? Should I start calling you 'boy' just 'cause you can't grow a proper beard?"

Evering turned a shade of reddish-purple as his hand went up to his chin again. "That's not my fault! It's an inherited trait! And anyway, what about that coat and hat you're wearing? They obviously weren't made for you. Are they supposed to make you look older?"

"Works better than that fuzz on your face. So what's the story with those two back there? How do opera singers get mixed up in the kind of trouble you're in?"

Evering shoved his hands into his pockets and shrugged. "The same way we all did."

Ink looked at him sidelong. "You do know that's not helpful, right?"

"Oh, I know. But look. There's Chester's house, just across the bridge."

They emerged from the grove into the southern end of the village. Here, Ink was met by the sight of a good crop of wheat bursting with ripe grain. As a breeze sent the golden stalks swaying, Ink realized he could still hear the sisters singing, though it was much fainter.

He followed Evering over a stone footbridge and saw a man sitting on the front steps of a house. As they approached, he raised a large glass full of crimson liquid towards them and removed the cigar from between his teeth.

"Honored guests! Welcome!"

"Good morning," Evering replied. "Ink, this is—"

"Oh, no!" the man cried, raising a hand to stop him. "No, Evering, please. Allow me."

He got to his feet and bowed dramatically.

"Chester Fortescue! Humble proprietor of the illustrious Riverfall vineyards. Producer, nay, architect!" He punched a triumphant fist into the air. "Of the finest spirits ever presented to the whole of the human world since the beginning of time! Unrivaled and unduplicatable—is that a word?—by any hand, mortal or otherwise! Keeper of ancient secrets of the vine! Herald of this wonderful gift which I deliver by holy charge to my fellow brothers and sisters. And—most importantly, and certainly in no way begrudgingly—sacred and most highly-appointed taste tester!" He raised his glass, took a huge swallow, then smacked his lips. "This is a good one."

Ink frowned and looked at Evering. "What does he do?"

"He makes wine and then drinks it all day."

Chester raised an eyebrow and sat back down. "Well, anybody can make it sound stupid. So Ink! Joining the cast, are we? Excellent. We're in desperate need of fresh blood up here . . . which I now realize is a very poor choice of words."

"Chester, it's just past eight o'clock in the morning," Evering said. "Do you really think it's a good idea to be drinking now?"

"Not only is it a good idea, it's the best idea. I've already got the latest harvest fermenting away. I'm due for a little reward. Got to have some balance in your life, you know."

"Does a lot of this 'balancing' go on around here?" Ink asked.

"With him? More often than not," Evering answered. "The wine is supposed to be used as payment to people from whom we . . . acquire supplies. That's the main reason we started making it in the first place."

"Keeps our consciences clear," Chester replied, then blew out a stream of cigar smoke. "Doesn't do a bad job keeping smiles on our faces either. The number of vices in which a fellow may indulge up here is . . . pitiable. But so long as we keep our glasses filled, you can ease the pain of doing without a few things. By the way, when's the last time that face of yours got past a smug smirk, Mr. Inkwell? Fancy a drop or two?"

"Actually, we're looking for Simon right now," Evering said. "Have you seen him?"

"I have not. You should ask the Plumsleys. Have you met my lovely ladies yet, Ink?"

"We were just there," Evering said. "They directed us to you."

"Oh, oh, wait, wait a minute . . ." Chester took another long draught from his glass. He leaned back and cocked his head, squinting up at the sky. "Oh, yes. Now I remember. I did see Simon. Heading towards the pipeworks, I think."

"Thank you," Evering said. He turned back towards the path. Ink followed.

"Ink?" Chester called out, tipping the glass towards him. "Sure you won't have a taste?"

"Oh, no wine for me," Ink answered. "I'm more of a gin man myself."

The sound of Chester's great belly-laughs resounded across the village—and long after he was out of sight.

As they continued along the path, the faint echoes of the

123

Plumsleys' song finally faded away. In its absence, Ink noticed the gentle murmuring of the nearby stream—and little else.

"It's so quiet," he said. "I don't think I've heard a single bird or cricket since I've been here."

"We're too high up for birds," Evering answered. "Leastways the smaller varieties. And as for crickets, I expect the chickens took care of them a long time ago. Anyway, here we are. The Pipeworks House."

He stepped up to another round building, which looked much the same as all the others, and produced a key. The symbol on the door was a clockwork gear.

Inside was a single large room—no hallway, no smaller rooms off to the side. There was a staircase in the center but there was also a wide door in the floor a few steps behind it. The room itself was filled with a variety of assorted items—tools, oil cans, coils of rope, crates of random components and mechanisms. Pieces of metal pipe were stacked on the far side, almost to the ceiling. It seemed to be more of a storage area than a proper house.

The door in the floor was propped open. Through it issued a sound of hissing and strange metallic clanking. Evering headed straight towards it.

"What's that noise?" Ink asked.

"You'll see. Come on. Down this way."

The stairs descended into one of the strangest places Ink had ever seen. It was a wide, cavernous chamber, carved out of clay and rock but with whole sections of the floor and walls missing. Through these great open spaces, the world below was visible. Ink looked down over the railing and saw a rolling expanse of green fields dotted with tiny white gaggles of sheep.

Morning light streamed in through the open back-end of the chamber. There were metal pipes everywhere—running along the walls, overhead, branching out from one another, and almost a third of them dripping water. They all seemed to stem from a gigantic black boiler in the middle of the place, like so many legs on a bulbous iron spider. Steam hissed out of vents near the top and around the sides. Below, a wooden walkway sprawled out like a labyrinth, reaching into every corner of the chamber. As Ink followed Evering onto it, he realized he'd been there the day before—heard the same strange noises—when Simon had first carried him to the infirmary.

"Sweet gravy!" he cried. "What is all this?"

"The plumbing system," Evering answered. "My dad came up with it. Took months of effort but he figured out how to get pipes up into the houses and the fountains in the garden. We actually thought we'd run out of water before we could get it all working. When the village first went up, the stream had nowhere to go but right over the edge. That's why we called the place 'Riverfall'. But then we figured how to make it so the water could be constantly cycling 'round, using pumps and things like that. That was a trial, I can tell you. We had to wait for a few good rain showers to fill the streambed up again, but it didn't take long. Now we got what only the richest folk in Altan can afford. That boiler there even gets heat to all the bedrooms and powers the propellers."

"Powers the what?"

Evering paused and pointed at the back of the chamber. Hanging out over the ledge were four huge spinning blades, each linked to the boiler by a series of large copper tubes.

"They're a fairly new invention," Evering went on. "We use them to move us forward. Steer us about. They don't have much power set against a large land mass like this—that's why we move so slowly—but we do our best with what we've got."

The wooden walkway twisted around four thick columns of earth supporting the roof, through which hung the ends of tree and plant roots. Passing the last of these pillars, Simon and Abner came into view. They stood beneath a large pipe which bent under its own weight and leaked water from three different places. The path beyond them dead-ended at a high wooden gate set with a heavy iron padlock.

"It's not the only one like this," Abner was saying, nodding towards the unfortunate pipe. "Another six months and the entire system could go bust. Not to mention we've only got coal enough for six weeks."

"We've run out before," Simon replied.

"Yes, and need I remind you how poor a substitute wood is for coal. I don't care to have anything like a repeat of our close encounter with a mountain last year."

Simon was the first to notice Evering and Ink approach. He made Abner a sign to cut the conversation short. "Morning, gentlemen."

Evering nodded to him. "Simon, Ink here was wanting to speak with you."

Simon glanced at Abner, whose solemn expression conveyed a sense of dread.

"Of course. Uh . . . we can talk over here. Follow me."

Ink glanced back to see Abner toss his son a coal shovel. Evering sighed and trudged obediently towards the boiler.

Simon led Ink towards the far corner of the chamber, away from the noise of steam and mechanical rumblings. As they went along, Ink took the opportunity to size up the Colonists' acting physician. He had a look of intelligence about him. Educated, as Evering had told him, tall and lean, but not thin. Ink thought he'd make a jolly good show in a boxing ring, but the gentleness in his eyes and the mildness in his voice told Ink the chances of that were very slim indeed.

When they came to a stop, Simon rested his hand on a railing and looked out into the vast expanse of sky ahead of them. "So, Ink?"

Ink took off his hat and blew out an exasperated breath. There was so much he wanted to know, but Delia's warning about asking the right kinds of questions echoed in his mind, making it hard to begin. He scratched the back of his neck and shook his head. "All right, I know . . . I know there's questions you can't answer. And I know there's some you *won't* answer. But you've gotta tell me how you knew about me and that Spektor in the lake, and how you found me in that flat afterwards. I don't like

126

being spied on. So if you've got some kind of . . . eavesdropping device or something to keep eyes on me, I want to know about it."

Simon nodded. "That's fair. The simple truth is that Evering saw the Spektor as we were passing over yesterday. He was busy repairing a pipe when he glanced down and spotted a huge shadow in the lake. He ran to get me and Caradoc, and we were able to identify it. Then we noticed you standing on the shore, saw it was headed towards you, and decided we had to jump into action. We watched Caradoc get to you first, then saw you run back into town and into that building. Evering even observed you through one of the windows, so we knew which flat you were in. But we weren't spying. Only trying to keep watch until we could get you to safety."

Ink leaned on the railing and scoffed. "Blimey. Makes me wonder how many other people are looking down from flying villages. How *do* you keep all this hidden, anyway? How has no one noticed a bloody big piece of rock flying through the sky?"

"Well, there's a kind of giant shroud around the whole place that makes us invisible. It's not solid, though. Rain passes through it. Sun rays, birds, and so on. If you were to toss something over the side, it would go straight through to the ground below. Chester once dropped a lantern and set a corn field on fire. That was a bad day."

Ink frowned. "So this . . . shroud thing . . . is that what made me black out?"

"Yes. It emits a certain energy which affects human equilibrium and other physiological senses . . ." He trailed off with a glance at Ink's puzzled expression. "To a degree."

"How do you get down?"

Simon was slower to answer this time. "We engineered a type of . . . lowering system. That's a bit more complicated to explain." He smiled as Ink's expression grew disgruntled. "Every time you get an answer, ten more questions crop up, don't they? Such is life."

"Such is *your* life," Ink retorted. "Me, I'm used to a simpler way of doing things. A better way. You have a question, you get an answer, you go on with life. If you don't get an answer, it means no one knows."

"What about lying?"

"Lying is an answer. It just ain't the right one. But at least it's an answer. That's why you people are so frustrating. I mean, you don't even lie! You don't even pretend not to know! It's no secret you've got the answers, it's just that you won't give 'em!"

"And you're used to getting what you want?"

"Well, if it ain't given, at least I can try to take it. Usually."

"Like you tried to last night? With your pistol?"

Ink glanced over the railing. A green river wound through a forest of yellow trees below.

Simon shook his head. "I don't blame you, you know. I don't think any of us do."

"Wouldn't be so sure of that," Ink replied, then turned and put his back to the railing. "Then again, I ain't sure of anything anymore. I thought I had my mind made up about you lot. But everything's been muddled. Too many things just don't add up."

"Such as?"

"Well, this place, for one. You're all Cassrians, so it's obvious you got an Entrian to do the enchantment for you. Unless there's another way of raising a village into the air and making it invisible that I don't know about. But what Entrian would lift a finger to help you? Of course you must've used force and threats and all that, knowing your reputation. But even then . . ."

"Reputation," Simon said, leaning on the railing and clasping his hands together. "Now that's an interesting word, isn't it? A great deal of reputation is based on opinions. On word-of-mouth. It can be manipulated, lied about, and all too easily."

"Well, you *have* all been acting out of character," Ink replied. "Risked your lives to get me away from those Spektor creatures. Haven't locked me up or given me a beating. Yet."

Simon smirked. "Yet."

"But then I wonder . . ." Ink bit his lip and dropped his gaze.

"You wonder what?"

"Well . . . you might've saved *me* from a sticky end, but how many corpses did you leave behind on that island all those years ago?"

Simon glanced away, grinding his jaw.

"I've also been wonderin'," Ink continued, "with all you've got up here, everything you'll ever need, why don't you just escape over the sea? Why hang around this world that hates you so much? Then I realize . . . the job ain't done yet, is it? There's still Entrians down there to kill."

"Ink—"

"You say you're good people. You say you're innocent, and you've put on a good show of it. But that's only 'cause you can. You're out of reach up here. But Bash wasn't, was he? And if those Spektor things went after him, then maybe they had the right idea. Maybe you really are the monsters the world says you are. And maybe you all really do deserve to die."

Simon stood from the railing and turned towards Ink. His face was stone but his eyes flickered with fire. "Don't you deserve to die as well?"

Ink felt his heart sink. As if threatening them with a pistol hadn't pushed the limits enough, he'd gone and finished the job with words. He gripped the railing as tight as he could, preparing to be thrown over the edge at any moment.

"Using your logic," Simon continued, "isn't a boy hunted by Spektors damned to our own fate? Doesn't a boy who carries a pistol and seems awfully adept at evading captors betray something about the nature of his life? You will say nothing of your family, nothing of where you come from, nothing of your actions. If we've been behaving a bit secretively, you have been a master of the game thus far. Was Martin right in wanting to lock you up? Should we be holding you prisoner? Should we be beating you?"

"No!"

"And why not? Because you're more innocent than you appear to be?"

". . . yes," Ink replied, though not as fast as he would've liked.

"But that's not what the facts show. And your reputation in this village has started out very poorly indeed."

Ink remained silent. The look in Simon's eye softened.

"But I'm willing to bet appearances aren't pointing to the truth here. I think you are innocent. I think you're a boy who got mixed up in a very bad business without meaning to. And I believe it because it's our story as well. I told you yesterday that we went to Damiras to prevent a massacre. That is the truth." He glanced out over the rail towards the horizon. "When we failed, we were shackled with so much pain and guilt you can't begin to imagine the weight of it. That the whole world accuses us of being murderers makes it all the worse."

Ink frowned. "Then why not just tell everyone?"

"We tried. But it made no difference. Like you, they had made their minds up about the truth in advance. So we had to flee. We had no choice. And we hang around this world that hates us so much because it's our home. Because we cling to the hope that one day all the wrongs will somehow be righted. That we will be free again." He rubbed his chin and shook his head. "Killing has never been our interest. Only preserving life. That's why we care what happens to you, Ink. You don't deserve to be at the mercy of the Spektors. No more than the Entrians deserved what happened to them on Damiras."

Ink's frown deepened. "But if you didn't do it, who did? Who was responsible?"

"We don't know. We have a few theories, but it's far too dangerous to investigate ourselves."

"Simon!" Abner shouted from across the chamber. "Give me a hand over here, will you? This ruddy valve won't budge!"

"On my way!" Simon called back.

"Wait," Ink said. "So . . . so you can look me in the eye and honestly say that no one here has blood on their hands? Not even a little?"

Simon stood from the railing and half turned away. Ink couldn't see his face, but the silence did not speak to the answer he was hoping to hear.

"No, Ink," he answered at last. "I can't say that."

He lingered a moment longer, then strode away. Ink let him go. There was too much to think about. Too much to sort out and keep straight in his memory. He needed a bit of time.

Unfortunately, it was starting to look like there would be plenty of it.

CHAPTER 14

THE NAVIGATOR RETURNS

The visit to the pipeworks turned out to be longer than Ink had intended. With both Simon and Evering present, Abner decided it was a good time to reroute a few of the pipe lines and fix some of the kinks in the heating system. Ink spent most of the time amusing himself by dropping pieces of coal through the huge gaps in the floor. The village was too high for him to tell if he'd actually hit any of his ground targets, but he was almost certain he'd clipped a passing bird on the tail at least once.

When he tired of this, he leaned against the railing with his hands in his pockets and tried to guess what might lay behind the padlocked wooden gates. Before he could put very much thought to the task, he realized there was something rather heavy in his left pocket. He glanced down as he began to pull it out, catching a glint of silver which quickly turned to emerald.

"Ink!"

At the sound of Evering's voice, he quickly dropped it into his pocket again and looked up. The young man beckoned to him from across the pipeworks. Simon and Abner were heading towards the stairs.

"It's almost twelve!" Evering cried over the noise of steam and the whirring propellors. "Let's get some lunch!"

Ink pushed himself off the railing and hurried across the walkway.

~

Back on the surface, the group parted ways to change clothes before heading to the Dining House. Ink started to follow Evering down the path but stopped soon after.

"What's the matter?" Evering asked.

"I'm not hungry."

Evering frowned. "Not hungry? You've not had anything to eat but a pancake and an apple for the last twelve hours."

Ink fidgeted. "I can't sit in there with all of 'em staring at me. Asking questions. Judging. Just thinking about it gives me indigestion. I won't do it. You go on."

Evering glanced back down the path. Simon had already rounded the bend and was out of sight. Abner had just stepped inside the house they shared.

"Go on," Ink urged again. "You don't gotta miss lunch on my account."

"I can't."

"Why not?"

"Hello, boys!" a woman's voice called.

Riva was coming towards them from the vegetable garden. She smiled at them from under her straw hat, removing a pair of gloves. "Shouldn't you both be at the Dining House?"

Evering hesitated, glancing at Ink. "Well, Ink isn't hungry and . . . I was going to stay with him. But now that you're here, do you think you could . . . keep—"

"Keep him company? Of course."

Evering thanked her and gave Ink a stern "be good" glare before hurrying on to his house. Riva smiled at Ink again, and it made him wonder if she was good-natured enough to be trusting. Perhaps he could wheedle a bit more out of her than Evering.

"Enjoying the sights?" she asked.

Ink nodded. "Quite impressive. Lots to see. And learn."

"Well if you like, I can take you around to see a bit more. Have you met Ed yet?"

"Was he at the meeting last night?"

Riva laughed. "Oh, no. Ed never moves from his post. You'll see why. Come on."

She led him on a stroll along the stream, passing into the garden grove under an arch of moss-covered oak branches. In the shadow of the trees the water was deep green and sparkled where the sunlight slipped through gaps in the leafy ceiling above.

"Out of interest," Ink said, hooking his thumbs over his belt as he stared down at the water, "is someone supposed to be keeping an eye on me at all times?"

There was a moment of silence before her answer came, somewhat apologetically.

"Yes. But only 'til we're sure you won't hurt yourself, or—"

"Or trip and go hurtling over the side," Ink finished. "Fair enough."

As they went on, his attention was drawn to the stone tower in the middle of the garden. They were heading straight for it.

"So what's this tower all about?" he asked. "Seems an odd thing to have in the middle of a little village."

"Oh, we use it for lots of things. The first level is where we stock firewood. The second is used for storage."

"Storage of what?"

She shrugged and tucked a stray lock of hair behind her ear. "Just bits of junk, really. No use throwing anything away up here. You never know when you might need it again. The third level is where Caradoc sleeps, and he works on the fourth—the glass chamber. That's the Navigation Room."

"But he's gone now, ain't he?" Ink replied. "So there's no one driving this thing?"

"Simon takes over his duties when he's gone. Which isn't very often, fortunately."

"Why Simon?" Ink asked. "Couldn't anyone do it? How much brain does it take to point a flying rock in the right direction?"

"It takes a great deal more brain than you would think," she answered. "Caradoc doesn't just point us in the right direction, he's our navigator. That means a lot more. You have to factor in wind currents and know things about direction-finding and course-plotting. You have to be able to read the skies for the weather and the stars to mark positions. It's complicated work."

Ink nodded, rubbing his chin. He may not have been getting answers to many serious questions, but learning anything he could about his surroundings was useful. Aside from theft, exploitation was one of the best tricks of his trade. Experience had taught him that even an answer to an 'innocent' question held the possibility of turning some kind of profit later on.

"And what about this village?" Ink continued. "These weird round houses and such. I've never seen anything like it."

She shrugged again. "Well, I suppose you've never been to an Entrian village before."

Ink's leisurely pace came to an abrupt halt. "A *what?*"

Riva smothered a smile. "No one told you? Evering's a worse guide than I thought."

"Hold on, hold on," Ink said, waving his hands as he stepped in front of her. "Are you standing there and telling me that this is an Entrian village? An actual Entrian village?"

"Rytram was its name before," she said. "We came upon it looking for a place to camp. And actually it isn't really a proper Entrian village. It's a kind of school."

Ink shuddered at the word. "This is a school?"

"That's why there's only one place for everyone to eat together, and why there's only one proper bedroom to every house. Each one was also designed with a particular subject of study in mind. Like the house we were all in last night? That's the Music House. If you had come to the school with the intent of

135

studying music, that's where you would live. I myself stay in the Literature House. There's a Mathematics House also, one for Philosophy, Natural Sciences, Medicine—that's Simon's place. You might have seen the symbols on the doors identifying them. The tower is meant for studying the stars."

"But if this is a school, what did you do—I mean . . ." Ink hesitated, but Riva looked at him with such earnestness he risked the question anyway. "What happened to all the people? The teachers and students?"

The light easiness in Riva's eyes dimmed, though she held her composure a great deal better than Simon had. Ink cringed, dreading to hear of the bloody scenario he was sure had taken place to make room for the desperate Colonists.

"They all went to the island of Damiras," she answered. "The school was still empty by the time we arrived."

Ink nodded. He needed no further explanation.

Moments later, they arrived at the base of the tower. The dark iron door gaped at them like an open mouth. Ink slowed his pace.

"Come on," she said with a small wave. "Round to the back."

Ink followed, half-expecting to see something horrible—like an old coot shackled to the stone walls or wasting away in a cage. But all he saw was a tree. It was a young birch with a canopy of leaves silvery dark and wide, spreading up and outwards from the stone wall. Upon closer inspection, he spied a list of about a dozen names scorched into the cream-colored bark.

Riva nodded towards the tree. "This is Ed."

Ink looked at her as though she'd lost her mind. She smiled again with a small laugh.

"I don't know why we call it that. Jeremy started it. The rest of us just sort of picked it up. This is our Memory Tree. Our memorial to those we've lost." She pointed to a name near the top. "This is Evering's mother."

Her finger moved down to another.

"Delia's husband . . ."

She used two fingers for a pair of names farther down.

"These are Jeremy's brothers. The eldest and the youngest."

Several of the markings shared surnames. It appeared entire families had been wiped out. Ink felt more confused than ever. He hadn't expected something as heartfelt as a Memory Tree from a gang of cutthroats. The more time he spent with the Colonists, the more it really seemed they were not what the rest of the world believed them to be. But how could he ever be certain?

Suddenly, a loud bell began to toll. Ink was so startled he clapped his hands over his ears and glanced around in fright. Riva smiled and beckoned for him to follow her. She led him on a short path towards the southern part of the glade, then turned and pointed up to a huge clock hanging on the third level of the tower.

"It sounds every hour from six in the morning to six at night," Riva said. "Keeps us synchronized with the rest of civilization."

Ink lowered his hands. "Ain't you afraid they'll hear that ruckus down below?"

"There's a silencing enchantment around the village. It stops the sound from—"

He glanced back at her. Her face had suddenly changed, fixed in an apprehensive stare that went straight past him. He followed her gaze and turned to see a dark figure staggering towards them through the trees. It was a man, walking heavily on his left leg and holding his right hand to his ribcage with a hat clutched tight in his fist. The other hand gripped the side of his neck. The next instant, Riva was off running towards him.

As Ink drew nearer, he was astonished to see it was the man who had pulled him away from the shadow in the water—the same one he'd thought drowned in the lake. The hat and jacket once discarded on the shore were now the only dry items about him. His shirt and trousers were soaked through and his hair was slicked back as though he'd just gone for a swim.

"What happened?" Riva cried.

"Now don't make a fuss," the man replied.

"Sit down. Right here. Sit down."

She grabbed his elbow, but he wrenched it out of her grasp. "I don't want to sit down. I want to go to my room."

She moved in front of him. "It's too far. Sit down."

"It's right behind you!"

"You are not going up two flights of stairs in this condition."

"Riva, I don't want to knock your head against a tree, but I will."

She moved aside the arm he held to his ribcage and opened his jacket. When Ink heard her gasp, he stepped closer and looked around her. The man's shirt was drenched in blood.

"For the love of God, Caradoc!"

"Keep your voice down!" he hissed at her.

"If you don't sit down right now, so help me, I'll kick your other leg out!"

He looked down into her stern, frightened face, and with a sigh, resigned himself to letting her help him sit at the base of a tree.

"How could you even think of walking all the way back here?" she said. "You should have signaled for help!"

"I wasn't dead."

"You don't look far from it. What's wrong with your neck? Let me see."

"Riva, I don't—"

"Let me see it, Caradoc!"

He lowered his hand. Riva gasped again. The man frowned at her. "Are you going to make that sound every time?"

"Do you know how close this is to your jugular vein?"

"Two fingertips away, as a matter of fact."

Ink couldn't see the wound itself for all the blood that slicked his skin. Riva put her hand to his neck and held it there for a few seconds. "What's wrong with your leg?"

"Tore up my calf on a rock."

"What else?"

"Bruised ribs, both sides. Collarbone, both sides." He went

silent, but her admonishing glare intensified until he begrudgingly continued. "Right shoulder . . ."

"Oh, for heaven's sake!"

"Look, it's nothing serious, just a lot of blood."

"That *is* serious!"

"I mean it looks worse than it is."

"I'll decide that. Move your hands."

"It's fine, Riva."

"Why are you being so difficult? How long have you been this way?"

"All my life."

"You know what I meant! How long have you been wounded?"

"I don't know. Four hours. Maybe five."

She reached for his jacket again, but he clamped his bloodied hands over the front of it. Ink noticed he was wearing a fingerless leather glove on his left hand.

"You're being a child," she said.

"And you're being a nag," Caradoc shot back.

She huffed through her teeth at him and moved down to his right leg, rolling up the trouser to inspect the torn flesh underneath. After a moment she held both hands to the injured muscle and pressed in. The man shut his eyes and leaned his head against the tree.

Ink was bewildered. He would have thought Riva the sort of girl to have fainted at the sight of blood, not plunge into the mess with all the vigor of a surgeon. What was more, he wasn't sure what good holding down on the man's injuries for a few moments was doing. A few seconds later, she released the pressure and rolled his trouser leg back down.

"Now move your hands," she said.

"That's not going to work here. Some of the wounds have started to burn. I think they might be infected."

Her anxious face fell into even deeper concern. "What happened to you?"

A pained expression crept into his eyes, and a long moment went by before he finally answered. "The shield broke."

Riva's face paled. "I didn't know that could happen."

The man's brow furrowed. "Neither did I."

None of this talk made any sense to Ink, but the weight of their words and the tone of their voices were enough to put a small shiver of dread in his heart.

"Stay put. I'm going to get Simon," Riva said to Caradoc. She rose to her feet and looked at Ink. "You stay here as well. If I find that you ran off—"

"Are you joking?" Ink said. "Now that something mildly interesting is happening?"

She gave him the same "be good" glare Evering had given him earlier, then hurried off through the trees.

Ink glanced down. The man had closed his eyes again and lain his head back against the tree, not so much in pain this time as in rest. He was about as tall as Simon, but dark-haired and with more weight in muscle. Owing to the heavy rings under his eyes, Ink guessed he hadn't slept much since they'd last met, but they were not the most noticeable marks he bore. Ink inched forward and peered closer.

Several cruel-looking gashes had been cut into his face, some of them deep. Two parallel scars on his right cheek were visible for a few inches before disappearing into his beard. Others near his left ear were so severe they couldn't be hidden by any amount of facial hair. Another cut went straight from the top of his right cheekbone almost to the inside of his ear, which was missing a small piece of its outer edge. The most noticeable scar had been carved above his left eye, short but deep, running jagged through the eyebrow. They were old wounds, no doubt set there for many years. Almost without thinking, Ink reached up and felt the scratch on his own cheek.

"So . . ."

Ink stepped back, startled. The man opened his eyes and looked at him with a mixture of amusement and irritation.

"You're the idiot who decided to put his face into the open mouth of a Spektor."

Ink didn't reply. Caradoc pushed himself into a straighter sitting position against the tree.

"What's your name?"

"Ink. Inkwell Featherfield."

"And what's your real name?"

"Ink-well Fea-ther-field," he said again. "What's your real name?"

Caradoc raised his eyebrows. "Victoria Meriwether."

Ink tipped his hat. "Glad to make your acquaintance, Miss Meriwether."

"Likewise, Mr. Featherfield. So . . .?" He straightened the front of his jacket and held his arms out wide. "What do you think?"

"Of what?"

"Well, you were eyeing me."

Ink shrugged. "You're a bloody mess."

Caradoc's stare grew so intense that Ink thought he might jump up, grab him by the shirt, and fling him over the tree line. Instead, the hint of a smirk flickered at the corner of his mouth.

"No thanks to you, little man."

"I heard screaming," Ink said. "I thought someone was drowning."

"Someone nearly did after you left. That was the Spektor screaming. One of the ways they lure their victims closer. Obviously to great effect."

"Have you been underwater all this time?"

The man nodded. Ink ventured a step forward.

"You can hold your breath for that long? Are you an Entrian?"

"No, I am not an Entrian," Caradoc said. He drew up his good knee and rested his left arm on it. "I'm a bloody mess, as you've said, and a God's-honest fool on top of that. Nothing more. There's a network of caves under Corvus Lake. Plenty of breathable air in them."

"What were you doing down there? You couldn't have been chasing it."

"No, that's impossible. Crazy. Only a lunatic would do that."

Ink swallowed. "Did you . . . did you get those wounds from the . . ."

"Yes," Caradoc finished. "And I'll tell you something else, Inkwell Featherfield. This isn't the first time I've taken a beating from a Spektor, but it's the worst I've been through in a very long time. I want you to tell me why."

Ink frowned. He glanced back, hoping to see Riva or Simon hurrying back through the grove, but the path was clear.

"I . . . I don't know," he answered at last.

Caradoc's gaze hardened. "Yes, you do. You just don't realize it yet. It may take some time to jog your memory, but the answer's in there."

"And what if it doesn't jog? You can't keep me here forever."

"Are you afraid?"

For a moment, Ink considered lying. It was always the preferred route when threatened with the possibility of losing face. But he got the sense that the blood-covered man on the ground would see through him in an instant, and probably did even now.

"Yes," he answered.

The man nodded. "Then you're not as stupid as I thought. Now . . ." He slicked back his wet hair with his good arm. "What were you doing before the Spektor drew you out to the lake?"

"I was sleeping. In a shed at the bottom of the hill."

"And how did you come to be in that particular shed near that particular hill?"

Ink dared a half-truth this time. "It was raining. I needed shelter."

"That was a happy discovery, being such a fair way from any road as you were."

"I don't always travel by roads."

Caradoc stared hard at the boy. Ink fidgeted, growing impatient. "Look, I don't have anything more to tell you. I don't know why it's chasing me."

"It?"

"Yeah, it. The *Spektor*."

"Oh, you are not dealing with an 'it', Mr. Featherfield. You think you only had one on your tail down there?"

Ink shrugged. "I don't know. Maybe two."

Caradoc shook his head. "You woke them all up. You have entire legions after you."

Ink felt a rush of cold panic. This whole thing had to be one big nightmare. It had to be. Any moment he was going to wake up, still under that tarp in that shed.

"This is ridiculous," he said. "This can't be real. It can't! I haven't *done* anything! I never even heard of Spektors 'til yesterday! It don't make any sense!"

"It doesn't have to," Caradoc replied. "In fact it's better for them that way."

"Look, maybe it was just . . . waiting."

"What do you mean?"

"Well, Bash had already been polished off by one. Maybe it was hanging around to see who else it could nab for dessert."

Caradoc nearly leapt to his feet, but thought better of it when he remembered his wounds.

"How do you know about Bash?"

"Everyone knows about him!" Ink said. "They were bloody well shouting his name through the streets yesterday. How he was a Colonist and how everyone ought to start looking twice at their neighbors and all that."

"They know how he died?"

"Well . . . no . . ."

"Then how do you?"

The panic rushed out of Ink with his next breath, deflating him like a balloon. He prided himself on keeping his wits through any conversation, even heated ones. But he'd been careless this time, and his calculated attempt at secrecy had smashed to pieces. His shoulders sagged.

"All right," he said with a sigh. "I was looking around in the house. Bash's house, I mean. I heard he'd died and I thought he might've left a valuable thing or two behind. Didn't get anything, though. Had to light out fast when these Entrians showed up."

"Entrians?" Caradoc repeated, a tone of strain coloring his voice.

"Yeah. A woman and two men, along with Bill Stone. He's the main reason I ended up in that shed. Got wind of me and started on the hunt."

"What did you hear?"

Ink's shoulders sagged even lower. Not only could this man see through him, he was several steps ahead. He shoved his hands in his pockets.

"They found Bash with his insides tore up. Bill didn't know what to make of it, but I think the others did. And they were more worried than happy about it. Frightened, even. I could see it."

"They talked of nothing else, this group?"

"Nothing I can remember. I was a little more worried about getting away from Bill."

"He saw you?"

"Heard me. I slipped on the ground and made a noise."

"And the others? Did they notice as well?"

Ink frowned. "I don't know."

Caradoc rubbed a hand across his face. Ink could practically see the gears of his mind turning. He shifted against the tree trunk and glanced up again.

"I know of only two things that will attract a Spektor's attention: hate and despair. If these become potent enough in a person's heart, Spektors will be drawn like vultures to carrion. Now think back, and tell me honestly—were you feeling either of these sentiments that morning? Even by the smallest degree?"

Ink thought back to the lake, to the fog, to the shed. Even to

144

Edgely Hill before it. He'd been frightened. Cold. Uncertain. But he hadn't despaired. And even his anger and annoyance with Spindler hadn't quite made it all the way to hatred.

"No," he finally answered. "I felt none of that."

Caradoc's dark eyes fell to the ground, searching it in thought. For a long time, there was no sound but the rush of the stream beyond the tower. Ink waited anxiously. Every minute he wasted in their village was a minute lost to his own business, and it was agonizing. He had risked so much and traveled so far. Now his only hope rested with the man in front of him, this infamous fugitive, who with a word could either set him on his way again or continue to keep him captive.

"It's not enough," Caradoc said at last.

Ink's heart sank. "What?"

"We don't have enough to put an answer together."

"But . . . I've told you everything. Everything I know."

"It doesn't matter."

Ink felt his face begin to flush. "Then what am I supposed to do? Are you just gonna keep me here? On this floating prison?"

Caradoc didn't answer. Any boy of lesser mettle might have begun to cry at that moment, but Ink would have nothing whatsoever to do with tears. When it came to showing emotion in the face of distress, he always erred on the side of anger.

"Well, that ain't good enough," Ink said. "No, sir. Not by a long shot. I ain't a criminal! I ain't on trial! And I've had it with all your secrets and lies! With all of you! I'm done here! You got it? Done! Spektors or no Spektors! You get me back to the ground right now or—"

"Or what?"

"Or . . . I'll take you all down with me!"

Ink didn't care how ridiculous he sounded. Rage filled him wherever the fear had not, and he stared down at the man on the ground with his fists balled up like a pint-sized prize fighter. Caradoc then did the worst thing imaginable in the face of a person at the full height of their fury. He laughed.

"You don't think I can?" Ink shouted. "I'll prove it! To all of you! *I'm* master of my own fate! Get it? Me! And no one else!"

Caradoc shot to his feet, causing fresh blood to flow from his wounds. That alone was enough to shut Ink up fast. Without a word, the man took a step forward and ripped the glove from his left hand. Here was another wound yet to be seen, and far more hideous than all the rest.

His palm had been mutilated, the skin slashed to ribbons. Bone, tendon, muscle and nerves were all visible where flesh should have been. But there was something even more alarming. A web-like pattern of gold strands had been set into the center of his hand, stretching from his wrist to the bottom of his fingers and gleaming like metal. Blood welled through it, running down his arm and dripping from his elbow. It was a horrifying sight. When Caradoc spoke again, Ink was astonished to hear not anger in his voice, but good humor.

"This, Mr. Featherfield," he said, "is what's keeping you alive. Why you are at the mercy of the Spektors without me. Why you are not master of your own fate. I am. And until that fact changes, you'll do what you're told while aboard this floating prison."

He stepped back and eased himself down against the tree again.

Ink shook his head. "I should've known. They tried so hard to make me think . . ."

"Make you think what?"

"That you're all innocent."

Caradoc replaced the glove on his hand. "If I've learned anything in this life it's that no one is truly innocent."

"What is that thing?" Ink demanded. "That thing on your hand?"

Caradoc leaned back against the tree and closed his eyes. "Something I did to myself."

"You did it . . . but why?"

The man didn't answer. His face was in such a perfect state of calm he might've been asleep.

Ink shook his head, anger once more overtaking his fear. "You're mad. You're mad is what you are. I know it when I see—"

Quick as lightning, Caradoc shot out his good arm and grabbed the front corner of his coat. Ink barely had time to react.

"Hey! Stop it! Let go!" he cried, trying to tear himself out of his grasp.

In another instant, Caradoc did exactly that. Ink's heart was beating in his throat.

"Whatcha do that for?"

"I was checking to see if there was a name sewn into the lining."

Ink's cheeks flushed with anger. "That's none of your business!"

The man settled back against the tree. "No. It's not."

With a barely-stifled curse, Ink straightened his coat and turned away.

"Where are you going?" Caradoc called after him.

"Away from you!"

He heard Caradoc chuckle. Ink ignored him and continued on. If this lunatic was going to be the one responsible for his fate on this ridiculous flying spit of land, it was going to be a very trying time. He paused for a moment when he heard another sound from behind, then glanced back in disbelief. The man was singing.

> *When I can't stand another hour*
> *When I can't bide another day*
> *When I can't bear a life this lonely*
> *Where do I find myself astray?*
> *I'm away from you*
> *Away from you*

Ink shook his head and hurried out of the grove.

CHAPTER 15

THE GREAT HALL

S pindler stared at the prison coach traveling ahead of his carriage. Two dozen men and women sat in silence along the coach walls, listless and hollow-eyed, each with their gaze cast to the floor. Some looked as if they were trying to sleep. Many looked ill. He wondered where they were going, as Talas Prison was many miles in the opposite direction. Both vehicles were headed towards the capital, but as far as he knew it contained only a small jail which was generally used as a holding cell and could not have accommodated them all. So it couldn't be a transfer. And it was definitely not a release.

As he pondered this, a dark-haired woman sitting in the rear corner of the coach lifted her head and looked at him with vapid, dreary eyes. He turned his head and pulled his coat tighter around himself, taking care not to jostle the driver beside him.

It had been four days since he'd left Harburg. Four days of bad roads and cold weather. Four nights of overpriced inns and food that turned his stomach sour simply by looking at it. He'd even been obliged to give up the comfort of the carriage's interior to a party of women who had boarded at the last town. The sound of their chatter and giggling had not ceased for the past two hours. But every time a bitter curse or grumble of complaint threatened to leave his lips, he had only to look up at the miserable cargo in front of him to put a stop to it.

"There it is," the driver said as the carriage crested a hill.

The next breeze that rushed over them carried with it the smell of the sea and the cry of gulls. Spindler sat straighter and looked out. Altan—the capital of Cassrian civilization—stood in the distance, perched atop a sheer-faced cliff which ran along the northern coast of the Talas Sea.

"You here for the cliffs?" the driver asked.

"No, I'm headed to the Great Hall."

The driver nodded. "Good. I'm supposed to report anyone going to the cliffs."

"Really? Why is that?"

"They're getting to be a popular destination for unsavory characters. Murderers and thieves and such. Anyone needing to rid themselves of evidence. And then of course there's the jumpers. I can't tell you how many fares I've had leave me a generous tip, go off for a nice meal, then take a short stroll off the edge."

"That's terrible."

"Aye. The bodies are getting to be a problem, too. Sometimes it takes a few days for the boats to come down and collect all the ones that float back to the top."

For the third time that day, Spindler felt his stomach turn.

The Great Hall was a formidable structure of iron and stone, built with two wings which curved away from the edge of the cliff like a mother shielding her children from the cruel wind and wild sea behind her. Spindler felt his courage abate as the carriage pulled up to the steps. He was taking a great risk in coming here, but he had no choice in the matter.

For the past few days his conscience had been tormenting him relentlessly, plaguing him even in sleep. It seemed his dealings with the boy in the oversized hat and coat—along with the consequences—were not to be ignored, no matter what Bill Stone said about the merits of dumb animals falling into traps. In fact, his comments had only inflamed Spindler's guilt, to the point where he had become unable to think about anything else.

As the Assembly was in recess, Spindler knew his options were limited regarding who he might speak to about his recent misadventures. He also knew, however, that Commissioner George Marlas was likely to still be in town. This was especially fortunate, as Marlas had made himself known as a politician who was always eager to talk to the press and was therefore the least likely to turn down an interview.

As Spindler descended from the carriage, he noticed that the prison coach had come to a stop only a few yards ahead. Each prisoner was being shackled at the ankles and wrists while a guardsman appeared to be giving them instructions. Too anxious to wonder over this, Spindler instead paid the driver, summoned every nerve he could muster, and walked up the steps.

The atrium inside the Great Hall was a magnificent chamber three stories high. Two sets of staircases spiraled up to the landings, each of which led to countless doors and passages. Huge marble columns reached up to the domed roof, while a set of silver-gilded double doors stood directly opposite the front entrance. A nervous-looking man wearing an expensive suit sat behind a tall desk in the middle of the chamber. Spindler removed his hat and approached him.

"Good morning."

"Yes?" the clerk replied without bothering to look up.

"I'm here to speak with Commissioner Marlas."

"Is he expecting you?"

"Uh, no. Not exactly. I did send a request a few days ago but never actually received a reply. As it is a matter of some importance I thought—"

"I'm afraid the commissioner is booked up for the week. You'll have to send another request to our Inquiry Department. Second floor."

"Please, if I could just have five minutes of his time. I'd be happy to wait if—"

"There is no possible way I can get you in to see him until next week," the clerk answered. "And certainly not today, of all days. Inquiry Department. Second floor."

Spindler put his hand on the desk. "Sir . . ."

The clerk glared at his hand with a look of great offense. Spindler removed it.

"Look, I understand he's very busy. But what I have to say to him is of potentially national importance. A very grave situation. Now I would hate to think of such an imperative report failing to reach the commissioner because of a denial of a five-minute space of time."

The clerk frowned at Spindler, regarding him with a little more interest. "National importance? Concerning what?"

"I dare not say more in open company. Now, please. Five minutes. That's all I ask. I could walk with him on his way out. I could bring him his tea. I don't care how it happens, so long as it happens."

The clerk sighed, then narrowed his eyes at Spindler, checked his pocket watch, scanned over his scheduling book, and rifled through a few more papers on his desk. "Very well," he answered at last. "I will pass your name along to the commissioner."

Spindler nodded. "Thank you. It's Spindler. John Spindler."

"Wait here."

The clerk crossed the chamber and stopped at an office door. Set into the wood was a polished golden plaque stamped with the words *The Honorable Commissioner George Reginald Marlas*. The clerk knocked twice, entered, and shut the door behind him.

Spindler smoothed down his hair and wandered toward a collection of paintings on the wall, each depicting any number of politicians in various scenes of self-congratulation. There was even a portrait of the Great Hall itself, as if to remind viewers what it looked like from the outside while standing inside.

A moment later, the clerk returned to the atrium, looking

even more ruffled and anxious than before. He carried a tall stack of papers to his desk and dropped them down with a great slap. Spindler hurried back to him.

"I regret to re-inform you that the commissioner is too busy to see you today," the clerk said as he began sorting through the papers. "Our Inquiry Department, however, would be more than happy to assist you. Second floor."

"But did you mention—"

"I mentioned everything you told me. Look, I don't mean to be rude, but I've got a lot of work to do here and we are expecting a very important visitor. Please, if you have an ounce of compassion within yourself, try back another time. All right? Can you do that for me?"

Before Spindler could answer, the front doors flew open. In marched the prisoners he had seen from the coach, flanked by a dozen armed guards.

"Oh, thank goodness, you're finally here!" the clerk wailed. "We've been waiting for over an hour!"

"We were told you wanted us at ten," one of the guards replied.

"You were told wrong, then. Well, never mind. The cabinet with all the cleaning supplies is through that door on your right."

"Prisoners?" Spindler said to the clerk. "You have prisoners clean the Great Hall?"

"That's right."

"But why?"

"Two words, sir. Free labor."

Another door slammed open. To everyone's surprise, Commissioner Marlas himself strode into the chamber, garbed in a splendid blue jacket with a heavy gold chain draped around his freshly-starched high collar. His white beard had been trimmed to perfection and his close-cropped hair tamed with scented oil. A large jeweled ring flashed from his right hand.

"What is the meaning of this tardiness, Captain?" he demanded.

"We were told ten o'clock, sir," the foremost guard answered.

"Our guest is to arrive in half an hour. That gives you only twenty minutes to make this room spotless. If it is otherwise, your command shall hear of it. Understood?"

"Yes, sir."

"And why are these prisoners wearing chains? They'll scratch the floor. That's unacceptable. Bind them with rope."

"Sir, our command dictates that the prisoners be bound in irons at all times. It is the law of our office—"

"Then I will change the law, here and now. They are to be bound in rope when in the Great Hall. And if they give you any trouble you will take them outside and shoot them through the head. Now is everything clear enough for you, Captain?"

Spindler saw the captain's eye twitch slightly.

"Yes, sir."

"Good. And see that you're all cleared out by the time our visitor arrives. There's plenty to be done around the grounds during that time. Mr. Quibly!"

The desk clerk nearly jumped off his seat. "Yes, sir?"

"Where are all my handkerchiefs? The silk ones? They were in my top desk drawer this morning and now they're gone."

"You asked me to get them cleaned for you, sir."

"Well, how long does it take to clean a little square patch of cloth? I can't meet our honored guest without a handkerchief!"

"No, sir. I'll take care of it, sir."

Without so much as a glance at Spindler, the commissioner whirled around, disappeared into his office, and slammed the door behind him. Straight away, several of the guards set to replacing the prisoners' iron bonds with rope. The others began distributing an assortment of mops, brooms, and brushes.

Above, a large group of people carrying papers and briefcases began filing out of a chamber room on the second floor. The guards hurried the prisoners to the farthest corner of the room, ordering their charges not to stare. More than a few snide comments and self-righteous glares of disapproval were directed their way as the crowd poured down the stairs to the ground floor. Spindler, meanwhile, had returned his attention to the clerk.

"So . . . he's got half an hour before this guest arrives."

The clerk pushed his wild hair away from his eyes. "Are you still here?"

"Let me just step into his office for a moment."

"Out of the question."

Spindler clenched his jaw and glanced around. Most of the passing crowd had left the Hall by now, but a few lingered behind, engaged in conversation with their colleagues. Spindler leaned in closer to the clerk and lowered his voice.

"All right, listen. Have you ever heard of a Spektor?"

"A specked? A specked what?"

"No, not a specked. A Spektor."

"Spektor?" the clerk repeated, loud enough that a man standing near one of the staircases broke off his conversation and looked towards them.

Spindler lowered his voice even further. "It's a kind of . . . spirit . . . thing."

The clerk raised an eyebrow. "A spirit thing? Mr. Spindler, I have been more than patient with you, and as you can see, there's a lot going on today. If this is the topic of conversation you wish to present to the commissioner, you needn't even bother with the Inquiry Department. Now will you kindly remove yourself from the premises? Or do I have to—"

"Mr. Quibly . . ." a voice interrupted.

Both Spindler and the clerk turned to see a young man approach the desk. His garments were almost as fine as the commissioner's, far exceeding the quality of the others around him. He even carried a walking cane made of ash wood and silver.

"Mr. Coram, sir," the clerk greeted in return. "Good morning."

"Is there a problem here?"

"This gentleman has been trying to get an audience with the commissioner. Some business about specked spirits or some other foolishness. But I have told him—*repeatedly*—that Mr. Marlas is far too busy for an audience today."

Spindler remained quiet, not wishing to damage his chances any further. The young man's piercing eyes brightened with interest. He held out his hand towards Spindler.

"Frederick Coram. And you are, sir?"

Spindler shook the man's hand, though baffled by the gesture. "Spindler. John Spindler."

"Well, Mr. John Spindler. Would you mind stepping into my office?"

Spindler followed the young man down a corridor, all the while trying to rack his brain. The name 'Frederick Coram' nagged at him like an itch but he could make no connection. His thoughts were further distracted when he stepped into the young man's office—an impressive room filled with marble busts, velvet-upholstered furniture, crystal lamps, and a huge window that overlooked the coastline. Coram paused by a plush chair behind a large desk.

"I am sorry the commissioner is not disposed to receive you today. Recent events have put more demands on his attention than usual, as I'm sure you understand. Please, sit." As Spindler did so, Coram took the seat behind his desk and folded his hands. "As an aide to Mr. Marlas, I hope you will not mind relating your business to me in his stead."

Spindler took a moment to consider this. He was all but certain it was his only chance of being heard. And if the aide believed him, he would surely pass it on to Commissioner Marlas. If not, he had done his duty in making a report to try to save the young thief's life. His conscience could demand nothing more.

He began by telling Coram a lie. While strolling to the bank one morning, he'd spied a young boy attempting to pick someone's pocket. Recognizing the youth as a runaway orphan, he took him off the streets and brought him home, giving him a warm bed and something to eat until he could be returned to the orphanage. Spindler then described the sudden appearance of a bloody streak on the boy's cheek, followed by the exploding front door and the arrival of the strange intruders. Coram sat straighter in his chair.

"Who were these people? Can you describe them to me?"

"There was a young man, maybe about your age, sir. Red hair. Sort of lanky. And an older man, lighter colored hair. Quite tall. Around forty years, I should think. A young woman was with them also. Long, blonde hair. Pale complexion. All in all, ordinary looking people if you ask me, sir. Nothing unusual about them . . . except I did think it strange that the younger man carried a lantern in the middle of the day."

"What happened next?"

"They had us out the door and running down the street as fast as we could. When we finally stopped, they started telling this fantastic story about dark spirits—Spektors, is what they called them. They said one was after the boy for some reason, but that they could take him to a place where he'd be safe."

"Did you believe them?"

"I hardly had time to think about it. Of course I tried to convince the boy to stay but they persuaded him in the end. I even tried to follow when they took off with him, but they disappeared too quickly."

Coram sat silent in his chair, tapping a finger against his cane.

Spindler fidgeted with his hat. "Since then, there's been no sign of them. No word. You can't begin to imagine the guilt I feel over having let the boy go off like that."

Coram sat forward in his chair and wrote something on a pad of paper. "You have nothing to feel guilty about, Mr. Spindler. You were placed in an impossible situation." He paused in his writing. "This boy . . . you say he was a runaway orphan?"

"Yes, sir. I recognized him from an advisory notice. His name is Anthony Revore, but he was using a different name at the time

156

we met. Inkwell Featherfield. The description on the notice matched him perfectly. Except for the height."

Coram waved a hand through the air and continued writing. "That's no great matter. They always manage to get some detail wrong."

Once finished, he sat back in his chair and laced his fingers together, regarding Spindler with a gaze that hinted on admiration. "You are very brave to come all this way to tell a story like that to a government official. But there's obviously something more you have yet to say."

"Yes, sir," Spindler replied, growing even more anxious. "I've gone over that day again and again in my mind. Every detail, every word I can remember. And the thing that keeps coming back to me is the door. I never saw anything like it before. Cracked into a hundred pieces but held together until the last moment when it just . . . blew apart."

"They used an explosive?"

"No. An explosive wouldn't make the door crack to pieces first. I thought it was . . . that is to say, it looked like . . ." Spindler scoffed at himself and glanced away.

"Go on," Coram urged.

"Well, it was like an enchantment, sir."

Coram's expression remained unchanged. "And so, Mr. Spindler . . . you think your door-breakers were Entrians."

Spindler pursed his lips for a moment before answering. "I think it's a very good possibility. As much as I hate to admit it."

Coram smiled, almost with glee. He rose from his chair and faced the window, gazing out over the coastline stretching away to the east under a darkening sky.

"Entrians kidnapping Cassrian children. That's a very serious charge."

Spindler nodded. "I know. That's why I came here. I figured if I was going to start a mass panic, I may as well start it at the highest level." He sat back in his chair and rubbed a hand over his face, wondering if his words had just ignited a war. "Will you tell the commissioner?"

"Yes," Coram answered, facing him again. "But I think you'll find a different effect than the one you imagine. A mass panic may indeed be stirred up over this, and I daresay . . . we should very well hope it does."

Spindler frowned. "How do you mean, sir?"

"I'm hesitant to say more without first speaking to the commissioner, and perhaps a few others. But rest assured, your trust has been well placed."

Spindler stared at the young man. There was much that was still childlike in his features, his eyes especially. Even the effect of his education—his manners and way of speaking—could not completely overcome the traces of tender adolescence that lingered in his voice.

"Excuse me, Mr. Coram," Spindler said, unable to stand the mystery any longer. "But I have to ask . . . how did you come to be in such a high position here? You can't be much older than twenty. And no new graduate, as surely you must be, could afford such fine clothing or have worked up to such a great office in so short a time."

The young man nodded. "I'm twenty-two, as a matter of fact."

"Frederick Coram . . ." Spindler repeated. "I've heard your name . . . ah!" The clouds over his memory parted. "Frederick Coram! Of course! You were the one who nearly captured the Colonists single-handedly! Down at that mining camp. What was it, six years ago?"

Coram grinned as he walked past Spindler to a bookcase in the corner of the room.

"You were a national hero," Spindler continued. "They convicted five Colonists in the span of a single week."

"And five heads rolled for it. That's more than Bill Stone ever collected at one time." Coram returned to Spindler with a silver medallion in his hand. "This is the award the Assembly gave me for my services. They paid for my education in full as well. The commissioner was most eager to recruit me, almost the minute I finished my studies."

Spindler looked over the medallion and shook his head in awe. "You managed to do what scores of Colonist-hunters could only dream of doing. Not to mention the Entrians. And you were just a boy."

"Boys are capable of a lot of anger," Coram replied, "and I had plenty to spare for what they did to my father. It's only a bloody shame we didn't leave that camp with all of them."

There was a knock at the door. Quibly stuck his head through, panting and looking pale.

"She's here, sir."

"Ah. Thank you, Mr. Quibly."

The clerk withdrew. Coram returned the medallion to the bookcase and looked at his reflection in the cabinet door, straightening his collar. "Mr. Spindler, I wonder if you wouldn't mind waiting here for a while longer? I should very much like to speak more with you on the matters we've discussed."

"Of course. I'd be happy to," Spindler said, merely thankful he had not been laughed out of the room.

Just then, the commissioner's voice rang through the outer corridor.

"Quibly! You have ten seconds to put a handkerchief into my hand!"

CHAPTER 16

THE COMMISSIONER AND HIS HANDKERCHIEF

By the time the carriage came to a stop in front of the Great Hall, every official in the building was standing in one of two long lines running from the base of the outside stair to the inner atrium. Commissioner Marlas positioned himself at the top of the steps with a diplomatic smile, his hands clasped before him, and a gold silk handkerchief in his left breast pocket.

The driver opened the carriage door, and Pallaton descended. As the Entrian lord's proud gaze settled on Marlas, the elder man bowed deeply at the waist. Pallaton turned and offered his hand to the lady inside the carriage.

"Are you still certain you want to go in there alone?" he said to her as she stepped down.

Seherene offered a gracious smile to the commissioner, who bowed even lower.

"This will be as short a visit as I can make it," she answered. "Besides, I know how much you dislike these particular functions."

"And if he implores you to stay?"

"I'll make up some excuse."

"Very well. Just don't say I didn't try to save you."

He began to move aside, but she gripped his hand a moment

longer. "If I'm in there for more than half an hour, come and get me out."

Pallaton smirked. "Understood. I'll start the count as soon as you get inside."

Seherene clutched the skirt of her cloak and ascended the stairs. Every head bowed as she passed. She tried to maintain an affably gracious expression, but the multitude of eyes fixed on her brought inevitable discomfort. She had never gotten used to this kind of attention. She suspected she never would.

"My lady Seherene," the commissioner said, taking a few steps down to meet her. "How wonderful to see you again. I hope nothing was amiss during your trip."

"Thank you, Commissioner. Nothing amiss whatsoever."

"I believe it's been some years since you last visited our humble Hall. We've made several improvements to it. My office, for one, has greatly benefited from the keen eyes of a company of expert decorators. I think you'll be most impressed by the results. Our main forum has also undergone revision. No more hard wooden benches. Individual chairs now, upholstered with the finest quality leather in the country . . ."

Marlas continued his commentary past the entrance, through the atrium, and all the way to his office, pausing only to dismiss the assembled company and shut the door behind them.

His chamber, for the most part, was just as she remembered it —a model of garish extravagance. From gold-trimmed silk curtains to the silver fox rug to the ebony tobacco box studded with rubies, there seemed no end to the excessive indulgences. But nothing compared with his newest accessories.

There were cages everywhere, most housing several rare birds with bright, jewel-like eyes, plumed with striking shades of blues, reds, purples, and greens. To the left were a pair of ring-tailed lemurs, staring out at them with large yellow eyes. To the right was a slender tree, its branches draped with the coils of a white-skinned snake half-hidden by leaves. The commissioner took great care introducing each animal to her by name, all but bursting with pride at his "immensely expensive" trophies. Seherene found herself particularly appalled to see a small black panther in a cage near his desk. When he grinned and rapped his knuckles on the bars, the cat did no more than flick her tail with her head lowered onto her paws, deep in melancholy resignation.

"Ah," Marlas said, gesturing to a pair of golden-headed eagles at the back of the room. "And there are Arterus and Andros, my great hunters of the heavens! I rescued them from a cliff-top nest, abandoned by the mother. They were just fledglings at the time and mere hours away from perishing of hunger."

The great birds sat perched on metal bars, each with a chain around its leg anchoring it to the floor. Seherene couldn't help but wonder if the eagles would have preferred such a fate to their present circumstances.

"And finally, there is Hast."

In a cage in the far corner of the room was a huge black vulture. Its naked head and unblinking stare were so unsettling that even the other animals in the room seemed to avoid its gaze. Seherene herself could not bear to look at the creature for more than a few moments.

"I know it's very unusual to keep a vulture," Marlas said. "But he stands as a sober reminder of my duty—an ever-present watchman over those we have yet to bring to justice."

Marlas gestured again to the corner. The Colonists' arrest warrants were posted beside the vulture cage, with several names crossed out in red ink. The topmost warrant bore the name of Isaac Caradoc. Marlas went to a cabinet and withdrew a bottle and two silver goblets.

"I regret, madam, that I am the only one present of our great Assembly to receive you today. We're in recess for the harvest holiday, you see." He set the goblets on a table in front of a large window overlooking the sea. "Will you have some wine?"

The obligation of politeness answered in place of her true feelings. "A small taste. I fear I cannot stay for long."

"Oh, for shame," Marlas replied. "I obtained this wine from a traveling merchant on my way back from Jaston last spring. It's called Cestriae. Impeccable quality and terrifically hard to come by. I've been saving this bottle for only the most important occasions."

"As I said, Commissioner, a taste. Thank you."

She took her seat and waited until he had filled his own goblet, then hurried to empty hers, if for no other reason than to shut him up about it. There was only enough for a mouthful, but even before the liquid touched her lips she realized she had made a dreadful mistake. The aroma was incredible. It was a rush of flower gardens, orchards, and crisp mountain air. The wine itself was as smooth as liquid silver, and the taste of it complex, with new flavors unfolding almost before she could begin to enjoy the last one. It was only after the last lingering traces had vanished that she noticed Marlas watching her with rapt attentiveness. A curious look of satisfaction passed across his face as she set the goblet down.

"It's extraordinary," she conceded.

He smiled. "I will make a gift of it the next time I have the fortune to come across it, though you are more than welcome to stay and enjoy the rest of this bottle. Now . . ." He took his glass and lifted it. "May I offer my congratulations on this great victory for your people, and our brotherhood of nations. This smile of fortune strikes upon the heart like a ray of sunlight."

"I thank you for the kind sentiment, Commissioner," Seherene answered. "But it is a dark victory we have achieved. One in which I cannot bring myself to rejoice."

"You refer to the *manner* in which it was accomplished?"

"More to the identity of the assassin."

"A hero worthy of great praise and honor, whomever they may be."

Seherene hesitated before answering, growing troubled. "Mr. Marlas, did you read the report on Bash's death?"

Marlas scoffed. "What a question. Of course! I didn't become head of this committee by ignoring pertinent information."

"No, Commissioner. I do not mean to imply you are not proficient in your duties. I am anxious, rather, to hear your thoughts on the facts."

Marlas stroked his beard as though struggling to remember. "Well . . ."

"The initial investigation turned up a crest jewel belonging to an Entrian family, all the members of which were murdered at the Battle of Damiras—"

"Yes, of course. The item which condemned him as a Colonist."

"That item alone was not enough to condemn him. There were two other points that moved me to more certainty on that score, one being a collection of verses found in his house. Do you recall it from the report?"

"My dear girl, that was a very long report which I haven't looked at for over a week. You can't possibly expect me to remember every little detail."

Seherene pulled a piece of paper from the folds of her cloak and held it out to him. "Would you mind re-familiarizing yourself with this page, if you would be so kind?"

Amused, Marlas took the paper and glanced through it. He failed to hide the surprise in his face as he did so, betraying the fact that it was the first time he had ever seen the words:

Heed not the love of Mortals
In truth, Betrayers all
Cast down the bonds of Brotherhood
Forsake the Woman's call
Deceit is dealt to goodly hands
And Harm with bloody fall
Sentenced hence to death in Life
A cold and lightless hall

"The crest jewel betrayed his past actions," Seherene said. "This betrayed what was in his heart. Despair, bitterness, condemnation. No one who has been questioned on Bash's character came close to describing him with these words—which tells me he was good at hiding."

"I'm inclined to agree with you," Marlas replied, handing the paper back to her. "And the final piece of evidence?"

She paused again, preparing to embark on a matter she knew might not be accepted, much less understood. But it was the sole reason she had decided to meet with him face to face.

"The third is Bash's assassin. From the . . . unusual way in which his death occurred, my investigations have led me to conclude that no human hand could have caused such destruction."

For the first time since their conversation began, the commissioner began to pay true attention. "No *human* hand?"

"I have come to believe, sir, that Bash was killed by something called a Spektor."

Marlas leaned back in his chair and raised an eyebrow. "I seem to recall that word from my days as a schoolboy. That was some years ago."

"Yes, I know the term has long since passed out of knowledge in Cassrian society, but not in ours. They are the spirits of the restless dead, wandering the earth to spread darkness wherever they may, delighting in hatred and despair. And on very rare occasions—so rare that only a few stories mention it—they will kill. Now it is true that Spektors are regarded largely as creatures of myth, but some of us know the myth to be a reality."

"I see," Marlas sighed, rubbing his brow. "Let me pose a question to you, madam. If these creatures are indeed so evil, how is it they have aided us in the disposal of a wanted criminal?"

"That is the most troubling thing of all," she answered. "I do not believe a Spektor would have any interest in murdering a Colonist. I believe it possible they are being . . . prompted."

"Prompted?" Marlas replied. "You mean controlled?"

"In so many words."

"Well . . . then that's fantastic!" Marlas said. "All right, so they may be using a less-than-orthodox method of doing the job, but effective nonetheless. Whoever's holding their reins is a very powerful ally for us indeed!"

Seherene choked back a frustrated sigh. "Allow me to remind you, Mr. Marlas, that the execution of a Colonist outside a court of law is illegal. We know that not everyone was taken into their service voluntarily, a point proved by your own self. There must be a thorough examination of the facts before any punishment is carried out."

"Perhaps this person controlling these Spektors knows they are guilty somehow. They're just a few steps ahead of the process. And, quite frankly, doing us all a favor."

"We have no proof of that," Seherene replied, her voice rising. She checked herself and began again. "And there is another matter of interest here, though little more than conjecture."

"Which is?"

"It is our thought—*my* thought especially—that the Colonists themselves are behind this attack. And that one in particular has learned to control the Spektors for their own advantage."

Marlas shook his head at the end of another long draught of wine. "Ridiculous. What reason could they have to murder one of their own?"

"It is entirely possible that Bash escaped from them himself. He had been living alone for many years before the time of his death."

"You think Bash turned traitor on the Colonists? If that was true, he would have gone to the nearest law office and confessed everything he knew."

"Not if he believed that staying silent might hold off any anger over his leaving. Moreover, if he had confessed to everything, it would have been all too easy for the Colonists to track him down and take their revenge. You know that no Colonist brought to a court of law has been able to avoid the public eye."

Marlas turned his gaze to the window, watching storm clouds arrive over the Great Hall. Seherene knew he was calculating the most tactful way to tell her what he thought of her rationale. Over his shoulder, a flurry of movement caught her attention. It was the vulture, ruffling its feathers before settling down to sleep.

"These are all interesting theories," Marlas said. "But perhaps —for the time being—you could keep such thoughts to yourself until there is a bit more evidence to stand on. I believe it is in our best interest to avoid any potential embarrassment, after all."

She narrowed her eyes and lifted her chin. "What else do you believe, Commissioner?"

"Well . . . I believe Bash must have been a middleman of some kind. A supply runner, perhaps. Further investigation into his background and activities may even lead us straight to the Colonists themselves. I find this potential *much* more troubling— that there may exist a network of support for these monstrous butchers. Who knows how extensive? For my part, I will see to it that a second and more thorough investigation is carried out, with special attention to this aspect. You are, of course, at liberty to conduct things on your end to your own liking, but . . . forgive me, madam . . . chasing after ghosts and shadows would be a waste of effort. Ah!" Marlas rose from his chair and went to the snake cage. "You've come out of hiding at last, have you, Abbis? Yes, it's nearly time for your lunch, isn't it, girl?"

It was Seherene's turn to gaze out the window, attempting to calm the anger churning inside her like the waves beneath the storm clouds. For nine long years, her sole mission in life had been to bring about the capture and prosecution of the Colonists. Not a day, not a waking hour went by that she did not think on it. But with each victory fewer and farther between, it was becoming harder to circumnavigate the obstacles she faced. Lord Pallaton was her best ally in dedication to the cause, but his aversion to the Cassrian race complicated efforts at every turn. Bill Stone used his particular skills to great effect but remained an unpredictable and often unstable associate, hard pressed to take any direction or accept any ideas apart from his own.

Commissioner Marlas had been a thorn in her side almost

from the very beginning. When he had first come forward declaring he had been tricked into joining the Colonists, he had been a great help offering every name, place, and date he could recall to memory. He was so determined to find his traitorous colleagues that the Assembly had not hesitated to put him in his present seat of power. But as the years passed, so had the zeal, and he now spent his working hours basking in the glory of his office, reveling in his expensive surroundings, and playing with animals. She hadn't expected him to accept her theories on the first hearing, especially regarding the Spektors, but she had hoped for more than a complete dismissal.

It wasn't until she looked away from the window that she realized he was standing right next to her, holding the three-foot serpent in his arms. She stood up fast and took a step back.

"Would you like to hold Abbis?" Marlas asked. "She's very friendly. She'll go right to sleep if you stroke her gently enough."

"No. No, that's all right. I . . . I have to be going."

"Oh, so soon? You must at least have another taste of the wine."

"Thank you, Commissioner, but my ship will be leaving port soon and I would hate to make it late." Marlas opened his mouth to protest, but Seherene managed to get another word in before he could do so. "Before I do go, however, there is something I would like your approval on. As you know, we Entrians commemorate the tragedy at Damiras every year through the Mourning Processions. This year, we thought to use our public shows of grief to aid the Cassrians against forgetfulness. We would like the Assembly's permission to take these processions down the main streets of several Cassrian cities."

Marlas cocked an eyebrow and nodded. "An inspired idea. I will pose it to the Assembly when we convene in a few days. I am certain they will offer no objections."

"Thank you."

"It's a pity you can't stay to propose the idea yourself. We see so little of you as it is. Of course you are an impossibly busy woman, but it is regrettable that your visits have become such a rarity. People like you and me—thinkers and motivators, comrades in common purpose—we ought to keep closer counsel together. Leastways as friends if not colleagues. And we are friends, are we not?"

Seherene offered a half-hearted smile. "Of course, Commissioner."

"Good. I am glad of that." He chuckled, feigning self-abashment. "I know I must seem like a very silly old man, living in this zoo here, but I find good companionship ever harder to come by. I feel these animals understand me somehow, at least better than most of my human compatriots. And I feel they understand you as well."

Seherene tilted her head. "Understand me?"

"I noticed a strange disposition settle over them as we came into the room together. A kind of sadness. Resignation. I believe they are mirroring what they sense in you."

She remained silent as another surge of anger flared inside her. Of course such sadness and resignation had nothing to do with being confined to a cage all hours of the day.

"I know how much you suffered that awful day," Marlas continued. "And how long you have carried the pain of loss. What happened on Damiras was a terrible blow to you and your people, most especially the murder of young Darian. I know you loved him very much. But you mustn't let your grief overtake you. I . . . wish merely to counsel you, as a friend, in easing your burden. After all, what has passed is passed."

"Not for me," Seherene replied. "Not until the last Colonist stands before us and hears the Elders pronounce their sentence."

"And if that never happens? If they continue to elude us? If all efforts from this day to the last prove utterly futile? What then?"

"You ask me to consider the impossible."

"My lady," Marlas said, "you answer like a woman blinded by ambition. You do yourself a disservice. You are far too wise not to consider every reasonable possibility."

"It is what I must believe, Commissioner, with all that I am. I have pledged my life to this cause. No less is required of me. And no less will be given." She stepped away from the table and gathered her cloak around her. "Thank you for your time and hospitality. I regret I must leave so soon but the morning grows late and my ship—"

"I understand, of course," Marlas replied. "But before you go, there is one final order of business."

He uncoiled the snake from his arm as he hurried across the chamber and returned it to its cage. Seherene stifled a sigh of impatience and wondered what the effect on diplomatic relations would be if she were to grab the bottle of wine and make a run for the door.

"Let me introduce you to my new deputy commissioner. I intend to put him in charge of all future investigations concerning the Colonists, beginning with the Bash case." Marlas threw open the chamber door and nodded at someone. "Mr. Coram . . ."

As Seherene stepped forward to meet the stranger, she was stunned to see he had barely ceased to be a boy. There was also something vaguely familiar about him, something fleeting around the edges of his courteous smile. It nearly put a crease in her masterful composure.

"Lady Seherene, may I introduce Mr. Frederick Coram. He is newly graduated from the College of Law here in Altan, a highly promising young man of enormous talent. We are most eager to see what great things he will do for our cause."

Coram bowed his head reverently before the Entress.

"You may remember him as the young hero who nearly ended the chase for us six years ago," Marlas continued, beaming with pride. "Led a group of hunters straight to the Colonists' hideout in the Ashing Mountains. Quite the feat."

"Yes, I remember," she replied, looking impressed. "Was it not also said that your father had been tricked into joining them?"

"Yes," Coram replied. "He was killed in the battle before he could redeem his error. But fortunately, my actions uncovered the truth of his innocence."

"I have just told the Lady Seherene of my intention to put you at the head of the Bash investigation," Marlas said to the young man.

"You honor me, sir," Coram replied.

"It will be a great opportunity for you to further prove your merit. I had hoped that we all might have discussed the arrangements of the investigation, but, alas, her Ladyship does not have much time to spare. Ah well. Not everything goes according to plan. Allow us to escort you to your carriage, my lady."

The atrium was empty, save for the desk clerk who bowed to the Entress again as they passed by his desk. Coram strode ahead and pushed open the front doors. The roar of a torrential rainstorm filled the chamber. Marlas hesitated, smoothing a hand down the front of his jacket. Seherene took advantage of the hesitation to be rid of him sooner than later.

"Do not trouble yourself, Commissioner. There is no need for you to go out into this."

"Well . . . but surely I cannot allow you to venture into that mess yourself."

"I have means enough to stay dry."

Marlas nodded. "Indeed. Well, perhaps that's best. Coram, can you at least see to it that our guest makes it down the stairs without breaking her neck?"

"Of course, sir."

"My lady, it has been a pleasure, as always. Do not hesitate to return at your earliest whim. Safe journey to you."

"Thank you, Commissioner."

Marlas bowed, then righted again at the sound of a loud squawk from his office.

"Ah, yes," he said. "Lunch time."

Coram smirked as the commissioner hurried away. Outside, Pallaton emerged from the carriage and drew a line in the air above himself with an outstretched hand. There the rain stopped.

"It's a great pity our fearless leader is such a fool, is it not, my lady?"

Seherene glanced back at the young man in surprise. "I'm sorry?"

"A search mission led by a blind man is a very sad thing to witness. Fortunately, there are those of us who notice even things that are not to be seen."

She frowned, her curiosity outpacing her impatience. "You speak in riddles, Mr. Coram."

"For instance," he continued, "just this morning a man came into my office and told me the most extraordinary story about a mysterious group of people capturing a runaway orphan."

"I'm afraid I don't see what this has to do with—"

"Kidnapped him, in broad daylight, after obliterating the front door and then warning him to run for his life from the Spektor that was in the room."

Astonishment overcame the Entress's composure. Coram went on.

"They disappeared soon afterward. According to the man, they professed to have been trying to save the boy. Quite the interesting story."

Seherene turned and made a signal to Pallaton, who acknowledged its meaning. She looked back to the deputy commissioner, her eyes bright with sudden hope.

"This man . . . where can I find him?"

"I thought to keep him here, should you be interested in speaking with him. I understand you are short on time, however—"

"Curse the time, Mr. Coram. Lead the way."

CHAPTER 17

NEW FRIENDS IN HIGH PLACES

I t wasn't until after having a stiff drink the next morning that Spindler would be able to reconcile himself to the shock of everything that happened at the Great Hall. He was already surprised to have been taken seriously by Frederick Coram, but standing before one of the most respected and powerful people in the country—and an Entress, no less—was far more than he could have imagined. His tongue twisted into a knot the moment they were introduced in Coram's office, and he didn't know whether to extend his hand or fall on his face. Fortunately, he didn't have to decide, as the Entress was eager to question him.

"What can you tell us about the people who broke into your flat, Mr. Spindler? Could you describe them to us? In as much detail as possible?"

"Well, there were three of them," Spindler said. "Two men, one quite young, and a lady. She was, uh, also young and . . . blonde." He flinched inwardly. He called himself a writer?

"And the others?" the Entress asked.

"The boy—the young man, I should say—he was red-headed. Had a patchy beard. Lanky. Carried a lantern . . . which, as I told Mr. Coram, I thought quite unusual at the time—"

"What of the man? The older man?"

Spindler shrugged. "Tall, lean, lighter hair. Maybe in his forties. Nothing unusual about him. Like any man you'd see in the street, I suppose."

"Did you notice any scars on his face? Or perhaps a glove on his left hand?"

"No. Nothing like that."

Coram stepped into the conversation. "I presume this man was either Simon Elias or Jeremy Stockton, by the description. The young, red-haired boy was no doubt Evering Hart, son of Abner."

"Mr. Spindler," the Entress said, "you say the front door was broken to pieces?"

"Yes, ma'am. It cracked and split, then blew all to bits. But I saw no flash or fire."

"The young girl . . ." Seherene repeated, beginning an anxious pace. "Could it be possible?" She looked at Coram, who was quick to catch the toss.

"The young runaway, Rivalia," he said.

Spindler frowned. "Wait . . . runaway? You think there's another kidnapped runaway among them?"

"Not exactly," Seherene answered. "A few years ago, she was pledged to marry a young man who was a friend to the family. The night before the wedding, she ran away from home and joined the Colonists."

In the next second, every drop of color drained from Spindler's face. His mustache twitched over his quivering mouth as his eyes went wide.

"Hold on. Wait a minute now," he said, raising his hands. "You're . . . you're saying that those people who broke through my door . . . they were . . . I-I let that poor boy get kidnapped by the . . . Colonists?" The level of his voice rose as he grew frantic. "Is that what you're saying?"

"Calm yourself, Mr. Spindler," Coram said.

"Oh, good God." Spindler clutched at his head, struggling to keep hold of his composure. How had a simple search for information on Bash led a trio of Colonists straight to his front door? And Ink? He had led him like a lamb to the slaughter. A strangulated cry left Spindler's throat. It was almost too much to bear. He may as well have slit the young boy's throat himself! Coram took Spindler by the elbow and led him to a chair—into which he quickly collapsed.

"I am curious, Mr. Coram," Seherene said. "How did you know to catch my attention by mentioning the Spektors? I would not suspect a young man born and bred in Cassrian society to have any knowledge of them."

Coram stepped towards her, swinging his gilded cane over his shoulder. "That's simple enough. When I came across the Colonists in the Ashing Mountains all those years ago I managed to gain the confidence of one of them—before turning them over to the hunters, of course. I learned much in that time, and discovered the link that exists between them and the demon creatures. I was reluctant to share it with anyone else then, particularly among my colleagues in the Assembly. I knew how unwilling they would be to accept such a thing. But I believe it to be a most crucial connection, a pathway that may very well guide us straight to the Colonists themselves, should we have the courage to venture into whatever places it may lead."

"I am much relieved to hear you say this," she said, "for it is my belief that the Colonists have found a way to control the Spektors to do their bidding."

Coram's calm gaze became a piercing stare. "Control them?"

"Yes. Possibly for—"

"Ahh!" Spindler cried. Seherene and Coram watched as he shot out of his chair and wheeled towards them, flailing his hands. "The man! The man in the lake!"

"What man?" Seherene asked.

"The boy . . . he told me about a man he saw dive into a lake. He said it looked like he was chasing a shadow in the water! I never put it together—"

"Isaac Caradoc," Coram finished, his dark eyes flashing. "I'd bet my life on it."

The Entress was too stunned to reply, but the look in her eyes went as cold as stone.

"Did the boy say where?" Coram asked.

"Somewhere along the shores of Corvus Lake," Spindler answered. "Just a few paces from Edgely Hill. It was the morning after Bash was killed."

"Incredible," Seherene said. "Mere hours and a few steps away from us."

"Isaac Caradoc," Spindler repeated. "He's the one described in the warrants as having a kind of golden mark on his hand, yes? I never knew what to make of that detail myself, but the boy said he saw him holding his hand out towards the shadow in the water."

Seherene and Coram both remained silent.

Spindler looked between them. "Does it hold some sort of power?"

Coram gripped the silver handle of his cane and rested his left fist on his hip. "The Colonist I met was most reluctant to reveal that secret. I found out very little, save that the mark is some kind of ancient talisman, the last remnant of a long-dead pagan cult. The mark keeps flesh from growing in its place, for what reason I'm not sure, but I saw it once or twice while in their company and it is a grotesque sight. Like a gilded bandage over a flesh-eating disease. Perhaps it allows for some sort of communion with these evil spirits, some radical form of worship, a mark of loyalty, or perhaps, as the lady says, a way of controlling them. Whatever the case, I believe it to be a thing of terrible demonic power. And the sooner we can get to Isaac Caradoc, the sooner we can send it back to Hell along with him."

Spindler glanced at Seherene for her word on the matter, but she remained silent.

Coram turned towards the Entress. "My lady, we can waste no more time. I will begin my investigation on Bash immediately, and concentrate all efforts on uncovering the mystery of the Spektors. I am sure now that this path will lead us straight to the end we seek."

"Agreed," she answered.

The next minute, they were walking back down the long corridor to the atrium. Spindler followed behind, still somewhat in a baffled daze.

"We must have new notices printed up for the recovery of this boy—what's his name?" Seherene asked.

"Anthony Revore," Spindler answered. "Going by the name of Inkwell Featherfield."

She raised an eyebrow. "That's a healthy imagination. We'll have both names printed, along with a complete description. I want them posted on every street corner, every government building, printed in every paper."

"I have already written the order," Coram answered.

"Good."

The rain had stopped. Pallaton re-emerged from the carriage as Seherene appeared at the top of the stairs. She gathered her cloak and began her descent. Coram and Spindler followed.

"Gentlemen," she said, "I cannot tell you what light you have brought to the world again. I am certain the identity of the boy's captors will be enough to incite total public outrage. It may be just the push we need to bring all of this to an end."

"Fresh blood on the trail at last," Coram replied. "A momentous day, indeed."

"Where do you intend to begin your investigation?" Seherene asked.

"I will make a visit to the Bash residence myself," he answered. "After which I will head west. I have a few contacts there to consult on the matter."

"And you, Mr. Spindler," Seherene said, pausing midway down

the stairs to look at the newspaperman. "I hope you will continue to aid us however you may. God knows it took a great deal of courage for you to come here today. I thank you for this. As do my people."

Spindler dipped his head in an awkward nod. "Of course. I'll do whatever I can."

"Do not hesitate to contact me directly should you learn anything more. That goes for you as well, Mr. Deputy Commissioner. We Entrians are fortunate indeed in our new allies."

Coram bowed his head. "It is only together that we will win this fight. And as for Isaac Caradoc . . . I will bring you his head on a pike for what he did that day."

Before the Entress could reply, a woman suddenly raced onto the stairs and fell at her feet. She was rain-soaked, her hair and clothes bedraggled, and her ankles and wrists bound by thick rope.

"Mercy, my lady! Mercy!" she cried, clutching at the hem of Seherene's cloak. "We are wronged! God help us, we are wronged!"

"Get back, dog!" Coram cried.

Pallaton rushed up the stairs and shouted at an armed man standing several yards away. "You there! Guard!"

At Pallaton's call, the guard realized his oversight and ran towards them with his hand on his pistol. Seherene tried to pull away, but the woman held tight and raised her face toward the Entress. Tears streamed down her sunken cheeks. Spindler recognized her as the woman who'd caught his gaze from the back of the prison coach.

"They say my husband and I aided the Colonists! They say we gave them food and shelter! It is a lie! We never did so, I swear it! We have been six years in chains! We have had no trial! Please! For the love of God, I beg you to help us!"

Before she could say another word, Coram took up his walking stick and cracked it hard against the woman's temple. With a cry, she fell and struck her head on the edge of the step.

"Sir!" Spindler cried, appalled.

"Mr. Coram!" Seherene said.

Pallaton reached them the next moment and took hold of Seherene, pulling her away. "She is lucky it was not an axe."

The guard arrived at last and yanked the prisoner to her feet. She swayed and staggered, her eyelids fluttering as blood trickled down the side of her face.

"See that you keep better charge over your inmates," Pallaton said. "The commissioner will hear of this, as will your superiors."

"I-I'm very sorry," the guard replied. "My most sincere apologies, my lady."

"Take her away," Coram commanded. "And see to it that she is given a thorough lesson on how to behave in public."

"Yes, sir," the guard nodded.

He jerked the woman around and led her away, ordering her to stop her tears. Spindler looked on in troubled silence. The Entress looked much the same.

"I apologize for this most regrettable incident," Coram said, straightening his fine jacket. "That's the first time we've ever had a problem with prison laborers, but—"

"Mr. Coram," Seherene interrupted, "that woman said she and her husband had received no trial."

"Yes. A statement which goes so much against the foundation of our laws that it can only be a lie," Coram answered. "I will have it looked into, of course—"

"Please do," the Entress replied. "And will you be so good as to send me your findings?"

He bowed slightly at the waist. "Consider it done."

At Pallaton's insistence, the company parted ways. Spindler and Coram remained on the stairs, watching as the carriage pulled away and passed out of the courtyard through the gate.

"As a new deputy commissioner," Coram said, "I find myself sorely in need of credible contacts. Trustworthy allies. I hope, Mr. Spindler, I may count you as one. Perhaps you might even share with me any worthwhile information you may come across, as the lady requested. You would be well-rewarded, I can assure you."

"Of course, sir," Spindler answered. He hoped it was only over-eagerness to please and impress that had caused the young man to act so roughly with the prisoner. But whatever the case, he would not test the deputy further by refusing his request.

Coram pursed his lips together and tapped his cane against the stairs. "It would, perhaps, also be prudent to keep secret the . . . spiritual matters we have discussed today. At least from anyone who might react badly to such things."

"By this you mean *everyone* else," Spindler replied.

Coram smiled. "I knew we understood one another. Now I hate to imagine you starting off immediately for home, such a long journey as it is. Here, take my card to the White Cliff Hotel. Stay as long as you like. Put everything on my account."

"Oh, but, sir—"

"Come, now. I insist. Such is the way of friends. And we are friends, are we not?"

Spindler tried to smile, but only one side of his mustache twitched. "Of course."

Coram smiled and shook his hand. "Good day, Mr. Spindler. I hope to be hearing a lot more from you in the future."

"Good day, sir. And thank you very much."

"My pleasure," Coram said, then turned on his heel and retreated into the Great Hall.

Spindler stood staring at the card in his hand. Only a week ago, he had given his own to a young boy in a café, setting him on a path from which he might now never return.

But how could he have known? How was he to know anything anymore? A crack had been opened in the side of the world, revealing an entire realm he never knew existed. Nothing was certain now. All was a mystery. There was only one truth he understood, and understood well; life had just become a lot more dangerous.

CHAPTER 18

WICKWIRE

The morning of his fifth day on Riverfall, Ink leaned on the balcony railing of the Hart residence. It was six o'clock, and already the sky was beginning to lighten. Evering was still asleep in the room they shared below, while the sound of his father's phlegm-rattling snores floated up from the bedchamber across the hall.

The chill air reddened his cheeks as it rushed over him. He took off his hat, letting his hair toss around his ears and lift from the back of his neck. They were traveling south now, heading towards a range of green mountains tinged with gold in the early morning light. He gazed out over the village and let his eyes come to rest on the tree-lined boundary.

For the first time since striking out on his own, Ink had no idea what to do. No matter how hard he tried, he couldn't understand why a host of dark spirits would seek to hurt him. And if the Spektors were nothing more than an elaborate hoax, it could only mean that the Colonists had a reason for luring him to the village. But what? He had no answer for that, either. They claimed to have saved him purely out of the goodness of their own hearts, yet this was nearly as difficult to believe as all the rest of it—if not more. People never did things for the sake of goodness. The very idea was laughable.

He ducked away the next moment when he heard voices from the path below. It was Delia and Jeremy, heading towards the garden with a collection of baskets, spades, and rakes. Ink stood again once he was sure they hadn't noticed him.

His short time among the Colonists had at least been relatively quiet, due in most part to his efforts to stay out of their way. Occasionally someone would attempt to make friendly conversation, but Ink didn't have much patience for it. On better days he saw only his roommate, though even this became trying when Evering took their growing familiarity as permission to hound him with questions. This annoyed Ink to such a degree that he began pretending to be asleep whenever he heard him coming.

A flutter of movement from the tower caught his eye. He glanced up in time to see a corner of one of the drapes fall back into place across a window on the third level.

Caradoc. The mysterious navigator had not been seen in open company since his return, having been confined to his room for recovery under strict orders from Simon. Cold anxiety gnawed at the pit of Ink's stomach as he recalled the image of the fleshless palm beneath the strange golden mark. Worse still had been his declaration that there was nothing for Ink to do but wait until they could make sense of his situation. But there had been surprises, too. It was Caradoc who had prevented Riva and Evering from scolding Ink for escaping the eye of supervision. Furthermore, he had granted Ink free rein of the entire village, no longer to be set under constant watch. Ink was very grateful for this new-found freedom, though of course he never said so. At the very least it was an encouraging sign that he hadn't yet offended anyone too badly.

As he slipped a hand into his coat pocket, his finger hit upon something cold and hard. Frowning, he pulled it out and looked down.

It was the pocket watch—the one he'd found behind the shed.

In the madness and chaos that had followed its discovery, as well as the Colonists' close initial observation of him, he'd had no time to give it a proper examination. He turned it this way and that, watching the beautiful case change from silver to gold, then to amethyst and ruby. The patterns across the surface gleamed like delicate spiderwebs. He hefted it from hand to hand, taken aback once more by the weight. It was no doubt bound with an enchantment or two to make it change appearance. Perhaps that's what made it so heavy.

He pressed the silver winding crown at the top, twisted it, pulled at it. He put his thumbs to the seam and again tried to pry it apart. He held it tight in his fist and tapped it against the hard stone floor. Still, it would not yield.

"Blasted thing," he grumbled.

He turned it over and closely examined the back. It looked much the same as the front side—save for one tiny detail he had missed. The etching in the very center was a series of letters. The script was peculiar, almost too elaborate to make out clearly. He rubbed at the spot with his thumb and squinted harder.

WICKWIRE

Ink swept the hair out of his eyes. He'd never heard that name before. Perhaps it was the name of the watchmaker. Or its former owner. Having made this discovery, he eased down onto the balcony floor and sat with his back against the outer wall of the glass room. The next few minutes were spent poring over every inch of the watch, turning it this way and that to see if there were any other words he had missed. The effort uncovered nothing else. He sighed, then knocked it against the ground a few more times as if trying to crack a particularly stubborn egg.

"Come on," he said. "Open for me, Wickwire. Open!"

And then, to his utter astonishment, something happened.

A strange light began to course through the patterns etched into the surface. It was a deep red-gold, like molten fire racing through the silver. Ink was mesmerized as he watched it. Once the case was entirely illuminated—the name last of all—the seam split wide. As if on a mechanized spring, the case opened with a single smooth motion and without a sound. Startled, Ink plucked his hand away and stared in disbelief as the watch tumbled to the ground. It seemed as though it had opened on his command.

But Ink made his most startling discovery after picking it up again. Inside, it looked nothing like a pocket watch. There were no numbers, no gears, no moving hands—only a smooth black surface inlaid with four rows of four small gold circles. Even more unusual was the curious image on the opposite face. It was a vast ocean of black water, dotted with sharp rocks jutting through the surface. Countless points of light quivered beneath the waves like shimmering grains of sand. At first, Ink took it to be the reflections of stars, but the sky was pitch black.

This curiosity, however, was nothing compared to the image's centerpiece. Out in the open sea, settled well beyond the horizon, was a dying sun. It was half-sunk in the dark water and glowed like an ember fighting for its last bit of life. The image was so life-like, its red light so vivid, Ink couldn't resist reaching out towards it.

"Ouch!" He drew back his stinging finger and stuck it in his mouth. "What the devil?"

His pain was soon overcome by awe. The waves of the dark sea seemed to be moving. Hesitant, he reached out his finger again. The breath caught in his chest. It felt . . . wet. He brushed against one of the rocks twisting out of the ocean. It felt solid. Real. He drew his hand away and looked at it. A drop of water ran down his fingertip.

"Bless my eyes," he said. "What is this?"

"There you are!" a voice cried out.

Ink snapped the watch shut and hid it behind his back just as Riva breezed onto the balcony, her good-natured smile in full force.

"Sorry. I didn't mean to startle you."

Ink got to his feet and tried to recover his usual attitude of indifference. "I'm fine. I'm fine. Did you want something?"

"Caradoc wants to see you in the garden. He's at the Memory Tree."

Ink nodded. "Oh. Goody. Must be feeling better, then."

"Yes, and thank God for it," she replied, then led the way into the glass room and towards the stairs.

As soon as she had turned away, Ink brought the watch out from behind his back and glanced down at it. The red-gold light had disappeared, the seam sealed tight again. The watch had gone back to sleep. With his heart still beating fast, Ink slipped it into his pocket and hurried after Riva.

He hoped she hadn't seen it.

Ink found Caradoc sitting on a stool in front of the Memory Tree. He was wearing a pair of spectacles and held a small knife to a bright flame inside an open lantern, heating the curved tip until it began to glow.

"Good morning," he said without looking up.

Ink remained silent. Caradoc withdrew the knife from the lantern, and with a practiced hand, scratched out an "S" into the soft white bark. The name '*Iophulis*' was completed.

"Aren't you going to wish me a good morning back?"

Ink shrugged. "Why should I?"

"Well," Caradoc said, making a deeper cut into the tree, "it's polite. A sign of good will and a good nature. Starting things out right."

Ink scoffed. "Fat lot of good that does me."

Caradoc returned the blade to the flame and glanced back at Ink. After a few moments he replied with a "hm" and returned his attention to the tree. Ink noticed he was still wearing the fingerless glove on his left hand, keeping the gold mark hidden.

"How have you been enjoying your freedom?" the scarred man asked.

Ink shoved his hands into his pockets. "It's boring, really. There ain't nothing to do but walk in circles 'round the garden and chase chickens . . . not that I have, by the way."

Caradoc answered with another "hm."

"Honestly, I expected a lot more action with you lot," Ink said, kicking at a half-buried rock. "Thieving and mischief and all that. Slit a few throats here, rob a few carriages there. But you don't act like fugitive murderers at all. More like . . . fugitive gardeners."

Caradoc chuckled. "There's something I'd like to see printed on a warrant."

Ink dislodged the rock and booted it as hard as he could into the stream a few feet away.

Caradoc finished engraving a *B* into the trunk, then reached into his pocket and withdrew a piece of folded paper. "Funny you should mention being bored. It so happens I spent some time last night coming up with a bit of action for you."

He held out the paper towards him. Fearing another trick, Ink dashed forward, snatched it out of his hand, then quickly stepped back again. Caradoc resumed his work at the tree, unfazed, while Ink glanced down at the paper.

Mon. - Mr. Jeremy Stockton & Ms. Rivalia
Tues. - Mr. Simon Elias
Wed. - Mr. Abner and Mr. Evering Hart
Thu. - Mr. Martin & Mrs. Harriet Whistler
Fri. - Mrs. Delia Ingleby
Sat. - Mr. Chester Fortescue & Ms. Wendolen and Ms. Josephina Plumsley

The second column read:

Clear dishes from dining table at all meals
Sweep all steps and balconies

Keep pathway clear of debris
Wind clock in tower

Ink looked up with a scowl of disdain. "Are you serious?"

"Immediately after breakfast and depending on the day," Caradoc said, "you will report to the person or persons I've marked on the list and take their directions, doing whatever they need you to do—be it cleaning the stable, pulling weeds, shoveling coal, and so on. However, any of them may enlist your help for any reason any day, and you will honor all such requests. In addition, the duties listed in the second column are to be completed every day after supper."

Ink stared at him in disbelief. "You are serious."

"I'm always serious," Caradoc answered. "Everyone earns their keep here."

"You can't honestly expect . . . after everything that's happened—"

"If you will not work, you will not eat."

"Then I'll steal."

"Then you'll be treated as a thief. I don't think you want that."

Caradoc turned his back and began cutting another letter into the tree. Ink's cheeks flushed as his anger began to burn hotter.

"Do you honestly think I'd waste a single *second* of my time doing *anything* for you? You snatch me away from my perfectly normal life, haul me up to this deathtrap in the sky, and now I'm to be a *slave*? I knew it! I knew there had to be some other reason for dragging me up here!" He stomped over to the edge of the stream. "I ain't lifting a finger to help anyone! And you and the rest of your fugitive gardening friends can just trot off to the hot gates of Hell!"

Caradoc glanced back in time to see Ink crumple the paper in his fist and toss it over his shoulder into the water. The boy crossed his arms and raised his chin, holding a defiant gaze against Caradoc's stern glare.

"Go get it," Caradoc said.

"Get it yourself," Ink retorted.

He tensed as Caradoc stood, removed his spectacles, and took a few steps towards him. The man could have burned the last letters into the tree with his eyes.

"Go get it," he said again.

"You heard me the first time, Miss Meriwether." Ink glanced down and saw the carving knife still in Caradoc's hand, glowing red at the tip. "And don't think I'm scared of that knife of yours, either, 'cause I ain't!"

Caradoc flung the knife away and strode up to him. A great deal of Ink's courage fled from him then. Although the others did not strike him as the violent type, he realized he had no idea what this man was capable of doing—even without a knife.

"I'm going to tell you once more," Caradoc said. "Go and get it."

Ink squared his shoulders and set his jaw, trying to appear much braver than he felt.

"No."

The next thing he knew, he was in the air—weightless, confused—until he plunged into the biting cold stream behind him.

CHAPTER 19

DROWNING BEFORE BREAKFAST

I nk convulsed with frenzied thrashing, choking as water entered his lungs. When his arm brushed against a fallen tree branch lodged into the bank he lunged for it, pulling himself above the surface. Spluttering and blinking the drops from his eyes, he looked up at Caradoc, who appeared almost phantom-like through the golden haze of the dissipating morning mist.

"I can't . . . I can't swim!" Ink cried between gasps.

"Really?" Caradoc replied with an air of indifference. "Well, that's a coincidence. I hear drowning is the best time to learn."

The swelling panic in Ink's chest threatened to suffocate him. "This branch . . . it's coming loose! Get me out of here!"

Caradoc crouched down. "Get my paper."

"Are you *insane?*"

Caradoc pointed to a spot downstream. "It's just there, clinging to a branch a few feet away from you, along with your hat. Go get it."

The branch under Ink bent and swayed. He grasped for another handhold farther up, his mouth barely above the water line. "You're . . . you're not going to help me?"

"Stop waving your arms around so much. Kick with your feet."

Just before Ink could release a well-rehearsed expletive, the branch broke away from the bank and dragged him back beneath the surface. He tried to struggle upward again, but his hysterical motions kept him underwater more often than above it.

"Help me!"

"Stop panicking!" Caradoc said. "Get control of yourself! Kick your legs wide. Slow your arms."

Ink breathed in another gulp of air and kicked his legs as hard as he could, doing his best to make smaller motions with his arms. In another minute he was treading water. Barely.

"Now go get the paper," Caradoc said. "Downstream, to your right."

Ink spied a part of the bank where tall grasses and shrubbery grew near the water's edge. His hat was caught in the clutches of a low-lying honeysuckle vine. The paper was just beyond.

"I . . . I can't! I don't want to move!"

"You have to."

Another stream of curses ran through Ink's mind, but he was too focused on trying to stay afloat to let them leave his mouth. Caradoc sauntered downstream, his hands in his pockets.

"Reach out with one arm at a time, slowly, like you're scooping the water away. And keep kicking your legs."

Ink took another deep breath and put an arm out in front of him, then the other. He didn't move an inch.

"Lean forward a bit."

That did it. Now he was moving. Caradoc crossed the stream over a narrow wooden footbridge and went closer to the water's edge near the honeysuckle vine, then crouched and laced his fingers together. As soon as Ink neared the bank, he made a quick lunge for his hat. But as his fist closed around the brim, he lost control and went under again.

He kicked wildly, and in an explosion of droplets, erupted through the surface, spewing water and thrashing like a wild mare. He made a blind grab for the paper but missed it by inches.

"Careful now!" Caradoc warned. "If you make it come loose and it floats away, you'll have a lot more swimming to do."

"You can reach it from there!" Ink gasped. "*You* get it!"

"Stop talking. Save your strength."

Ink's oversized clothes were fully waterlogged and he fought hard against their weight. His throat and nostrils burned. Every limb ached. He swam another two strokes, grabbed the paper with his free hand, and dipped beneath the surface again. This time, he could not fight his way out. He squeezed his eyes shut as he sank down, the breath leaving his lungs between puffed cheeks. This was it. All was lost. He had gone and died for a piece of paper.

Just as the darkness closed in around him, a pair of hands grasped his coat and heaved him out of the water. Ink collapsed backward onto the bank, but Caradoc rolled him onto his side and held him there, waiting as the boy expelled the water from his lungs in a series of violent coughs and sputters. Every gasp set Ink's lungs and throat afire. He flopped over onto his belly, pushed himself up from the ground and vomited. Tears rolled down his cheeks in great big drops. He wiped his mouth with the back of a shaking hand.

Caradoc sat by in silence. Once Ink's fit was over, he reached for the soggy piece of paper and stood. The parchment was awash in blue dye, the writing hopelessly blurred. He tucked it back into his pocket. "You can write out another copy during breakfast."

Ink's ears buzzed. He shook his head a few times, his chest still heaving as he shivered. Caradoc grabbed him by the front of his coat and lifted him to his feet. Ink wasn't sure he had regained the strength to stand, but it was a passing concern. Caradoc wasn't letting go.

"I heard about the incident with your little firearm," he said in a low voice. "If you ever, *ever* threaten to harm any one of my fugitive gardening friends again, I will turn you loose to the ground for Spektor sport as fast as it takes you to fall there. Understand?"

Ink nodded. He didn't dare doubt his sincerity now.

"Now go get changed. I expect to see you at breakfast in half an hour."

He released his hold on Ink and strode back to the tower. Ink stood on his own for all of three seconds, then crumpled to the ground as his legs buckled beneath him, utterly spent. He wondered if he would live long enough to make it to breakfast.

Caradoc was waiting for him outside the Dining House when he arrived. The clock on the tower was just striking seven. Ink clenched his jaw as he approached, wondering what kind of apology the insidious man would offer for nearly drowning him. He raised his chin, preparing to make a sharp refusal of forgiveness. But as he neared the steps, Caradoc only turned towards the door and waited for him to enter with simple expectation.

The moment they crossed the threshold, the room erupted into a chorus of cheers and warm welcomes. Caradoc returned the greetings but Ink stayed silent, feeling his ears burn beneath the brim of his still-damp hat.

"So the truant returns at last!" Chester said, clapping Caradoc on the arm as he passed.

"I ought to be truant more often if the reception's as good as this," Caradoc said, nodding towards the table. He steered Ink towards a chair and took the hat from his head.

"We thought we'd do something special this morning, now that you're both here," Harriet said. "In honor of Mr. Bash."

It wasn't until Ink plunked down at the far end of the table that he noticed the "reception" to which Caradoc had referred. Before him was the largest spread he had ever seen. There were fried eggs with tomatoes, flaky rolls smothered with fresh butter, toast with apricot and raspberry jams, diced plums and pears, thick, creamy porridge, fried potato slices, an assortment of cheeses, boiled eggs, and as many rashers of piping hot bacon as one could ever want. There were also several jars of fresh-squeezed orange juice, pots of coffee and hot tea, jugs of fresh milk, and even a few bottles of wine. It seemed enough to feed everyone for a week.

"How old was Bash when he joined us?" Caradoc asked, pouring wine into his glass.

"In his late seventies, I believe," Abner answered. "Had a stout heart for the job that had to be done."

"He was a good man," Delia said. "Very kind."

"A bit shy, too, as I remember," Wendolen replied.

"Except when it came to his trade," her sister said with a laugh. "Lord, he could prattle on for hours about his precious pens and pencils!"

Simon smiled. "I always enjoyed hearing him talk about it, if only to watch his face light up. I have to admit I was a bit sad when he decided not to stay with us."

Ink noted this bit of information with interest. So Bash had not been forced out after all.

"I nominate Simon to do the honors, then," Martin said. "Before the food gets cold."

The rest of the table agreed, so Simon took up his glass and stood. The others copied the motion with revered silence. Ink didn't move. One of the pens he'd stolen from the dead man's house was still in his pocket. No use adding insult to injury.

"To his courage," Simon said. "To his friendship and loyalty. We thank God for the honor of his aid and trust, and we rejoice in the knowledge that he is now at rest. At peace. And that he will keep the lights burning bright for the rest of us." He raised his glass. "To Mr. Iophulis Bash."

After this, Ink was made to copy out the note he had ruined. Once he was finished and finally allowed to eat, he attacked his plate with such gusto it was as though he had never seen breakfast before. Up until now he had taken his meals in his room, and half of them had gone uneaten. But the morning swim had summoned back his appetite with a vengeance. He was nearly half done before he realized the room had gone silent. He looked up and glanced around, horrified to find everyone looking at him.

Chester let out a loud chuckle. "You'd better be careful eating like that, boy! Otherwise you'll end up looking like Martin here!"

The others burst into laughter. Ink breathed a quiet sigh of relief.

Overall, his first experience dining with the Colonists was not so terrible as he'd anticipated. Despite their dark pasts and unhappy circumstances, he was amazed to find a kind of joy and contentment in their attitudes. They did not cease to offer each other another rasher of bacon or piece of toast, and jested and teased each other like the best of siblings. It was almost as though all was good and right with the world. From the start of the meal, Ink had been preparing himself for another round of questions about his personal life, but apart from being made by Caradoc to say "thank you" whenever he received something, he was mostly left alone.

They talked of the weather, the crops, the upcoming harvest, the state of the cow pen. Ink came briefly to attention when Caradoc announced his new work arrangement, and not a few were surprised by it. Harriet in particular questioned the wisdom of the decision, unsure whether a boy Ink's age ought to be made to do such labor, but most of the others expressed grateful enthusiasm for the new help.

After this, they began to press Caradoc for the account of his adventure at the lake, now that he was fit to relate the story in detail. He started by narrating his first encounter with Ink on the shore, then told of his decision to follow the Spektor into the water.

"I knew there were underwater caves in the area from a survey expedition I'd done a long time ago. What I failed to remember, however, was Corvus's reputation as one of the biggest lakes in the North Country. Needless to say, the chase took a bit longer than I planned."

Ink wanted to ask why an evil spirit would flee from a mortal man, but decided against opening his mouth and drawing more attention to his ignorance.

"I finally caught it in a grotto near the western shore," Caradoc continued. "I asked why it had gone after the boy, but it only let off a string of less-than-courteous phrases and attacked."

"It's that face of yours that puts them off," Simon said. "You best take someone prettier with you from now on."

"Look, Simon, if you want to go along next time, all you have to do is ask."

Simon threw a grape at him as the table erupted into another chorus of laughter.

"Now, boys!" Delia reprimanded, despite laughing herself.

"Don't let him get to you, Simon," Riva said while grinning at Caradoc. "You wouldn't believe the fuss he made when he got back. He was the biggest baby you can imagine."

Caradoc picked up Simon's grape and threw it at Riva. She dodged, laughing.

Wendolen took a sip of wine and shook her head. "First Bash gets the Spektors on his tail, now this young boy. What on earth is going on?"

"Nothing good," Martin answered.

"Well, thank you, Martin. That helps a lot," Chester said, pouring a second glass of wine.

Abner sat forward in his chair and nodded towards Caradoc. "You've said before you don't believe the Spektors would have any interest in hurting us because we're Colonists."

"That's right," he replied.

"Do you believe it still?"

"I do. Spektors aren't concerned with politics, or who did what against another. They care only about spreading misery and feeding on the darkness that follows. As for Mr. Bash . . . I don't know why he was attacked." He nodded across the table. "Nor why they turned on young Mr. Featherfield. Nothing about it makes sense. Not from what I know about Spektors. But then my education on them was fragmentary at best."

"Perhaps there are other circumstances which might cause them to kill," Riva said. "Ones we don't yet know about."

"In my opinion, that's all the more reason for us to stay up here together," Harriet said, bunching up her napkin in her fist. "No more of this cavorting to and fro down below. Including you, Caradoc. You of all people."

"I agree," Martin said.

"But that's not always possible, or practical," Abner replied.

"Then we should try to make it so," she answered. "We all know what happens when one of us is put to the mercy of the Assembly or the High Council. That's awful enough. But I would rather meet Bill Stone himself than share poor Mr. Bash's fate."

The company fell silent. Ink looked down. A large yellow eye was glaring up at him from under the table. He'd almost forgotten about the old gray cat, not having seen it in several days. He took a piece of bacon from his plate and flung it under the table. The yellow eye disappeared back into the shadows.

"While I'd like nothing better than to agree with Harriet's idea," Delia said, "I can't believe that hiding is the best solution. These are black deeds being done, and though we may not know the cause, we must at least try to stop the effects. Isn't that the reason we all came together in the first place?"

"She's right," Jeremy said.

Everyone, including Ink, was startled to hear the quiet man finally speak. He cleared his throat nervously as all eyes turned his way.

"Although," he continued, "there's not much to be done about it from up here."

The table went quiet again, save for the sound of spoons stirring in teacups. Ink pushed the food around on his plate, feeling useless.

"What about that man?" Evering said, pointing his fork at Ink and flinging bits of egg. "That man you were with in the flat? Could he help us?"

Caradoc frowned. "Man? What man? Someone else was there when you picked him up?"

Evering raised a red eyebrow. "Well, yes, but . . . I don't think he recognized us. And anyway, we couldn't just leave him. We had to get him out of there, too."

"Did you tell him why?" Martin asked.

Simon took a silent breath before nodding. "We had to explain the situation to Ink in front of him."

"And if he reports it to someone?" Caradoc asked. He looked hard at Simon, conveying a second part to the question that went unspoken. Simon understood his meaning and looked away.

"Aw, come on. Who's he going to tell?" Chester said. "Nobody buys this Spektor business the first time they hear it."

"And besides that," Josephina added, "no one would ever put two and two together. Who would ever think to connect us with the Spektors?"

"A great many people may," Caradoc said, "now that Bash is dead and everyone knows who he was. The cause of his death must have been discovered by now, and while the Cassrians might write off a theory about a man being eaten alive by a dark spirit, the Entrians wouldn't."

"That's true," Riva said, lines of worry creasing her brow.

Caradoc settled back in his chair with a quiet sigh. "Well, there's nothing to be done about it now. But we will have to tighten our defenses and try to limit our—as Harriet put it— cavorting to and fro down below. Although that does make my one and only idea difficult to suggest."

"That's one more idea than we've got," Abner said. "Let's hear it."

"Mastmarner," Caradoc said. "We go back to Mastmarner."

"I thought you promised you'd never set foot there again," Delia said.

Caradoc nodded towards the far end of the table. "Technically, Simon promised."

"She's not going to appreciate a visit," Simon replied.

"If anyone knows why Ink is being hunted, she will," Caradoc said. "She'll help us."

"If she doesn't shoot us first, you mean."

Caradoc smirked. "Naturally. But that's the chance we always take, isn't it?"

Abner glanced out the large window on the far side of the room. "We're passing west of the Ashing Mountains just now. How many weeks does that put between us and Mastmarner?"

"With no delays, three, three and a half," Caradoc replied. "What does everyone think?"

"It's a good plan," Delia said. "Even if she doesn't like the fact of us turning up, she'll try to help us if she can."

Caradoc looked around to see the rest nodding in agreement. All but one.

"Simon?" he asked.

"I don't have a better idea, so I suppose we'll have to try it," Simon said at last. "Just don't expect me to tag along. I prefer holding to my promises."

"In the meantime," Martin said, staring at Ink, "perhaps our young guest could put a little more time and effort into thinking about what happened that day at the lake. Anything he might have missed."

Once more, eleven sets of eyes turned towards the boy, with only Caradoc gracious enough to spare him the discomfort. Ink managed a slight nod.

"Well," Chester said after another long silence, "I think I've had just enough of this talk to sour my digestion. Wendolen, would you be a dear and pass down the wine?"

CHAPTER 20

INK IS PUT TO WORK

As it was Monday, Ink spent the first half of the day under Jeremy's command. It started with a lesson on how to use a scythe. It was a terribly awkward thing to hold and even harder to properly sweep about, but when Jeremy was satisfied that Ink wouldn't do himself harm, they set to cutting the tall grass around the stone path. The excess mulch would later be gathered up, dried, then used to fuel the kitchen oven. It was tedious, unnatural work. Ink tried to get out of it by complaining, but Jeremy only smiled and shrugged in response, which eventually caused the boy to give up the effort altogether. It was no fun whining to someone who took it so well.

As they set to work outside Delia's place, they heard raised voices arguing through the walls of Simon's house next door. Ink halted his scythe in mid-swing and listened.

"Who's that?"

"Simon," Jeremy answered without looking up. "And Caradoc."

Ink listened again. "How can you tell?"

"Something passed between them. At breakfast."

Ink propped up his scythe and leaned against it. "So . . . d'you think they got secrets? Things they keep from the rest of you?"

Jeremy wiped his brow with the back of his sleeve. "Oh, I know they do."

Just then, the noise inside Simon's house died away and the front door opened. Caradoc came down the steps carrying two long-necked bottles, one containing a blue liquid, the other amber-colored. He strode across the path without so much as a glance at the laborers nearby and disappeared into the garden grove. Ink looked back at Jeremy.

"Don't suppose you could tell me what's in those bottles, could you?"

Jeremy smiled and pointed to the next house. "Oh, look. More grass to cut."

Ink snorted and shook his head. He swung the scythe up to rest on his shoulder but nearly tumbled over from its weight. He looked around, hoping no one had seen him, and caught sight of Oswald sitting in the window of Delia's house. The old gray cat stared at him over a saucer of milk, his yellow eye unblinking. Ink stuck his tongue out at him before returning to work.

So began Ink's first week of manual labor. Each day held the test of some new skill to learn, while each hour promised some inevitable mistake. He broke three plates trying to clear the dining table as fast as possible, ruined a batch of Chester's wine by adding too much sugar, and got his first kick from a cow during a milking lesson with Delia. He had bruises everywhere, aches in every muscle, even a proper sunburn on his nose and ears. His pride took some knocks as well. As Riva insisted on a supply of fresh flowers in every house, Ink found himself standing on the Plumsleys' doorstep one afternoon with an armful of marigolds. He got such a ribbing from the giggling sisters that he made Riva swear to make her own deliveries from then on.

Then at the end of each day, when he felt he couldn't lift another finger, there was still the matter of daily chores. With heavy steps he would walk the stone path, kicking away loose stones and fallen branches. After this he would haul himself up ten sets of stairs to sweep the balconies of every house, and each night the climb seemed to grow a little longer and steeper. The one balcony he was spared from cleaning was the tower's. Ink was too relieved to ask Caradoc the reason for this omission, but he was aware his presence was neither wanted nor welcome on the fourth level. It was one of many useful discoveries he had made during that first week.

One of the most interesting concerned doors. While most places in the village were unlocked and unbarred, there were three doors which needed keys. One was the front door to the Pipeworks House. The other two were the high wooden gates which stood on either side of the enormous propellors down below. His inquiries into what lay behind these gates were always deflected, and the only thing he was able to get out of Evering on the matter was the existence of two copies of each key, entrusted to a select few.

Another important observation he made was that the Colonists didn't mind questions so much when they were trying to concentrate on something else—an advantage Ink was quick to exploit whenever helping with chores. He learned of their past professions, their families, their habits and tendencies. Some were more willing to talk than others. Riva, for instance, would say nothing of her past, only that she had not been with the Colonists from the beginning. And Martin seemed to grow so disgruntled whenever Ink was in the same room, the boy gave up hope of any conversation whatsoever. Still, it wasn't hard to notice that the more they talked to him, the more they eased their guard.

Of all the discoveries he made those first few days, the strangest and most unexpected was that his fugitive captors had a fondness for sing-alongs. If the weather was good after dinner, they would throw open the glass doors of the Music House and serenade the night with a seemingly endless repertoire. The noise of their merrymaking often climbed to such a volume that Ink feared it would breach the silencing enchantment and float down for all the world to hear. Wendolen and Josephina always took center stage with a duet or two, often with an inebriated Chester banging away on the piano with a broad smile on his flushed face. Ink found it so amusing that he began to time his chores so that he would be close to the Music House when the revelry commenced. After a few days of this, however, he was forced to keep his distance when the boisterous musicians started including his name in every song whenever they caught sight of him.

Aside from these brief diversions, Ink's days were wearisome and maddening. Some nights he was so exhausted that he would fall into bed fully-clothed and go straight to sleep. There would be no time to plot his way out of his problems or worry about getting back down to Eriaris, and he soon began to wonder if that wasn't exactly the intent. 'Keep the boy busy.' And busy they kept him. Ink had little choice but to go along with it. After the incident at the stream, he didn't fancy testing Caradoc's patience again. Not for a while, anyway. At night, when Ink had finished the last chore, it was Caradoc who would look over his work, noting mistakes and neglect. Ink always tried to amend what he had done wrong by the next day, but even if he did manage to get it right there would be no acknowledgement from his cruel taskmaster. The man may have saved his life, but Ink found it hard to be grateful to someone so heartless.

The great clock that kept time for the village required winding once every seven days. On his tenth night on Riverfall, Ink entered the stone tower for the first time. The ground level contained only firewood, stacked high against the walls. As Ink climbed the curving stairs and passed through the second-floor doorway, the light from his lantern fell on a huge collection of schoolhouse things. There were maps, easels, chalkboards, portraits, even birdcages and marble busts. Books overflowed the place, every table and shelf packed full. What didn't fit was heaped in piles on the floor. Ink clucked his tongue as he looked out over the mess. At least no one had asked him to tidy up in here. Yet.

He came to the third-level door and knocked.

"Come in."

Ink stepped into the room. It was an odd, makeshift bedchamber which shared its space with the cogged machinery of the tower clock. A low bed was pushed up against the far wall, accompanied by a small bookcase, dresser, and wash basin. Moonlight streamed in through a narrow glass door leading out to a ledge where the clock face could be accessed. Caradoc sat at a table on the far side of the room, copying notes from a book by lantern light. He glanced up briefly and looked at Ink through his spectacles.

"Ah. Inkpen. Here for the clock?"

"Yeah. And it's Ink*well*."

"Know how to do it? You've got to wind the gears with that ratchet hanging on the wall there. Just attach it to that rod sticking out from the middle."

Ink set his lantern on the floor. After finding the ratchet he slid it onto the rod, braced his footing, and attempted to turn the crank. It didn't budge. He snuck a glance at Caradoc, who was engrossed in his book. Ink gritted his teeth and took a deep breath before trying again, determined not to look like a weakling. This time, he heard a single metallic click as the gear rotated half an inch. He rubbed his red hands together and went for it again, shutting his eyes and practically hanging off the crank with his full weight. One more click. The gear would yield no more.

When Ink opened his eyes, Caradoc was standing in front of him. With a good-natured glint in his eye, he reached forward and cranked the gear in a matter of seconds. The heavy weight rose overhead, suspended on a pulley system of thick rope. Caradoc removed the ratchet and handed it back to Ink.

"Maybe we'll wait a bit longer 'til we give you this job. But you can still check the oil. Clear away the dust. And do me a favor by staying out from under that weight."

"Fine by me," Ink said with a shrug, determined not to let the show of strength get to him. He jabbed his thumb back at the contraption. "Shouldn't this thing be ticking?"

"There's an enchantment around it to keep the noise from driving me mad."

"Huh," Ink said. "It must be broken, then."

"By the way," Caradoc said, heading back to the table, "I don't mind if you neglect to extend the proper courtesies to me, but I'd like you to start practicing your 'yes, sirs' and 'no, ma'ams' with the others."

Ink scowled. Unless he needed a dose of charm, he usually avoided using terms of respect, never having met anyone truly deserving of the honor. He shrugged again. "I'll try."

"No. You will. And I'll have my spies keep tabs on you while I'm gone."

"What? You skipping off again?"

"For a few days. Abner and I are going down to see if the Entrians have connected Bash's death with the Spektors. If they have, it's possible they might have discovered the motive for it, which might then lead to solving your own case. Simon will inspect your work in the meantime. I know you're crushed."

"Devastated. Why Simon?"

"Because we've known each other since we were children. He knows my mind almost as well as I do."

Ink filed away this piece of information in his head. Jeremy's comment about the two of them keeping secrets from the others now made a bit more sense.

Caradoc opened another book on his desk and flipped through the pages. "Oh, I've been meaning to ask . . . what's your age? Thirteen? Fourteen? I can't work it out myself."

Ink frowned, irritated by the recurring question. "Well, how old are you?"

"You're answering a question with a question."

"What, are slaves not allowed to do that now?"

"I'm forty-one."

Ink let out a low whistle. "Sweet gravy, I certainly ain't as old as that. Forty-one! Blimey, old man, do you take your teeth out before you go to bed at night?"

"All right, all right, you've made your point. Keep your secret. Only take care not to say anything like that in front of Martin. We're the same age."

"No worries there," Ink replied. "I try not to say anything to him at all if I can help it."

Caradoc closed the book and pulled a chart down from the corner of the table. Curious, Ink moved closer. A map of Eriaris and several star charts were spread out in front of him. A sextant and an open compass lay nearby.

"Is this what you do all day, this navigational stuff?" Ink asked, picking up the sextant.

"Yes. Navigational stuff is my trade. I studied navigational stuff at school."

"Well ain't that kind of a joke up here? I mean, you got the whole sky to move around in. There ain't no icebergs or sandbars to get stuck in."

"We're still low enough to get stuck in a mountain. Besides that, we've got to know where we are. Can't just drift about. Especially not if we've got to get you to Mastmarner."

"Hopefully sooner than later," Ink replied. "Don't think I could take another week of this. You know you're a right slave driver? Getting me to do all this muck for you? I ain't a common work-horse, you know."

"You've got tomorrow off."

Ink paused at the start of another gripe. "What?"

"Tomorrow. Off. I suggest you use it wisely. As a matter of fact, the only thing I am going to require you to do is take a bath."

"A bath?"

"You're right about not being a common work-horse. They smell better than you do."

Ink glared at him, open revolt burning in his eyes.

Caradoc cocked his head. "It's either that or more swimming lessons. Your choice."

Ink rubbed a tired hand over his tired face, then held out his arms in defeat. "Fine."

Caradoc went back to his charts. "Oh, and one other thing. While Abner and I are down below, we'll be able to get a message sent out, if you'd like us to. If there's anyone you want to contact, anyone who might be worried about you, friends, family—"

"No," Ink answered. "No, I don't . . . I mean . . . it wouldn't do much good . . ."

The scarred man gave him a look of concern but waited patiently for the rest of the answer. Ink felt a flush of embarrassment and shook his head.

"No messages."

Caradoc's concern did not lessen, but he nodded in understanding. "All right. Well, I'm a bit pressed for time at present. I'll have Simon look over your work in the morning. I expect you to keep up the same standards while I'm gone. No slacking off or skipping out on chores. I can make it very unpleasant for you if I find that's what you've been doing. Understand?"

"Yeah, I get the point."

"Good," Caradoc said. "You can go to bed now."

Ink trudged back to the door. He was losing ground in this contest of wills. No matter how hard he tried to defy this beastly man, not once had he ever seen a victory. Not once had any of his usual tricks worked. It was like kicking against a wall of stone. Ink glanced back as he set his hand to the doorknob, trying for a final jab.

"Would you like me to say 'good night, sir'?"

Caradoc didn't miss a beat. "Only if you mean it."

Ink nodded. "All right, then."

He left the room without another word.

CHAPTER 21

REVERBERATIONS

By all accounts, October in Eriaris that year was much the same as all the others that had come and gone. It was a time of feasts and harvests. Dragging mittens and scarves out of trunks and wardrobes. Baking all sorts of sweet and sticky things, plucking turkeys and pheasants, and sealing up the last jars of fruit preserves. In the city, the folk with more money and less useful things to do were in the shops snapping up the latest cold-season fashions. Blankets were held tighter to chins. Cloaks wrapped snugly around shoulders. Trees and shrubbery began to stretch their limbs and yawn, dropping nettles and leaves. And never in all that time—neither in the darkest dream nor the wildest corner of imagination—did anyone have the faintest idea that a village of fugitives was drifting silently overhead.

The air was quicker to turn cold at the higher elevation, and the Colonists paid special attention now to gathering extra fire-wood and preparing for the harvests of the gardens and vineyard. Ink found himself constantly on the move with hardly a moment to stop for breath between chores. Despite this, the work was getting easier to do. His muscles didn't ache as much, the bumps and bruises were less frequent, and his ears and nose no longer burned now that the sun had turned the full gaze of her face away.

The days were especially sweet now that Caradoc had gone, leaving a kinder, gentler overseer in his stead. Not only did Simon constantly praise Ink's efforts, he seemed loathe to criticize any mistake at all and was even averse to making him work after the sun went down. A blind eye was turned. Corners were cut. Apparently, Caradoc's closest friend did not know his mind so well as he thought. Here, at last, was a victory.

Even better was the day Ink realized he no longer feared for his life. No longer worried about his throat being cut in the middle of the night or his cup being poisoned. His captors had become more relaxed around him, more trusting. On days when he had been working particularly long and hard, Chester would even pass him a glass spiked with a bit of wine, along with a wink. The practice was soon banned after Delia caught him in the act, but Ink appreciated the gesture all the same. Though, of course, he never said so.

But not all things were improving. Martin was still openly hostile towards him. No matter how Ink's rate of dish-breaking improved, there was not a comment or look not filled to the brim with vitriol and animosity. Whenever giving directions, he was particularly fond of adding the phrase "or are you going to try and shoot me again?"

Thus far, Ink had never given him the satisfaction of a response.

~

"All right, listen," Ink said as he pushed through the door, squaring his shoulders. It had taken much too long to gather up the courage to do what should've been done long ago. "I've put up with your rubbish for a good two weeks now and I've had enough. You know I'm forced to do hard labor, innocent though I am, but you insist on making things bloody impossible for me. So it looks like I'll have to be the bigger man here. I'm calling a truce. A term of peace—look, can't you shut up for two minutes?

Thank you. Now I don't want to be here any more than you do, but none of us have a choice. So I think it's best if we just try to get along."

The row of chickens in front of him blinked, replying only with soft clucks.

"So here's what's going to happen," Ink continued. He paced down the coop with his hands behind his back, sidestepping piles of gooey white refuse on the floor. "No more pecking, no more clawing, no more shrieking. The faster you let me clean this stinking coop, the faster I can be on my way again. Get it? Matter o'fact, why don't you all just clear out whenever you see me coming? Take some exercise! Stretch your legs a bit! There's plenty to do out there!" He paused to brush a feather from his coat, then resumed his pacing, sticking out his chest like a court prosecutor. "So! Bottom line here is . . . if we can't be friends, we can at least be civil to one another. Agreed?"

"Mmm*bawk*! Agreed!"

Ink pitched backwards against the wall, upsetting an open bag of feed. "What? Who said that? Which one of you said that?"

"I did! I did!"

Ink flattened himself against the wall and sidled towards the door, his face stricken with horror. "Saints above, I knew it! I knew it all along! You're possessed! You're possessed chickens!"

Chester stuck his face through the door just as Ink came alongside it.

"*Bawk*! That we are!"

"*Baaaaaaahh*!" Ink slipped on the spilled feed and fell to the ground.

Chester stepped back from the coop door, doubled over in laughter alongside Riva. Ink picked himself up and charged outside.

"You filthy swine!" he shouted, taking a hard swipe at the oily-haired man with his hat. "You lunatic! The last thing—the *last* thing I need are *demonic chickens*!"

"Such a performance!" Chester howled. "Such bravado!"

Ink hurled his hat at him. "How long have you two been listening? How long?"

"We're sorry, Ink," Riva said, wiping tears from her eyes. "We didn't mean . . ."

Her words dissolved into laughter. The tower clock began to strike noon, signaling the mid-day meal. Delia stepped through the back door of her house, wiping her hands on her apron.

"What's going on?" she asked.

Chester and Riva were still chuckling when they reached the doorstep of the Dining House, and even Delia couldn't help but smile. Ink, still red-faced, busied himself with thinking of a way to take his revenge.

"Hey!" a voice shouted from down the stone path. "Hey!"

"Evering?" Riva said. "What's wrong?"

The young man came sliding to a halt in front of them, nearly stumbling. He gestured frantically towards the southern end of the village with a panicked expression.

"Lowcloudsonthehorizon!" he rushed, out of breath.

"What?" Delia asked.

"Slow down, you loony," Chester said.

Evering leaned over and put his hands on his knees, panting. "Low . . . clouds . . . on the horizon. Coming towards us. From the south."

Ink saw Delia shoot him an uncertain glance. She leaned into the house.

"Simon, you might want to step outside."

"What's going on?" Wendolen asked, arriving with her sister at that moment.

Simon was out in a few seconds, along with Martin and Harriet. Evering repeated his message and frantic pointing.

"I saw it coming from down in the pipeworks. Thought you'd want to know, now that . . . well, now that . . ."

"Oh, dear," Josephina said, glancing at Ink with an air of dread. Her reaction quickly spread to the rest of the group.

"No. Listen now," Simon said. "We've been through this. They know we're up here. They've never bothered us before. This is nothing."

"It may have been nothing before, but now you've let *him* aboard," Martin shot back.

"What did I do now?" Ink asked.

"But would they even risk it?" Harriet asked. "Knowing Caradoc might be here?"

"They will as soon as they find he's not!" Martin replied.

Simon put a hand on Ink's shoulder and began leading him away from the Dining House. "I'm taking him down to the pipeworks. How long have we got, Evering?"

Evering hurried along the path to catch up. "Five minutes at most."

"What are you doing?" Martin said, jogging up behind them. "You think you can hide?"

"They might not know about the pipeworks. It's our best chance."

"Well I'm coming with you," Martin replied. "I'm not waiting around for them to look through the stragglers."

The others stood in uneasy silence until Chester finally said what everyone was thinking.

"Uh, what say we go along, too? For . . . moral support."

"Yes," Riva agreed. "Something like that."

They all made a mad dash for the Pipeworks House.

"Oooh! Slow up a bit!" Josephina called out. "You know I can't run in these heels!"

Ahead, Ink struggled to keep up with Simon's long strides. "You gonna tell me what's going on? Or is it up to me to guess again?"

"We know of only one way the Spektors can pass between worlds. Vapor. They use it as a passageway. They can summon it or make use of what's already there. That means smoke, mist, steam—"

"Or clouds," Ink finished, feeling his knees weaken.

They came at last to the Pipeworks House. Evering flew through the front door, caught up a nearby lantern, and made for the descending stair.

"You first, Ink," Simon said. "Follow him."

A few minutes later, the Colonists were huddled together on the stairs of the pipeworks, gazing out at the fast-approaching mass of dark clouds. Ink gripped one of the balusters, trying to steady his nerves. The temperature dropped as the first traces of misty haze began trickling in through the far side of the chamber. Everyone pulled their coats and cloaks tighter. Riva was bare-armed, but Delia hugged her close and spread her shawl around them both. Evering raised the lantern to his eye, gazing intently at the flame.

"Whatcha doing that for?" Ink asked.

"Looking through fire or water is the only way to see Spektors that don't want to be seen," Evering answered.

A tense hush fell over the group as thin, wispy tendrils of vapor began drifting over the walkways and curling around the pipes. Mist poured into the chamber from behind, swallowing the propellers whole in seconds.

"This was a mistake," Martin said, his voice starting to shake. "I knew it from the beginning. We never should have taken him in. Should've left him where he was."

Harriet tried to shush him, but he didn't hear her. All his attention was focused on the boy sitting a few steps in front of him.

"Do you think they'll leave us alone if they find him?" he continued. "They'll know! They'll know we helped him! And then we all end up like Bash, ripped up from the inside! You know I'm right!"

"Calm down, man!" Chester said.

"Quiet!" Delia hissed.

Harriet put an arm around his shoulder. Martin bit his tongue, but his eyes burned through the growing gloom.

A moment later, Riverfall was enveloped in cloud. The damp cold settled over them like a slow-moving rain shower, making their clothes heavy with dew. The gray swirl became so thick they could barely see one another, and every sound but their own breaths faded into silence.

"Clever boy."

Ink turned his head. "What?"

He could no longer see the flame from Evering's lantern. Shivering, he drew his knees to his chest and hunched his shoulders up around his ears, trying hard not to think of the fog that had surrounded him at Corvus Lake.

"My time is now yours. Use it."

The words came close to his ear, soft and gentle. Ink snapped his head around.

"What? Did someone say something?"

"No one said anything, Ink." Evering's voice sounded faint and far away.

Ink shifted, ready to accuse Chester of another trick, then realized the voice had belonged to a woman. But none of the ladies were sitting anywhere near him.

"Name your enemy."

He squeezed his eyes shut and tried to convince himself it was only the wind. He had nearly succeeded when the voice came again.

"Name your enemy."

Without thinking he shuddered back against Simon, so alarmed by the mysterious voice that he didn't bother to right himself again. Simon reached forward and pressed a reassuring hand on his shoulder.

"Name your enemy. And live forever."

The words were inside his head, a whisper carried on the

slightest breath, reverberating between his ears. He tried to shove it away, tried to think of anything else. A song. A loud noise. But there was no need, for the voice did not come again.

In another minute they passed out of the cloud. Sighs of relief echoed behind him, the more so when Evering reported he had seen nothing through the flame. But Ink had already guessed as much. The voice, had it been real, could not have belonged to any Spektor. He would not be breathing otherwise.

～

Together they made their way back to the Dining House. The sky had darkened and a damp chill remained in the air, threatening rain. Conversation was sporadic during lunch. Uneasy. No one said a word about the incident, and those who tried to encourage Ink with a smile or a kind word couldn't help but feel uncomfortable afterward. In the past few days of teaching the boy to milk cows, grow herbs, and cut grass, they had almost forgotten he was such a dangerous liability.

As soon as Ink finished eating he rose to clear away the dishes, having learned to start the chore as early as possible. He entered the kitchen with an armful of plates, avoided looking at Martin as he set them on the counter, then hurried out again. This continued for a good ten minutes before he realized the dishes piling up beside the sink were not moving. On his way out again, he snuck a glance at the dish-washer.

Martin was hunched over the sink, clutching the edge of the counter with his eyes shut, taking deep, shuddering breaths. Ink hated to show a single smidgeon of concern for the man, but he couldn't help himself.

"You all right . . . sir?" Ink added the last word grudgingly.

Martin started and turned fast, as if spooked by his voice. "What? What did you say?"

"I was just asking if . . . if you were all right."

"Oh," Martin said, nodding. "Oh, so . . . you're finally showing some concern about someone other than yourself?"

Ink frowned. "I just—"

"You're starting to notice you're not the only one around here with problems? Is that it? Well that is a wonder. A kindness indeed. What charity! What . . . what *benevolence!*"

Ink took a step back. Something wild flashed in Martin's eyes.

"How extraordinary!" he continued, his brow beginning to glisten with sweat. "To think that you should grace us with such compassion! You! Who has suffered far more than any mortal should be made to bear!"

"Look, I'm sorry I asked!"

Martin swooped towards him and put his hands on his knees, now at eye-level with the boy. "And what's this? An apology for your behavior? Showing some regret for your conduct? And here I thought you never erred! Here I thought you had life all figured out!"

Ink stayed silent, knowing better than to take the bait.

"Well, don't you? Don't you have it all planned out? Don't you have us all pegged as either fools or tyrants? We who live to either serve you or get out of your way?"

Ink was startled when he bumped against the wall. He hadn't noticed he'd been backing away. He glanced around the room, looking for something he could use as a weapon if it came down to it. The only thing nearby was a wooden spoon.

"You know," Martin said, straightening again and stepping back, "I'm not convinced you're a mere human. Not with the way you treat the rest of us. You must be something more. An immortal, perhaps? A god? Maybe that's your secret. Maybe that's why you've got a host of demons after you. Maybe that's why Caradoc found you all alone, wandering the wilderness with nothing but the clothes on your back. Or is it just that no one wants you around? That no one can stand to be in your presence? Oh, ho! I think that's it! I think I've hit the nail right on the head! What do you say to that, *Mr. Featherfield?*"

Ink froze against the wall, unable to speak or even run from the room. Something terrible was happening. The veins in Martin's severed arm were bulging under his skin. Red and purple lines twisted up from his stunted elbow, the blood vessels popping out like filaments of scarlet thread. Martin clutched at his arm and let out a choked cry of fury. Upon catching sight of Ink's horrified expression, he became even more enraged.

"What are you looking at?" he shouted. "Get out!"

He picked up a large plate and hurled it towards him. Ink ducked as it crashed into the wall just inches from his face.

"Get out, I said!" Martin roared. *"Get out!"*

Another dish crashed over Ink's head. He backed away towards the door and ran into Harriet, who put a hand on his shoulder.

"Ink, go outside," she said. "Simon, Chester, your help, please."

She hurried into the kitchen, followed soon after by the two men. Martin was now throwing every dish within reach, yelling in anguished rage, flecks of spit flying from his mouth.

"I'll get the chloroform!" Harriet said above the noise. "You two restrain him!"

Chester swore as a large cup exploded in front of them. Shards of porcelain flew in every direction. Harriet rushed to a small cabinet in the far corner of the room.

"Come away, Ink," Delia said, tugging him by the arm. "Let's go."

Ink was so shocked he could barely tear himself from the scene, but at her urging finally turned away and allowed her to guide him. She led him straight through the room, past the dining table, and out the front door. Riva and the Plumsleys followed.

"Are you all right?" Riva asked, checking his face for cuts.

"I'm fine," Ink replied, though not sure if he really was.

"That brute!" Delia said as she paced back and forth with her hands on her hips. "He ought to be chained up if he can't be trusted to control himself!"

"Delia . . ." Riva said, her tone bordering on reprimand.

"Well, he should! These outbursts are coming more and more often. And you know he struck poor Harriet once in this state. He can't keep putting her through this! Nor the rest of us!"

"Pay no mind to anything unkind he might've said to you in there, Ink," Wendolen said. "He doesn't mean it. Really."

"Like our Uncle Bailey," Josephina said. "Used to get raging drunk after only a few glasses of port and didn't know a thing he was saying. So you just forget all about it, all right?"

Ink didn't answer. He was too busy listening to the terrible sounds of struggle coming from inside the house. It was another full minute until the noise of breaking dishes stopped.

CHAPTER 22

THE SAGA OF MARTIN AND HARRIET WHISTLER

Though it was only one o'clock, Simon cut Ink loose from his chores for the rest of the day. It was just as well, as it had begun to rain. Feeling the need to be alone, Ink wandered to the uninhabited Music House and climbed the stairs to the glass room. The effect of water pouring over the transparent walls made him feel as though he were standing inside an invisible bubble under a waterfall, the droplets streaming down the sloping panes like thousands of tiny pearls.

He strolled towards the instruments and went to each one, plucking every string, tapping every drum, brushing his fingers against the woodwinds. Some bore cracks and dents, chipped paint and tarnished keys, but these were the marks of regular use, not neglect. They were loved, treasured, played instead of merely displayed. More than that, they were needed. Standing there among them, in their own private sanctuary, Ink had the feeling they knew it too, and were bloody proud of it.

He drifted across the room and sat down at the piano, accidentally kicking over an empty wine bottle as he did so. The sheet music on the stand was so old the paper had begun to yellow and curl. Ink smirked as he read the title. *Merry in the Springtime*. The phrase "o'er the hills of lingering white" had been underlined in red ink, the last word circled several times. He pushed the brim of his hat back, squinted at the black circles scattered along the first four measures, then tried a few of the keys before striking a proper chord. Just as he did, someone entered the room. It was Harriet.

"I'm sorry," she said. "Am I interrupting?"

"No. I mean," Ink stumbled, trying to answer as he'd been taught, "no, *ma'am.*"

She approached the piano almost shyly. "Mind if I sit?"

"Go ahead . . . uh, ma'am."

"It's all right. You don't have to call me that," she said with a smile. She sat next to him and set her cane against the side of the piano. "Do you play?"

Ink shrugged and looked over the music again. "Not really. Had an old piano in the house I used to plunk around on a bit. But I can't read all these markings and such."

Harriet nodded. "My mother made me learn when I was young. I try to keep it up, but I'm certainly not proficient."

She looked down and brushed her fingers over the keys. Ink snuck a glance at her face. She was troubled, her gentle eyes deep in thought.

"Ink, I need to apologize to you. For my husband. He's a good man. It's just that sometimes . . . he doesn't always remember it."

Ink stayed quiet, even though he wasn't sure he understood her.

"Martin doesn't like me talking too much or too freely about our personal history," she said, hesitation in her voice. "But I think you have a right to understand what happened."

Ink knew that out of all the Colonists, she was the one who felt the sorriest for him. He had never once hesitated to exploit that compassion—to get an extra bite to eat or leave work early—and it now appeared that this same sympathy would finally give him some worthwhile information. He sat straighter on the piano bench.

"His troubles started long before we ever came to Riverfall," she began. "Before we ever became Colonists. We lived in the South Country then. Martin was a high-level manager at Williams and Glenn, one of the biggest banks in the country. All the most important politicians and society figures do business there. Six months after we were married he got word an executive officer was retiring, and that the board had chosen Martin to be his replacement. We were both overjoyed. It meant a better life for us, and for the . . . child I was carrying . . ."

Her eyes dropped to her hands for a moment.

"He was so proud the day he took over the post. We even had a big banquet to celebrate with all our friends and family. And Martin was a great success at the job. The youngest officer in the bank's history, in fact. It was a very high honor. And it wasn't long afterwards we started hearing rumors that he was being considered for a seat in the Assembly. A great many things changed for us. We moved into a bigger house on a nicer street. We were able to afford more servants, a larger kitchen staff . . ." The corners of her mouth turned up in amusement. "Isn't it funny? Now we're the kitchen staff."

"So what happened?" Ink asked. "Did he take to the bottle? I hear a lot of them business types do."

"No. It wasn't so obvious as that. It was little things at first. Staying later at work. Not getting enough rest. He had to travel a lot, though he always hated being far from home. Then it was office politics, and getting into rows over employee pay, and being obliged to attend social engagements full of people he disliked. Even when he had time to himself he was never let alone. There was always someone wanting to speak with him about a problem or ask his advice. Once when we had gone out for a picnic, someone came to fetch him because a cigar had caused a fire in one of the offices. Most nights he came home so tired he could barely stay awake through supper. He started losing weight, getting gray hairs. In just a few months he seemed ten years older. I asked him to rest, suggested we take a holiday together. But he said he couldn't be seen lying idle. There was too much pressure from the bank's investors. Pressure to be constantly ahead of the competition, to always be striving to make things better, more efficient. And there were those around him who were always watching for a mistake. Waiting for an opportunity to spread vicious gossip about him. He had to uphold a solid image of strength at all times. I believe it was this, more than anything else, that started breaking him on the inside. But he was so proud. And so unwilling to let anyone help him."

A long moment of quiet followed. Ink sensed a terrible anxiety rising within her, as though she were preparing to venture into a dark place she usually avoided. He remained silent, waiting for her to continue.

"The worst of it came . . . after we lost the baby. Near the end of the term. Martin was devastated." She bowed her head for a moment. "He went to work the next day, though I begged and pleaded with him to stay at home. When he returned that evening, I saw something had happened to him. Something had changed. It was in his manner, the way he carried himself, the way he spoke. He became more impatient. More distant. There was a bitterness and harshness in him I'd never seen before. During the course of the next year, the man I knew and loved disappeared almost completely."

She looked away and wiped at a corner of her eye, rushing on to her next sentence to forestall any further outpouring of emotion. "I didn't know what to do. No one else seemed to see what was happening, or didn't want to mention it if they did. I went every day to prayers for a time, pleading for guidance, asking what I could do to help him, but I always left feeling even more helpless than before."

She paused, looking out through the rain-soaked window.

"The day I decided to stop praying was the day Caradoc turned up on our doorstep."

"Caradoc?" Ink echoed in surprise.

She nodded. "He said he had passed Martin in the street and had . . . seen something, sensed something . . . wrong. A sort of darkness. I asked him into the house immediately, and he did his best to explain the situation without scaring the wits out of me. Do you know, Ink, there are far worse things a Spektor may do to a person than kill them?"

Ink frowned and shook his head.

"There is a way for them to . . . get inside your head. They try to take control of you, try to make you do things you wouldn't normally do, see and hear things that aren't really there. They can change you. Once I learned this, I was sure it had happened to Martin. Caradoc said he could help him, that he had a way of removing the Spektor, but only if Martin consented to cooperate in the process. I almost lost hope then. I couldn't imagine convincing him to agree to it. Caradoc had been called away on a job and was due to leave the following morning, but said he would delay another two days to give us time. He told me where I might find him, then left."

The rain began to fall harder, washing down the glass with all the noise of a rushing river. Neither of them took any notice. The remaining warmth and light in Harriet's eyes had stolen away, retreating inside her soul like a candle being taken into an inner room. She stared down at the piano for a long time, pensive in silence, and when she spoke again, her voice was barely above a whisper.

"It was very late when Martin came home that night. And just as well. It took me hours to gather the courage to talk to him once I realized I didn't have a choice. I wouldn't lose my husband without a fight. So I told him everything. Told him about the changes I saw in him, the hours spent in prayer. About Caradoc and about the Spektor. I begged and pleaded with him to get rid of it. For the sake of his happiness. His life." Her expression grew pained. "But he just sat there, silent, staring at me as though I'd betrayed him. When I exhausted myself on words, I had only my tears and my hands pressing on his to implore him. It must have been nearly half an hour before he finally spoke. And when he did . . . he was angrier than I had ever seen him in my life. He accused

222

me of terrible things, condemned me, cursed the day I ever became his wife, all the while using language I had never heard him use before. He became violent; he never touched me, but he made a mess of the room. Then he walked out of the house, into the dead of winter without so much as a hat or coat. When he didn't return, I sent some of our servants out to look for him the next day. They only learned that he had not been to the bank. I became frantic then. I called the police, told them only what they needed to know and asked them to keep the matter private for as long as they could. But they had no better luck. On the second night I went out to look for him myself. I called on all our friends and family who lived close by and made up some pretense to avoid arousing their suspicion. But no one had seen or heard from him. By the time I returned home, I was all but convinced he was dead."

She shut her eyes and let a few moments pass before continuing.

"I was preparing to visit Caradoc that night to tell him what had happened, when there was a knock at the front door. It was Martin. I was so relieved, so grateful to have him back I was even ready to apologize for the whole business that had prompted him to leave in the first place. But I was so shocked by what I saw I could hardly speak. There were bruises on his face and arms, dark rings under his eyes. He was so pale you could almost see the veins beneath his skin. And he couldn't stop shaking. Couldn't stop glancing around as though he were searching for something, as though his eyes couldn't focus on any one thing. He wouldn't speak, wouldn't answer any of my questions about where he'd been or what he'd done. He just came towards me and put his arms around me. I could feel him shivering. His clothes were torn in places, caked in mud. Finally, after what seemed like an eternity, he said he was ready to get rid of it. I wasted no time in taking him to see Caradoc." She straightened her posture and smoothed out the folds of her dress. "And that was it."

Ink stared at her, stunned. "That was it? What, just like that?"

"I wasn't allowed in the room when Caradoc performed the expulsion. I wanted to be, but I was expressly instructed not to interfere with the process. It nearly drove me mad. Especially when I heard Martin scream."

"Scream?"

She nodded. "Once a Spektor has made itself at home, it is very unwilling to leave. And when it is forced out, it will do its best to take their captive down with them. So it was with Martin. The Spektor tried to make an end of him in the same way our friend Mr. Bash came to his." She hesitated, casting a concerned glance at the young boy beside her. "It started on Martin's arm, you see, and . . . well, Caradoc had to act quickly before it could get any further. He says he wouldn't have had the courage to do it at all had Martin himself not insisted upon it."

Ink sat quietly, taking in the full significance of her story. For the first time since it had happened, he felt genuinely thankful to have escaped Spindler's flat with only a scratch.

"I hope I haven't frightened you too badly," she said, her anxious eyes searching his.

"Don't worry," he replied. "I'm used to it by now. But there's something I don't understand. If Martin was saved . . ."

"Yes, the rage attacks," Harriet replied. "That part remains a mystery. He had his first one almost two years after the Spektor had been expelled, and since then it seems they're happening more and more often. Caradoc doesn't know what's wrong. Simon has examined his arm several times but can find no answer for it. Obviously we don't dare take him to a proper physician. I'm hoping our visit to Mastmarner will prove helpful in some way. We have a friend there who knows about such things. But until then, I'm afraid nothing more can be done. His mood and behavior improved a great deal after the Spektor was gone, but he never completely returned to his old self. The pain of the injury and the shame of how it came about made him bitter and afraid. He's become so terrified of another Spektor attack he refuses to set foot down in Eriaris again. It's also the reason he reacted badly towards you, and for that I am truly sorry."

Ink looked out the window towards the Dining House, barely visible in the heavy rain. The glow of a candle burned in the second story window.

"Does he know you're here?" he asked. "Did he send you to apologize?"

"No," Harriet answered ruefully, "and he mustn't know that I've told you. I only wanted you to understand why he is the way he is. Perhaps now—whenever he shouts at you or looks cross with something you've said or done—perhaps it will be just a little easier to bear."

Ink didn't answer, still gazing out the window. Harriet moved to put her hand on his shoulder, but thought better of it and pulled away. She took up her cane and rose from the bench.

"Did he do that to you?" Ink asked, glancing back at the cane.

The implication of the question brought a brief look of pained regret to her eyes.

"No. I had a bad fall from a horse when I was a young girl. The injury never quite healed properly."

Ink nodded, though he wasn't sure he believed her.

She smiled at him sadly. "You are a very brave boy to have endured all the things that have happened to you, Ink. I hope that one day you may be rewarded for your courage. If not in this life, then certainly the next."

"Is that why you've stayed with him?" Ink asked. "'Cause you think things will be better in the next life?"

She shook her head. "I stay because the man I fell in love with still exists inside of him. And if the one you love must walk through Hell itself, you do not abandon them at the gates."

Martin joked about the incident at dinner that night, calling it a mere "tantrum", all too eager for it to be forgotten. Harriet and

Ink locked eyes for a few moments, sharing a look of understanding. As Ink went about his chores later on, Martin scolded him on his speed and lack of efficiency, as usual, but the reprimands came less often and he never once raised his voice.

Ink spent the rest of the night trying to decide if that was a good enough apology.

HARVEST TIME

"Time to get up, Inkpot."

There it was. That dreaded voice. A boot kicked at one of the legs of the bed frame. Ink stifled a perturbed grunt and rolled over. There stood Caradoc, holding the old gray cat in his arms and scratching behind its ears.

"Let's go. Come on."

Ink got out of bed, griping under his breath, and grabbed his clothes from the bedpost. "So you've come back, have you?"

"Had to. Oswald here couldn't bear another day without me."

Ink pulled on his coat with a worried frown. "Did you find anything out? 'Bout me or Mr. Bash?"

Caradoc's expression sobered into regret. He shook his head. "Nothing yet, I'm afraid. But we'll keep trying."

Ink slumped his shoulders. The hope of being free again was floating ever farther out of reach, like the scrap of paper in the stream. As he tugged on his hat, he turned his sullen gaze to the one-eyed cat. "You'd better not let Evering see you've brought him in here. He'll go mental."

"He was already here. Just sitting at the foot of your bed, sort of watching you."

Ink shrugged into his suspenders. "Shoulda known you'd set him guard over me, too."

∽

It wasn't until Ink caught a glimpse of the clock tower that he realized he'd been woken a full hour earlier than usual. Caradoc informed him the time would be used to showcase all the work he'd done in the past few days. Ink cringed. This would not be pleasant. He'd been lazy and Simon lax, though he knew he wouldn't be able to lay the blame on his more merciful benefactor.

Despite Ink's best efforts to distract him with questions and chatter, his eagle-eyed inspector found every single mistake, every trace of carelessness. Some tasks had been so neglected Ink couldn't even come up with a half-decent excuse. The chicken coop was a mess, the cow pen hadn't been mucked out in days, and the dust balls in some of the less frequented rooms were starting to look like tumbleweeds.

At a quarter to eight, with the sun blinking through the trees on the southern side of the village, the inspection came to an end. Ink bit his lip as they halted on the stone path, waiting for the explosion of outrage that was sure to follow.

Caradoc scratched his beard and squinted up into the sky. "What's today? Wednesday? I think you're supposed to be under Abner and Evering's supervision, but things will be a bit different. You'll be working with me for the next few days, preparing for harvest time. All right?"

"All right," Ink replied warily, baffled by his reaction.

"All right," Caradoc said again, smiling. "See you at breakfast."

He put his hands into his pockets and turned away.

Ink called out after him. "Wait! Wait a minute! Hold on!"

Caradoc turned back.

"That's it?" Ink said. "That's all you've got to say? Ain't you gonna yell at me? Ain't you gonna say how horrible I've been?"

"No."

"Well, why not? Ain't you angry?"

"Not really."

"But . . . look what a terrible person I've been! I slacked off! Cut corners! Did exactly what you told me *not* to do!"

Caradoc smiled again. "I know."

Ink pointed at his face. "And why the smiling? What's that about?"

Caradoc shrugged. "It's a beautiful morning. And I'm back home again."

"I know what this is," Ink said. "This is another way to torment me! Another way to drive me up the wall! That's what this is!"

Caradoc laughed as he turned and walked off. "Isn't it exhausting to be so suspicious all the time?"

Ink shook his head and muttered a reply beneath his breath. "Ain't it exhausting to be such a loony all the time?"

"Sometimes!" Caradoc called back from down the path.

Ink frowned, then turned and tramped away in the opposite direction. One the one hand, he was relieved to have escaped the wrath and punishment he knew he was due, but on the other, it made him uneasy to realize he was dealing with someone he couldn't begin to predict.

At breakfast, Abner and Caradoc revealed what they had discovered during their excursion below. The source of their intelligence, oddly enough, had been a lately-recruited Colonist-hunter who spilled everything he knew after being bought a round of ale in a quiet pub. According to him, sixteen days after the death of a Colonist, life in the North Country had mostly returned to normal. The doubled street patrols in the major towns were now taken for granted. The newly re-printed arrest warrants had caught the public's attention for a week or two, but soon faded from thought. With Bash gone and the Entrians having returned to the West Country, the only new development was the appoint-ment of a deputy commissioner who would serve under Marlas—a young man by the name of Frederick Coram.

Upon hearing this, reactions from the Colonists were immedi-ately passionate. Scorn. Contempt. Disgust. Chester went so far as to utter a crude insult for which he was made to apologize, and the mood only darkened further when Abner revealed that Coram was now leading a special secondary investigation into Bash's death. The room went silent, all eyes turning towards the scarred man at the end of the table.

"All the more reason to get to Mastmarner as quickly as we can," Caradoc said.

On top of this, every effort to track down what conclusions the Entrians might have made about Bash's death had proved unsuccessful. Officially, the cause had been listed as 'internal hemorrhaging aggravated by severe heart attack'.

"What of the body?" Simon asked. "Was he at least buried?"

Abner shook his head grimly. "Burned, and the ashes scattered in secret. Like all the others."

No one had much of an appetite after that.

When the meal was over, Harriet pulled Caradoc aside and asked him to wait. As Ink began collecting an armful of dishes, he watched her go into the kitchen and speak to Martin. He couldn't make out what was said but saw Martin shake his head, then nod in approval. When Harriet returned to the dining room, she approached Ink and asked if he would mind finishing things up while she had a word with Caradoc. He told her he wouldn't, and made sure Caradoc heard him use the word "ma'am".

Watching them climb the stairs to the second story, Ink felt a sense of satisfaction. The cruel treatment he'd suffered would now surely be made known, no matter how badly Martin had wanted to hide it. A hint of swagger even entered the boy's step as he went about his chore, and especially whenever he went into the kitchen to drop off another pile of dishes. If Martin even noticed the effrontery, he was too deep in thought to show it.

They returned to the dining room just as Ink finished brushing the crumbs from the table, and he saw right away that Caradoc's previously sunny disposition had sobered. He stopped next to Ink and nodded.

"I was wrong to go off and leave you so defenseless. No one should have to fear for their life up here, you least of all. I promise, from now on, never to put so much distance between us again that I can't protect you."

Ink's triumph deflated in an instant. Now he would never be free of the man.

"Fantastic," he replied flatly.

"I knew you'd be excited," Caradoc said, then went to the kitchen for a word with Martin.

Harriet glanced over the table. "Wonderful job, Ink. You've finished in record time."

"And gone three whole days without breaking a dish," Ink replied. "You can make that public as well."

She smiled. "I knew you'd get the hang of it. You're a clever boy."

Ink felt a chill run through his heart. He'd been so preoccupied with Martin he'd almost forgotten about the strange voice he'd heard in the clouds—the one he'd convinced himself hadn't been real. His instinctive reaction to Harriet's words, however, said otherwise. And he was suddenly, and reluctantly, feeling glad of Caradoc's promise.

Harvest time came once a year, the sole occasion when everyone worked together to reap the treasures of the orchards, gardens, and vineyard. Their ability to survive the winter would depend heavily on the successes or failures of the next three days, and everyone devoted their time to making preparations. Ink spent the rest of the morning hauling boxes, baskets, and bags out to the orchards, laid ready to be filled a dozen times over. In the afternoon, he helped prepare a heap of sandwiches to cover the next few days, and by evening was so sick of the sight of them he wasn't sure he would be able to eat any when the time came.

It was a gorgeous day that dawned the next morning. The sun shone in full force but the altitude kept the air mercifully cool—perfect conditions for a solid day of manual labor, or so said Caradoc as he got Ink out of bed at sunrise. The others had already gathered in the garden grove by the time they arrived and were divvying up the baskets and boxes. Almost everyone had brought a hat to shield their faces as they worked, and Josephina had taken the opportunity to debut a ridiculous handmade creation with a huge straw brim pinned with flowers and feathers. Ink had to stifle a laugh. It looked like a large bird's nest.

After a breakfast of fruit and boiled eggs, they went to the apple orchard and began working their way up the trees. Everyone seemed to be in good spirits, taking to their tasks with vigor and energy, and enlivened all the more by Abner's declaration that this year's harvest looked to turn an even better profit than the last. The hours flew by. When their sacks and baskets were filled to the brim, they dumped them into wheelbarrows. Once those were full, Abner, Simon, and Caradoc took them to the kitchen and unloaded them into large metal tubs. Chester was expected to be part of the wheelbarrow brigade but managed to evade this duty by declaring he had "somehow" pulled a muscle in his shoulder the night before.

But what labor was lost by his injury he made up for in entertainment. Unable to abide long periods of silence, he endeavored to lead everyone in an endless procession of ballads, hymns, and shanties. Only Martin and Ink did not join in. Chester bore down particularly hard on Ink to sing along, until Ink insisted he'd "somehow" pulled a muscle in his throat the night before. He was left alone then, but not before being called a "cheeky scamp".

Later in the morning, Ink lugged two shoulder bags over to the nearest wheelbarrow. Simon stood next to it, fishing a twig out of one of his work gloves.

"Ho there, Mr. Inkwell. How goes it?"

Ink grunted as he struggled to lift one of the bags over the lip of the wheelbarrow. "Yesterday, after making about six hundred sandwiches, I swore I'd never touch another one. I just added apples to that list."

Simon smiled. "I say the same every year. Never lasts long. I wonder—now that you're here—if you wouldn't mind doing a small side job for me."

"Oh, no. I live for work."

"Jeremy was just telling me he's not sure the apples at the tops are quite ripe yet. When you get a chance would you mind going up one of the trees and taking a few for us to look at?"

"Sure."

"But listen, I want you to wear a rope around your waist when you go up. Tie it around the trunk somewhere halfway, and over at least one solid-looking branch as well."

"Oh, come on, Simon," Riva said as she stepped beside him and emptied a basket into the wheelbarrow, "you're talking like he's never climbed a tree before."

"That's not the point. I don't want to have to set any bones or treat any concussions today. And I don't need any dissent from you, either." He playfully poked her shoulder on his way back to the trees.

"He can be such a spoilsport," she said to Ink, smiling as she walked away.

Ink tipped his hat back and wiped his sleeve across his brow. From the moment he'd first set eyes on the trees he had harbored a secret desire to climb them, but fearing it would make him appear childish, he had resisted. Now there was a purpose for it. An excuse. He glanced at the tree a few feet in front of him. The boughs were broad and sturdy with plenty of knots and forks for footholds. A tethering rope would be an insult. He laid his hat atop the wheelbarrow, put a bag over his shoulder, and went to the tree. After glancing around to make sure no one was watching, he raised his arms and closed his hands around the lowest branch.

The next moment he was off the ground, skittering up among the leaves and branches with all the dexterity of a young squirrel. His face flushed with excitement the higher he climbed, the limbs bending beneath his weight. When he had climbed almost to the top, he straddled himself against the trunk and plucked three apples, each near to bursting with juicy sweetness. He placed them in the sack and took a moment to savor his accomplishment. A breeze rushed through the orchard, parting the branches and letting through a warm shower of golden sunlight. He took a deep breath, inhaling the delicious scent and vowing never to keep himself from climbing another tree again. He fantasized about how long he could stay there before anyone noticed, but only for a few moments. He didn't care to find out what kind of punishment Caradoc would think up for a boy who insisted on spending so much time in a tree.

"Rope, ha!" he said to himself as he began to make his way down. "Maybe for you, old man, but not me! No, sir! I'm agile as a duck in water! Nimble as a Wood Spirit! Skillful as an *ahhhhh . . .!*"

His foot slipped on a patch of moss as he reached for the next branch. He had only a second to cry out before he flipped backwards and crashed through the boughs, sending down a shower of leaves as he fell. He tried desperately to grab onto something but the only branches he could reach were newer shoots that snapped off at his touch. Before he knew it, he was seconds away from smashing into the ground head-first. With a gasp he squeezed his eyes shut, flung his arms over his head, and waited for the end.

And waited.

And . . . waited.

He had stopped falling, but no crash had come. How was that possible? He opened one eye and dared a peek. A thick carpet of grass lay above his head.

"What?" he cried out.

He opened both eyes and looked down at his feet. The tree was upside-down.

"What?" he cried again.

It was then he saw Riva crouching by the wheelbarrow, holding her hands out towards him as though she were waiting to catch something. A basket had fallen at her feet, spilling apples to the ground. Ink's eyes popped wide open.

"*What?*"

A great gasp left her lips as her hands fell to her sides. Ink completed his fall, bumping his head lightly against the ground and tumbling forward over himself. Riva rushed towards him and helped him up. Her face was as white as a sheet.

"Don't ever make me do that again!" she said. "I wasn't the least bit prepared!"

"But . . . but . . . you—"

"Are you hurt? Anything bleeding or broken? Simon's going to kill me. This is all my fault!"

"You . . . you . . .!" Ink pointed at her, unable to formulate a full sentence. "You're a—"

"Yes! Yes! I know!" she said. "Believe me, I know!"

Ink stared at her with his mouth agape. She sat back and looked around. No one else had witnessed the incident. She sighed with relief and pushed the hair away from her face.

"Listen, this stays between you and me, all right?"

"But . . ." Ink said, still in shock, "but how can you be . . . *what?*"

"Come on. We should get back to work."

She returned to the wheelbarrow and crouched beside her fallen basket. Ink got to his feet and followed her on shaking legs.

"Oh," he said, revelation dawning on him like a burst of light. "Oh . . . that's it. That's it! That's how you broke down Spindler's door! That's why you know so much about this place, this Entrian school! That's how this blazing big chunk of earth is floating up in the sky! It was all you! All of it!"

"Shh!" she hissed. "Don't shout at the top of your lungs."

"Why?" Ink asked, lowering his voice to a whisper as he glanced around. "Did they tell you to keep it a secret from me? Did they kidnap you, too?"

"Don't be ridiculous." She stood and went to the next tree. Ink followed close behind.

"Well, why else would you be up here? And why haven't I ever seen you use your magic before now?"

"First of all, never use the word 'magic' in front of an Entrian."

"Why not?"

"Magic is false. It's tricks and illusions and deception. What we practice is far more than that. There are no special words or foolish rituals."

"Can you do anything you want?" Ink asked. "Like conjure things out of thin air? Or . . . throw fire at people?"

"What?"

"You know, like they do in stories."

"Don't be absurd."

"You didn't answer the question!"

She sighed. "In theory, Entrians have the ability to do anything they can imagine. We're limited only by what we lack in faith and discipline."

She moved to the next tree. Ink followed.

"So you could kill someone with a word if you wanted?"

"You should get back to work."

"Or blind someone with a terrible stare?"

"Look, I'd really prefer not to talk about it."

"Why ever not?" Ink replied. "You Entrians are the most powerful beings on earth! You could have this entire world in the palm of your hand if you wanted! You're gods!"

"Don't!" Riva said, turning sharply on him and raising a finger. "Don't ever say that! It is so far from the truth it is profane!"

Ink shut his mouth and shrank back, surprised by a fierceness he had never seen in her. She lowered her hand, looking apologetic the next moment, and spoke with a softer tone.

"I take no pride in what I am, or where I come from. Entrians are not so extraordinary as you think. We were entrusted with our gifts to make this world good, to protect it, to preserve peace. But by greed, by pettiness and pride, we've failed that calling. They all make themselves out to be such martyrs, but they haven't suffered any more than they've deserved."

Ink's mouth fell open again. "How can you say that? After everything that happened? Half the people on that island wiped from the face of the earth!"

"They brought it upon themselves!" she said, anger coloring her cheeks. "After decades of clan wars and blood spilling into neighbors' houses! They are a broken people. A nation of hypocrites too concerned with tending to their own self-righteous indignation. That is the truth. That is their legacy . . . as well as mine."

She set her basket down in the middle of the orchard, too upset to continue on, then plopped down and put a hand to her brow. Ink sat next to her and pulled the sack of apples from his shoulder, knowing that for once the fury was not aimed at him.

"I'm sorry," she said. "I just don't like to be reminded of it."

Ink furrowed his brow, incredulous. "You're ashamed of 'em?"

She had only to think for a moment. "Yes. I'm ashamed."

Ink shook his head. It was another piece to the puzzle of the Colonists' existence. But what good was finally getting an answer when the questions kept piling up?

CHAPTER 24

DOWNRIGHT EVIL

"You two all right?"

Riva and Ink both looked up to see Delia coming towards them.

"We're fine," Riva answered, trying to brighten herself up again. "Ink was clever enough to discover my secret identity a few moments ago."

"It's finally out, eh?" Delia said, removing her straw hat and wiping a hand across her brow. "So where have we got to now? Have you told him about Berwick yet?"

"Ber-what?" Ink asked.

Riva rolled her eyes. "I was hoping to avoid that particular story."

"Oh no, you can't do that!" Delia said. "It's one of my favorites! One of triumph over adversity!"

"Well? Go on," Ink said to Riva, grateful for any respite from labor. Delia grinned as she sat beside him on the grass.

Riva sighed. "All right. Well . . . I'm not sure if you know this, Ink, but in Entrian society, parents still hold the right to arrange marriages for their children. Several years ago, my parents pledged me to a boy named Berwick. He was considered a great catch—as my parents constantly reminded me—but we had attended the same school since we were very young and I was already well aware of his qualities. I witnessed firsthand his transition from a whining, wretched little bully into a sniveling, cowardly bully of a man."

Delia scoffed. "Arranged marriages. And some call Cassrians uncivilized."

"There was no way out of it," Riva continued. "At least, not by any legal means. So I resigned myself to the idea. I had no choice. But I started feeling this growing sense of doom, like my life was coming to an end. My happiness at the very least. Everyone kept telling me how lucky I was, but I could never convince myself of it. I grew frantic as the wedding day neared. Then at the rehearsal party, I heard Berwick make a particularly disgusting comment to his friends about our future life together. Never mind what. After that, I went straight to my father and told him I wouldn't marry Berwick. Not for anything in the world. But because the marriage laws are so strictly enforced, it meant that if I did not marry him, I would have to sit in a prison cell until I no longer refused."

"Blimey," Ink said. "Just for not wanting to get married?"

Riva nodded, then dropped her gaze as a wave of sadness passed across her face. Ink glanced at Delia, who looked on with sympathy.

"My father made it clear he would uphold the law to the fullest extent," Riva continued, "no matter that I was his only child. So that night, I decided I had to make a run for it."

"And what is this?" a voice interrupted.

Josephina shuffled towards them, looking tired and drawn. Her hat was crushed in a few places along the brim and her curls unkempt and frizzled.

"Riva's telling Ink about Berwick," Delia said.

"Oh," Josephina said, half-sighing, half-groaning as she let the sack of apples slip from her shoulder to the ground. "Mind if I join you? I'm afraid my stamina's not what it was." She knelt, fell heavily to her side, then whipped off her hat. "Sweet mercy. All this bending and lifting and crouching and pulling. I don't know how much longer I can last."

"We're only apple picking, Jo," Riva said with a smile.

"We may as well be rolling stones up hills for all the difference it makes to me! I was not built for this kind of work. Oh, my poor back. Sorry, what were we all talking about?"

"Berwick," Ink said.

"Oh, yes. Why didn't you marry that boy, Riva? You could've had a nice house full of nice things and a nice-looking husband."

"Is that all life is about?" Riva replied.

"Oh, how I wish it were!" the large lady said, throwing up her hands to the heavens. "If only it were! Put me at the front of the queue on that day!"

"Go on, Riva," Delia said.

"Well," she continued, "I needed two things to make my escape. Money and transport. I didn't want to steal anything from my parents, so I came to the next best solution—becoming a Colonist-hunter."

"A Colonist-hunter?" Ink cried. "You?"

"The High Council grants every Entrian Colonist-hunter a horse and a regular fee, so long as they report back to their home office every three months. I waited as soon as the nearest office was open, then rushed down and signed myself up. I thought the money might get me through a week or two while I sought employment in a Cassrian city, but this turned out to be very naive thinking. For one thing, I had no skills of any use to offer, and using my gifts was out of the question since I was trying to hide my identity. For another thing, the money didn't carry as far as I thought it would. Only a few days later I was down to my last few coins and beginning to despair, until I found myself sharing a bench with Simon outside an apothecary shop."

Josephina chuckled. "The only Colonist-hunter *not* looking for the Colonists and she ends up sitting right next to one. Incredible luck, that is."

"I don't think it was luck at all," Delia said, smiling.

240

"We started talking," Riva said. "About the weather, the town. I asked if he knew of any work. He said I might have better luck if I exchanged my Entrian clothing for something a bit more humble."

"I'll bet he thought he was so clever," Delia said.

"He did," Riva said. "'Til I told him he might be better off if he started using a stronger glue for that fake beard he was wearing."

Delia and Josephina cackled, reveling in the image of a shame-faced Simon. Ink looked around to make sure the man himself was nowhere nearby.

"I asked why he was hiding," Riva went on, "and as a joke, I suggested he might be a Colonist. He laughed and said no, that he was an actor on a lunch break and just hadn't bothered to change out of his costume."

"He's always been terrible at lying, bless him," Delia said.

"No," Riva replied. "I mean, I might have believed him if not for the gift."

"Whatcha mean 'gift'?" Ink asked.

"Oooh," Josephina said, giggling as she raised her eyebrows. "I don't think you should tell him this bit. Might come useful later."

"You shouldn't have told any of the boys," Delia agreed.

"Aw, you can't leave me out if everyone else knows!" Ink insisted. "That just ain't fair!"

"So?" Delia said. "There's a lot of things we know that you don't."

"Ain't it time to break the cycle? Come on, ladies," Ink pleaded, clutching at his heart theatrically. "You can trust me. Haven't I got one of those honest faces?"

"Oh, he's good, this one," Josephina said.

"Entrian women have a special ability that the men don't possess," Riva said, too kind-hearted to keep yet another secret from him. "The ability to detect a lie. And it's infallible, no matter how well you hold your expression steady, or your hands still, or your eyes sincere. No Entress has ever failed a test to determine what is true and what is a lie. Never."

Ink sat back. He never dreamed Entrians could possess powers over the mind as well as over matter. He would have to be better about keeping his guard up around Riva from now on.

"That's how I knew Simon was lying, from the very first word," she said. "And once I realized it, I had to think quickly. I had no chance of surviving away from home for much longer, and returning was out of the question. So I decided to follow him. I honestly didn't know whether or not I believed they were responsible for the massacre, but I was so desperate I hardly cared. I reasoned that if the Colonists did not accept me or the aid I could offer them with my gifts, they would simply kill me for discovering them. I had begun to believe death a better fate than marriage to Berwick."

Josephina let out a loud snort of disapproval.

"You of all people can't reproach her for that," Delia said to her. "You once told me an empty theatre on opening night was a fate worse than death."

"Oh, that's absolutely true!" Josephina replied, pushing herself up to a sitting position with great effort.

Riva shrugged. "Maybe I'd have felt differently if I'd actually been on Damiras that day. My uncle was head of our clan at the time, and he was one of the lucky few who made it back alive."

"I've been meaning to ask," Ink said. "How'd they all fit onto that island? It's a small spit of land, ain't it? Did they do some enchantment to float over each others' heads to make room?"

"The island used to be a lot bigger," Delia answered. "Easily holding a hundred thousand of them. But over the past ten years it's been slowly falling into the sea, piece by piece."

Ink frowned. "How d'you mean?"

"No one can quite explain it," Riva said. "It's happening much faster than natural erosion. Many people say the land is cursed for what happened there."

Ink glanced at the ground. Any time he questioned the

Colonists about Damiras, they insisted they had gone to prevent a massacre, not cause one. Problem was, he still didn't know if he believed them. So he changed the subject.

"Right, so . . . you followed Simon back to the others. And they just welcomed you with open arms?"

"Well, not at first," Josephina said. "Simon, poor man, got a serious reprimand for being followed, and we were terrified at having been found out by a young girl. Never mind the fact that she was a certified Colonist-hunter."

"Is that normal?" Ink asked. "I mean . . . are there many lady Colonist-hunters out there?"

"Why shouldn't there be?" Delia said. "Women make far better hunters than men."

"Oh that's rubbish, Delia," Josephina said.

"No, it's not. Women are better attuned to what's going on around them. Better at paying attention to things, keeping track of details, having an eye on every little space and corner that needs it. Why else do you think they've got what's-her-name leading the chase on the Entrian side? I'd be far more terrified to find myself facing her than Bill Stone."

Ink perked up, his heart beating faster in his chest. "What's-her-name? Who's that?"

"Ask Riva. I can never say her name right."

"Seherene," Riva answered. "Probably the most powerful person in Entrian society, apart from the Elders of the High Council."

Ink repeated the name aloud twice, the syllables rolling off his tongue like a holy word.

"Why *do* you people have such strange names?" Josephina asked. "I've never once heard of a Mary or a Tom."

"We don't use family surnames like you do," Riva answered. "And no two Entrians are ever given the same name. It's a point of pride. Helps us remember that we're all unique. So after thousands of years we've sort of had to move beyond 'Mary' and 'Tom'."

"This . . . Seherene," Ink said. "Have you ever talked to her? I mean, since you're all innocent, wouldn't you be able to convince her of that? Get the price off your heads?"

"We tried," Riva said. "Not with her, specifically, but after finding out the Colonists were good people, I went back to the Entrians and tried to tell them. But word of my actions against Berwick and my family had spread, and they accused me of betrayal and treason for having taken up with the Colonists. That's how I got my own name added to the arrest warrants."

Delia shook her head. "Of all the people in this grand tragedy, that Entress is the one who ought to be made to answer to treachery. She's been willfully ignoring that lie detection ability all these years, looking so many of us in the face and declaring us guilty. It's downright evil. Our blood has been spilled for it. Our heads have rolled for it. There is no justice practiced in any court they bring us into, no matter how fair they claim to be."

She was cut short when another apple-picker approached.

"Hey, what's this?" Chester cried. "I want to sit down, too!"

"You're always welcome at any party," Josephina said, making room for him between her and Riva.

He sat down with a grunt and took a silver flask from his belt. "So what's the gossip today?"

"We were talking about Se . . . Ser . . ." Josephina faltered. "That Entress woman."

"Ah!" Chester cried, rocking backward and tipping his hat skywards. "Seherene! That woman running us ragged 'round the world! Have you seen her, Inkwell?" He let out a low whistle. "Don't mind having a beautiful woman like that chasing after *me* for once!"

"Oh, she's nothing special," Josephina said.

Chester nudged Riva in the arm. "She should be called *Sirene*. You know what I mean?"

"Delia's just been telling us how 'downright evil' she is," Ink said.

"Evil? Naw, she ain't evil," Chester replied. "Just lets her emotions get the best of her sometimes. Like any woman." He glanced at Ink and winked, as if knowing the comment would get a rise out of someone.

"Please tell me you're joking," Delia said, instantly annoyed.

"Well, our gifts *are* tied to our emotional state," Riva said. "The more an Entrian feels—whether it be anxiety, anger, passion, anything really—the less effective their gifts are. Maybe her emotions really are interfering with her ability to detect a lie."

"Which proves my point," Delia said. "A decent person would resign under those circumstances."

"Oi, Caradoc!" Chester cried.

They turned and saw the scarred man passing near a fountain, steering a wheelbarrow piled high with apples. Ink grimaced, hoping he wouldn't be scolded for sitting down on the job.

"Oi, Chester!" he called back.

"That Seherene woman . . . that's a gorgeous bird right there! Am I right? These uptights here won't admit to it! Now you can't say you'd mind getting caught by someone with a face and a figure like that, can you?"

Caradoc set the wheelbarrow down by the fountain and removed his hat. "Personally, Chester, I'm a little more concerned with watching my own backside these days."

"Well put!" Delia said as the others burst into laughter.

Caradoc stooped over the fountain and threw water over his head and neck. When Josephina chided him for messing up his hair, he ran his hand over it and made it even worse. She clucked her tongue at him as he picked up the wheelbarrow and grinned, moving off into the garden grove. Delia shook her head as he passed out of sight.

"I'd hate to think of what would happen if that woman ever got her hands on him."

"That's easy," Chester answered. "The torture would be longer and slower. Might even have him burned alive instead of a nice quick chop to the neck."

Ink frowned, disturbed and somehow surprised. "They torture you?"

"Oh, please, let's not go into that," Josephina said.

"But . . . what did Caradoc do that was any worse than what the rest of you did?" Ink asked, then corrected himself. "Or what everyone says you did."

A solemn look passed around the group.

"What's the harm in telling me?" he said. "I mean, if he didn't really do it . . ."

"This is an exception," Delia replied.

"What makes it an exception?"

The uncomfortable glance went around the circle again.

"Because," Chester said, "it's one of the few things the stories about us actually get right."

"He ain't a cannibal, is he?" Ink asked. "They got some nasty cannibal stories about you."

"Oh, how awful!" Josephina said.

"Don't joke about it," Riva said to Ink, smacking him lightly in the arm.

"It's not our place to say what he's done," Delia said. "If you learn it from anyone, it ought to be him."

"You think he'd actually tell me if I asked him? He won't. He don't tell me nothing. Except what I do wrong every day."

Chester raised an eyebrow as he noticed something over Delia's shoulder. "Speaking of wrongdoing, here comes an unhappy-looking chap about to give us an earful for it."

Abner stomped towards them with a frown, carrying four sacks of apples near to bursting. "And what's this? Early lunch?"

"Gossiping like sinners as usual, Abner," Chester said, leading the group to their feet.

"There's no time to be lagging about! We've got a lot to do and little time to do it! You know that! I'm surprised at all of you."

"Oh, don't chide us like children," Delia said as she picked up her basket and turned back to the orchard.

The others followed, disappointed to have their conversation cut short. Ink slung his apple sacks over his shoulder and trailed behind Riva.

"I knew he wasn't safe."

She turned her head. "Who?"

"Caradoc. I could tell he had some loose change rattling around in his head the first time we met. He's the one who ought to be watched day and night. Not me. Do you know he threw me into the stream just to fetch a stupid little piece of paper? Me! Who don't swim! And he just stood there while I nearly drowned!"

Riva stopped under a tree and began to fill her basket. "Yes, he told me."

She tried to hide a smile, but Ink noticed everything.

"What? You think it's funny?"

"No, it's just . . . that's what Caradoc does. He asks the impossible. But it's nothing he doesn't also demand of himself. He may have his odd moments, and he can be hard to predict at times, but he's always kept his promises and proved faithful to us a hundred times over. All the while suffering what none of us can imagine."

Ink frowned at her. "Because of that thing on his hand?"

She hesitated a moment, weighing her words. "Because of a lot of things. But listen, Ink, that's a man you want on your side. Not one to push away. Don't rush to judge him too harshly."

Ink let her go as she stepped away to the next tree. He would not be made to feel pity, nor guilt. He knew the truth. Caradoc was no more a saint than Seherene was evil.

He shoved his hands into his pockets and strolled away, kicking at a rotten apple on the ground. He longed for another encounter with her; that mysterious goddess offering a taste of the divine with her mere presence. Every day the sound of her voice faded a little more from his memory, like a strain of music slipping away into silence.

"Inkwell!"

Chester clapped a hand on his shoulder, startling him.

"I've got the perfect song for you. You're gonna love this one. It's called 'If I Never Had to Work Again'. Now listen carefully and repeat after me . . ."

Chester began to sing. Before Ink could protest, he caught sight of Caradoc returning to the grove with the wheelbarrow. He stopped at one of the garden fountains and stooped over, gripping the stone rim and breathing as hard as a man twice his age. But why? The wheelbarrow was empty. Ink watched as he seemed to curse under his breath, then began splashing water onto his face. His gloved left hand shook.

Ink made himself look away. He would not be made to feel pity. Not for anything.

CHAPTER 25

CAPTAIN VICTORIOUS

"Oh, damnation," Chester was the first to lament the next morning.

The world had frozen over. The houses were coated in a layer of sparkling frost, the bushes and vines dusted white. Every tree stood slicked with ice and the ladders propped against them stuck fast to the trunks. The grass was a sickly shade of blue. Curtains of icicles hung from the fountains. The Colonists made their way across the grove in stunned silence as they surveyed the disaster. The wheat and corn were ravaged, most of the stalks bent or snapped under the weight of the ice. The vegetable garden hadn't fared any better, nor the last crop of their beloved vineyard.

Damnation indeed.

There had been no warning—not one sign or hint of an approaching cold snap. But there was little to be done now. The frozen vegetable garden would have to be dug up to salvage what they could. Others would go through the cornfield, raking through the ears now fallen to the ground. The ruined wheat field would be hewn down to fuel the oven and boiler.

After breakfast, Ink was sent to the cornfield with Evering, Chester, and the Plumsleys. Chester tried to resume his cheery attitude, whistling brightly as they worked, but no one else had the heart to join him. Ink hadn't seen such low spirits since the day he'd announced the death of Mr. Bash.

"We needed this harvest. We were running low as it was," Harriet remarked to her husband as they passed by.

Ink turned to Evering. "So what happens now?"

"Now?" the red-haired lad replied, tossing aside yet another ear of spoiled corn. "Now we'll have to go down and pillage and plunder what we need."

"Well, that's not so bad," Ink said. "Plenty of folk pinch things now and then when they ain't got the coin for it."

Evering raised an eyebrow. "That may be. But the difference is when they get caught, it only means a bit of time locked up somewhere. We wouldn't be so lucky."

As the morning wore on, the frost began to melt away. The topsoil of the vegetable garden turned to mud as the spades worked the ground. Martin walked around with a hammer and broke up the ice in the fountains, bringing them to life again. By late afternoon, they'd saved just under half a wheelbarrow of carrots, a handful of radishes, and five cabbages. None of the corn had survived.

They gathered around the wheelbarrow and stared down at the pitiful crop with faces so forlorn anyone else would've thought they were looking into an open coffin.

Caradoc removed his hat and sighed. "I'll start looking for a suitable town for us to visit. Fortunately, we've still got a few days before we head into the mountain pass."

"It's so strange," Delia said. "We've never had a sudden frost this early in the year. It almost seems . . . I don't know . . . malicious."

Simon nodded. "Well, we've had hard luck before. We'll make it through again."

"There's still apple preserves to be made," Harriet replied. "Plenty of work for tomorrow."

Wendolen let out a long sigh. "I suppose this means no Harvest Feast. I was rather looking forward to that."

The group went silent again. Evering kicked at a rock. Ink wiped his nose on his sleeve. The wind rustled through the leaves. A bird called.

Caradoc frowned. He cocked his head, then leaned to his left.

"Evering . . . did you just hear a bird?"

Evering shrugged. But then he began to think. There were no birds on Riverfall.

"Yeah. I did. Sounded kind of big, too."

Knowing it would be folly to make any sudden movements, everyone began to slowly turn their heads this way and that, searching for the source of the noise. Ink grew bewildered when their gazes came to rest on something just over his shoulder. He turned to look behind him.

A flock of large, gray geese had landed in the vegetable garden, pecking around at the uprooted spoil left behind. Ink counted fifteen of them. Enough for a slew of Harvest Feasts.

"Let's all stay calm," Simon said. "We've got to spread out and get around them, then push them towards the trees so they can't fly off."

"Ink!" Chester hissed. "You have that pistol on you?"

"Simon's still got it."

"Damn!"

The Colonists began to close in, bending low and sweeping their hats gently towards the birds. Growing anxious, the geese made chortling sounds and clustered together, then turned and started padding towards the orchard.

"Get around them in front!" Delia said. "Hurry!"

Everyone rushed to close the gap, but the geese had caught on to their scheme. With a loud, panicked honk their leader sounded the alarm, instantly scattering the flock and inciting them to make a mad dash for the trees.

"It's every man for himself!" Chester cried, breaking formation and chasing after the nearest frightened fowl. The others followed, catching up the sacks still lying around the orchard.

It was pandemonium. They whooped and hollered and bellowed out war cries and goose calls, honking and cooing and clucking. The birds were terrified, but the trees were so close it was impossible for them to fly more than a few feet at a time.

The Whistlers were closest to making the first catch. They got alongside one of the larger geese and, after a count of three, lunged for it at the same time. But it made a sudden jerk to the left and swerved away under Martin's short arm. Jeremy managed to throw a bag over one of the birds but lost his hold on it. The goose went lumbering away, trailing the bag along the ground. Josephina nearly gave up the chase altogether when one of the birds turned and hissed at her. She shrieked and pulled back, letting it pass by unchallenged. Evering was so determined in his efforts he forgot to watch where he was going and almost ran head-first into a tree. Riva, who had nearly coaxed a goose motionless with an enchantment, lost her focus as she fell to laughing at him. A few feet away, Caradoc cursed as the bird he was chasing suddenly doubled back and flapped out of sight. He changed course and went after Simon's prey instead, trying to push him out of the way. Simon pushed back, then stumbled, giving the bird a chance to zip away to the left before either of them could catch it.

It was Ink who had the first victory. He waited behind a tree until a goose waddled by, then leapt out and brought an apple sack down over its head. It struggled violently at first but Ink held on until it became calm. Abner hurried over, pocketing a handkerchief he'd been using to mop his red face.

"Here, Ink! I'll hold that for you. I'm too old for this sport anyway. Go on! Get another one!"

A few minutes later, Ink claimed a second victory using the same method. Jeremy ran up and took hold of the bird with a smile. "Well done! You've got the trick of it!"

"Yeah," Ink said. "Not bellowing my guts out like an idiot!"

Jeremy laughed as the boy ran off again. Riva, meanwhile, managed to calm one of the geese long enough for Delia to whip a bag over its head. Chester had picked up a scythe and was shouting like a crazed warrior, trying to bring the blade down on anything gray and once coming dangerously close to shearing the tail off Oswald the cat, who had joined the hunt.

On the far side of the grove, Simon made a mighty leap and came down onto the back of one of the larger geese, which promptly turned its head and bit him on the fleshy web of his hand. Caradoc overturned a nearby wheelbarrow and helped shove the bitter captive underneath. They collapsed on the ground against it, ignoring the angry squawks coming from within. Simon put his hand to his mouth and sucked on the wound. Caradoc bit his lip to keep from laughing.

"Don't you say a word," Simon warned.

Martin, Harriet, and Wendolen cornered a bird by the stream. It panicked as they closed in, spitting out angry hisses and ruffling its feathers. As the Whistlers came towards it with open bags, it let out a squawk and hurried in the opposite direction. Wendolen held her arms wide, lengthening the blockade made by her already sizeable figure. She chuckled.

"Oh, there's no getting past this wall, darling!"

At the same time, Ink caught up with Jeremy's pre-bagged bird, still trailing the sack from around its neck. Within seconds he flipped the bag over its head, then scooped it up into his arms and ran back towards the others.

"Here!" he cried, dumping the treasure into Caradoc's lap and taking off again.

Simon smiled as he watched the others scurry after the remaining flock. "There now. That was just what we needed. A bit of excitement to raise our spirits."

Just then, Chester ran by with his scythe raised high and his greased hair sticking out in all directions, screaming like a madman as he chased after a bird barely taller than his knee.

Caradoc looked back at Simon. "Should we be worried about him?"

～

They captured eight geese in the end—four of them thanks to Ink's craftiness. As they marched towards the coop to incarcerate their prisoners, Chester and Abner rushed forward and raised the boy up onto their shoulders.

"Ladies and gentlemen!" Chester cried, still wild-haired. "All hail to Riverfall's conquering hero! The one and only . . . Captain Victorious!"

"Let me down," Ink complained while the others clapped and cheered.

"Don't worry, I'm very good at this. No keener eye on earth! No swifter hand or foot! Tremble before him all ye beaked and feathered! Cower and fear all ye villains and scoundrels!"

"Careful there," Martin said, "I think *we* fall into that last category."

"Oh," Chester said. "Right you are."

～

In celebration of their good fortune, and despite the meager pickings from the fields and gardens, preparations for the Harvest Feast commenced in full force later that afternoon. All traces of ice had long since vanished, and the weather turned so mild again they declared it the most peculiar frost they had ever seen.

Ink followed Jeremy and Delia to a clearing in the meadow behind the Dining House where there sat a large canvas tarp, and just beyond, a shallow pit littered with charred wood and ash. Ink helped them remove the canvas and was surprised to find a huge table beneath. The craftsmanship was magnificent. A menagerie of animals had been etched into the surface, showing scenes of frolicking deer, wolves on the hunt, bears fishing in a river, and a hundred others.

"Bless my eyes," Ink said, running his fingers over the table's sleek surface.

"This is one of our most treasured possessions," Delia said. "We use it only for very special occasions."

"Did you steal it?"

"No, we did not steal it. We once had a pair of talented wood-workers among us. This is their creation, as well as the table in the Dining House."

Ink clucked his tongue, staring at a great shaggy wolf carved into the back of one of the chairs. "Now that's skill halfway worth something."

Delia's eyes grew solemn. "Yes, well . . . that Entress woman certainly put an end to it quickly enough."

She turned and went back towards the house with Jeremy. Ink shook his head at her, tracing his fingers over the image of a flock of geese in flight.

By six o'clock the next evening, the table was fully furnished with every delicious thing they could afford to serve. Each of the Colonists came to the table wearing their finest apparel—tailored jackets, waistcoats, neckties, gowns touched with ruffles and lace, cotton gloves, and even a few choice pieces of jewelry. Ink stuck to his usual attire of oversized hat and coat, much to the chagrin of the Plumsleys, who never ceased offering him stylish things to wear.

When the prizes of the goose-catch were brought to the table, golden brown and dripping with juice, cheers and applause broke out. Once everyone's plate was filled, Martin poured the first round of wine. This particular matter was one of special signifi-cance as it was Chester's "top shelf stuff" which he always saved for the occasion of the Harvest Feast. Ink, Jeremy, and Simon's glasses, however, were filled with water.

Then came a toast to Captain Victorious, who was made to sit at the very middle of the table. Ink's ears reddened as everyone stood and raised their glasses to him, but he played to the crowd and accepted the praise with arms raised in mock-graciousness.

"Merely a trifle," he said. "Give me a challenge next time, eh?"

CHAPTER 26

SOMETHING TO HOPE FOR

T he evening was sublime. From the moment they took their places at the table, the beleaguered, world-weary fugitives transformed into a merry group of party-goers. The laughter flowed as freely as the wine, every eye bright, every face shining with mirth. The simple goodwill and affection among them could not have been more generous. Even the old gray cat was treated to a plump leg of goose for his part in the hunt. For those few precious hours, every ache and burden was carried off, as though they had stepped into a world where trouble had never darkened their door.

Upon finishing her second helping, Josephina rose from her seat and led the group in an exuberant toast and round of cheers to the Whistler's much-appreciated culinary skills.

"Making it all worthwhile!" her sister added with a grin.

Chester cleared his throat with dramatic flair as he helped himself to another glass of wine. "And speaking of skills . . ."

"What? You found some?" Simon teased.

Chester laid a hand on his shoulder. "Jealousy is a terrible thing to waste, Simon. Save it for a woman, all right?"

Simon shook his head as a round of laughter followed.

"As I was saying," Chester continued, "I've been thinking

about that job we've got to do downstairs. Now, because we managed to get most of the vineyard harvest in—thanks be to God for that—we've got plenty of merchandise to do a proper show to a proper-sized crowd. We've got to be somewhere close to Burgess Valley by now. I think that's our best bet."

"Oooh!" Josephina said, placing an excited hand on his arm. "Absolutely superb! Wen and I have perfected the most wonderful little operetta. Sure to draw the attention of the masses!"

"Attention?" Ink said. "Ain't that dangerous for you?"

"Not a bit," Wendolen answered. "When Jo and I heard about the chance to help on Damiras, we had to slip out the back door so no one would try to stop us. And when it became clear to our dear, enterprising manager that we were nowhere to be found, he wasted little time in replacing us with look-alikes to keep raking in the coins."

"What?" Ink said. "So there's another pair of Plumsleys out there?"

"Of course, neither one of them can sing worth a pint of frog spit," Josephina said. "But they solved that problem by having them mouth along to recordings we made before we left."

"But it also means we can show up anywhere we like and reveal our identities without consequence," Wendolen said, "so long as we don't appear in the same town as the false Plumsleys. Comes in handy every now and then." She nodded down the table. "Chester's in the same boat."

"Really?" Ink said. "There's a bunch of fake Chesters running around down there?"

"There's not enough hair cream in the world," Caradoc replied.

Chester hooked his thumbs under his lapels. "As a traveling purveyor of . . . unique merchandise, I never stayed in one place for more than a week or two. Wasn't missed when a handful of Cassrians were unaccounted for after that debacle on the island, so I was never suspected of playing a part."

"And you're sure Burgess Valley is the best spot for a raid?"

Martin said. "Last I heard it was one of the fastest-growing cities in the river valley."

"Big towns are always best," Abner answered. "Easier to get lost in them. Go unnoticed."

After a good deal of debate, it was decided in the end that Simon, Jeremy, and Delia would do the actual pillaging and plundering, while Chester and the Plumsleys would be on hand to provide a distraction. That still left them two bodies short of a proper raiding party. Their number had to be small enough to avoid notice, but large enough to help one another load up the goods and be on the lookout for trouble.

Martin, as usual, refused to set foot down on Eriaris, and Harriet wouldn't leave his side. Evering's eager offer to volunteer was instantly shot down by his father, and Riva declared she was too nervous to show her face in a city so close to Entrian Country, which lay just over the mountains they were fast approaching.

"Well," Abner said, "Guess that leaves me and you, Caradoc."

Ink glanced across the table. Would Caradoc keep his promise never to put too much distance between them? Would he stay behind and leave the others one man short? Or would he leave Ink locked up somewhere for safe keeping while he was gone? Ink searched his face for a clue, but the man was impossible to read.

At last, he began to nod. "Why don't you stay, Abner? Ink and I will go down."

The movement of cutlery and glasses stopped. Eleven bewildered expressions turned towards the boy, then back to Caradoc. Ink's eyes had gone as wide as his dinner plate.

"We were just talking about skills," Caradoc continued. "We saw Ink put his own to use yesterday. I think he could be a great help."

Harriet glared at him from across the table. "You wouldn't possibly be using this as an opportunity to bait a Spektor with him, now would you?"

"Of course not. I think it would be good for him is all. Us as well. And if a Spektor *should* happen to come along—"

"Oh, for heaven's sake," she said, shaking her head in exasperation.

"I'm not forcing him. Do you want to go, Ink?"

"Yes, I want to go!" the boy cried. "Got the quickest hands in the country! I could do the whole job for you with my eyes closed!"

"He's just a child, Caradoc," Delia said, making Ink scowl.

"Aw, let the boy go," Chester said. "There's kids less than half his age out in the streets picking pockets. He can do it, no problem."

"And if he gets caught, what then?" Delia said.

"He won't get caught," Chester said.

"How can you know that?" Martin replied.

"All right, listen!" Ink said, putting up his hands. "I can put an end to this quick. Just answer me this. Have I been sitting here since dinner began? This entire time?"

Everyone thought for a moment, then agreed he had.

"I haven't moved from this spot?"

Everyone agreed he hadn't.

"Then . . . how did I get this?" With all the flourish of a circus ringmaster, he pulled a silver flask from beneath his coat and held it up for all to see.

"Hey, that's mine!" Chester cried from the far end of the table. "How'd *you* get it?"

"Easy," Riva said. "He pinched it from your room before dinner."

"He did not! It was on me when I sat down!" Chester replied, checking his belt.

As the others puzzled over the trick, Evering began to laugh.

"Way to teach 'em, Ink."

After that, no one attempted to argue any further over the matter. Ink sat back in his chair with a smug grin as Chester stomped over to retrieve his property. His fortunes were improving at last. Soon he would be down on free soil again—and

Spektors or no Spektors—it was hard not to think of making a run for it.

He snuck a glance at Caradoc, only to find the man already looking at him. Ink's heart sank. His overseer knew exactly what he was thinking. Allowing him to join the raiding party was no act of mere goodwill. It was a test of trust. Reliability. And Caradoc would be there every step of the way to make sure he passed it.

The feast carried on well after the sun had dipped below the mountains in the west. Once the geese had been picked clean and the plates scraped clear, everyone was treated to a slice of apple pie for dessert, made with the last bit of sugar they had. As darkness spread overhead, Jeremy loaded a pile of logs into the pit beyond the table. No one felt like fetching a matchbox, so Riva went to the pit, crouched on her heels, and put a hand on the bottom-most log.

Ink watched her carefully. She closed her eyes and relaxed her posture. There was no immediate spark or burst of flame. In fact, several moments passed with nothing happening at all. Her lips did not move. Her hand did not waver. What was the trick of it? Was it an act of willing the fire into being? Or chanting some kind of incantation inside her head?

At last, the piece of wood under her hand began to glow—a faint red deep within its center. Then it brightened, becoming amber. The color spread towards the outer edges of the bark, lightening to a deep gold, then bright yellow. Riva opened her eyes and pulled her hand back just as a spurt of fire licked up into the air and spread down along the limbs and branches, crackling merrily.

They took up their chairs and placed them around the fire. Although the victuals were gone, there was still plenty of wine to be drunk, and drunk it was. As the night wore on, shoulders relaxed, defenses came down, and Ink made sure to keep his ears open.

"I have to say," Delia said, her words drawling out a bit longer than usual, "this place has been looking a great deal better since we've had Ink here to help us take care of things."

"Hear, hear!" Josephina agreed. "He's been brilliant!"

"Psshh!" Martin scoffed. "He's a menace with that broom of his. Every time I pass under a balcony, whoosh! Out goes a cloud of dust right over my head!"

At this, they chuckled and giggled, and Ink guessed that some of them thought the one-armed man jolly well deserved it.

"He's done a fantastic job. Especially under the circumstances," Simon said. He looked at Caradoc. "Wouldn't you say so, taskmaster?"

"He's done well enough," Caradoc answered.

Delia smiled back at Ink. "That's ample praise coming from him, believe me. Nothing's ever going to measure up to merchant sailor standards in his eyes."

"What?" Ink cried, sitting straighter in his chair. "So *that's* it? That's the reason I'm worked as hard as a ruddy mule? Mr. Tally-Marks over there was a sailor?"

"Heh," Chester snickered as he attempted to light the cigar between his teeth. "Mr. Tally-Marks. That's good."

"That's the reason you're worked proper," Caradoc said, then smirked into his cup as he took another draught. The others let out a chorus of boos, rejecting his reasoning.

"I don't know if I even believe it," Ink said. "I can't imagine you taking orders from anyone."

"Well, what did you think I did with all that navigational stuff before?" Caradoc asked.

Ink shrugged. "I figured you got lost a lot."

"The way I heard it," Harriet said with a small grin, "the word 'sailor' ought to be applied very loosely in his case."

"That's true!" Chester cried, wine sloshing out over the rim of his glass. "That's all true!"

"There's some ammunition for you, Ink," Abner said.

"Why do you like to get me into trouble, Harriet?" Caradoc said, putting a hand over his face.

"Why? What do you mean?" Ink asked.

"I think you'll find the proper term less 'sailor'," Wendolen answered, "and more . . . what would you say . . . brigand?"

Ink's eyes tripled in size. "You mean . . . *pirate?*"

Caradoc sat straighter and raised a finger. "Technically, the term is 'smuggler'."

"Ha," Simon said. "That's not what your father called you."

"Yes, well my father called me a lot of things."

As the others continued to laugh and joke, Ink looked at Caradoc with new eyes. He saw the sailor plainly now. It was in the way he walked, in his manner, in the way he sometimes threw his gaze far and wide, as if seeing or hearing something beyond the reach of human senses.

"So why'd you turn smuggler?" Ink asked. "Did you fail out of school or something?"

"No," Caradoc answered. "I started out honest, as a matter of fact. Went to work for my father on one of his fleets. He was the most successful merchant in the country at one time. I think he was even considered for a seat on the Assembly."

"Good Lord, Caradoc," Martin said. "You don't mean Ambrose and Sons? Ambrose was your father? His company was the bank's biggest investor. Still is, as far as I know."

"Sons?" Harriet said. "Did you have brothers?"

Caradoc laughed, a note of scorn in his voice. "No. It was just me. Dad thought the name sounded better in plural form."

"So what happened?" Evering asked. "If things were going so well, why'd you leave?"

Ink watched as Caradoc took another sip of wine. Something strange flashed behind his eyes for an instant, then was gone.

"One day, he decided to stop all dealings with the Entrians," he said. "Cut them off entirely, and then rallied a lot of other businesses in the country to do the same. It led to the end of what good remained in our relationship with the Entrians back then. Dealt a serious blow to their economy and put a lot of families into poverty. I couldn't forgive him for that. Couldn't look away as it was being done. And nothing I said could convince him he was wrong, so I left. Found work elsewhere."

"As a criminal," Ink finished.

"It's not as bad as it sounds. I helped run merchandise to Entrian ports along the coast. Didn't have a choice, really. Felt I had to do something to atone for my father's offenses." He paused for a moment, a dark mood threatening to linger over him. "Anyway," he said, waving a hand as he shifted in his chair, "my smuggling career didn't last long. I got a respectable job as a cartographer a few years after that."

"Do you miss it?" Abner asked. "That life, I mean. Out at sea."

Caradoc glanced up at the stars, a sigh leaving his chest. "Oh Lord, do I miss it. The creaking timbers. The canvas snapping in the wind. The light playing on the water. This travel-by-air is a shoddy substitute." He raised his glass to Riva. "Though I'm very grateful for it."

"What about the rest of you?" Abner asked, looking around. "What do you miss the most? Obviously we all miss our loved ones. But apart from that."

A long moment of silence passed before anyone answered.

"The post office," Simon answered.

Riva nearly choked on her wine as she laughed. "The *what?*"

"I know it sounds ridiculous," he said, "but I used to look forward to going to the post office every day. Getting new books in for my students. Chatting with the postmaster. Hearing the town news. It's little things like that I miss. Simple things."

"For me, the walk to work," Martin said. "The bank wasn't far from our home so I could take my time. It was a lovely path down a nice tree-covered lane. There was a bridge with all these vendors and their carts and stalls across it. I'd buy my breakfast there, get a copy of the paper. The streets were always busy with people going to and fro. I always liked that. The signs of a world in forward motion." He looked at his wife. "I know what you miss the most."

She nodded, smiling. "Riding. Over open country at full gallop, on a fine young steed raised properly. Not bred for the racetrack, mind you, but one that's been brought up free, and knows it's free."

Delia sighed. "I don't need much beyond simple common sense and a good rolling pin. But I do miss the farm. The house. The barns. The stables. Not that I don't take pleasure in what we've got here, but my husband and I built our life together on that land. It's where I raised my children. And I miss walking the fields. Watching the summer storms crossing the horizon."

"It's the city we miss," Wendolen said, looking at her sister, who nodded in agreement. "And of course there's nothing in the world like an evening at the opera. Especially if you're the stars of the show. All the applause, the smiles, the flowers and gifts, everyone out in their finest fashions."

"The backstage drama," Josephina said with a sigh. "I even miss the backstage drama."

The group went quiet again, reflecting on their long-lost treasures.

"Well, this might sound even odder than missing the post office," Riva said, "but I miss going to prayers. I know a lot of people don't like to go, but that's mostly from being *made* to go. I always enjoyed it, always felt safe in the temples. At peace. And they were so beautiful. You felt God himself was there, walking the halls and admiring the place right beside you."

"I miss the factories," Abner said. "Those were my temples. The machinery. The sound of the gears grinding. Working by the sweat of your brow and the smarts of your intellect. Nothing like it. I never minded having grease on my clothes so long as there was a wrench in my hand. Suppose I still don't."

"Summer holidays," Evering said.

"What?" Ink said. "Aren't you a bit old for that?"

"I was still in school when we left for Damiras. I never went back. Never finished. But it's not school I miss. I miss what came at the end. The long break of freedom. Nothing to do but whatever you wanted. Even during school, there was always the *promise* of the holidays. And even the promise of them was better than not having them at all. It was something to hope for." He clasped his hands around his arms with a small sigh. "I miss having something to hope for."

Wine glasses lowered from lips. Gazes fell to the fire. No one had realized it before. Or at least, they had never put it to words. But every one of them felt the same way.

"Well," Chester said, removing the cigar from between his teeth. "If you want to know what *I* happen to miss the most . . ."

"Easy now, Chester," Delia warned, raising a hand. "There are young ones among us."

"Please!" he said. "I was merely going to express my wishes through a little poem I learned long ago." He stood and cleared his throat. "I once knew a sweet girl named Cass, who had a magnificent—"

"Chester!" half of them cried out. The other half were beside themselves with laughter.

"Well, *excuse* me!" Chester said. "I thought we were all being honest here!"

"What about you, Jeremy?" Riva asked. "What do you miss most?"

The meek man offered a sheepish smile at the attention. He'd been in equally high spirits, laughing with the others and enjoying his share of good food, but in his usual manner had stayed mostly silent.

"I don't know," he said. "It's hard not to think of loved ones. But . . . I suppose there's the fair. My parents and brothers and me . . . we'd all go to the autumn fair around this time of year. I always liked that."

Ink fidgeted in his chair. He missed knowing what the devil was going on. He missed knowing up from down and left from right. Thanks to the Colonists, he was completely flummoxed, with nothing to do but wait. He slumped back in his chair and wondered if he could get away with sneaking a bit more wine into his glass.

Talk soon turned to what to do with the leftover goose parts. The grease and lard collected would be made into soap. The feathers would be stuffed into pillows. This latter idea got them so excited they decided to make a toast to goose-feather pillows. Then to the soap. Then even to the grease and the lard. The wine ran out soon after, at which point the least inebriated members of the company brought instruments down from the Music House, and the evening frivolity continued with singing. The Plumsleys even honored Ink's victory with a song of heroic deeds borrowed from a favorite opera.

Despite himself, the boy was seen to almost smile.

CHAPTER 27

HOW TO FALL

The darkness swirled thickly, the air heavy and close. All was silent. Cold. Nothing moved. Nothing called. Every light had gone out. Every mind captive to dreaming.

"S-stop . . . stop . . . I can't see you . . ."

A small voice quivered through the stillness.

"Wait! I can't . . . I can't go that far!"

Someone lit a flame and brought it to the bedside.

"No, don't! Don't! Come back! *Come back!*"

"Ink, wake up! Wake up, mate!"

Ink shot upright as someone grabbed his shoulder. He clutched at his shirt, drenched in cold sweat, his heart pounding in his chest. Evering stood by the bed with a candle.

"Good gracious, I've never heard you make such a racket before. You all right?"

Ink leaned back against the pillow and rubbed his hands across his face.

"Do you want me to get my dad?" Evering asked. "Or Caradoc?"

"No! No. It's . . . it's nothing."

Evering blinked and stood back. "All right. Well, everything's fine now. Just a dream."

He set the candle on the washstand, returned to bed, and was fast asleep in two minutes.

For a long time afterwards, Ink sat staring at the flickering flame, hugging his knees and shivering. He fought back tears, tried to think of anything else but the images from his dream. Guilt settled so heavily upon him he felt he could hardly breathe.

It was an hour before he was able to drift back to sleep again, and quite against his will.

~

He spent the better part of the next day trying to forget the nightmare, though it played over and over in his thoughts, voices echoing ceaselessly. The dark feeling of dread had burrowed itself into a corner of his mind, unwilling to be forgotten or ignored. He attacked his chores early that morning with angry vigor, determined to distract himself.

A few hours later, the ground gave out a slight shudder beneath his feet. Jeremy explained that Riverfall was being "anchored", meaning that the four giant propellers in the pipeworks were being shut down to make the village slow to a halt near their desired destination. It became riskier every time it was done, as the pipes always sprung new leaks once the propellers were engaged again.

Once the Colonists agreed upon a finalized list of supplies to be acquired, the members of the raiding party met in Chester's house to prepare. Ink was particularly interested to find himself at the door of the room left of the staircase—one of the few places he had never been allowed to enter.

"I have everything perfectly organized in there," Chester had said. "Can't abide the thought of anyone putting even one thing out of place. So sue me."

Beyond that hallowed door was a large collection of costumes. There were racks of clothing, hats, shoes, wigs, and no meager assortment of accessories. Mirrored dressing tables were scattered around the room, along with half a dozen partitions. The place had a curious smell, a mixture of musty cloth, cheap perfumes, and slightly melted rubber. Ink looked into a tray on top of a dresser near the door. It was full of false noses.

"Welcome, Mr. Featherfield, to my humble domain of true expertise!" Chester spread his arms wide as he moved down the middle of the room. "The ageless art of illusion! The magic of show! The time-honored mastery of—"

"Deceit?" Simon offered.

Chester deflated as his momentous boast was cut short. He huffed a curt sigh. "Yes, deceit. Thank you, Simon. Take a seat, Ink. Anywhere you like."

"Thanks, but I think I'm all right," Ink said, glancing into a drawer of fake teeth.

Chester frowned and put a fist on his hip. "You can't be serious."

"Look, I know the rest of you have to get dressed up, but nobody'll recognize me."

"But this is half the fun of a raid!" Chester exclaimed. "Taking on another identity! Playing a part! Come on, don't you at least want to try anything on?"

"I'm afraid you've got to, Ink," Caradoc said. "Delia and Simon are going as a pair of well-to-do bluebloods. You're going to be Simon's son."

Ink frowned. "What?"

"You can skip the makeup if you want, but you'll have to wear something a bit higher class than your usual things."

"And you need a name," Simon added.

"Pick something you'll remember," Delia said, pinning up her hair. "You'll use it every time you go down. We try never to wear the same disguise twice, but we always use the same false name. It's easy to forget if you change it too often, and we've all got to remember each other's names as well as our own."

"That's no problem for him," Caradoc said. "He's good at answering to fake names, aren't you, Inkwell?"

Ink sneered at him before turning to Simon. "Why weren't you in disguise the day you came to get me?"

"There wasn't time," Simon said. "That Spektor was moving awfully fast."

"Going down like that was one of the riskiest things they've ever done," Delia said, looking at Ink with a grave expression. "There have been a lot of sacrifices made for you, young man. It won't kill you to put on a nice jacket and pair of shoes for a few hours."

Ink sighed. He'd lost that battle before it had begun.

The Plumsley sisters arrived shortly afterward, picked out two armfuls of dresses with nothing short of glee in their faces, then rushed to another room to try them all. As the others took a more measured approach to picking out their apparel, they went over the details of their backstory. Simon would be Wentworth Douglas, a wealthy lawyer from a neighboring town. Delia would be his aunt Fanny, come to help her nephew pick out furnishings for his newly-bought home. Jeremy and Caradoc were to be Christopher Rusby and Tom Rawlings, their ever-faithful menservants. For Ink, they decided on the name "Edward", which was at once posh-sounding and easy enough for everyone to remember.

They attended to every detail of their disguises, from the style and color of the wigs to ensuring their shoes were appropriate for their stations. Ink begrudgingly accepted a pair of polished brown boots with a small heel, along with a green jacket arrayed with large gold buttons. Makeup was next. Simon and Delia's sun-tanned skin would need to be paled, as the Douglas family would no doubt be accustomed to spending most of their time indoors. Ink refused to let even a smidgen of powder touch his cheek, but it wasn't seen as a problem. They reasoned that Simon's spirited boy would have some color from playing out in the garden.

Ink sat slumped in a chair with his hands in his pockets as he watched the others put the finishing touches on their new faces. Caradoc was closest to him, applying a false beard over his own that was much bushier and bristlier. A thick layer of makeup covered most of the scars on his face. Chester came up and dropped what looked like two hairy caterpillars onto the table in front of him. "There's a pair of eyebrows to match your wig."

"You know I hate the wigs. It's like wearing a cat on my head."

"Well? You like cats. And this one hasn't been drinking any water, so put it on."

Ink smirked as Chester moved off.

Caradoc dipped a small brush into a pot of glue and began applying it to his cheek. "You were quite enthusiastic in your work today, Mr. Inkwell."

Ink shrugged, already equipped with a convincing lie. "Tried to finish up early. Figured you wouldn't let me go down 'til everything was done."

"That's all it was?"

"That's all."

Caradoc leaned towards the mirror and pressed the beard to his skin. "Well, good. You had me a bit concerned."

"What for?"

"You had the look of someone trying to push something out of their mind and keep it out. Overworking the body so there'd be no energy left for thought. I know a bit about that."

For a split second, Ink considered mentioning the nightmare. Instead, he looked away and pretended to interest himself in a collection of silk scarves.

An hour later, the rest of the Colonists met them at the door of the Pipeworks House. Abner and Jeremy handed out weapons to the members of the raiding party—all except Ink, who was only told to stay close to the others, despite his protests. Riva made sure Simon's false sideburns were properly glued to his face. Evering double-checked the supply list to make sure bacon had been included. The Plumsleys complimented Ink on how handsome he looked in his green jacket.

They said their goodbyes and wished each other well, shaking hands and exchanging hugs and kisses. Ink would only exchange nods. When Harriet's turn came, she moved forward as if to embrace him, but thought better of it and settled for a gentle hand on his shoulder.

"Are you still certain you want to go? It's not too late to change your mind."

"Oh no, ma'am," he answered. "Been looking forward to it."

Abner and Riva led the way down to the pipeworks. At a fork in the wooden walkway, just a few steps from where the massive propellers stood silent and still, the company halted. Chester and the Plumsleys agreed to go down first to prepare the diversion ahead of time, and Ink listened to talk of "having enough fuel" and "tying off", though he had no idea what it all meant.

After wishing each other a safe journey, Caradoc handed Chester a bronze key, and the two parties each made for the wooden doors on either side of the chamber. Ink held his breath as Delia produced a bronze key of her own and turned it in the lock. These were the same doors Ink had puzzled over ever since he'd arrived, chained with the locks he'd tried countless times to pick. He peered around her as she pushed the door open.

Past the threshold lay thirty feet of solid ground, and beyond that, open sky.

"This is it?" the boy said. "This is the big secret? You just fall off the edge and hope you don't hit the ground too hard?"

"Here." Riva pulled a small object from her pocket and held it out to him. "Take this."

It was a small, round piece of blue glass, rimmed by a wire-thin layer of bronze and attached to a thin chain. The surface was rippled and warped, as though the glass had been cooled too soon after taking shape.

"We call them spyglasses," she said. "We use them mainly to

signal one another. If you hold your thumb to the center, the glass will glow. The ray of light it sends up is only visible through another spyglass, but you can see it from any distance, in any weather."

Ink pressed his thumb to the glass. A pale blue glow appeared in the center, then surged into a brightness so dazzling it seemed he'd caught the sun in a mirror, forcing him to glance away. A moment later, it faded again.

"I never did get the enchantment quite right," Riva continued. "The glow wasn't meant to be quite so blinding. We usually hold the glass between our hands after we've activated it, or tuck it behind our coat or neckline."

Ink glanced down at the object again, then put the chain around his neck. "Well, this is useful. But how's it supposed to help you get down?"

"They also allow us to see through any of Riva's shroud enchantments," Caradoc answered. "Hold it to your eye and take a look through the doorway."

Ink did as he said. "Oh! Blimey! Well that's a better way to fall, now ain't it?"

At the end of the landing was a thirty-foot airship, staked down with half a dozen ropes. The hull was solid oak, and the balloon above seemed to be a patchwork of various fabrics and materials. A small propeller was set at the stern of the ship. Ink followed Simon towards it.

"Did you build it yourselves?" Ink asked him.

"We did. There's one behind that second door as well."

Ink felt a wave of queasiness pass over him. He paused for a moment, lowered the spyglass, and realized he was now able to see the airship with his own eyes.

"You all right?" Simon asked.

"Yeah. I think so. Did the enchantment do that to me?"

Simon nodded. "That was a vast improvement over the first time you crossed it."

Ink dropped the spyglass beneath his shirt. "When I passed out, you mean?"

"Yes. But don't worry. Most people do the first time they walk through a shroud."

Ink followed him onboard. Lanterns hung over the edge of the hull. Crates of wine had been stowed under the starboard gunwales, with tankards of fuel on the port side. The helm consisted of a tiller-like device which appeared connected to the propeller in the stern.

"Are these things usually this small?" he asked. "I thought most normal ones could fit whole crews of people."

"They usually can," Caradoc answered, boarding last. "This one holds only six. We call it Drifter One. The other is Drifter Two, even smaller. Holds only three."

Ink held onto his hat as he craned his neck to look up at the balloon. "You were right to hide this from me at the start. I'll give you that."

Caradoc smirked at Simon.

"That's why you've all got different keys to different doors," Ink said. "So no one person's got access to these things. That right?"

"That's the idea," Jeremy answered.

Ink watched as they lit the burner, spewing gas into the balloon overhead. Delia started the propeller. Jeremy sat across from Ink and showed him a safety rope that ran the length of the hull. "Just in case," he said.

"Why do you call 'em Drifters?" Ink asked.

"Because that's all we could do with them when they were first built," Simon said. "Until we could make them steerable, we were at the mercy of the wind. They still give us trouble sometimes. Evering, Riva and I were supposed to follow Caradoc straight down to the lakeshore the day we found you, but the fuel tank wasn't working properly."

"Oh yes, blame it on the tank, Simon," Delia teased, adjusting the brim of her bonnet.

Abner stepped through the wooden gate and approached the ship. "Ready to go, mates?"

"We're ready," Caradoc answered. "Drifter Two is away?"

"Without a hitch."

"Good."

"Best of luck to you all down there. And don't forget my coal."

He and Riva began untying the tethering ropes. Almost before Ink knew it, they were airborne. Caradoc sat at the stern working the tiller while Delia posted herself at the prow, ready to call out directions as soon as they neared the ground. Simon's hand remained on the switch of the fuel tank, keeping careful watch on the balloon's pressure. Ink glanced back at Riverfall and watched the two figures grow smaller. Riva waved. The mutton-chopped man cupped his hands to his mouth.

"You take care of yourself down there, Mr. Inkwell!"

"My good man!" Ink shouted back. "That's what I do best!"

CHAPTER 28

THE RAID

"Let us walk."

The priest gestured down a long corridor which ran to the far end of the temple. Spindler nodded, and they started on a slow stroll across the stone floor.

The temple was an open place—in both design and principle—consisting of a flat roof, an abundance of pillars, and a broad, shallow staircase which ringed the entire building and allowed access from any direction. It was much the same as all the others Spindler had visited in the past few weeks.

The priest tugged at his silver beard, his heavy brow furrowed. "In truth," he said at last, "it is a word I have not heard since I was a young child."

"So you have heard of them?" Spindler said. "You're the first clergyman I've met in over a dozen cities who's said as much."

The priest chuckled. "How very old I must be, then. I can recall having heard them mentioned in stories and rhymes, most often told to frighten impressionable children. They never seemed to me anything more than creatures of imagination, in the same realm as fairies and ogres."

"I've heard that the Entrians still talk of Spektors. Often with great seriousness."

"It's entirely possible," the priest replied with a nod. "The Entrians have insights into the spiritual world that we Cassrians may never fully possess. But in all the holy texts passed down to us, not once have Spektors been mentioned. And as you may know, the clergy is hard pressed to put our faith in anything outside the written word. Though I've been increasingly moved to believe this a great danger."

Spindler looked at him with a touch of surprise. "Oh, yes? How so?"

"Well, it leaves no room for the possibility of new evils. Just because something did not exist a thousand years ago, or even yesterday, does not make it any less real or true. Who knows how many things have passed in and out of being since the ink dried on the last holy text?"

"So then . . . you believe there's a possibility Spektors might actually exist."

The priest fell silent for a moment, his eyes tracing the ground. "For this, I cannot give you an answer one way or the other. But I would say that a person who makes themselves certain of matters unseen, unknown, and unexplored is a fool."

Spindler smoothed down his hair and glanced to his right as they passed by the altar, shrouded by a dozen silk veils and sitting atop a high pedestal in the temple's innermost chamber. "Now, these tales, the ones you heard as a child, what do you remember about them? Any details on the Spektors themselves? What they do? Where they come from?"

"Well, it was so long ago, I fear I'd give you details too inaccurate to be of any use."

"Anything will help, sir."

The priest sighed and cocked his head. "I remember hearing them described as spirits not at rest. Beings that were once human but who had met their death full of rage and bitterness. They were not demons, and that was always a very important distinction in the stories. They were more fearful somehow, startled easily. Not that it made them any less frightening. They knew well the minds of men to cause torment and strife which, if I recall correctly, was their chief ambition. Instilling a deep-rooted sense of darkness and dread. Planting seeds of despair. Even now I don't find it any less disturbing than when I was a boy." He furrowed his brow again, then shook his shaggy head. "Alas, I can remember no more. You would do better to take the matter to the Entrian priests."

"I intend to," Spindler said.

The priest glanced at him with a raised eyebrow. "You're very determined. Beyond the point of mere curiosity, I think. Have you . . . had an encounter of some kind?"

Spindler tapped his hat against his leg. "That's one of the things I'm trying to decide."

The priest nodded. "In that case, there may be another avenue to seek out. There are always fanatical groups cropping up every now and then, often fading away before anyone knows they exist. People who take it into their heads to worship whatever captures their fancy—stars, trees, beasts, even demons. I shouldn't wonder if there was just such a group devoted to the Spektors, particularly in Entrian society."

"Any idea how one would find them?"

They slowed to a halt as they came to the end of the corridor. The priest shrugged.

"You look in all the wrong places. Being a priest, I'm not too familiar with such things, but I imagine a determined newspaperman wouldn't have to search very long to find them out."

Spindler nodded. He had suspected his investigation would eventually lead down darker, less-traveled paths, but he had been hoping for an easier way all the same. "There was one other thing I wanted to ask. Do you recall anything about a talisman? A sort of gold mark upon the hand. Something to do with having some kind of power over the Spektors."

The priest stroked his beard again. "There are passages in the holy texts which describe angels having symbols on the palms of their right hands, all with different meanings and purposes."

"This would be on the left hand. With the flesh underneath eaten away. Decayed."

The priest's expression became stern. He hooked his thumbs onto his belt and made a quick glance around them. "You have . . . seen someone like this?"

Spindler hesitated for a moment. "No. Not exactly."

The priest's troubled stare darkened. "Such a thing strikes me as an object of outright corruption. Of wickedness. Even if the thing had once been of holy purpose, decay would indicate a perversion of its original nature. I would not stand within a hundred leagues of whatever person or creature carried such a curse."

At these words, Spindler felt the blood drain from his face. It now seemed he had not sent the young boy into a den of lions, but to a place far more infernal. The priest took a step towards him, passing a hand over his face in an effort to lighten his brow.

"Go to the Entrians," he said. "Find out what you can. If you do nothing else, pay a visit to Mastmarner. There they have texts even older than the ones within these walls."

"Thank you, sir," Spindler said as the priest took his hand and pressed it. "You've been more help than you know."

Spindler sighed as he made his way down the stairs. He'd found precious few answers for the effort he was putting into this strange inquiry. It did nothing to inspire any confidence, no matter what the Lady Seherene had said about the value of his aid. The thought of crossing into Entrian territory made him anxious, but he had little choice. It was the next logical step in his hunt for information, though he was beginning to wonder if he was chasing down a long dark hall, only to come up against a dead end at the finish.

A few steps from the bottom of the stairs, a noise of rising volume drew his attention to something farther down the road. A crowd was gathering around a wagon in the middle of the town square, and its three occupants—a man and two ladies—were making great flourishing gestures as they handed bottles to people standing near them. Curious, Spindler began moving towards the scene. The streets were so busy he hardly noticed when a man leading a horse on foot brushed by him a little too closely.

"Beg pardon, sir," the man said, touching a gloved hand to his cap.

Spindler grunted a response and moved on towards the square.

The man led the horse past the temple to a collection of shops farther down the road. Here, he stopped the horse and went to the carriage behind. After opening one of the side doors he brought down a short stair for the passengers, then held out a hand to assist the lady inside.

"Thank you, Tom," she said.

"May I humbly suggest we not hang about for more than an hour? People start to notice missing things right about then."

"Like carriages?" quipped the boy who hopped down after the lady.

"Exactly like carriages. Thank you, Master Edward."

"I hardly think we need advice from hired help," said the well-dressed gentleman still in the carriage, putting on his best air of snobbery. "As you can plainly see, we've done very well for ourselves thus far without your aid."

"Right, sir," the manservant responded, taking the short stair away from the carriage. "I trust you can get down by yourself, then."

The servant on the other side of the carriage snickered as he unloaded crates of wine. The gentleman hopped down onto the road and offered his arm to his aunt, which she took.

"Stay close behind, Edward," she said, then lifted a small sun umbrella above her head.

Ink followed them into half a dozen shops, watching Simon and Delia put on a show of expressing interest in various bits of merchandise. The game was one of distraction. While the salesmen were busy trying to win them over, Jeremy and Caradoc would slip to the far end of the establishment and help themselves to whatever they really needed. If there was a clerk hanging around close by, Ink would put on his most bothersome, petulant air and pepper them with irritating questions. It was also an opportunity for him to put his quick hands to use, for the clerks would often become so annoyed they'd soon find any pretense to escape to the backroom. Sometimes, Simon or Delia would ask for a look at the back stock and instruct their servants to wait patiently in the front. Then, if Ink had already done his job, there was no one to watch as they set to work filling their hands and pockets. Although the Douglas family never made any actual purchases, they always left with the promise of returning, along with a crate or two of wine at the back door.

As the scheme progressed, Ink found himself admiring the Colonists' skills—particularly their brilliant performances. Delia and Simon played up their station with an ever-present air of haughtiness and pride, somehow making the merchants all the more eager to please them. Even the way they carried themselves as they walked along the street prompted others to make way for them. Jeremy and Caradoc were equally convincing, if not more so. They bowed and scraped, keeping their eyes lowered to the ground and their shoulders slumped, spouting off every courtesy to those who spoke to them, including—much to Ink's great amusement—a constable whom they directed to the town square upon his inquiry of the emptying streets.

Chester and the Plumsleys were doing a much better job at causing a distraction than anyone had anticipated. The free samples of wine were attracting attention from every direction, drawing steady traffic into the square as word-of-mouth spread.

And once the Plumsley sisters lifted their voices in song, the entire town seemed to disappear from their homes and storefronts.

With a quarter of an hour left on their timetable, the raiding party split up to obtain the last few items on their list. Delia and Simon made for the local physician's office, while Jeremy, Caradoc, and Ink were left with the wagon, responsible for finding coal. A hotel or restaurant seemed their best bet for the amount they needed, but there was a high risk of being noticed by managers and clerks who were all-too accustomed to keeping a sharp eye on strangers. In the end, they decided to try an unassuming pub down the street.

Curtains were drawn over the windows, but the glow of a hearth fire still flickered inside. The door was locked. Just as they had suspected, it had been temporarily abandoned for the show in the square. Within seconds, Ink made use of his lockpick and pushed the door open.

Caradoc nodded at Jeremy. "Meet us at the back with the wagon."

The place was empty. Cigars still smoldered in ashtrays. Glasses sat half-full on the tables. Caradoc went to the door beside the bar and peered into the back room.

"Furnace room," he said. "Must be two dozen bags back here. Easy pickings."

A bottle clattered to the ground. Caradoc's gaze came to rest on something behind the counter. Ink stepped up beside him and saw a man slumped against the wall with a bottle in each hand. A third one near his leg was spilling out onto the floor.

"Is he asleep?" Caradoc whispered.

The man raised his head and stared blankly ahead, his eyes watery and bloodshot. A soft tap came at the window of the furnace room's back door. Jeremy stood ready with the wagon.

"Don't worry," Ink said. "I'll take care of this."

Caradoc raised an eyebrow. "Oh, you will?"

"Please. I've been doing this since I was a kid."

Ink stepped behind the counter. The man was moderately well-dressed, sporting a pressed pinstripe suit. A new bowler hat lay atop the counter. Ink sat down next to him, righted the fallen bottle, then waved Caradoc away. "Go on!"

Caradoc hesitated for a moment, then disappeared into the back room. Ink turned his attention to the drunkard and cleared his throat.

"Afternoon."

The man did nothing more than grunt.

"Not gone to see the show outside, eh?" Ink said.

No answer. The man puffed out heavy breaths, as though he struggled to fill his lungs with air. He seemed coherent but didn't show the slightest concern over having been locked inside a pub that had just been broken into.

"Everyone else has gone," Ink continued. "Whatcha doing here all on your own?"

The man jerked his head and muttered.

Ink shook his head. "I have to tell you. This don't look too good. You sitting here like this. Up to some mischief, I should think."

"No. No m-mischief," the man said, slurring his words. "My brother's place. Left me the key. All . . . f-fair and legal."

"Right. So what's the story with wasting all this whiskey, then?"

The man's head drooped to his chest. "I c-couldn't do it. I tried. God knows I did."

"Tried what?" Ink took a swig from one of the bottles and choked on the contents.

"Going to the t-temple. You can see it from here. Standing all s-straight and good and honest. But I couldn't go inside. They'd find me out in a second." He hung his head again, then began to cry. "I never meant any harm. I never m-meant any wickedness."

"Oh, come on. It can't be all that bad."

"But you don't know! You . . . don't know!"

There was a sound of scuffling in the furnace room as Caradoc and Jeremy started hauling the coal bags into the wagon. Ink cleared his throat again to distract the inebriated man from the noise, though he knew he probably needn't have bothered.

"So? Tell me, then. What's this thing you've done?"

The man's eyes grew wide. The bottles shook in his hands. "I can't. S-secret, you see? No. Can't tell. Can't tell anyone." His brow wrinkled in anguish, and he let out a sob. "God forgive me. God f-forgive me. She never will. Never."

"Forgive *what?*" Ink said, growing impatient. "Did you cheat someone? Steal? Get a lady in trouble?"

"Poor Margaret," the man said, putting a fist to his eye to wipe away the tears. "I didn't even tell her. Didn't say a word. Now it's too late. And I can't go back. I can never go back." He burst into another round of tears, spilling whiskey down the front of his shirt.

Ink grabbed the bottle away, then took the handkerchief from the man's vest pocket and tried to clean him up. "Aw, brighten up, mate. Get a hold of yourself." He snuck a glance at the furnace room door, wishing his fellow thieves would hurry.

"You wouldn't say that if you knew. You didn't see it like I did. It was there! Right in front of my face! Straight through the f-fire!"

Ink froze. "What do you mean 'through the fire'?"

"I fell asleep . . . with my head on the table. When I woke, there was a lantern in front of me . . ." The man trailed off again. The remaining bottle in his hand slipped to the floor.

Ink chucked the handkerchief down. "What did you see? Tell me what you saw!"

The man shook his head. "I can't . . . I can't . . ."

"Did you see it when you wasn't looking through the lantern? Over it or around it?"

"No. No, only through the fire. And that's . . . that's how I knew . . ."

"How you knew what?"

The man lowered his voice. "It was evil."

Ink's voice began to rise in panic. "When did this happen? When? Was it nearby?"

The man didn't answer. Ink got to his knees and grabbed him by the lapels of his coat.

"Did it happen here? Is it still in here? You've got to tell me!"

"No!" the man cried. "Not here! At *her* place! At Margaret's!"

"Where is she? Where is Margaret?"

"Sh-she lives on the edge of town! Runs a boarding house!"

Ink sat back against the wall. The edge of town. That was far away enough to stay calm for now—but not enough to relax completely.

The man beside him sniffed. "Such a good soul, that Margaret. Or at least . . . was. 'Til I stuck my greedy nose in her business. Oh, God forgive me."

"What are you talking about?"

"Nearly lost everything . . . when she became a widow. Taking in boarders weren't bringing in enough money, so she set up a gambling room. That's where I saw it. That's where it was. Probably s-still there. And it's all my fault. I could've given her more time. Postponed her payments. Reduced her debt. But no! Something had to be gotten out of it for me! And I went and made it a thousand times worse!" He hung his head again and sobbed. "I brought it in! I brought it to her house!"

"All right! All right, just calm yourself down!" Ink said, tired of the man's blubbering and frightened by the possibility of a nearby Spektor. Fortunately, there was a solution to both dilemmas. "Now I happen to be a well-connected gentleman, and I just might be able to pull a few strings to help you out here."

The man looked up at Ink, his wet eyes skeptical. "Really? You'd do that for me?"

"Sure I would. Just don't think it won't cost you nothing."

The man pulled a wallet from his pocket and held it out. "Take it! All of it! Please!"

Ink snatched it up and rifled through the contents. "Boy, you are sloshed."

"You need a p-password. To get into the gambling room. Here." He reached into another pocket and withdrew a pen and a small pad of paper. "Write it down."

The password turned out to be a lengthy dialogue full of keywords and cues. Ink knew it couldn't possibly be accurate, considering the man's state of health, but he humored him and took comfort in the feel of the heavy wallet in his coat pocket. When the task was done, the man sat back against the wall and wiped his brow with his whiskey-drenched handkerchief.

"Now, make sure to put that in a safe p-place."

Ink ripped out the page and made a show of putting it into his pocket.

"Oh," the man said, "and you might need to give her my name. So she knows who s-sent you. It's Lime. Leonard Lime. Write that down as well."

Ink did so on a new sheet of paper, then crumpled it up and tossed it over his shoulder. "Got it."

"Edward," a voice called from the back door. Caradoc appeared and beckoned to Ink. "Time to go."

Ink stood and straightened his coat. "Well, it was nice talking with you, Mr. Lime. Don't hang 'round here all day. Go across the street and get some coffee in you. Oh, and there's some excellent wine outside the back door by now, but wait a while before you dip into that stuff, all right?"

He turned to go, but the man scrambled to his knees, swaying unsteadily as he did so.

"Wait! One more thing! Please!" The man clasped his hands together in desperation, fear filling his glazed eyes. "On my life, whatever you do, p-please . . . don't tell Bill. Don't tell him I spoke to you about all this. Never. God only knows what he'd do to me."

"Bill?" Ink repeated. "Bill who?"

Before the man could answer, Caradoc swooped in, grabbed Ink by the collar, and pulled him out of the room.

~

Delia and Simon had already returned from their visit to the physician's office and were seated in the front of the wagon, which was now loaded with a mound of coal bags.

"Edward, get into the back with Mr. Rusby," Delia said.

Ink frowned as Jeremy helped him into the wagon. "Are we not leaving in the carriage?"

"There's no time to fiddle with two vehicles," she answered. "We've got to make a quick exit. Mr. Rawlings here had to knock out a clergyman who asked one too many questions."

Alarmed, Ink glanced around the alley and spied a bearded man lying prostrate on a heap of burlap sacks. "You laid out a priest?" he cried.

"I just relaxed him a bit," Caradoc said, then swung up into the driver's seat.

They set off at a moderate pace, keeping to the far side of the road as they traveled down the main thoroughfare and into the square. The Plumsley sisters were on their fifth song, with Chester passing out the contents of their twelfth crate of wine. The surrounding crowd was well pleased, charmed by the sudden festival interrupting their daily routines. A few even swayed to the music with their arms around one another. Caradoc tipped his hat to Chester as they passed. Chester nodded in return.

The main road ran under a large stone bridge braced between two rocky hills. Just as the Colonists neared it, the traffic ahead of them came to a sudden stop beneath the archway. People turned and began to hurry off the road, looking anxious and alarmed. Some were even frightened. Delia was the first to see the cause.

"Stop," she said, putting a hand on Caradoc's shoulder.

"What?"

"Stop. Pull us over. Take us off the road. Now."

He urged the horse into a grassy patch a few yards away and brought the wagon to a halt. Ink peered over his shoulder. Ahead, two strangely dressed men stood underneath the bridge, each holding a large white banner that looked as though it were streaked with blood.

"Jeremy, Caradoc, get down. Hide behind the wagon," Delia instructed. "Ink, you stay where you are. Simon, keep your face turned away."

Without a word of question, they followed her instructions. A third man appeared between the banner-bearers, wearing a white robe that appeared to be spattered with blood and carrying a large, ridged horn that twisted upwards at the end. He brought it to his lips and blew out a long, mournful note that pierced through the air and silenced the merriment in the square. Every head turned to the bridge. Ink saw Chester mouth a curse.

The men beneath the archway began to move forward, and it was then Ink saw an entire procession of people following behind. They began a slow march, looking out at the bystanders along the roadside with sorrowful eyes and drawn faces. Each was clothed in a blood-soaked robe, and many were drawing up handfuls of dust from the ground which they rubbed over their faces. The horn blew again. Another answered it. Then another.

Jeremy put his hands to his face. Simon began to tremble. Caradoc's expression turned to hard stone. Delia pulled the brim of her bonnet low over her eyes and tried to remain motionless. Ink edged over to her.

"What is this?" he asked in a whisper.

"Entrians," she answered. "A Mourning Procession."

She paused, hesitating on the edge of her next words.

"To commemorate the day we killed them."

CHAPTER 29

THE BLOODY PARADE

The solemn procession came steadily on. Some of the Entrians walked arm-in-arm. Some held hands. Others had their arms around one another's shoulders. Ink noticed several children among them, all clothed in the same blood-spattered garments. Many had tears in their eyes yet kept a dignified composure. They made no show of loud weeping or sobbing. There was only the sound of the mournful horns as they swept their gazes across the dumbfounded Cassrians on either side of the road. An older woman caught Ink's eye, her lined face drawn in silent anguish, her pained eyes staring straight into his own. He looked away.

After a while, the noise of the horns stopped, and a single voice began to rise from somewhere in the middle of the procession. It was the sound of a woman singing. Quiet at first, almost timid, uncertain. But it strengthened as the song carried on, becoming a raw, beautiful cry of lamentation. Others around her began to join in, their voices intertwining with different harmonies. The tune itself had no words of any meaning—at least none that Ink could understand—but the feeling conveyed was not lost on anyone, and it wasn't long before a few of the Cassrians along the road were wiping tears from their own eyes.

Then, something beneath the archway caught Ink's eye. It was a wheeled platform, moved forward by three Entrians on either side. Atop the platform was an altar bearing a human figure, draped entirely in a cloth of red silk. The Cassrians watched its approach with silent dismay.

As the song ended, the procession came to a halt with the platform in the middle of the square. Chester and the Plumsleys clambered down from their makeshift stage, avoiding eye contact, while an Entrian man climbed onto the platform and stood next to the altar. The city had gone dead silent. No one dared move. Those who had turned their eyes from the disturbing sight could do so no longer, and even the children in the crowd knew better than to fidget or make a sound. The Entrian man lifted his chin, and with a strong, clear voice, began to speak.

"Mothers and fathers. Brothers and sisters. Sons and daughters. Friends and neighbors." He looked around, his eyes making deliberate contact with every face in sight. "Each of us is one of these at the least. And we are each to one another."

A few murmurs of disapproval rose from the watching crowd, but the man continued.

"Many years ago, our two great nations were driven apart. I do not think I err in saying that each side has been the worse for it. In times past we shared in each other's joys. In each other's love and hope. We long to do so again. We long to restore those bonds that were broken between us. Today, we take a step closer towards that purpose. Today, we humbly offer you a part in sharing those things which have struck our hearts so deeply. Our sorrow. Our loss. Our anger."

Ink could not tear his eyes away. It was as though he was being held in a trance.

"Nine years ago we Entrians gathered together on the island of Damiras, seeking an end to the clan wars that were tearing us apart. That island was meant to be a symbol of great promise. Our hope for a peaceful future. A place to repent our sins before the eyes of God as one people. But something else happened.

Something no one could have imagined in their darkest dreams. That day, nine years ago, thirty-three people calling themselves 'The Colonists' decided to make history in their own way. In the very worst way."

Ink stole a glance at Delia and Simon. They hadn't moved a muscle.

"It doesn't matter who they were," the man continued. "Where they were born, how they were raised. Whether or not they said their prayers. What matters is that they struck a blow so grievous, it wounded Time itself, allowing the effects of their terrible deeds to bleed into all the Ages. Defiling the past, mocking our present pains, and staining unborn generations to come."

There were no more murmurs from the Cassrian crowd. No disapproval. They were hardly even breathing. The man on the platform gestured to one of the twisted horns.

"The horn serves to beseech the ears of God to hear the depth of our grief, and to come and heal our wounds." He held out the hem of his garment. "The blood . . . to remember that there is not one among us left untouched by the violence done that day."

He approached the body on the litter and laid a hand on the head. "The burial shroud . . . for our first martyr. A young man by the name of Darian. Many of you can still remember the messages he spread calling for brotherly love, peace and unity. To our deep shame and regret, he was wronged for it. Wronged in rejection. In misunderstanding. But none wronged him more than the ones who ultimately took his life."

The man paused for a moment as he reached inside the altar. When he looked out again, he was clutching two sheaves of paper.

"That day, the number of those on the island was cut down by half. And written here are the names of those who committed not only the crime of murder, but the crime of hate. Of treachery. Crimes against mankind. Against goodness and decency. Against God himself."

Chester sat with his back to the procession, hunched down over the ground as though he might be sick. The Plumsleys leaned against one another for support, their eyes downcast. The Entrian looked down at the papers in his hand, clenching them in his fists.

"Whenever this world loses a soul, it is not only family and friends who are robbed of the joys that person brought to them. You are as well. We all are. Gone is a smile you might have received passing them in the street. Gone is a kind word you might have heard in simple thanks. Gone is a single voice of unique and irreplaceable beauty, forever silenced from the chorus of life." Angry tears began to well in the man's eyes. "And what mocks the memory of those we've loved and lost . . . what brings fresh pain to our deepest wounds . . . is this. Listen, my friends. *The Colonists . . . are . . . free!*"

Almost at once, the heat of anger rose from the crowd. It was almost visible, like a swirling red cloud overhead. Ink felt his cheeks flush with it. He clutched the side of the wagon.

"The Colonists are free!" the man said again. "And their atrocities did not come to an end nine years ago! They continue to murder! They continue to blaspheme and desecrate! And that is why we need your help!" He held up the papers in his hands. "Listed along with their crimes are the names and physical descriptions of every known Colonist. We humbly implore you to help us put an end to these servants of evil, once and for all. Help us to bring the sun to set on that terrible day. And never forget that what tragedy happens to one of us, truly happens to us all."

Ink blinked. There was no more to be said. There was no need to even give it a second thought. Every day he spent tolerating their existence, he was sharing in their guilt, taking part in their sins. And he would suffer it no longer. Without so much as a backwards glance, he jumped down from the wagon and rushed into the throng of people gathering around the platform.

The Cassrians were practically climbing over one another for a copy of the papers being passed around. After snatching up one of the warrants for himself, Ink pushed forward through the crowd. With only a few words he would end the Entrians' torment. He would be a hero in their eyes . . . in *her* eyes. All he needed was the attention of the man on the platform.

"Alas!" the man cried, raising his arms to quiet the crowd. "There is yet another crime to be added to this list. So new there was not time to amend our records. The crime of kidnapping." He reached down inside the altar and pulled out another stack of papers. "One of your own! A Cassrian child! Snatched in the prime of his youthful innocence only a short time ago!"

A cry of outraged surprise went up from the crowd. Ink halted in his tracks.

"Witnesses say the poor boy was tricked into trusting them, then taken away from everyone he ever knew or loved. God alone knows the purpose of this new transgression, but we pray for the boy's safety until he is found again. Let us all be on the lookout for young Anthony Revore. Let us bring this sweet child home as soon as possible, and his monstrous kidnappers to their final judgment."

He handed the new papers down to the crowd. They spread faster than wildfire, the people roused to righteous anger. The Entrian man stepped back to the center of the platform and put a hand over his heart.

"We thank you from the depths of our hearts. We thank you for hearing us. For sharing this burden with us. The wounds we have suffered may be slow to heal, but we need not bear the pain alone. Blessings to you all. And may God grant us justice."

He turned and descended from the platform. The horn at the front of the procession sounded again, and the Entrians were on the move once more. Behind their wake a swell of people swarmed the square like flies, poring over the warrants like precious treasure maps. Ink spied a copy of the kidnapping notice on the ground and picked it up.

Printed in large, bold letters was a detailed—and finally accurate—physical description of him, as well as a list of individuals to

294

contact with any information on his whereabouts. The first was Ivan Mewes of Kinsington Orphanage, followed by Commissioner George Marlas, Deputy Commissioner Frederick Coram, and Mr. Bill Stone. Ink felt a chill of horror.

Spindler. That wretched hack. He'd spilled everything.

He pulled his cap lower over his face, wishing with all his might that he'd taken Chester's offer of a better disguise. He looked back and watched as the procession wound away and out of sight. The sound of the somber horns still resonated through the air, even vibrating through the stones underfoot. Soon his chance would be gone. But his chance for what? He was having trouble remembering now. The only thing he could comprehend were those two words in bold staring up at him from the paper in his hand:

KINSINGTON ORPHANAGE

They would send him straight back once he revealed his identity. Then he would be placed under supervision, watched all hours of the day and night. They would keep him apart from the other children, perhaps even add a few more locks to the outside of his door. And that was the catch. Giving up the Colonists would also mean giving up what freedom he had left. Not to mention the total abandonment of the mission he'd sworn to fulfill. Would the Entrians' promise of honor and glory be enough to ease the torment of such utter failure? He wasn't so certain now.

"There you are, Edward."

Almost before Ink had time to react, an arm went around his shoulders and wheeled him back towards the road.

"Thought we'd lost you for a minute there."

It was Caradoc. His face was even paler than the day he'd returned to Riverfall covered in blood. He lifted Ink up into the wagon. Jeremy helped him to a seat near the front.

"What were you doing?" Delia hissed over her shoulder.

"I . . . just wanted a notice," Ink answered, holding up the papers.

Caradoc cracked the reins and set them off at a near-gallop out of Burgess Valley. From the time they left the square until the moment they set foot back on Riverfall, barely a single word was spoken.

~

It was sunset by the time they finished storing the last of their plunder. The raid had been a success—but hardly a victory. Those who had stayed on Riverfall were unsettled by the dark mood fallen over the returning company, and once told what happened, the darkness spread, casting shadows over every face. Dinner that night was barely eaten. Ink could only stare at his plate, his mind a thousand miles away.

"Was it real blood on their clothes?" Josephina asked.

The others looked up at her, almost surprised to hear a voice after yet another long bout of silence.

"From animals," Riva said bitterly. She looked away and shook her head. "The brutes."

Wendolen fidgeted next to her sister. "And . . . was it really that prophet boy under the covering?"

"Not likely," Chester said. "Probably some kind of statue or something."

"Even so," Harriet said, "how dreadful."

Martin stirred at last, moving his hand from his brow. "Well . . . at least you all got out of there safely. No other problems?"

"No," Delia replied, eager to answer before Caradoc's scuffle with the priest could be mentioned. "Everything else went as planned."

Chester took a sip from his flask. "Would've been out of there ahead of schedule, too, if not for that bloody parade."

Abner shook his head. "Bash's death must have unleashed the full power of their desperation."

"I'd bet my life this was all her doing. That sainted Entress of theirs," Delia said. The look of sorrow in her eyes had turned to anger. "And if parading bloodstained children around in the streets is only the first act of that desperation, what comes next?"

The room went silent again. Ink squirmed in his chair, still wrestling with his actions in the square. For a few brief moments he'd held their fate in his hands. Ready to end it all. Now, he couldn't even bring himself to look any of them in the eye.

"Are you all right, Ink?" Riva asked from beside him.

Ink scratched the back of his head, trying to act casual. "Fine. I'm fine."

"He did us proud down there," Delia said with a small smile. "I never saw someone so handy with a lockpick in all my life."

"He even helped us out of a tight spot getting your coal, Abner," Simon said. "Just how drunk was that man, Ink? Caradoc said he could hardly speak."

Ink frowned. He'd forgotten all about Leonard Lime and his terrible story. He slipped a hand into his pocket. The scrap of paper was still there.

"He . . . just told me about something he saw," Ink replied. "In some woman's house. Didn't make much sense."

Evering leaned forward with his elbows on the table. "Must've been pretty bad to make him drink that much. Did he tell you what it was?"

Ink thought about fibbing, in no way eager to dredge up any more ill feeling in the room. But Riva was watching him too closely. She'd know in a second if he lied.

"Well, sort of. Described it, more like."

"As what?" Riva asked.

Ink fidgeted again, hesitating until he felt everyone's expectant gaze on him. No good playing it off as unimportant now. He cast his eyes to the table, almost ashamed.

"Something he saw . . . behind a lantern flame."

All eyes turned to Caradoc.

The scarred man hadn't said more than two words since

returning to Riverfall, and now sat at the far end of the table with his chair turned to the window, watching the bronze-gold sunset splash across the forest on the border. He returned none of the stares.

"But," Ink continued, "he was so plastered he probably didn't know what he was talking about. I mean, it could've been his own shadow for all the sense he was making."

The table remained silent. It was far too serious a matter to shrug off or let pass. They could only wait for Caradoc's word now. After a minute that seemed an eternity, he drew a slow breath and spoke at last with a voice of utter dejection.

"Where is the house?"

"On the outskirts of town somewhere," Ink answered. "A boarding house, I think he said. Run by a widow who's got a gambling business going on the side. Probably all rubbish. The barmy old coot even had me write down the password to get in." He scoffed as he pulled the piece of paper from his pocket and held it up.

After another long moment, Caradoc lowered his arm onto the table and beckoned for it, still staring out the window. Ink held the paper out to Riva. She took it, then passed it over to Delia, who passed it to Abner, who passed it to Harriet—where it stopped.

"No," she said quietly, clutching the paper in her hand.

The others looked at her, surprised.

"No," she said again, looking at Caradoc beside her. "You can't do this. Not again. Not after all that's happened."

"Harriet," her husband chided, "give the man the paper."

"She's right," Chester said, evoking another round of surprised glances. "Why should he risk his life for some old broad down there? Maybe she brought it on herself. Maybe she deserves what's living in her house."

"Or maybe she's completely innocent," Riva said.

"Whatever the case," Harriet continued, "it's too dangerous. You don't know how long it's been there, or how many there are."

"It doesn't matter," Caradoc answered, still looking out the window.

"It does," she said. "Because every time you come back from these expulsions it seems a little more of you is gone somehow. How long before nothing is left at all?" She looked around the table. "I can't be the only who sees this."

"He's made a choice to help others in this way," Delia answered.

"Damn the others," Chester said, rising from his seat. "Why should he care? Why should any of us care any more?"

"Sit down, Chester," Abner said, trying to calm the situation.

"What about *our* losses? What about *our* suffering? What about laying our lives on the line for all those people and never giving a second thought to whether or not we'd even make it off that island? And did you hear them call us *free*? Did you catch that bit?"

"That's exactly what we are," Delia replied sternly. "Free to make the choices that others refuse to make. That's why we're all here."

With a quick swing of the hand, Chester threw his chair back against the wall. "Please, Delia, please! Spare me the lecture!"

He stalked out of the house, spitting curses between his teeth. A moment later, Jeremy stood from his chair, wringing his cap in his hands as he looked at Caradoc. All traces of his ever-ready smile had long since vanished.

"Don't do it," he said simply, then left the table and walked out the door.

Martin turned again to his wife. "Don't take this any farther. It's his choice to make, not yours."

"How can you say that and still call yourself his friend?" she snapped angrily.

"Stop it!" Riva said, bewildered in alarm. "What's the matter with all of you? I know it's frightening for the rest of us, but hasn't he proved he can take care of himself?"

"That's what I say," Delia replied.

"You're both forgetting a very important factor," Abner said. "This is a house expulsion."

"What difference does that make?" Riva asked.

Simon sighed, passing a hand over his weary brow. "Spektors who decide to anchor themselves in a specific place are a great deal more dangerous to expel. They've 'staked a claim', so to speak, and are harder pressed to leave it. Adding to that is the fact that it usually must be done in a residential area. Not our favorite set of circumstances."

"Yes," Harriet said, turning back to Caradoc. "And how long has it been since you've done such an expulsion? Five years? Six?"

"Seven," he answered.

She kept her gaze on him, hoping the implications would sink in far enough for him to abandon the plan. His eyes lowered at last from the window and settled on the rug.

"We'll wait five days," he said. "The ruckus in town will have gone quiet by then."

Harriet began to shake her head, but he ignored her.

"I'll take a team of four with me. Simon, you'll accompany me to the house, if you will."

"I will."

"Ink stays near me at all times. This is no exception," he continued, scratching his beard. "It'll be our best chance to try to get some answers out of a Spektor, if there's really one down there. Abner, you and Evering will round us out."

Abner nodded. "Of course."

Evering looked between Caradoc and his father. "Really? You're letting me go along?"

"Never to leave my sight the entire time," Abner replied with a look of warning.

Caradoc put a hand over his brow and fell silent again.

One by one, they each took their leave, saying a 'good night' with whatever cordiality they could muster. The Plumsleys excused themselves first. Then Abner and his son. Then Delia, followed by Simon and Riva. Martin went into the kitchen and started washing up the dinner things. Ink was uncertain whether or not he ought to start clearing the table. He looked at the two Colonists left sitting at the far end of the table, wondering if they even remembered he was there.

"Ink," Caradoc said, "show me those papers you picked up."

Ink rose from his chair and pulled the notices from his pocket. He handed them over without a word.

"Good work today," Caradoc said. He folded up the papers without even glancing at them and put them into his own pocket. "Get some rest."

Ink nodded, then turned and hurried out of the Dining House, more eager to leave it than he'd ever been before.

Once the boy was gone, Caradoc finally brought his gaze to rest on Harriet. She sat with her head bowed, her gentle face wrought with sorrow. Her hands were folded together on the table, still clutching the slip of paper. He turned and reached forward, taking one of her hands in his.

"Do you remember the very first words I ever said to you?"

A hint of a smile brightened her face. Her eyes met his.

"Good afternoon, ma'am. My name is Isaac Caradoc. I'm here to save your husband's life."

He smiled gently back. "Could you really deny someone else that chance?"

There was no tone of accusation. No rebuke. Only a simple question which knocked down her reasoning with a single blow. The smile faded from her lips. She looked away.

"Forgive me," she said. "Forgive me for being so weak."

He gripped her hand a little tighter.

"I see no weakness," he answered. "I never have."

With his gloved hand, he reached out for the piece of paper. A silent sigh went out from her heart, and she gave it to him.

CHAPTER 30

THE WEIGHT OF THE WORLD

Things were bad for the rest of the week. The morning after their trip to Burgess Valley, Jeremy was found by the Memory Tree wearing nothing but a long nightshirt and with a forehead bruised and bloody from having bashed it into the trunk. He was so drunk it took three of them to carry him to the infirmary. Ink had been working with Simon when they brought him in. He was a pitiful sight, crying and rocking back and forth as blood trickled down his face. No one admonished him for drinking. They only asked how he had gotten hold of the wine. He claimed he couldn't remember, but everyone suspected Chester was to blame.

By the next day, Chester still had not come out of his house. Even the Plumsleys—his closest companions—could not persuade him to appear, or even unlock his front door. Jeremy remained silent on the matter, but the guilty expression on his face at the mere mention of Chester's name told them more than enough.

Ink and Evering were headed to the pipeworks when they saw Martin, Caradoc, and Abner stride up to Chester's house and demand entrance. When nothing but a long bout of silence answered them, they kicked open the door and let themselves in. The ensuing noise of scuffling and shouting was enough to draw the Plumsleys out of the garden and up to the edge of the stone path.

"What's going on?" Josephina asked before even noticing the broken door across the way.

"Oh, dear," Wendolen sighed, always a few steps ahead of her sister.

Bottles were breaking inside the house amid a string of loud insults and curses.

"Poor Chester," Josephina said. "He only meant to show Jeremy some kindness."

"Rubbish," Evering replied. "He knew better than to do what he did. He'll get no sympathy from me."

"Honestly, I'm surprised this didn't happen sooner," Wendolen said. "God knows it's been eating away at us all for the past nine years."

Ink looked at her. "What has?"

She kept her eyes on the house ahead, her features set in unwavering solemnity. "The misery. The hopelessness. Made all the worse when you remember how useless you are. And Chester feels that just as well as we do."

"What do you mean by that?" Evering asked.

A bitter smile came to her lips. "My sister and I have no delusions about how much we're worth aboard this flying rock. Two fat old ladies who must eat twice a proper share of rations and can't do much more than clip a few twigs all day."

"Come on, Wen," her sister said. "Don't talk that way."

"You two were with us from the very beginning," Evering said. "You stepped up to the frontlines when few others would. That's worth more than what can be measured."

"It's worth a dead man under a cloth. And a few thousand blood-stained robes."

Evering opened his mouth to speak again, but nothing came out. Ink looked between them, disconcerted. The after-effects of what they had witnessed in Burgess Valley only seemed to be growing stronger rather than fading.

Wendolen plucked off her work gloves and stuffed them into her apron pocket. "You should never try to be more than you are. Especially if it doesn't amount to much in the first place." She pulled off her hat and stalked away.

Josephina looked back at Evering and Ink. "Don't worry. She'll be . . . fine."

She gathered up her skirts and hurried after her sister.

The third day, Chester made his long-awaited appearance, showing up to breakfast clean-shaven, washed, sober, and properly shamed. Before the meal commenced, he stood from his chair and made a heartfelt apology, first to Jeremy, then to the others. His manners were impeccable throughout the meal. He even opted for a glass of water instead of wine, which no one had seen him do in recent memory.

Ink spent that day under the direction of the Whistlers, weeding the herb garden, peeling potatoes, and scouring pots and pans. Overall, it was a lighter workload than usual. But what had not lightened was the verbal abuse from Martin. It seemed there was nothing Ink could do fast enough or smart enough. There were even times he knew he'd done a job to perfection but nevertheless had to endure a tirade of criticism. He did his best to bite his tongue, fearing one word would be excuse enough to send the man into another violent rage. Harriet was there to defend Ink at every turn, but her husband only brushed her comments aside. Ink didn't know why she bothered.

The tension came to a breaking point after dinner. While clearing the dishes from the table, Ink put a stack of plates an inch farther away from the sink than Martin would have liked. Anyone else might have thought the boy had just spit on his shoes.

"Hey!" he barked.

Ink's shoulders slumped as he turned around.

"What's this?" Martin said, nodding at the plates. "Are we doing things only halfway through now?"

Ink stayed quiet, avoiding eye contact. Martin stepped towards him, his face full of scorn.

"Does it bloody *look* like I can reach that far?" he jeered, waving the stump of his left arm. "For God's sake. I know you're an orphan but can't you at least *pretend* to be useful?"

Ink felt his cheeks flush. It was all he could do to keep himself from grabbing a rolling pin and beating the man senseless. But as it turned out, there was no need for him to act. Not a second later, Harriet marched up to her husband and slapped him across the face.

Both Martin and Ink stood frozen in utter shock—so rare was it that the tender-hearted woman dare any amount of defiance towards her husband.

"Inkwell," she said, her steel-eyed glare fixed on Martin, "would you give us a moment?"

"S-sure."

"And close the door on your way out."

Ink had heard the Whistlers argue before—usually only small spats lasting no more than a few minutes and nearly always ending with Harriet backing down to appease Martin's temper. This time, however, it was nothing less than an all-out battle. Ink wandered to the back of the Dining Room, dropped into his usual seat at the end of the table, and laid his head down on his folded arms.

It was twenty minutes before the kitchen door opened again. Ink raised his head just in time to see Harriet take up her cane from beside the door and storm out of the house in silent fury. He stood, expecting to see Martin fly out after her. But the man never appeared.

Once again, Ink found himself in the uncomfortable situation of not knowing whether or not he'd been remembered. He crossed the room and stopped at the kitchen door, peering inside. Martin was still at the sink, leaning against it with his hand over his face. After a long moment he stirred to wipe at a corner of his eye. It was only then he noticed Ink.

"You can go," he said, his voice hoarse and dejected. "You're done for today."

Ink lingered for a moment at the door—though he wasn't sure why—then turned and hurried out of the house.

As he made his way back to his own room, kicking at sticks that had fallen onto the path, a sound caught his ear that made him pause. Someone was having a furious go at the piano in the Music House. The melody was strikingly beautiful, but tempestuous, streaming out overhead like a storm cloud. He knew it was Harriet at the keys.

The next morning, Ink went to Delia's house for his day's labor. They spent the first few hours mucking out the cow pen together, fixed a hole in the roof of the chicken coop, then turned their attention to cheese-making. Delia had never been one for small talk, which made it a very quiet morning and left entirely too much time for thinking. And worrying.

As Ink moved a small vat from a shelf to the counter, his eye caught Delia's. The elder woman sighed and set her cheese knife down with a *clank*.

"All right. What is it? You've been stealing glances at me all day."

Ink frowned and dropped his gaze. "Oh. Have I?"

"Like you're expecting my head to catch fire. Do you know something I don't? Did Chester put something in my tea?"

She was teasing now, but Ink didn't much feel like teasing back. Delia's smirk faded when she realized it.

He shrugged. "It's just . . . everyone else has gone a bit mad since we came back from that town. Figured it was only a matter of time before you went off, too."

Delia pushed a wisp of hair from her face. "Well, that's the thing about me, Ink. I don't go off. I'm the sensible one."

She pushed away from the counter and moved to the back window, looking out with a hand on her face. The wind was picking up outside, tossing the long grass in the meadow beyond the cow pen. The fire crackled under the cauldron of milk in the corner of the room.

"Oh, Ink," she said. "We've done it all wrong, haven't we?"

He looked back at her, surprised. She turned and sank into the chair beneath the window.

"We wanted to protect you. Keep you from carrying more than you should bear. Then you go down and see that monstrous parade. Hear all those horrible things. The Entrians could make the Devil himself look like a victim if they wanted, no matter the truth. And the way we've all been acting this week . . . God knows what you must be thinking of us now."

Ink stood silent for a moment, then moved to the window and sat in the chair beside her. "I've been thinking the Colonists ain't gonna make it another nine years. Not by the looks I saw on those faces down there. Or the ones up here, as a matter of fact."

Delia lifted her chin, regarding him with a hint of astonishment. "That's certainly not the observation of a child. Which must mean you're a lot more grown up than the rest of us think you are. Or want to believe you are."

Her face fell with her gaze, and she gave out a heavy sigh. A long moment of silence passed before she spoke again. "Nine years ago, Simon and Caradoc discovered a plot to murder half the Entrians in all of Eriaris, not just on Damiras. But it was to begin on that island, by way of a black spell spoken sometime during the peace gathering."

Ink sat straighter in his chair, stunned. She was telling him. Someone was finally telling him the Colonists' side of the story.

"Entrians have always been forbidden from performing black spells," she continued. "But someone—never mind who—had re-discovered some of the old words. There was also a plot to ensure the deaths of the Elders if the spell didn't kill them off. At the time, it was believed the High Council was the only thing keeping the clans from tearing one another apart, and that without them the West would have fallen into total chaos, possibly even leading to war. Simon and Caradoc rushed to bring their findings to the Elders but were turned away at the city gates when the guards realized they were Cassrians, the times being what they were. They turned next to the Assembly, pleading for aid, and were laughed out of the chamber by all but one politician."

"Who was that?" Ink asked.

Her face hardened. "A cowardly, repulsive, lowlife of a serpent. George Marlas. At first, he seemed an angel of mercy. He offered to provide a ship to get us to the island and vowed to cover all the expenses himself. But he never cared about the Entrians. All he really wanted was the chance to come out looking like a hero. Meanwhile, Simon and Caradoc began the real hard work of gathering a rescue party. My husband Henry and I had long been good friends with Simon's parents and we happened to be visiting them when Simon came to beg their help. His family wanted nothing to do with the matter. But Henry and I couldn't refuse."

"Why?" Ink asked. "What was in it for you?"

Her brow furrowed as she glanced out the opposite window, watching the treetops sway over the garden grove. "Most people are content to let misfortune happen if they believe it has nothing to do with them. Henry and I never could abide that kind of thinking. We had hoped to have at least two hundred fellow rescuers by the time we had to take ship, but when the moment came, there were only thirty-three of us. That, to me, was the first great tragedy of the day. I remember Caradoc didn't even want to set out then, the risk to our lives being much higher with so few of us. But we convinced him to let us press on. And so we did."

"I heard you were in disguise when you landed on the island," Ink said. "Is that true?"

"It is," she answered. "Somehow, Caradoc came into contact with an Entrian Elder who not only heard his story but believed him as well. Unfortunately, he had no success convincing his fellow Elders of the truth. Yet he continued to do what he could to help us. Through his efforts, we gained access to the island, donned convincing disguises, and walked among the crowds without raising suspicion. Some of us went to guard the High Council's tent. Others tried to locate those Entrians whom our Elder friend suspected might have learned the black spell."

She turned her face away, shaking her head as though trying to forget the memory she was attempting to relate.

"I was posted at the tent. I couldn't see much from where I stood. All I heard was a gunshot, a scream, and then everything went dark as night, as if the sun had suddenly dropped from the sky. Before we could react, the High Council's tent was attacked. We could hardly see their faces, whoever they were. There must have been a dozen or so. And of course, we tried to stop them, but we were too late, and too few." Her brow creased in pain as she lifted her eyes to the window again. "The Elders were all killed. Every last one. And then, whether out of panic or intent, the violence spread. We tried to help as many as possible before rushing back to the ship, but it was utter chaos."

She took a deep breath, rubbing the back of her neck as she rose from the chair and paced a few steps away. "The rest you know. We ran from that island as fast as we could, and we've been running ever since."

Ink frowned, sitting forward in his chair. "And what about Marlas?"

Delia crossed her arms. "George Marlas was so terrified after that day—so concerned with saving his own skin, not to mention his reputation—that he went back to the Assembly and told them we had tricked him into coming to the island. He betrayed us, implicating us as the murderers, and even offered to help catch those of us who'd survived, which is why they let him sit there in that cozy office to this day. On his orders, our friends and family members were interrogated, sometimes even imprisoned. They seized our houses. Our properties. Took everything we ever had.

And ever were. Two of our company attempted to return to their families and spread the truth, but no one believed their word against Marlas's. They were turned over to the Entrians and executed soon after."

She wiped at a corner of her eye and leaned back against the counter. "And that's why we've all been going off our heads. The world deemed us guilty, pronounced our sentence, and forced us into exile without any defense. Our one and only consolation is that the black spell was never used. But when you are left to carry the cost of sins you never committed, when you have the weight of the world bearing down on you, after a while, the cracks begin to show. It's why Abner won't leave his work for two minutes. Why Martin acts so beastly. Why Chester breathes alcohol instead of oxygen. We all have our ways of trying to kill what makes us feel it."

Ink tilted his head. "What's yours?"

Delia nodded at the room. "Never giving myself a moment's rest."

Ink's gaze dropped to the floor. He felt worse than he had in a long time. He was never quick to believe anyone's word at first, but neither did he think she was lying. And he had almost given them up—almost turned them over in front of the entire town—and only stopped when he realized they would chuck him straight back into the orphanage.

"So . . . will the others be upset you told me?" he asked.

"I don't believe so," she said. "But if they are, they'll have me to deal with."

She untied her apron, lifted it over her head, and slung it over the counter. Her face was drawn and her eyes were wet. She moved to the door, then paused to glance back.

"We'll leave this work for another day. Put out the cauldron fire before you leave."

He nodded. She turned and disappeared into her room across the hall.

Things were different by the end of the week. Nerves settled, tempers calmed, and everyone was a little kinder to Ink. He figured they'd learned what Delia had told him. Most even seemed relieved. It was one less secret to keep. One more person who knew the truth. Not that they wanted to talk any more about it. Indeed, Ink was not eager to hear any more. Not yet anyway. He was still trying to sort things out in his own head—never mind the approaching Spektor expulsion he was supposed to be worrying about.

The night before the dreaded event, he found Simon and Caradoc on the second level of the tower. They sat on the ground amidst tall stacks of books, leafing through the pages and tossing them this way and that once they were finished. Candles had been lit to supplement the fading sunlight. Ink cleared his throat as he stepped forward.

Simon looked up. His expression softened almost instantly. "Oh. Hello, Ink. Need to speak with your supervisor?"

Ink nodded. Simon glanced at Caradoc, who only picked up another book and began to flip through the pages.

"Isaac," Simon said louder. He threw a book towards him. "Isaac!"

"Mm?" Caradoc grunted, finally looking up through his spectacles. "Oh. You."

Ink jerked his thumb back towards the door. "I got work needs to be checked."

Caradoc looked back down at the book. "That's all over with."

Ink's face lit up. "What? You mean work?"

"No. The checking bit. You know by now what you're supposed to do and how well you're expected to do it. Understand, however, that slacking off will remain strictly forbidden."

"All clear to me, Admiral," Ink said, though without his usual relish of mockery. This was another sudden act of kindness, and from a pirate, no less. He wasn't about to push his luck.

He walked over to the pile of books near Simon and crouched down, looking over the spines. They held such titles as *A Brief History of Industrial Engineering, Physics and Physiology*, and *On Becoming an Effective Orator*. Other subjects ranged from music theory all the way to animal husbandry.

Ink frowned. "What's all this?"

"We're looking for anything that might help us with the Spektor expulsion tomorrow," Simon replied. He tossed another book onto the pile. Ink picked it up, read the cover, then looked back at him with a raised eyebrow.

"'One Hundred Classic Dances'? Ain't you got something a bit more fitting? Holy texts and stuff like that?"

"Holy texts aren't the only way God gives inspiration," Caradoc answered without looking up from his book. "Did you find that one on children's fairy tales yet?"

"Got it right here," Simon replied, thumping a hand on one of the books. "So, Mr. Featherfield, are you ready for tomorrow?"

"I don't even know what to be ready for. 'Specially not if dancing's involved. But then I figure we've got to be all right with you coming along."

Simon looked at him in surprise. "Why do you say that?"

"You're the closest thing we've got to a priest up here."

He smiled and continued his work. "Is that so?"

"Yeah," Ink answered, sitting down on a stack of books. "I mean, you never swear. You never drink. You're always making sure everyone's got their head screwed on straight—"

"It's been a tough week for that one, I can tell you."

"You don't gossip. You don't hardly argue. You even turn down dessert every time we get the chance to have it! Now that just ain't normal."

"There," Caradoc said. "He's pegged you down in three words. Just. Ain't. Normal."

"Have you ever hit anyone?" Ink asked, leaning forward with his elbows on his knees.

Simon sighed. "Where are you going with this, Ink?"

"Just trying to prove my point. It's a simple 'yes' or 'no'."

"How about this one?" Simon said, holding up a book for Caradoc to see.

"What is it?"

"'Big Cats and their Natural Habitats.'"

"That's good. Keep that one."

Ink huffed in frustration. "Well then, what about *thinking* about hitting someone? Have you ever even thought about it?"

"Save your energy, Inkling," Caradoc said. "You'll need it for the big day tomorrow. Now go get some sleep."

"All right. All right." Ink stood and trudged back to the door.

But as he did, every step grew heavier. There it was. That question that kept popping up in his mind, refusing to stay away. It galled him. Mostly because it meant bringing up emotions he didn't want to feel again. Or cause again. But he couldn't help it. He had to know. A foot from the door, he stopped in his tracks with his head bowed.

"What about revenge?"

The sound of ruffling paper stopped.

"What?" Caradoc asked.

Ink still couldn't bring himself to look at them. "Ain't you ever thought about revenge?"

Neither of them answered.

Ink shook his head as he turned back. "All those people telling lies. Setting everyone against you like that. Marlas. Bill Stone. Going after your family and friends. And what about her? That Entress woman? Seherene."

Something flashed in Caradoc's eyes. He set his book down. "What about her?"

"Well . . . Delia says she's evil. That she knows you're all innocent and just doesn't care. And that she wants to see *you* dead above all the others." He frowned in both concern and curiosity. "Is it true?"

The wind whistled outside the tower walls. Caradoc's gaze fell, his brow furrowed and his face grief-stricken. Simon closed his book and moved his worried glance from Caradoc to Ink.

"Go on, Ink. Off to bed now. Big day tomorrow."

Ink turned and pulled the door open.

"Goodnight, Anthony," Simon said.

"Don't," Ink said, quietly but with an undercurrent of anger. "That ain't my name. That ain't me. You got that?"

Simon nodded. "If you say so."

Evering had not yet gone to bed. Ink was glad. It meant he had the room to himself, at least for a few minutes. He washed his face and got changed into his bedclothes, trying all the while to empty his mind of the thoughts swirling around it. As he slung his coat over the bed post, a sound of clanking metal rang out. Something far heavier than brass buttons had hit against it.

An inside pocket revealed the culprit. It was the watch. The one with the mysterious name of "Wickwire" engraved into the case. Once again, he'd forgotten all about it. Goosebumps covered his arms when he recalled how it had seemed to open at his command. How his finger had come away wet from the picture of the sea and singed from a touch of the sun. But of course, that had only been his imagination. Hadn't it?

He tried again to pry it open with his fingers. Pressed the winding crown a dozen times or more. Still, it did not open. He placed it in the middle of his bed and stared at it with a wary eye. Dare he try it?

"Open, Wickwire," he whispered.

His breath caught as the red-gold light flared to life again, spreading through the etched crevices. The case squeaked open. The strange markings on the right side of the watch were just as he remembered. Four rows of small gold circles set in black stone.

But the other side had changed. Ink's hand trembled as he picked it up and looked closer. The fallen sun in the dark sea was

314

gone. In its place was a forest of dead trees, every last one stripped of its leaves and standing in what appeared to be a solid layer of ash.

Ink brought his finger up to the image. Hardly daring to breath, he touched the bottom edge. It felt soft and smooth. He pulled it away, terrified to look. But he did. And there it was—ash on the tip of his finger. He turned and swung his legs over the side of the bed, his heart racing.

Wait. What was this? The picture had changed again. Now he looked upon a huge black mountain, looming high in the distance.

A scratch came at the bedroom door. Ink started, jerking his hand. At the same time, the mountain moved. When the sound did not come again he jumped to his feet, beginning to feel he had just made an important discovery. He turned in circles, facing every direction. It was true. Whenever he turned, the image turned with him. To the east lay the forest of dead trees. To the south, the dark mountain. To the west, the dying sun in the sea of fallen stars.

Turning northward, another astonishing sight came into view. It was a harbor town, set on the edge of the dark sea. Docks ran out to empty ships that lingered in the bay. Ink peered harder at the image. It was impossible to tell if there were any people to be found. It was all outlines and shadows, everything black against the background of a peculiar red light flickering behind it all. Was something on fire?

Movement caught his eye in the center of the image. A figure on a horse was galloping down the beach in his direction, spraying up sand from the beasts' black hooves. He stood still, certain it would pass to his left.

But to his horror, the rider pulled up the reins and came to a stop directly in front of him. As he took a step back, the harbor town grew smaller. His mind began to race. If looking at the images worked as though he were standing there himself, perhaps he could turn and run away if the rider came any closer. He glanced over his shoulder.

Of course. A wall *would* be there.

The rider stood up in the stirrups, their face hidden beneath a hooded cloak.

"What now, clever boy?"

Ink froze in terror, every hair rising on the back of his neck. The voice floating out of the watch was the same one he'd heard that day in the pipeworks as they'd passed through the low clouds. The same one he'd convinced himself he'd only imagined. A woman's voice. The rider regarded him with an air of perplexity.

"Why have you not used the gift?"

Ink couldn't answer. He'd forgotten how to speak.

"Name your enemy," the rider said. *"Name your enemy . . . and live forever."*

Suddenly, Evering rushed into the room and slammed the door behind him. The watch flew up into the air. Ink fumbled for it and snapped it shut, then hurried to the bedpost and shoved it into his coat pocket. His heart was in his mouth.

"That damned infernal cat!" Evering said as he stalked in. "It was waiting for me outside the door! I told you that thing has it in for me!"

Ink couldn't respond. He was too busy trying to recover from the heart attack he was sure he was having. Evering glanced at his face as he moved around him to the wash basin.

"You all right?"

"Y-yeah. I'm . . . I'm fine. You startled me is all." He got into bed, turned towards the wall, and pulled the covers over his head.

It was a trick. It was just a trick. Like the changing appearance of the watch's case, the rider and her strange surroundings were only a bit of enchantment. A clever illusion. It was a joke. A hoax. That was all. Nothing more.

CHAPTER 31

MOMENTUM

In the weeks following her visit to the Great Hall, Seherene had traveled the North Country with Pallaton and Drystan, meeting with various Colonist-hunters to inquire after their progress and ascertain if there were any new leads. Most had been Entrians, chiefly upon Pallaton's insistence that they were far more likely to be successful in their task. Seherene did not bother to waste any significant energy arguing this point, especially since she knew the result would be the same no matter whom they spoke with. And indeed she was right. No one had anything new to report. Everything had gone quiet again.

They were now headed back to Ciras to report their findings to the High Council. Seherene was not particularly eager to return. The news they brought was difficult enough—from the worrying prospect of a Spektor assassin to a Cassrian boy kidnapped by the Colonists—but there would also be a tremendous increase of pressure to keep the momentum of action going, to be plotting their next tactics and strategies, and to bring another great victory hard upon the first. Because of this, she had resolved to make the most of every free hour afforded her during the course of the return trip, enjoying whatever small comforts and quiet moments which might help her to unwind.

Fortunately, the private parlor of their vessel was a perfectly lovely place to spend an idle evening. Seherene had gone every night to sit by the fire with a cup of tea or a glass of wine and read. Pallaton and Drystan often joined her in the room, usually for a game of cards or billiards. Tonight they had settled on the latter. At the top of every hour, an attendant would appear to offer more refreshments and sometimes to change out the wax disc spinning on the phonograph in the corner. At the moment, a jangly piano and reedy violin were playing a slow, sweet waltz.

She knew the tune. The last time she'd heard it, she was happier than she had ever been. It transported her instantly to that time and place, so vividly that she soon forgot all about her correspondences and fell to gazing at the hearth fire instead. The grief that quickly followed was acute, but she tried to focus on what fond sentiments the memory had first brought to mind, determined to keep as much of the bitterness at bay as she could.

"Anything interesting?"

Pallaton's voice brought her back into the present, but it was several moments before she realized he was referring to the letters in her lap.

"Oh," she said, "all interesting, to varying degrees." She picked up the first one and reviewed the contents. "Mr. Stone writes that there has been no revenge killing following Mr. Bash's demise, so that's something to be thankful for. He says he'll likely stay in the North Country a while longer and then make his way west."

"Splendid," Pallaton replied, resting his cue stick on his shoulder. "And does he mention any particular places I'll need to avoid in the near future?"

"Really, Pallaton. Do you not feel even the smallest ounce of gratitude towards him after all he's done? How many Colonists has he brought in for us, Lord Drystan?"

"Five on his own. Ten if you consider he led the group who acted on young Mr. Coram's tip."

"I can be grateful enough," Pallaton said, "so long as I don't have to speak to him again. I swear if he thought any more highly of himself he'd make people kiss his hand before addressing him."

Drystan laughed. Seherene turned to the second note in the small pile.

"I've also had a letter from Mr. Spindler. He writes of his intent to seek out any fanatical groups who might have an interest in the Spektors and possess insight into their behavior. Lord, I dread the very thought of such people existing."

"I dread the thought of relying so heavily on Cassrian informants," Pallaton said before taking his next shot with the cue. "They don't even believe in the Spektors, which proves their insight and judgement are far more limited and therefore of little worth. They are like children blundering about, merely playing at being adults in a world they don't truly understand."

"Until they bring us ten Colonists in custody," Seherene shot back with an arched eyebrow.

"Several of which," he continued, "were undoubtedly apprehended with no small amount of luck. Wouldn't you agree, Drystan?"

"Oh, no. I'm staying out of this one."

"Little worth you say," the Entress continued, "yet here we sit in a ship of their own invention and design, listening to their remarkable musical device, while you and Drystan play for the third night in a row at a game they created. Or were these also done with no small amount of luck?"

Pallaton responded with a look of annoyance, which pleased Seherene so much that she smiled as she enjoyed another sip of wine.

"Well said, my lady," Drystan replied. "But along with such praises of their inventiveness, surely there must also be a degree of pity. It is painfully obvious that these creations are merely an effort to make up for what they lack. They can pray all day at the altars of science and technology but they will never know the privilege of true power."

"I heartily agree," Pallaton said. "You could not compare a

hundred of their crude devices to the splendor of even one enchantment."

"Oh, yes, they are terribly splendid," Seherene answered. "And what have we been doing with them? Staving off inconveniences, supplementing our indolence by wielding them for even the smallest tasks, and—correct me if I am mistaken—using them to kill one another up until ten years ago."

Pallaton answered with a shake of his head. "With such opinions as these, I wonder that you return to the West Country at all. You ought to find a nice little home in Altan. You could chat with your friend Commissioner Marlas every day."

She winced at the suggestion. "Oh, don't even think of it."

"Or perhaps go even farther to the lawless East," Drystan said, smiling. "You could set yourself up as a pirate queen on some distant island, never to bother with your foolish Entrian brethren ever again."

"Now that is a far more appealing prospect," she replied, then tapped her chin with an exaggerated expression of reflection. "In fact, I'm half-tempted to tell the captain to turn the ship around right now."

Pallaton nodded at Drystan. "Now you've done it. She'll think of nothing else for the rest of the journey."

"Not just yet," she said. "Not until I've thoroughly routed your assertions of Cassrians being worthless."

"Oh, so you have more for me, do you?" he asked, turning to her with a fist on his hip. "Pray tell. I am all a-quiver to hear it."

"Only this." She lifted the letter again. "That Mr. John Spindler has become our one and only link to our one and only lead. If that boy really has been taken by the Colonists—and there is every indication of this being the truth—then he is the beacon which may lead us straight to all the rest of them. We must be watching for him in all places at all times."

"*If* they have taken him," Pallaton said, "the truth of which hinges on the claim that he really was attacked by a Spektor. But Spektors do not attack children."

"The Spektors have been around for two thousand years," she replied. "I am not sure anyone can say anything absolute about such creatures unless they had been there from the beginning. For all we know, they are stirring up new evils all the time that we have not yet heard of."

Drystan glanced down at the billiards table with a troubled frown. "That is a logical conclusion. Terrifying, but logical."

Pallaton rounded the table and studied the trajectory of his next shot. "Well . . . despite my perfectly reasonable doubts, I do hope you're right about all this. Nine years is far too long to be chasing anything without regular success."

Drystan nodded. "I wonder how the Mourning Processions were received. That was six days ago. There should be some word of the results by now."

"Fortunately, Mr. Spindler has answered this as well," Seherene replied. "He was in Burgess Valley six days ago and witnessed a procession first-hand. Apparently it was done to great effect. He says he never saw so many people so quickly roused to grief and anger all at once. There were eight new recruits to the Colonist-hunters' ranks. Daily prayer gatherings specifically for the cause were established in the local temple. And the warrant list now hangs in at least one window in every house across town."

"Fine sentiments," Pallaton said. "I only wonder how long they will last."

"Perhaps we ought to go and see for ourselves," Drystan replied. "It's only been a few days since we sailed past Burgess Valley. By the time we return to it, we might be able to get a good sense of the effect's longevity. Decide if it is an approach worth continuing."

"No objections from me," Seherene said. "But I'm afraid you may have a difficult time convincing our friend Pallaton. Every moment east of the Lockhorns is a torment for him."

And of course, she would not say how very eager she was for any opportunity to delay their return to Ciras.

"I do not deny it," Pallaton said with a sigh. "But I have also been in the legal profession long enough to know that there is a time to fight and a time to bite one's tongue—most especially whenever outnumbered."

"Speaking of the legal profession," Drystan said, "did you ever consider the field yourself, Lady Seherene? You held your own very well against us just now. I think I should like to see you making a case in the inner ring of a court some time."

She laughed. "Thank you for the compliment, but I'd much rather go the way of the pirate queen before then. Honestly, if it were up to me, I would have a profession as far away from law and judicial matters as humanly possible."

"What?" Pallaton said with a teasing scoff. "Are you trying to tell us that your highly-honored position with all its great power and influence, all its boundless glory and distinction, is entrusted to you against your will? Now that I could never believe."

She maintained her smile until he glanced away, then let it fade until all that remained was a half-hearted expression of geniality, signaling her unwillingness to continue the subject. Fortunately, she was soon aided by the entrance of another attendant who had come with his hourly offering of drinks and sandwiches.

"Ah, perfect timing," Drystan said to him. "Would you fetch your captain to come and speak with us? We require a change of course as soon as possible."

The attendant acknowledged this and offered a small bow before retreating to fulfill the request.

As Pallaton and Drystan once again gave their full attentions to the game, Seherene returned to her letters. She had been relieved by Mr. Stone's, heartened by Mr. Spindler's, but disconcerted by the third. She would not share it with the others, not least of all because it would likely prove to be a conspicuous flaw in her defense of the Cassrians.

The letter was from Deputy Commissioner Frederick Coram. Most of it consisted of cordial pleasantries and flattering encouragements of her continued success. At its conclusion, however, were two small lines which gave the message its only real worth.

As to the woman who begged your assistance on the steps of the Great Hall, I can now give you complete assurance that her claims of having no trial were entirely false and that her guilt over aiding the Colonists was confirmed in a fair and legal hearing. She serves a thirty-year sentence.

Reading it a second time, Seherene felt her sense of disconcertion turn to anxiety. She had seen no lie in the desperate woman's eyes. Heard nothing of it in her voice. But in Coram's letter—though they were many miles apart and she could not reasonably assert her suspicion—there was an air of falsehood. It was nothing very specific, and certainly nothing she could make either one of her lawyerly colleagues see or support her by. It was only a feeling. A vague hunch. But one so persistent that she hoped—with all her might—that she was terribly, terribly wrong.

CHAPTER 32

MARGARET'S HOUSE

The good citizens of Burgess Valley were not as disgruntled as the Colonists had expected to find them. The Mourning Procession had laid a heavy air of grim sobriety over the town, and finding they'd been robbed in the self-same hour did nothing to ease that ill-feeling. But their collective outrage died away almost as soon as it had begun. No one could help but be pleased by the gifts left at their back doors, and many declared that the crates of high-quality wine far outweighed the value of the stolen goods. The pub owner in particular was thrilled to receive his generous share at the cost of only a few bags of coal. The chief constable even declared the crime spree to be nothing more than a "well-orchestrated act of mischief", though many attributed this leniency to the half-dozen crates left at the station house.

By now, everyone had made the connection between the robberies and the smooth-talking showman who'd passed out 'free samples' with his opera-singing assistants. But no one in their wildest dreams suspected the Colonists were to blame. Not in their town. Not when arrest warrants were now hanging on every lamp post and in every window. Not when sketches of the poor kidnapped orphan graced the front page of every newspaper.

They had even gone so far as to hang a huge banner over the main road that read *BRING ANTHONY HOME*.

"Well," Simon said, pulling his cap lower over his eyes, "whatever we might think of the Entrians' new strategy, it was certainly an effective one."

They were back in disguise, this time dressed to look like common workmen searching for jobs in town. Ink, Simon, and Caradoc retained the false names from their last visit, and Abner and Evering had become Walter Fleck and Charlie Watkins—the latter of whom finally bore a full beard on his face with the aid of an adhesive. They carried three lanterns among them, hidden inside knapsacks.

After receiving directions to the boarding house, they started down a street which led them out of the main part of town and toward a collection of smaller houses set apart by swaths of pasture. The workday was fast coming to an end. Farmers brought in their cattle from the fields. Children were called in to supper. Sheds were locked and barns latched. It was time to rest. Time to put aside all worries for another day.

If only the same could have been true for the Colonists. They were nervous wrecks, each busy imagining all the terrible and frightening things that could go wrong during the impending expulsion. Abner kept mopping his forehead with his handkerchief. Simon was rigid with tension, his eyes constantly darting around for signs of trouble. Evering was even paler than usual and walked with his eyes fixed on the ground, clenching his hands inside his jacket pockets. Ink kept adjusting his fake spectacles and fidgeting with his cap. After seeing his name on the kidnapping notice, he hadn't hesitated to don a complete disguise this time. He even allowed himself to suffer the indignity of wearing a wig, though the curly locks kept falling into his eyes. At least it distracted him from the rising collective fear.

Well . . . nearly collective.

"Oh, look at this!" Caradoc said, bounding back to them from the side of the road with a small pink flower in his hand. "These are called Stag's Heart. They're the only wildflowers in this part of the country to survive all year round. Even under a foot of snow. Amazing little things."

He'd been like this all day, pointing out minute details in nature with great delight, complimenting a flower seller on her hat, even rejoicing in the lowered prices of cotton in the business section of the paper. He whistled snatches of merry tunes as they walked along and tipped his cap with a friendly smile to anyone who looked their way. The others couldn't comprehend how a man who would soon risk death at the hands of a Spektor could be in such high spirits. Yet here he was, marveling at the wonder of a tiny pink blossom.

"We should try to grow some in the village," he said, putting the flower into his waistcoat pocket. "We'll have to pick up a few seeds the next time we go for supplies."

"What—by all that is holy—is going on with you?" Simon said, unable to bear it any longer. "Yesterday you were acting as though you wouldn't live to see another sunrise. Now you're behaving like we're on the way to a garden party. You're not cracking up, are you?"

"It's that neckerchief he's wearing," Abner said. "Cutting off the blood to his brain."

"Aren't you nervous at all?" Evering asked.

"What's there to be nervous about when you're all here with me?" Caradoc answered with a grin, putting his arms around Simon and Evering.

"Oh, no," Simon said with an expression of dread. "Please, *please* tell me you didn't decide to do this drunk."

Caradoc laughed and took his arms down from their shoulders. "Not this time."

Ink shook his head and hit Simon in the arm. "Forget the lunatic for now. Have you got the password down? You remember what you're to say? And what answers to wait for?"

"I think so. Yes."

"Best go over it again now," Abner said. "Just to be sure."

Simon nodded. "All right. When we get in, I'm to say, 'I understand you're in need of a house carpenter'. Then, if we make it past the first test of scrutiny, we're presented to the owner of the place. The widow. What's her name?"

"Margaret," Ink said, pushing the wig out of his eyes again.

"Margaret. Right. Then she'll say, 'Well met. It's been a long time since I last saw you.' Then I say, 'Well met, ma'am. Uh . . . I've been at sea, on errand to' . . . where was it?"

"King's Island."

"King's Island . . . where I might have stayed . . . but . . ." He narrowed his eyes and twisted his mouth. "Oh, what's the rest?"

"But I missed my loved ones too much," Ink finished.

Simon nodded. "Yes. I missed my loved ones too much."

"How sweet," Caradoc said.

Simon ignored him. "Then she's to say, 'It's good to have you back again.' And then she lets us through to the gambling room."

"And remember," Ink said, "if she changes that last line, it either means you screwed the whole thing up too horribly, or it's not safe to go in."

"Right."

"And another thing. The exact order of words ain't important. Just key phrases and meanings. Like that 'well met' bit at the beginning."

"Blimey, Ink," Evering said, "you could give lectures on password strategy."

Ink tucked his thumbs into his belt. "Who says I haven't?"

The shadows reached out over the fields as they continued down the lane. Hearths and lanterns blazed to life inside parlors and dining rooms, and still they hadn't seen the house. It had been described as a two-story residence, painted white, with a sign at the front gate. But as time wore on they began to wonder if they hadn't misheard the directions.

A little while later they passed by an old man sitting outside his front door, smoking a pipe. He nodded to them and called out. "You boys looking for Margaret's place?"

"We are," Abner called back.

"Almost there," the man answered. "Another six houses down. On your right. Just be sure to head for home before your pockets run dry."

As they continued down the road, the feelings of nervous anxiety began to build again.

"Ink," Simon said, "what else did that man at the pub say about this Margaret person? What else do you know about her?"

Ink shrugged. "Just that she's an old widow, and that when boarders weren't bringing in enough money to pay her debts, she turned to the gambling business."

"If we lived in a decent world, they'd cancel widows' debts," Abner said. "Shame she had nowhere else to turn. Shame the banks wouldn't help her. And what if she gets caught, the poor woman?"

"Doesn't seem like much of a secret," Caradoc said, glancing back at the man on the porch.

"And did you see the look that woman gave us when we asked for directions back in town?" Evering said. "Practically turned her nose up at the mention of the place."

"Yes, well it's all too easy for the so-called 'good folk' to judge," Abner answered. "Especially the ones who've never been close to losing everything they've got."

In another minute, the house came into view. They stopped in front of the fence, noting the sign posted on the gate:

MARGARET'S BOARDING HOUSE
ROOMS TO LET

Simon looked at Caradoc, who was staring at the house with a thoughtful expression.

"Anything?" he asked.

Caradoc nodded. "Oh, yes."

An air of dread fell over them all.

"I can't tell how many," he continued, "but the anchor's been set here at least a year. Maybe longer."

He pushed through the gate and started towards the house. The others began to follow, but froze the moment they set foot past the fence line. The world had gone silent. There were no crickets chirping in the tall grass. No night birds making calls from their roosts. No wind through the trees. It was as though a heavy blanket had suddenly settled over everything, muffling all sounds of life. They were used to this kind of quiet on Riverfall, but down here, it was outright disturbing. They started forward again with cautious steps. Evering's hands shook so badly the lantern rattled inside his knapsack.

"Damn," he said. "I was hoping there'd be nothing to find here."

Ink glanced back at him. "But you've done this before, haven't you?"

"With free-rein Spektors, yes. Those that go where they please when they please. Expulsions are like . . . hunting a lion. If it's out in the open, you can run and hide if it comes after you. You can keep watch on it from a distance. But this . . . this is like going after a lion in its own den. That's an entirely different game altogether."

Ink felt his mouth go dry. Why did he have to keep asking questions?

"What if she recognizes you by your hand?" Abner asked Caradoc as they neared the front door. "It's described in all the warrants."

"We'll just have to risk it on the fact that most people don't usually read the fine print. Especially a widow who's got more pressing matters to worry about. You ready, Simon?"

"As ready as I can be."

Caradoc stepped onto the porch and turned back to them. "The rest of you keep watch here. Space yourselves out so you can see anyone approaching from any direction. And try to look casual, at least until we've got the house clear. Don't light your lanterns 'til then, either."

"Don't worry about us. We've got it handled," Abner said. "Just make sure the two of you come out again in one piece."

"Ink," Caradoc said, "the Spektors here are fixed on the people inside the house. As long as you don't draw attention to yourself, they won't know you're here. Stay near the others, but if anything goes wrong, you yell for us. Scream your bloody lungs out. Understand?"

Ink felt like curling up into a ball and hiding, much as he'd done in the rundown shack near Edgely Hill. But this time, he swallowed past his fear and nodded. Caradoc stepped up to the front door and put a hand on the knob.

Suddenly, what little daylight remained went dim, as though a veil had been drawn over the sun. A vibration went through the air like an electric shock, pricking up the hair on the backs of their necks. The air became so thick and heavy it was harder to breathe. The foundations creaked and shuddered as a slow, deep groan issued from the house.

"Well," Caradoc said, raising an eyebrow, "someone knows I'm here."

The next moment, the world went back to normal. The air lightened. The dark shadow passed away from the sun. Everyone could breathe again. Ink's heart raced in fear, and he wondered how fast he could run back to the Drifter.

"Oh, look!" Caradoc said as he pushed through the front door. "She's got Stag's Heart growing around the house here. Isn't that lovely?"

"I feel safer already," Ink muttered.

Once inside, Simon and Caradoc found themselves in a quaint, well-kept place full of decorative touches which lent an air of easy

330

familiarity. Simon felt as though he'd just set foot in his old family home again and half-expected to see his mother come rushing towards him from around the corner. They stood at the front of a long hall set with doors on either side. A tidy little parlor room was visible through an open door on the left. To their right, a small desk sat near the foot of a staircase. They stepped forward, removing their hats.

"Hello?" Simon called out.

A girl emerged from one of the doors farther down the hall. She approached them with her hands folded in front of her.

"Good evening, gentlemen. How may I help you?"

Simon cleared his throat, his mouth twitching up into an uneasy smile. The test had begun. He worked to control his nerves, determined not to make a mess of it.

"Will you be wanting a room?" the girl asked when he did not answer right away.

"Uh . . . no," he replied. "I . . . or . . . rather *we*, that is . . . we understand that, uh, that you're in need of a h-house carpenter?"

He ended weakly, unable to remember whether the line was supposed to be a question or a statement. He held his breath, hoping the blunder hadn't cost them their chance.

"I will fetch my lady, sir. Wait here."

After a small curtsey, she disappeared through a door to their right. Simon breathed a sigh of relief. Caradoc whacked him in the shoulder with his hat.

"You are *the* worst liar I've ever known in my life. We should've had Ink do this."

"I'm sorry. I don't have a lot of experience with these pass-word situations."

"Just relax."

Simon nodded, then shifted his weight to his left leg and stood with a hand in his pocket, trying to affect a casual air. "I just hope I won't have to shout to make the old bat hear me."

A moment later, the door opened, and the old bat herself

331

came into the hall. As Simon turned to greet her, the smirk dropped dead away from his face.

The woman who stood before them could not have been more than thirty years old. Her blonde locks were swept up into a pretty, modern style, and a pinch of red on her cheeks drew attention to her sparkling blue eyes, brimming with energy and intelligence. Her graceful poise and composure were so well-polished it was as though she had come to greet royalty.

"Well met, sir," she said, studying them both with a practiced eye. "Long has it been since last I saw you."

The timbre of her voice was like liquid amber, dulcet and rich, enough to lay a spell with a single word. Or so thought Simon. He stood staring, too overcome to remember where he was or what he was supposed to be doing. Caradoc hit him in the back of the shoulder again. Simon blinked and shook his head.

"Uh . . . well m-met, madam. I . . . I . . . uh . . ."

The so-called priest let fly a sudden curse in his frustration. Caradoc brought a hand to his brow. A tiny corner of the widow's mouth turned upward.

"Forgive me," Simon said. "I . . . oh! Oh yes. I-I was at sea . . . uh . . . on a ship . . . uh . . . well, of course on a ship. For a long time. Don't remember how long, exactly." He chuckled nervously. "The sea air will do that, I suppose."

He fell silent again as he struggled to remember the rest.

"And," she said, trying to help him along, "you have come from . . .?"

"Oh, yes!" he said. "From King's Island. Yes. That's it. And I-I might have stayed there, but, uh . . . but . . ." His mind went blank again. Beads of sweat popped out onto his forehead. He cleared his throat. "I . . . I, uh . . ."

Both Caradoc and the widow looked at him with encouragement, urging the poor sap to finish the last line.

"I can get this," he said, raising a hand. "I can. Uh . . . I might have stayed, but . . ." He squeezed his eyes shut. "I, um . . . uh . . ."

Caradoc couldn't take it any longer. He leaned around Simon.

"We'd like to visit the illegal gambling room, please."

The woman smiled wide, barely containing a burst of laughter.

"Of course," she said, more than willing to mercifully cut the scene short. "Follow me."

She turned and led the way into the parlor. A large, unusually wide grandfather clock was set against the wall on the far side of the room. She went to it, pulled open the front casing, and stood aside, revealing a passageway where the pendulum, weights, and pulley system ought to have been. Caradoc passed through first. Simon hung back, shaking his head in embarrassment.

"I-I'm so sorry."

"Don't worry," she said, chuckling. "You're not the first to have mucked it up."

The gambling room was an impressive size for a hidden chamber. There were half a dozen tables topped with cards, coins, and dice, each with four or five patrons sitting around them. The room was hazy with the smoke of their pipes and cigars. A hearth at the back of the room blazed brightly.

"Here we are, gentlemen," the woman said as she closed the passageway behind her. "The room is open until half past midnight. Anyone refusing to leave by then will be banned from the tables indefinitely. We do not supply alcohol here but you are welcome to bring your own in the future, so long as nothing gets out of hand. I must also ask that you turn over any weapons you may be carrying."

"Oh, we carry none," Simon said. He and Caradoc opened their coats to prove it.

"Well enough," she said, nodding in satisfaction. "There's no fighting or threatening of any kind allowed here. At the first instance of such behavior you will be banned from the tables."

Caradoc moved away as she spoke, cocking his head this way and that as though listening to a noise no one else could hear. The widow glanced at him quizzically for a moment, but continued her speech to Simon.

"If you're accused of cheating by no less than two separate witnesses, you'll be banned from the tables, as well as at the first suspicion of theft. Is that understood?"

"Absolutely," Simon answered. He hadn't heard a thing.

She looked over at Caradoc again, who was now running the tips of his fingers across the wall as he walked alongside it. At one point, he put his ear to a space near a wall sconce. The gamblers at the tables were too engrossed in their games to notice him.

"I'm . . . Margaret," she said, frowning at the strange actions. "Call on me if you have need of anything."

"Thank you very much. You are most kind," Simon said, using an eager tone to try to catch her attention away.

She looked back at him. "And you are?"

"Wentworth Douglas."

"And your curious companion?"

"That's Tom. Tom Rawlings. He's harmless. Had a little too much of the sea air as well."

She watched as Caradoc withdrew a compass from his coat and stood in the middle of the room, frowning down at it as he turned in different directions. She looked back at Simon.

"Does he still think he's at sea?"

"Oh no. He just . . . likes to keep track of where he is. So! This is a very nice place. We were admiring the flowers out front before we came in. H-have you lived here long?"

"Long enough."

"Ah," Simon said, nodding as if her answer had been informative. "Yes, well . . . we're actually looking to buy a place like this sometime soon. Run a little business of our own. Would you be able to give us any advice on the matter?"

"What's he doing with that feather?"

Simon looked back at Caradoc. He was down on one knee, staring hard at a small gray feather between his fingers.

"Oh, that's just a little good luck ritual he does before hitting the tables. It's nothing to worry about." Simon winced. This wasn't working. He had to try something else. "By the way, I'm . . . I'm very sorry for your loss."

She looked back at him, perplexed between the two distractions. "My what?"

"Well, we were told you were a . . . widow. I'm sorry for your husband's passing."

"Would you excuse me?"

She began to make her way through the tables towards Caradoc, who was now on his hands and knees with his head in the fireplace. Simon cringed as he followed, casting anxious glances at the others in the room. No one even looked up. Margaret stopped next to the hearth, crossing her arms as she waited for Caradoc to notice her, but he was far too busy inspecting the black granules he held in his hand.

"Mind telling me what you're after?" she asked, trying to sound both friendly and obviously perturbed at the same time.

"Signs," he said, almost to himself. "The signs are all here. But I still can't figure out where it's anchored."

She looked at Simon. "Is he mad?"

"That's sort of a complicated question," he answered.

Caradoc leaned over the fireplace and brushed his hands together, then stood and put an arm across the mantle overhead, mumbling figures to himself.

"What are you doing?" she demanded.

He continued his calculations, oblivious to her.

"Sir, when I ask a question, I expect to be answered, not ignored."

"Sixteen months," he finally said.

"What?"

"Sixteen months," he said again, turning to her. "Three weeks. And . . . six days. That sounds right, doesn't it?"

She frowned at him. "I don't know what you mean."

"Something happened here. Something that invited darkness

335

into this house. Something you played a hand in. Sixteen months, three weeks, and six days ago."

Her face went deathly pale. The brightness in her eyes and smile turned ice cold as a great wall of iron reserve rose up around her. Caradoc raised an eyebrow.

"By the look on your face I'm guessing it wasn't this gambling business."

"Who are you?" she asked, her voice sharpened steel. "Where do you come from? How did you find out about this place?"

Caradoc stood back from the hearth and glanced at Simon.

"Who told you about it?" she said, growing angrier. "Who sent you? I want a name!"

"Look," Simon said, unwilling to risk drawing the gamblers' attentions, "is there somewhere we can be alone?"

"I think you've got the wrong idea about what sort of place this is, Mr. Douglas."

Simon turned beet red.

"So you haven't noticed all the strange things going on around here?" Caradoc asked.

"Apart from you two? No. Now I want you both out of here. Right now. I don't care how far you've traveled or how much money you've got to spend. I won't have two deranged fortunetellers trying to frighten me in my own house. Get out."

Neither of them moved. The fury in her eyes burned even brighter.

"You can either walk out of here on your own two legs or be shown out through a window. Your choice."

"That's an interesting point, isn't it?" Caradoc said.

He pulled the feather from his pocket and held it up. The light fibers shuddered on the stem, bending as though in a breeze.

"Interesting," he repeated, "because there are no windows in this room. No doors left open. And what little air there is in here is being sucked up the chimney through the hearth. Not blown out of it." He stepped around the room, raising and lowering the feather, pointing it at the corners of the room. "Anywhere I move it, the same thing happens. Even on the ground."

He let it fall to the floor, leaning down to watch as the feather continued to sway and curl. He looked back up at Margaret.

"How do you explain that? Where is the draft coming from?"

"What kind of idiotic—"

"And another thing." He stooped down and took a handful of black residue from the hearth.

"Soot?" she said. "What? I suppose it contains magical powers?"

"Look closer," he said, stepping towards her. She looked down into his hand. He moved the granules around with his finger, pushing them back and forth across his palm.

"It isn't soot," he said. "It's sand."

There was no mistake. The fine grains did not smudge like soot, nor clump in powdery heaps like ash.

"Sand?" she replied, frowning at the evidence in his hand.

"A great deal of it, as a matter of fact."

She folded her arms. "Is this what you two do? Travel around with feathers and heaps of sand in your pockets for a laugh? And what are you expecting for a third-rate trick like that? Money? Applause?"

"We don't want anything," Simon replied.

"Good. Then allow me to show you out."

She turned and hurried back towards the passageway door.

CHAPTER 33

A GIRL CAN'T BE TOO CAREFUL

"I trust you can see yourselves out the rest of the way?" she said once they'd returned to the parlor room. "And I hope you won't be too offended if I ask you never to come back."

"You can't keep the rooms heated, can you?" Caradoc said.

She looked at him, stunned again.

"That must be hard to endure," he continued. "Especially with winter coming on. You can get by on a little heat for now, but what will your customers say when they have to start showing up in fur coats and woolen mittens?"

"I'm not going to tell you again. Get out."

"Wouldn't you like to know why that is?" he said, moving towards the hearth in the corner of the room. He crouched down in front of the fire, drew back his sleeve, and without a moment's hesitation, thrust his right hand into the middle of the flames.

"What are you doing?" she cried. "Are you insane?"

"Calm down. Here. See for yourself."

She hesitated for a moment, but seeing he did not draw his face in pain or take his hand back from the fire, she crossed the room and crouched down beside him.

"There's hardly any warmth at all," he said as he moved his hand back and forth across the flames. "It's nearly cold. There's more black sand here as well." He pulled his hand out and showed it to her, completely unharmed. "You try it."

"Do I really look that stupid? I know you've put some kind of . . . protective chemical on your hand or something."

"No, ma'am. All clean."

He offered his hand to her. She looked down at it for a moment, then took it into her own and inspected it. Finding no evidence of anything unusual, she glanced back at Simon, unsure.

"It's all right," he said with a reassuring nod. "I promise."

She turned back to the fire and rolled up a sleeve. "If this is some kind of joke," she said, glaring at Caradoc, "I hope you made peace with your Maker before coming here."

Slowly, she moved her hand towards the fire, pausing as she got closer, expecting at any moment to feel the heat of it. But it never came. Not even when her fingertips hovered just above the licking flames. After a long moment of hesitation, she took a deep breath and swept her hand as quick as lightning through the fire. Then again. Then a third time, slower, plunging her fingers down into the heart of the blaze with a frown. She pulled her hand out again and stared at it.

"But . . . that's impossible."

She backed away from the hearth and sank into a chair, staring at her hand in sheer confusion. When she looked at them again after a long moment of silence, there was a touch of anxious fear in her eyes, as well as suspicion.

"All right," she said at last. "Tell me why."

Caradoc rose to his feet, his cap in his hands. He shared a look of apprehension with Simon before answering. "Sixteen months, three weeks, and six days ago a malicious presence entered this house, invited by you. Unknowingly, of course, but since then it's been working its influence over everything and everyone."

"Malicious presence?" she echoed. "What, like some kind of . . . demon?"

"Not a demon," Simon answered. "A Spektor. They share similarities but with an important distinction. Spektors were once mortal. They are the spirits of those who died so full of hate and bitterness they couldn't bear to leave this world behind without making others feel their pain and suffering."

"Ghosts?" she said. "You're telling me my house is haunted by angry ghosts?"

"Oh, it's much worse than that," Caradoc replied. "All that fighting and cheating and stealing you talked about earlier in the gambling room. How often does that happen here?"

"I don't know. I suppose as often as anywhere else."

"But it's gotten worse over the past sixteen months, hasn't it?"

"Well . . . come to think of it, yes. But times have been hard—"

"And nowhere more than here," Caradoc said. "Your customers know it, too. I sensed it. They're on edge. Anxious. Something is making them uneasy as soon as they set foot in this house, though no one can quite put their finger on it."

She scoffed. "You actually expect me to believe that some evil spirit is hovering over everyone? Whispering into their ears?"

"Into their hearts, actually," Caradoc replied.

"We know how ridiculous this sounds," Simon said. "But we wouldn't be here if we weren't willing to risk a little embarrassment on our part to help you out of this."

"Oh, is that what you're going to do? Help me out of it?" she replied. "You two are some kind of . . . Spektor fighters? Is that it?"

"In a manner of speaking," Simon answered.

She laughed, rising from her seat. "Well, what a lucky girl I am! Two stalwart heroes showing up on my doorstep to rescue me from evil? I thought that only happened in stories." She crossed the room and stopped in the doorway, gesturing out towards the hall. "As entertaining as your tales and parlor tricks have been, gentlemen, I have other business to attend to, so if you'll excuse me . . ."

"You hide it very well," Caradoc said. "Better than most I've seen."

She frowned at him, baffled. "What?"

"The despair. The shadow over your heart. The pain you can't quite put a name to."

She crossed her arms in a show of indignation, but the hard look in her eye softened. She shifted uncomfortably. "Is this the next part of your act? Pretending you know me?"

"You feel it all the time," he continued. "Everywhere. Even in broad daylight. Like a heavy cloak you can't cast off. The sun isn't as bright as it once was. The things you loved no longer bring you joy. And no matter what you do, no matter how many times you try to re-ignite a spark of hope or happiness inside you, sooner or later the flame always goes out again."

She looked away, unsettled. The two men could tell she was trying to decide between reacting in fear or anger.

"You've heard I am a widow," she said, shaking her head while avoiding their eyes. "You're making conjectures based upon grief."

"Your grief is one of the things the Spektor used to gain access to you," Caradoc answered. "That's how they operate, lurking about the world to take advantage of the vulnerable. And once they find a place to make themselves at home, they start to work spreading sorrow and discord. They try to make you feel alone. Put ideas into your head, words into your mouth. They set temptations in front of you. Try to make you do things you don't want to do. Things you wouldn't have even considered before they came. Like what happened sixteen months ago."

Despite the woman's best efforts to remain unmoved, her resolve was clearly crumbling. She put a hand to her throat and drew her eyebrows together. "How can you know that?"

"We'll leave if you really want us to," Caradoc continued. "If you're content to continue living under this kind of darkness, that's your choice. But if you'd rather take the chance to be free from it, we'll stay and help. That's what we came here to offer."

She put her arms around herself, considering his words. The look on her face was almost tortured, as though she struggled with the very thought of hope. She shook her head. "Why? Why would you want to help me? You don't know what I've done. What I'm . . . doing."

"And we won't ask you to tell us," he answered.

She stood straighter, trying to regain her business-like manner and refined composure. "All right. Let's say . . . I believed you. What exactly do you charge for this kind of service?"

Caradoc stepped closer, his expression grave but his voice kind. "If you're serious about this, it could cost you everything. You must be willing to see the truth, and that means stepping through a Veil very few people know about. You'll find out all you are. And all you're not."

She remained silent for a long moment, growing ever more anxious. "What about Rosie? The girl who helps me here? Has she been affected too?"

"Everyone has," Simon answered. "Everyone who's set foot inside this house in the past sixteen months. But they'll all be freed once the Spektor is gone."

Her eyes grew wet for a moment, and she brushed at a tear before it could fall. She nodded, taking a deep breath. "So . . . what's first?"

"First, you'll have to send everyone away," Caradoc said. "The more people there are in the house, the more dangerous it will be."

Margaret returned to the gambling room and announced that two men had come to warn her of a police raid about to descend upon the house. The gamblers needed no further encouragement to depart. They raked their coins into their purses, grabbed up their hats and coats, and were gone faster than a group of school-children at the last bell. This done, she then went to Rosie and asked her to escort the four resident boarders out of the house.

"But why, ma'am?" the young girl asked.

"Just tell them two gentlemen have come to inspect the house and have asked for it to be cleared out. They can return in an hour. You may go home for the night."

"What kind of inspection?"

"I can't explain it all now," Margaret replied. "But we're all going to be a lot better off for it. Trust me."

Rosie did what was requested of her, even convincing the four disgruntled tenants to take in a show at a theatre in town. Once she had gathered her own things for the night, she returned and reported to her mistress, who thanked her, and then suddenly embraced her.

"Oh, Rosie! I'm so sorry."

"For what, ma'am?"

She pulled back from the girl and looked hard at her innocent face, wondering how well she had learned to hide the ill feelings in her own heart.

"Never mind," Margaret said. She clasped the girl's hands in affection. "Someday I'll tell you. For now, go home to your family. Hold them close tonight. I'll see you in the morning."

After everything was done, she found the two men in the hallway. Caradoc was taking long, deliberate strides up and down the corridor, holding his hands out as though he expected to catch on to something. She stepped up to Simon.

"What's he doing now?"

Before he could answer, Caradoc cried out. "Aha!"

He stopped next to a door at the end of the hall and continued to pace in front of it. "Yes. Yes. Definitely here," he said to himself, then looked up. "What's in this room?"

"It's my bedroom," Margaret answered.

He held his left hand in front of the door as though feeling for the direction of the wind. "Hm. Interesting." He stepped away and glanced back at her. "How do you sleep?"

"Alone," she replied, piqued at the question. Simon bit his lip to keep from smiling.

"No, I mean do you have a lot of nightmares? Strange dreams?"

"Yes. I do. Does that have to do with . . . it?"

"Very likely. This is where it's anchored." He put his hand to the knob and turned it. It wouldn't budge. He tried again. "Locked."

"How can that be?" she said, going over to try the knob herself. "It can only be locked from the inside." Upon this grim realization, she plucked her hand away and hurried back.

"You're sure everyone's out of the house?" Simon said.

She nodded. Her mouth had gone too dry to speak.

"Well, not everyone," Caradoc remarked. He tried the door again, throwing his weight against it as he twisted the knob. "That's just pathetic." He turned and shouted at the door. "You really think that's going to keep me out?"

Simon raised his eyebrows. "It's getting desperate."

In another minute the door was kicked open, and the three of them stepped inside. Caradoc walked the room, inspecting the walls and corners in the same fashion he'd done in the gambling quarters. The fire Rosie had lit in the hearth still burned.

"I've never noticed anything unusual in here," Margaret said.

"You wouldn't," Caradoc replied. "It's been here so long you've gotten used to it."

She put her arms around herself again, trying to keep from trembling, and looked at the man beside her. "You trust him, right? He does . . . know what he's doing?"

Simon nodded, trying to smile. "He knows."

Caradoc went to the hearth and reached inside, grasping through the fire among the logs in the grate. "Hm. A lot more sand here. Which direction does the house face?"

"East," she answered.

He rose from the hearth, deep in thought as he brushed the sand from his hands. "All right. I need a song."

She stared at him. "A what?"

"A song. Any song. Hymns are best, but anything will do so long as it means something to you."

"Are you serious?"

"Haven't told a joke yet."

"He's not that funny," Simon said.

"That's how you're going to get it out of the house?" she said in disbelief. "With music?"

"It's more for you than for them," Caradoc answered.

She looked to Simon, but he only offered another unhelpful smile. "I know it seems unorthodox, but it could help a great deal. Try to think."

A tense moment passed as she pondered how to answer them.

"'Weather the Wind'," she said at last. "My mother used to sing it."

Simon dipped his head approvingly. "That's a good one."

"Very good," Caradoc agreed. "How does it go? *'If they send me 'cross the deepest ocean, send me 'cross the wildest sea'* . . . what's the rest?"

"*'I won't be afraid, no I will not falter,'*" Simon added.

They finished the last verse together. "*'Give me a sail and I will weather the wind.'*"

Satisfied, Caradoc nodded at Simon. "All right. That's it then, Mr. Douglas. Thank you."

Margaret turned to him in surprise. "You're leaving?"

Simon pressed his lips together, looking reluctant, then finally answered. "The only way past the Veil is by the use of a special Key, but it doesn't allow for more than two to go through, one of whom must be the Keyholder—that's him." He nodded at Caradoc. "The other is usually a Defender. And since it's your property which lies in the balance, that must be you. I'll be waiting in the hall. We've got three others watching outside the house as well, so try not to worry." He attempted to smile again. "You'll be all right."

He cast a final glance at Caradoc, nodded once more, then

hurried out of the room and shut the door behind him. Caradoc, meanwhile, was busy removing a fingerless glove from his left hand. Margaret backed across the room as she waited, casually trying to put some distance between them.

"I'm afraid we're going to have to be a bit closer for this to work," he said. "And there's no need for that pistol, either."

"What are you talking about? What pistol?"

"The one you picked up from that drawer in the parlor."

"Well . . . a girl can't be too careful these days," she admitted, glancing around the room. "You do realize how this looks, don't you?"

He smiled good-naturedly. "Keep it then, if it makes you feel better. All I've got is this."

He moved to the middle of the room and stopped, holding out his left hand. Something gold glinted in his palm. Cautiously, she approached.

Upon closer inspection, she was horrified to discover that a metal webbing of some kind was biting into the flesh of his hand and meshing out over an open wound. She could tell he was being careful not to move his fingers, no doubt to avoid disturbing her further by shifting the exposed tendons and muscles beneath the gold mark.

"That's the Key?" she said.

He nodded. "I know it doesn't look very nice. But it will take us through the Veil."

She stared at it a few moments longer. "Does it hurt?"

"No," he answered. "Not yet."

The tone of sudden vulnerability in his voice made her look up at his face. She was surprised to see a troubled look in his eyes, which he then tried to dismiss with a shake of his head.

"When you're ready," he said, "put your hand in mine."

She scoffed and put a hand to her throat. "Is anyone ever ready?"

He cocked his head. "Not really."

She drew in a deep breath, trying to calm her anxious heart, then began to move her hand towards his. Halfway, she stopped and looked up again, searching his eyes.

"Are you certain *you* want to do this?"

The question seemed to catch him by surprise.

"No one's ever asked me that before."

"Well?" she said. "Do you really want to face God-knows-what, all for the sake of saving a stranger?"

He considered this for a moment, then shook his head again. "I don't have a choice. Especially not when I meet someone worth saving."

His hand had begun to tremble. She covered it with her own, then lifted her other hand to support it from underneath. "I'm ready."

He nodded. "Once this starts, don't let go. If you become frightened, just hold on tighter. Trust you'll get through all right. I'll be beside you the entire time."

"I trust you," she said. "Although I can hardly believe I just said that."

"Do you permit me to both speak and act on your behalf?"

"Yes."

"Do you give me authority to speak for you and your household?"

"I do. So long as you give it back."

A light was starting to glow beneath her skin, dimly at first, but growing stronger until the image of the gold mark shone bright on the back of her own hand. She looked up at him, alarmed.

"Don't worry," he said. "It's not permanent. You won't end up looking like me."

Suddenly, the room began to fill with swirling vapor, growing thicker every moment as it closed in around them. At first she thought it might be coming from the fire, but soon realized her mistake when it passed over her bare arms. It was mist.

"What is that? Where's it coming from?"

"It was always here," he said. "You just couldn't see it before.

It's the reason your fires are all turning cold, and why the feather moved in the closed room."

"And the sand?" she asked, trying to keep her gaze focused on his face. "The black sand? Where did that come from?"

The gold mark on their hands began to burn brighter.

"You'll see soon," he said.

CHAPTER 34

WHIRLWIND

A bner opened his knapsack and pulled out the lantern.
"All right, boys. Let's light 'em up."
Evering and Ink took out their own lanterns as Abner struck a match and held it inside each one. They'd barely spoken to one another since Simon and Caradoc had gone into the house, too anxious to bother with chatter. The gamblers had left the house in such a hurry they'd hardly noticed the strange trio standing awkwardly by the bushes. The boarders who passed by a few minutes later only glanced at them and muttered something about "inconveniencing paying customers". The last to leave had been a young girl, eyeing them with enough suspicion that Abner and Evering attempted innocent smiles at her as she walked away.

"I'll post at the front corner here," Abner said. "Evering, you go and stand at the northern side of the house. Ink, you'll be around the back corner, but stay near enough for Evering to be able to hear you. That way, we can see anyone approaching from any direction."

"Is that a good idea? Splitting up like that?" Evering asked.

"We don't have to worry about anything coming after us, believe me," Abner replied. "In another few minutes nothing in Heaven or Hell will want to be anywhere near this house. Our only concern is to keep prying eyes away until it's done. Now get a move on. And don't stand too close to the house. Keep a good ten feet away at least."

They both nodded and turned away. Evering fell into step beside Ink as they moved toward their positions.

"Don't worry," he said. "You'll only be a few feet away from me. And I'll pop round from time to time and make sure you're all right."

"Thanks," Ink replied half-heartedly. It was small consolation to know that if any dark spirits came rushing out, it was Evering who would be his first line of defense.

When they reached the far corner, Evering halted and began to fiddle with his lantern. Ink stepped around him, intent on continuing towards his own post, but paused when the young man spoke again.

"By the way . . . I heard you having another nightmare this morning. That's the third one this week. Sounded pretty bad, too."

Ink frowned in irritation. "So what? I'm not allowed to have bad dreams now?"

Evering looked up from the lantern and fixed him with a stare of exasperation. "Good grief, Ink. Why do you do that? Why do you let everything get you riled up so fast? You act like the whole world is against you all the time."

"Who says it ain't?"

"I do," Evering said, stepping closer. "Come on. You can't go biting people's heads off when they try to show a bit of concern. I know you probably think it makes you seem tough, but you're only hurting yourself in the end. I was just trying to say I'm worried about you. And if you're wanting to talk about it—"

"I'm not," Ink said. "It ain't nobody's business but mine."

"But what if others could help you?"

"They can't. No one can. So there's no point wasting any breath on it." He began to turn away again, but Evering moved in front of him.

"Of course there is," he said. "If you keep things bottled up like that, they can take hold of you in the worst way. Eat you up from the inside, like a black spell over your heart. Most times the only way to break it is to say it aloud. Get it out into the open. I had to learn that when my mum passed on. It felt so much better to talk about things, even though nothing could be changed."

Ink drew his eyebrows together. "Maybe that's what *you* had to learn. But my lesson was quite different. I got taught that if you show your feelings, you open yourself up to getting hurt even worse. And who wants that?"

"No one," Evering conceded. "But I think there's an even worse danger. If you keep your heart inside a wall like that, you'll never get healing for what's already in pain. Not really. Look, it doesn't even have to be me you talk to. It could be anybody. Just . . . think about it, all right? That's all I'm asking."

Ink considered this for a long moment, then finally nodded. Evering's expression filled with a look of relief. It seemed as though he wanted to say more, but before he could Ink turned and marched off towards the back corner of the house. All this foolish talk had gone on long enough. They had much bigger things to worry about.

He stopped as soon as Evering had gone out of sight, though he was still close enough to be heard fiddling with his lantern again. Ink glanced around. The meadow beyond the widow's house was empty. The neighbors' residences were all far away, each with soft lights glowing in the windows. Nearby, he spied a water trough beneath a covered hitching post, as well as a few deep wheel ruts betraying the departure of the gamblers' carriages and wagons. His thoughts soon began to drift back to Evering's words, but he shook his head with a noise of disgust and stomped even farther away.

Suddenly, he felt himself start to sink into the ground. He looked down and saw he was standing in a puddle of mud. The soles of his boots made sucking noises as he pulled them out and

351

moved to drier ground. He grumbled a curse and scowled as he wiped his feet in the grass.

"What the blazes am I doing here?" he said aloud to himself. "I ain't got no qualifications to be dealing with the supernatural. I ain't even supposed to be in this part of the country. I was going North. I was making progress. Now look at me. If this weren't mud, that'd just about say it all."

He sighed and looked up. All was still and quiet. He raised his lantern to his eye and looked through the flame, turning a slow circle. It was then he noticed the flickering glow of a hearth fire through one of the back windows of the house. He ventured closer, then set his lantern on the ground and moved a wooden crate beneath it. As he stepped up, the curly locks fell into his eyes again. With a curse he pulled the wig and cap from his head, tossed them to the ground, and looked back through the window. The room was filled with smoke. He pulled off his false spectacles and pushed his nose up against the glass, squinting. Then again, it didn't move like smoke. More like . . . fog. But it couldn't be.

He could see nothing of the room itself, apart from the dim flicker of firelight on the far side. There were no shadows or silhouettes. No hint of any movement whatsoever.

Suddenly, a tremor shuddered through the ground, rattling the glass pane in front of him. Ink clung to the windowsill as the crate shook beneath his feet. Then it stopped.

"Right," he said, taking his hands off the windowsill. "Backing away now."

Ink had always done a masterful job at convincing himself of nearly anything he wanted to believe. The tremor around the house? It was only the shoddy foundations of an old building crumbling away. The pocket watch with the moving pictures? Entrian enchantments and trickery. That was all. And the strange voice calling him a "clever boy"? He'd been ill. Hallucinating under stress and exhaustion. Any excuse would work, for any number of things. It didn't matter if his heart was beating so hard he felt as though it would run straight out of his chest. When it came right down to it, there was no one Inkwell Featherfield was better at lying to than himself.

Until then—when he turned away from the mist-filled house in the silent darkness, and came face-to-face with a living nightmare.

A man had been standing right behind him. Or at least, what looked like a man. It had more a skull than a face, the pale and waxen skin transparent in places, with veins and withered muscle visible beneath. His thin, matted hair fell long around his shoulders, and he wore what had once been a fine tailcoat, now frayed and ragged. Two emerald rings on his right hand hung loose around his skeletal fingers, still bright, but by no means his most conspicuous adornment.

That fell to the gruesome silver chains twisted around his body. They were heavy and thick, with huge spikes fashioned all along their length, like the cruel teeth of some hideous creature. If they were causing him any pain, he didn't show it. He towered over Ink with an almost tangible air of menace, staring down through silver eyes that were at once hungry and hollow. A vapor-like darkness hung around his shoulders like wisps of smoke in constant motion, reaching out with sinister tendrils one moment and curling inward the next. Behind him, a horse waited patiently. Its eyes were missing.

Ink had only seconds to take it all in. As he stared in horror, the man's upper lip began to curl into a snarl.

He had silver teeth.

Ink opened his mouth to scream his bloody lungs out. But before the sound could form, the man reached forward, took him by the throat, and threw him onto the back of the horse.

The next moment they were at a full gallop away from the house. Ink clutched at the horse's mane. The arms of the ghostly man reached around him, holding the reins in his fists, but Ink couldn't feel them—neither his arms, nor any breath on the back of his neck, nor the terrible chains, though he knew they were right against his back.

Suddenly, a flash of bright light blazed out from somewhere ahead, so intense it drowned out the world around them. Ink shut his eyes, unable to bear it. The horse did not falter for a moment.

When the light faded, Ink opened his eyes. A half-choked cry tore from his throat and he reeled in the saddle, thunderstruck.

They were no longer in a dark, empty meadow, but on a bridge strung high above a misty ravine. The shadows of great mountains were visible on either side, while ahead a beautiful city gleamed like a jewel in the sun, its shimmering towers encircled by wisps of pale pink cloud. Ink had no more than few moments to witness the astonishing sight, for the bright flash of light came again, bleeding over everything in view, and he was forced to shut his eyes once more.

When he opened them again, they were in a desert valley, arid and windswept beneath a dull gray sky. The ground below was a labyrinth of deep cracks that ran as far as the eye could see. A black river wound away to their left, smoking and bubbling towards a line of foothills to the west. Eastward, a curious fortress built of massive bones sat atop a mud-slicked ridge. Ink clenched the horse's mane tighter between his fists. What was happening? Was he hallucinating? Had he slipped off the crate beneath the window and hit his head?

Another bright flash wiped the scene away.

Now they were in a great forest, surrounded by a host of enormous trees, taller than any he had ever seen before. Tiny blossoms swirled down through the air from the dark green canopy above. Purple and yellow ferns spanned their feather-like leaves between mossy stones. The air was full of birdsong. Far off in the distance, Ink caught sight of people moving among the trees in a dream-like dance. The place was so enchanting he wanted to grab hold of the reins and stop the horse himself, but before he had even finished the thought, the forest vanished in a burst of light.

Curiosity had begun to overtake Ink's terror somewhat, and he was almost eager to open his eyes again to see what lay behind the

354

fading light. But the next moment, his blood turned to ice. They were now riding alongside a high wall of sheer black stone, upon which hung a slew of chained corpses in various stages of desiccation. Ink brought his sleeve to his nose and mouth, choking on the putrid smell. At the base of the wall ran a broad moat filled to the brim with blood. Ink squeezed his eyes shut and tried not to be sick, waiting for the flash to come. He saw it from behind his eyelids.

Opening them again—this time with great hesitation—he found himself in the middle of a young wheat field, still green and spread across rolling hills that sloped away for miles in every direction. A tree-lined road curved towards a beautiful manor house on a distant hill. The sky swelled with dark clouds.

It was here the man finally brought the horse to a halt. He then took hold of Ink by the shoulders and flung him to the ground. The boy lay paralyzed with terror as his ghastly captor dismounted and fixed him with an unblinking stare. Ink tried to think of something bold to say, even impertinent. Something to prove to the man, as well as to himself, that he wasn't afraid. But it was too great a lie to tell, even for his prodigious talents.

The sound of clanking chains approached from behind. Three others were galloping towards them on eyeless horses—a man and two women—all wearing the same chains of metal thorns, all with silver eyes and teeth, all with the same expressions of unrelenting scorn. The black vapor hovering around them pulsed with impatient energy as they stopped beside Ink.

"Did he see you?" the younger of the two women said to Ink's captor.

"No," he answered with an air of contempt. "There was no time for him to detect us."

The second man dismounted from his horse, his chains clanging together with grating coldness. He was young, perhaps Evering's age, and carried a maniacal glint in his eye as he stalked towards the boy. Ink's terror jolted him into action and he began to crawl backwards.

"So much risk for such a pathetic thing," the man said, sneering down at him.

"We do as the Mistress commands," the captor replied.

Their voices were strange. Thin and hollow, like sinister whispers in a cave. Ink turned over and began to crawl faster on his hands and knees, breaking clear of the ring of horses and trying to regain his footing to escape at a full run. A whizzing sound whistled overhead. Ink's breath caught in his throat as a huge black blade stuck fast into the ground just inches from his nose. The young man strode forward, grabbed him by the neck, and hoisted him into the air. Ink pulled at his hands. They were stiff and ice-cold.

"What a waste of effort!" the man cried. "He doesn't even have it on him!"

The man dropped Ink back to the ground, then held a hand out towards the blade. Within seconds it dissolved into a black mist which returned to his withered frame and hung about his shoulders. At the same time, the younger woman dismounted and moved towards Ink.

"We must do a thorough search," she said, her pupils enlarging as she looked down at him. "Limb by limb. Bone by bone."

"No, Zarada!" the captor cried. "Not a scratch. You acted too soon once before. It will not happen again."

The woman's mouth curved into a deranged smirk as she crouched low and reached for Ink's jacket lapels. "Shame," she said, pulling him close and bringing her mouth to his ear. "I barely got a taste the last time."

Ink brought a hand to his cheek where the scratch had appeared in Spindler's flat. The look of utter horror on his face seemed to give her pleasure, and she chuckled as she backed away, making room for the fourth rider who joined them.

She was an old woman in a long cloak, wearing half a dozen jeweled bracelets and a collection of diamond rings on her bone-white fingers. Her chains were coiled around her neck. The deep wrinkles lining her face attested to a lifetime spent in nothing but displeasure and gave her face the appearance of being cracked and broken.

"Stand up, you wretch," she hissed at Ink. "Don't lie there gawping like a fish."

Ink shot to his feet, eager to avoid being the target of another sharp metal object. The Spektors closed in around him, hovering like predators.

"Do you know who we are?" she asked.

"Of course he knows!" the younger man spat. "How else could he have lived this long?"

"No credit to him," Zarada said with a sneer. "He's only lucky to have made an ally of the Broken One."

A great peal of thunder boomed in the distance, echoing through the fields. The four riders looked eastward. Rainclouds were beginning to swirl over a small hillock a few hundred feet away. Lightning flashed from ground to sky—the wrong way around.

"It has begun," the first man said. "We do not have much time."

"Look here!" the old woman said, turning her sour gaze back to Ink. "Let us not squander words. You must bring us Wickwire's watch."

"What?" Ink said, finding his voice.

The younger man cuffed him hard across the ear with a claw-like hand. "The *watch*, you little worm! The one you stole from that shack! Don't you dare pretend ignorance!"

The older man reached towards the younger's neck. A shred of dark vapor flew out from around him and settled into his grip, taking the shape of a dagger. He tipped the point against the other's throat. "Touch him again, Marcus, and I will expel you myself."

"Enough, you fools!" the old woman cried, then turned back to Ink. "We know the watch has awakened. We know you've seen its power with your own eyes—and had your fun with it. But that time is over. Retrieve the watch, get as far away from the Broken

357

One as you can, then wait for us to find you. Do this, and we will forget that you ever got in the way."

Ink tried to stand straighter. It was difficult with his legs shaking beneath him. "And wh-why should I? If you're really . . . what you're supposed to be . . . why should I help you?"

"Don't bother explaining," Zarada said. "How could a stupid child possibly understand?"

Marcus brought his waxen face close to Ink's. "If you don't do as we ask, we'll see to it that you never have a moment's peace for the rest of your worthless life, which we will bring to an end whenever it so pleases us."

Ink gathered enough nerve to laugh in his face. "Ha! Well that's a load of rubbish! You can't do nothing of the sort! I know all about you lot. You can't harm me. They said so. Said it's against the rules."

The silver eyes around him began to shine in rage.

"And what's more," Ink said, hooking his thumbs into his belt, "I know full well you don't got the guts to come within spitting distance of the bloke back there in that house, and I'm with him now. Just wait 'til he finds out what you've done. I expect he'll be here any minute."

A tremor rumbled through the ground beneath them. The churning clouds over the hillock began to swirl faster as a great gust of wind whipped across the meadow, bending the wheat almost flat to the ground. Three bolts of red lightning flashed from sky to earth. Zarada let out a choked gasp and clutched at her chains, fear overcoming her arrogant sneer as she lunged for her horse. Marcus grabbed her by the arm.

"Stand fast, you weakling!"

"I'm not waiting around for him to find us!" she cried. "I can't go back! I won't!"

"The boy's not frightened enough," the old woman said to the first man. "A few more worlds might loosen his resolve. Or take him back to Hejr Sheddeth. Let him sit on his own for a while by the river of blood and the wall of corpses. Perhaps then he'll have a change of heart."

Before Ink could react, the first man's hand darted out and grasped him by his collar.

"I know of worse places to make him obey."

Ink fell to his knees, trying desperately to pull the shriveled hand away. His own went straight through it.

"You will leave him to me!"

A loud voice rang out behind them. Ink felt a surge of hope. Could it be? Had Caradoc come to save him at last?

The others parted, revealing a fifth horseman riding towards them. Ink's heart sank at the sight of the silver chains wrapped around his chest and arms. He was just like the others, save for the fact that he was also accompanied by a large, wolf-like creature which kept pace at its master's side. The eyes of the beast glowed green, and a pair of sharp horns curled behind its ears. Upon reaching them, the rider reined in his horse and looked down.

Ink had thought the nightmare could grow no worse, but he was wrong yet again. He knew those clothes. The arched bridge of that nose and the curved ends of that gray mustache. Even the slant of that top hat over his left eye. Ink gaped in wide-eyed horror, unwilling to believe what stood before his eyes.

"But . . ." he said, "you . . . you can't be. You *can't* be!"

The rider reached out a hand. "Bring him up to me."

The others did as he commanded, and Ink was once more hauled onto the back of a blind horse.

"Do what you must, Eamon," the old woman said. "He would not yield to us."

"Of course he wouldn't, you stupid old bat," the horseman shot back, his deep voice full of derision. "He'd never do anything merely for the sake of being told. I did not raise my grandson to be a fool."

And with a crack of the reins they were off, racing across the green fields towards the chaos forming above the hillock.

CHAPTER 35

THE HIDDEN CITY

The air began to shimmer in the far distance, bending and warping like melted glass. The wind whipped around the hillock, raising up bits of wheat and dust into the air. An eerie blue light filtered down through the middle of the swirling vortex of cloud above it. Ink's grandfather halted his horse and dismounted.

"Get down. Quickly."

Ink cast a wary glance at the wolf-beast standing nearby. When he saw it took no notice of him he clambered down, then grabbed the spyglass from under his shirt. He'd hardly thought about the device since Riva had given it to him before the raid. Now he pressed his thumb against the center, desperate to alert the others. But nothing happened. He tried a second time, then a third.

"That won't work here," the Spektor said. "You've gone too far from them."

Ink slipped the spyglass back under his shirt. "And . . . just how far would that be?"

Eamon raised his chin, his silver eyes fixed on the whirlwind atop the hill.

Beyond the roads that e'er I traveled
Past the stars that e'er I read
'Cross the lands 'twixt dream and waking
To walk the ground that none have tread

The words, spoken in that chilling and hollow voice, made goosebumps rise on Ink's arms. He rubbed at them, shuddering. "You're saying . . . this is actually a whole other world? This is all real? Not some kind of trick or illusion? Or me hitting my head back there?"

"You best start believing in the truth now," the Spektor answered, "no matter how far-fetched it seems."

Ink stepped forward. "What happened, Granddad? I don't . . . I don't understand. How can you be here? Who did this to you? And why—"

"Fewer questions and more paying attention," Eamon snapped. He pointed an emaciated finger towards the horizon. "Nothing and no one in the world is more important than what is happening right there."

"But you were dead!" Ink cried with a shaking voice. "You died two winters ago in the High Country! I picked out that suit you're wearing! And the coffin you were buried in! I even had Mr. Wilkins from the clerk's office do the funeral 'stead of a priest, just like you told me. Now here you are, standing right in front of me with those chains 'round you. Saints above, Granddad, what have you done?"

Eamon went to his grandson and stooped down, removing his rotted top hat as he did so. His cold eyes pierced through the boy's own. "No man is ever ready to face his Maker when the time comes. I was no exception. So I did what anyone with a brain would do. I bartered my way out of it. Made a deal. If you're smart, you'll do the same one day."

"And become an evil spirit?"

"Evil is a point of view."

"Tormenting people?" Ink said, unable to mask his horror.

"Driving 'em to madness? Spreading darkness just for the fun of it? You're telling me that's the way to do things?"

"And what if I am?" Eamon cried fiercely, making Ink shrink back. "Since when did you care about people? What did the little maggots ever do for you? What did they ever do for me? Maybe I was tired of seeing all the filthy, lying cheats get away with it all! Maybe I couldn't accept a world so damnably unjust it made me sick to my stomach every godforsaken day! Maybe I decided to do something about it!"

Ink shook his head in disbelief. "And this is the best you could think of? Becoming a Spektor?"

"And what have *you* done?" The black vapor around the Spektor's shoulders flared in a burst of fury, the whites of his eyes darkening around his silver irises. "Sold yourself into slavery! Let yourself be taken in by sob stories and baseless promises! Do they make you feel loved? Do they make you feel wanted? Is that it? And I suppose you told them everything! I suppose you spilled your guts! Laid everything bare on the butcher's block! Is that what I taught you?"

"No, sir! I didn't! I swear!"

"And what about your mission? The great duty to which I charged you? Have you abandoned that completely now? Have you decided they aren't worth the effort?"

"No, sir!"

"Then what the devil are you doing twiddling your thumbs up on a floating rock?"

"They said they could protect me!"

"And you believed them! How can . . ." Eamon stopped short, his fury dying away as he regarded Ink with an air of bafflement. "Since when did you start saying, 'sir'?"

Ink felt his cheeks flush. The old Spektor sneered, baring his silver teeth, then began to laugh. It was a terrible, grating sound.

"You poor, sorry sap. They got to you. Got inside your head. If that's not the saddest thing I ever heard."

Ink shut his eyes and shook his head. "This can't be real. It can't be."

Eamon arched an eyebrow. "I know I taught you to question everything and everyone. But it's time you learned the world is a great deal more than it seems." He reached forward, took Ink by the collar, and dragged him forward. "Now *look . . . out . . . there!*"

A black cloud of dust had risen from the ground, meeting the vortex above. Lightning flashed within, sending tremors through the ground that rippled out like waves.

"What's happening?" Ink asked.

"The battle being fought back in that house is creating a tear through the Veil," the old man answered. "In countless other lands and realms—places you could not begin to imagine—the same is happening in that very spot. The creatures who are laying eyes on it in their own Otherworlds will think it only a bit of irregular weather. They'll call it a squall or a cyclone or a lightning storm. Only we Spektors know better."

Each time the lightning flashed, a collection of fast-moving shadows became visible in the center of the cloud. Flames began to swirl around the outer edges. The sound of faint screaming broke out across the open meadow and a loud crack resounded across the sky. Ink jerked back a step and glanced up at his grand-dad. The Spektor was already looking at him.

"You don't know who your Protector really is, do you?" he said.

Ink had to raise his voice over the howling winds. "I suppose you're going to tell me."

"Better than that. I'm going to show you. Get on."

Ink followed him back to the horse, eager to leave the place. The hellhound waited patiently and regarded him with a dead-eyed stare as he approached.

"What's this?" Ink asked. "Your pet?"

"A gift," Eamon answered as he swung into the saddle, then pulled Ink up after him.

"A gift? For what?"

"For being good at what I do."

Ink felt his stomach turn. They sped off, heading northward as the ground shook beneath them once more. Another scream broke from the swirling vortex in the distance. This time, it didn't sound human.

A bright flash wiped the green meadow away.

They came to a stop on a narrow mountain ledge. The horse whinnied and pulled up its head, trying to back away from the brink. Eamon calmed it with a word. The hellhound stood alert, its ears pricked forward on its shaggy head.

"Stay on the horse," Eamon commanded. "You're likely to lose your footing otherwise."

Ink felt his head swim as he glanced down. A large bay spread out before them, encircled by a ring of mountains. The highest peak in the chain had been split down the center, creating a wide rift in the barrier. Beyond lay a boundless sea.

"What is it I'm meant to be looking at?"

"Wait," Eamon answered. "We must wait for the tide to go out."

"But . . . won't that take hours? It can't be midday yet."

"Not all worlds play by the same rules as yours."

A minute later, the sound of breaking waves suddenly changed to that of a huge, rushing river. The water level was dropping, as though someone had pulled a plug from a bathtub drain. In a matter of minutes, the bay poured itself through the chasm in the mountain chain and out to the sea beyond. And there, in the center of the miry basin left in its wake, lay a dark secret which the waves had hidden.

It was the ruins of an ancient city. A place of stone pillars and marble porticoes, statues and grand stairs. But nothing stood in one piece. The houses were smashed, the temples had caved in. Stairs had cracked down the middle. The destruction was so complete that no corner of the city had been left intact. Most appalling of all was a river of liquid fire which swept down every thoroughfare and lane, circling in a never-ending, never-ceasing current. There was something about it that reminded Ink of the strange light which appeared on the case of the Wickwire Watch before it opened.

"This was the city of Krymenos," Eamon said. "The site of an expulsion that happened many years ago. The battle was long and fierce, neither side making any headway. Until, in utter desperation, the Broken One—your Protector—called down fire from the sky to vanquish the Spektor he pursued. The entire city was destroyed in a moments. Thousands were killed."

Ink looked on in horror. He could almost hear screaming above the roar of the rushing fire.

"In a final act of shame," Eamon continued, "he brought down part of the mountain and let the sea cover all evidence of what he'd done. Only a few years have passed in your world since the time of that expulsion, but here, that fire has been burning for over a thousand years. The water will not quench it. And as far as anyone knows, it will burn forever."

The distant roar grew louder. Whether it came from the sea or from the fire, Ink couldn't tell. He stared down with unblinking eyes, unable to tear his gaze away.

"Do the others know? The Colonists, I mean. Is this the terrible thing they say he did?"

"No," Eamon answered. "Apart from the Broken One, you are the only other living soul who has seen this place and heard its history."

Ink swallowed. "Why do you call him the Broken One?"

"You would know if you saw him."

"I have seen him."

Eamon ground his teeth in his jaw. "Only in your world."

The reply sent a chill down Ink's spine. A rumble echoed overhead. In the blue sky above the mountain on which they stood, a thunderhead of dark cloud suddenly appeared.

"Another tear," Eamon said before Ink could ask. "The battle is bleeding through to this world as well. Now listen to me. Whatever this man has told you about protecting you or helping others, it's only an attempt to conceal his true purpose. Control."

"Control?" Ink repeated. "Of what?"

Eamon drew himself up to his full height and swept his silver eyes across the ruined city. "Us. For years he's been seeking the grounds in which our bodies are kept—a place we call the Crypt. If he finds it, he will have the means to control every soul he's ever expelled. That's why he's been so ruthless in going after us, even if it means the destruction of entire cities like this one. The more he expels, the more he will have under his command. And you were the perfect bait. When he saw how the other Spektors swarmed to you he knew he had to take you under his wing and keep you there. Use you to lure as many as he could."

Ink stared back at the fiery city, remembering Caradoc's promise never to leave him. Eamon clamped his hand down upon Ink's shoulder, his grip like an iron vice. He leaned closer.

"No one should ever have that kind of power. We would put an end to the threat ourselves if we thought we could. But he's grown too strong. Too dangerous."

The blood drained from Ink's face. "Are you asking me to . . .?"

"Kill him," Eamon finished. "Before he can find the Crypt and take control. Before he rains eternal fire down on a thousand Otherworlds."

The ground shook, scattering rocks and dust over the edge of the ridge. The hellhound growled. Far overhead, a burst of lightning struck the side of the mountain, sending a mass of boulders sliding towards them.

Ink looked back at his granddad. "Can we get out of here?"

"What's your answer?"

"What? *Now?*" He glanced up again. The rocks were picking up speed.

"The man who makes slaves of us makes slaves of all," Eamon said. "Surely you can see that."

"I can see that! I can see that!" Ink cried, trying to urge the horse forward himself.

Eamon grabbed the reins back. "He's already begun to wreak havoc in your own world! You know this! Don't be a fool! Do it for the reward if nothing else. You'll have all you ever dreamed of! All you ever wanted!"

"I can't do anything with my head bashed in!"

"If you don't have the guts to kill him yourself then hand over the watch!"

"No!"

"Why not?"

"'Cause I don't trust you! Not any of you! And you're not my granddad!"

Eamon spurred the horse forward. The sound of crashing rocks echoed in Ink's ears as the world flashed bright.

He was flung to the ground once more. They had returned to the widow's house in Burgess Valley. All was silent and dim. The ground no longer shook. There were no shadows or hearth fires or swirling clouds now. Just a silver-eyed Spektor on the back of a blind horse. Eamon looked down at Ink with an air of amusement.

"You turned out better than I thought you would. You remember well the first lesson I ever taught you."

Ink stood and brushed the dust from his clothes, relieved he had not inspired his granddad to another burst of rage. "Trust no one."

"Trust no one," Eamon repeated. "No matter how good they seem. No matter how loving, how kind, how faithful . . . they will let you down. It's inevitable. And even if they should call you 'friend', what is a friend, really?"

Ink sighed. "A friend is an enemy you always keep in sight."

"Remember that. And heed not the love of mortals."

Ink glanced up at him in surprise. "I know those words! I saw them in Bash's house! They were written on some strange piece of stone!"

Eamon raised an eyebrow. "Bash stuck his nose in many places it did not belong."

Ink frowned, trying to keep his voice steady as he ventured to ask yet another question he wasn't sure he wanted answered. "Is that why you . . . killed him?"

The Spektor narrowed his eyes, the silver orbs becoming slits. "That is not for you to know."

He drew up the reins and turned to face the house. Ink followed his gaze. The same curious blue light he had seen bleeding through the center of the swirling cloud was now growing bright through the windows. The wind picked up around them, moaning eerily through the tall grass in the meadow beyond. The horse snorted, growing anxious.

"Why are the Spektors coming after me?" Ink said. "Is it the watch? The Wickwire Watch? Is that all they want?"

"They're coming after you because you became important," Eamon answered, "and no matter the original reason, there is nothing now that will make you free of them. You know too much. You've seen what no living eyes are meant to see."

"But I never asked to see!" Ink cried. "I don't want to be important! None of this is any of my business!"

"Wrong," Eamon said. He leaned down over the saddle and pointed a bony finger at the house. "He is your business now. The fate of things both flesh and spirit are your business now. One day you'll see him for what he truly is, and once you decide to do something about it there will be three paths to take. Kill him. Give us the watch. Or take the Spider Key for yourself."

"The what?"

"The mark on his hand. Without it he won't be able to control us. But it can't be taken by force, it must be passed from one to another. There is small chance of defeating him that way, but if you see an opportunity, you must have his trust before he will give it to you. Draw him in close. Only don't allow yourself to be drawn in as well." He sat up in the saddle again. "You're wise to keep the watch for yourself. Have the courage to use it. It's the only thing you can rely on to tell you the truth."

Ink glanced back at the house as the windows began to rattle. The hellhound growled, raising its hackles and baring its teeth. Eamon tugged at the reins, turning the horse away.

"One last thing," he said, glaring down at Ink in stern reproach. "I will always be your granddad. Always. Death does not change that."

A groan issued from the house, as though it were in pain. The walls were starting to bend outward. Frightened, Ink turned back to his granddad.

He was gone.

CHAPTER 36

AND GREAT WAS THE FALL
OF IT

I nk had little time to recover from his terrifying adventure. Not a moment later, Evering came running towards him from around the corner of the house with wild shocks of red hair sticking out from under his cap.

"Ink! We've gotta move! Something's wrong! Grab your lantern and follow me!"

"Where have *you* been? You said you'd pop 'round the corner and make sure I was all right!"

"What, you scared of the dark? It's only been a few minutes. Where's your wig?"

"Come on, boys!" Abner cried, stepping around the house. "This way! Hurry!"

They rushed to the front gate as the house buckled and shook. The air began to shimmer with flashes of fire as a great wind rose up. Then all at once, every window exploded with a great crash, shooting shards of glass in every direction. Abner stepped in front of the two boys and tried to shield them as they all covered their faces. A tremor rumbled through the ground, accompanied by a sound like grating iron that set their teeth on edge. Abner raised his lantern to his eye.

"Be ready for anything now!" he cried out over the noise.

The boys looked at each other wide-eyed, then raised their own lanterns. Ink forced himself to look through the flame. He didn't want to see another Spektor again for as long as he lived. He didn't even want to believe they existed. But now he had no choice. The old world he thought he'd known was gone forever.

The walls of the house cracked and crumbled. Deep fissures appeared in the earth around the foundations, and with a mighty *crack,* the front door split down the middle. Everyone held their breath. Suddenly, a figure burst through, breaking it to pieces. It was Simon, waving madly as he ran towards them.

"Back! Farther back! Across the road!"

He ran past them and jumped the fence. The others hurried after. A high-pitched squeal issued from the house as the walls convulsed and quivered like sheets of paper. Unable to take the strain any longer, the chimney collapsed in a heap, scattering stones from the roof. The noise became unbearable, like the sound of overworked machinery on the brink of an explosion. The blue light inside the house went blindingly bright.

"Get down!" Simon cried.

They dropped to the ground in a shallow ditch beside the road and covered their heads. The air pressure plunged so low and so suddenly, each thought they had gone deaf.

The next moment, the house imploded with a thunderous crash. Columns and support beams snapped like twigs as the house caved it on itself, throwing up a cloud of dust fifty feet high. In a matter of seconds, the entire structure was utterly flattened.

The wind died away. The noises were silenced. The four grovelers in the ditch looked up. Evering could only make a small squeaking sound in his throat.

"Mother's love!" Abner said, slack-jawed in astonishment.

Ink looked at Simon, his heart pounding in his ears. "Does this usually happen?"

Simon's eyes did not leave the house. "No. Not usually."

"So . . . what about them, then?" Abner asked. "Are they . . .?"

Someone called from inside the dust cloud. Caradoc emerged moments later, carrying in his arms a woman on the brink of unconsciousness. Simon got to his feet and flew back across the road towards them. The others followed. As Caradoc eased the woman onto the grass, Simon rushed to her side and dropped to his knees.

"Stay awake. Stay with us," he said, gently patting her cheek as her eyelids fluttered.

Evering stared at the widow in disbelief, then turned to Ink. "You said she was old!"

Ink smacked him in the arm. "And *you* said you'd make sure I was all right!"

A change came over the woman. She jerked violently, as if flinching from an unseen attacker, her breath quickening as her face twisted in panic. With her eyes still shut, she began to flail with her fists. Simon and Caradoc each caught a wrist.

"It's over!" Simon said. "It's all over! They've gone!"

"God help her," Abner said.

She went into an even madder frenzy, trying to wrench her arms free of their grasp. Caradoc looked down at her face and spoke in a firm, commanding voice.

"Margaret."

With a gasp she awoke, becoming still. She looked between the two men with wide eyes.

"It's all right," Simon said. "It's all right now. You're safe."

They released her arms. Instantly, she reached toward Caradoc and clutched at the front of his shirt.

"I'm sorry," she said in a choked voice. "I shouldn't have let go. I shouldn't have let go."

"It doesn't matter now," he replied, gently taking her hands from his shirt.

She caught his arm and held it fast. "Why did you do this? No one's ever fought for me before. No one."

A tear slid down her cheek. He pressed her hands in comforting reassurance, then moved away and got unsteadily to his feet, listing sideways as he put a hand on his thigh to support himself. His face was beaded with sweat. Blood welled through the gold mark on his left hand and dripped onto the ground. There was also a jagged gash on his brow. Ink shuddered as he thought of the black Spektor blade that had struck the ground just inches from his own face.

"I'd ask how you're doing," Abner said to the scarred man, "but that's probably a stupid question."

Caradoc answered with a weak smile and looked back at the rubble behind him. "Hm. That could've gone better." He tore a strip of cloth from his shirt and set to wrapping it around his injured hand. "How went the watch?"

"All quiet out here," Abner reported. "Up until the last five minutes."

"Got attention coming from that way," Evering said, nodding down the road.

Several people had ventured out of their homes, wondering over the source of the terrible noise they'd heard. The bolder of the curious began to gather in the street.

Caradoc nodded. "Time to make our exit."

Abner went to Margaret's side as Simon helped her to a sitting position. "Miss, is there anyone we can leave you in the care of close by? Friends? Relatives? A neighbor?"

She shook her head. "There's no one. My family and friends have all gone. And what neighbors I have would sooner leave me to lie here than take me in."

Abner glanced up at Simon. "Didn't we pass an infirmary in town?"

"There's the temple as well," Evering offered.

Margaret looked at the man beside her with an expression of renewed terror. "You mean to leave me?"

Simon didn't reply, but she found her answer in the faces around her.

"But you can't!" she said, growing hysterical. "You can't! Not now! Not after everything that's happened! How can I live with what I've seen? What I've heard? What would a doctor do but shut me up in a madhouse? What would a priest do but force me to pray all hours of the day and night? They wouldn't know! They wouldn't understand!"

The sound of distant voices began to draw nearer. Ink jabbed a thumb towards the street.

"They're getting closer."

Caradoc nodded. "Abner, you and the boys get back to the Drifter. Simon and I will stay to make sure these people take care of her."

Margaret looked back at Simon, her eyes making a desperate plea straight to his heart as she grasped his arm. "Please. They may be my neighbors but they are not my friends. They've never shown me a moment's kindness. If they ever spoke to me, it was only to shame me for the business I ran and the company I kept. I have no one to depend upon. No one in the world. Only you."

He gazed back at her, his brow wrinkled, his mind in turmoil. Helpless, then angry, then resolute, all in a matter of seconds.

"She's coming with us!" he announced.

The others froze in their tracks, then turned back to him.

"Have you gone *mad?*" Abner exclaimed. "You know she can't!"

"We did it with Ink."

"That was different!"

"We can't abandon her. We won't. And if she's not coming, then I'm staying."

"But you can't!" Evering said. "Don't you know what that would mean?"

Simon clenched his jaw, resolute, and looked to Caradoc.

The scarred man passed a hand across his face, too weak to argue, then glanced back at Margaret. "Can you walk?"

She nodded. "I think so."

"Then let's get going. All of us."

"What?" Abner said. "You can't be serious!"

"There's no time to argue. We can't all be here when those people turn up."

"And what are they going to say when they do? When they discover a flattened house and a missing woman?" Abner stepped closer to him and lowered his voice. "Another kidnapped victim of the Colonists? Another grand headline to sell papers with."

"We'll burn the wreckage. They can mark it down to a disgruntled customer." Caradoc looked at Margaret again. "With your permission, of course."

She nodded. "And good riddance."

This being decided, Abner, Evering, and Ink went back to the ruins of the house and poured out what remained of their lantern oil. In so doing, Ink's sharp eyes did not fail to notice everything that glittered and sparkled in the wreckage.

"No sense letting it *all* go to waste," he said to himself, pocketing a silver hair comb and a pearl-encrusted brooch from a demolished dressing table.

Abner smashed his lantern over a broken chair. Evering broke his over the remains of a stair railing. Flames spurted up among the glass. Ink brought his lantern down over a pile of drapes.

"Let's go!" Abner shouted and hurried back towards the street. Simon, Caradoc, and Margaret had already passed through the front gate.

Just as he was about to step away, Ink spied something glinting in the firelight near his foot. It was a silver ring, half-buried in dust. He scooped it up and looked it over, marveling at the weight of the tiny object. The thick band was inlaid with a flowering vine of pure emerald. Ink let out a soft whistle. It had to be worth more than the sum total of the last ten wallets he'd swiped.

"Ink! Watch'ya dawdling for?" Evering called out.

He slipped the ring into his pocket and ran after them.

Margaret lost consciousness as soon as they passed through the shroud enchantment around the Drifter. Simon caught her up in his arms, carried her the rest of the way, and laid her on a canvas tarp in the bow. Abner took post at the burner. As they ascended into the night sky, Evering lit the lanterns around the hull. Caradoc sat by the tiller in the stern.

Ink stared at him. Was he reveling in his victory? Tallying up the number of Spektors he would soon have under his control? In life, his granddad had often tricked and deceived him in order to test his wits and cleverness, and for all Ink knew, his warnings and stories about Caradoc were simply more of the same old guff. But the more he thought about it, the more sense it made. His granddad had been genuinely disturbed at the prospect of Caradoc finding the Crypt, and the other Spektors had done their best to threaten him into handing over the Wickwire Watch to put a stop to it. Then there was the business of Caradoc's remarkably high spirits on their way to the house. So whether true or false, the simple facts did not fall in his protector's favor.

"You've been quiet, Mr. Featherfield," Caradoc said, feeling Ink's eyes on him.

"Got a lot on my mind," Ink replied. "You seem pleased with yourself."

Caradoc sat back against the hull and winced. "Any day with fewer Spektors in the world is a good one."

Ink raised an eyebrow and glanced back at the woman on the tarp. "Might not be so good once the others see what kind of souvenir we've picked up."

"They'll come around. Didn't exactly sit well with me to leave her behind, either. A person who lives through something as harrowing as a Spektor expulsion needs care and compassion afterward. Leaving them to sort things out on their own can be dangerous."

Ink shifted uncomfortably on the bench, then glanced at the blood-soaked bandage around the navigator's hand. "That mark you've got . . . I heard it was called the Spider Key."

"Did you?" Caradoc said. He pulled out the spyglass from under his shirt and held it to his eye as he looked out across the prow, moving the tiller to adjust the Drifter's course.

Ink furrowed his brow. "So where are they now? These Spektors you've taken care of."

Caradoc let the spyglass fall back against his chest. "Tucked back in their coffins, waiting in the dark until their turn for judgment. Should be some time around the end of this world if I remember the old texts correctly."

Ink bowed his head, fidgeting with his hands. Caradoc glanced back at him, and his hard gaze softened.

"It's good you were there to see what you did," he said. "Maybe now you'll appreciate your situation a bit more."

Ink scoffed. "What, you mean having the good fortune of your company?"

"Don't know if I'd call that 'good' fortune."

Suddenly, Caradoc grimaced and reeled over, clutching at his heart. The airship swerved as the tiller began to slide to one side. Abner glanced back and saw what was happening.

"Ink! Grab that! Evering, take my post!"

Ink rushed over and took hold of the lever, pulling it straight again.

"I'm fine, Abner," Caradoc said. "I'll be fine. It's passing."

Abner halted in his steps, but the worry in his face did not diminish.

The others on Riverfall were waiting to meet them on the steps of the Pipeworks House. Knowing this, Caradoc made sure to don his cap again to hide the gash on his brow. At first there was a general outcry of relief at seeing the returning party still in one piece, but this was soon stifled upon sight of the stranger Simon carried in his arms.

"Who is that?" Martin said, his voice on the edge of alarm.

"Who indeed," Abner grunted.

"It's the widow," Evering answered. "Simon decided to invite her to our humble abode."

"*That's* the widow?" Chester exclaimed as he looked the unconscious woman over.

"I'm taking her to the infirmary," Simon said, moving past the others without showing the slightest regard for their shock. "Can someone give me a hand?"

"I'll go!" Chester said and followed after him.

"Are the rest of you all right?" Harriet asked, casting concerned glances at Ink and Caradoc in particular.

"We're fine," Caradoc said. "Jo, Wendolen, do you know 'Weather the Wind'?"

The sisters looked at one another.

"Well, of course we do," Josephina said. "Why?"

"Go with them to the infirmary, if you will. It'll help her if she goes into another fit."

"But why is she here at all?" Wendolen asked.

"Yes," Martin said, assuming his old acerbic tone, "are we now opening a resort for hard-luck cases?"

Caradoc pulled off his neckerchief and began to wipe the makeup off his face, bringing his scars back into view. "There was no one to leave her with. Simon insisted on bringing her along. We didn't have time to argue."

"Doesn't he know what this could do to us?" Delia said. "What *she* could do to us? What was he thinking?"

"Look, we can handle this," Caradoc said. "Just don't let her wander off too far and she'll think she's in any other village."

"Oh, that's right," Martin said with a scoff. "You weren't here to see Ink figure out where he was in less than ten minutes."

Ink considered replying to this with a smart remark but found he didn't have the heart. Caradoc nodded at the Plumsleys, who dutifully took off down the path after Simon and Chester. Abner sighed and pulled off his false nose, along with a pair of spectacles. He left the bushy black beard on his face as he turned back towards the Pipeworks House.

"Come on, Evering," he said, "let's get those propellers started up again."

Caradoc stepped towards the young man before he could move away and gripped his hand in a firm shake. "Thanks for your help, Evering."

Surprised, Evering nodded and mumbled something in return. Ink watched as he followed his father through the door. He hadn't noticed until then, but the events of the evening had shaken Evering up as well, and he was hiding it better than Ink had thought him capable.

"Well," Riva said to Caradoc after Abner and Evering had gone, "at least you look a right sight better than you did after the last expulsion."

"The Spektor must have been weak," Delia said. "It was just the one, wasn't it?"

Caradoc looked down and fidgeted with the makeshift bandage on his hand.

"Caradoc," Delia said, her brow furrowing, "how many were there?"

"A few," he answered cryptically.

"How many is a few?" Harriet asked.

Caradoc stuffed a hand into his pocket and scratched at his beard with the other, twisting his mouth as he glanced away. "Seven."

They stared at him in shock.

"*Seven?*" Delia echoed.

Martin looked skyward and put a hand on his brow. "Seven. The man just said 'seven'."

"What?" Ink said, looking up at Caradoc. "Ain't that a normal workload for you?"

"I've never taken on more than two at one time."

Ink frowned. "Is that why the house got flattened?"

"*Flattened?*" the others cried all at once. Caradoc cringed and shot Ink a look.

"You should be dead!" Jeremy exclaimed.

"Yes. I should be," Caradoc said, "if not for Margaret. She has such fire in her spirit, even in the face of the unknown.

Hardly showed any fear at all—until we were about to leave her."

Harriet stepped closer and gently pulled the cap from his head, revealing a blood-soaked bandage over his brow. "Good heavens, Caradoc, why do you always insist on hiding the worst of your injuries?"

"Sit down," Delia said to him. "Here on the steps. Riva . . ."

This time, he did not protest. Riva unwrapped the bandage, then placed her hand over the wound and closed her eyes. The others looked on anxiously. Even Ink stepped closer to see if the enchantment was working. After a minute had passed, she shook her head.

"It's deep. And there is some sort of . . . remnant . . . from the weapon that did this."

Ink trembled again, recalling the black vapor that hung around the Spektors like a living cloud of poison.

"Come on," Harriet said, nodding to the others.

They gathered around the wounded man. Harriet sat beside him and clasped his right hand between both of hers. Jeremy and Martin crouched down and each put a hand on one of his shoulders. Delia touched his arm. Riva took a deep breath and moved her hand to the side of Caradoc's face.

Ink stood back, confounded at first, then astonished as he watched the wound begin to heal. Muscle and tissue knitted themselves together. Skin grew back into place. In a matter of seconds, the horrible injury was no more. Only a trace of smeared blood remained. Caradoc put his fingers to his brow, feeling the new flesh.

"Thank you," he said.

Before he could say anything more, his face twisted in pain and he clutched at his chest once more. Blood spilled through the bandage on his left hand, spattering onto the stone steps.

"Someone go and fetch Simon!" Harriet cried.

"No," Caradoc said, short of breath. "No. I'll be fine. I just need to get to my room."

Delia went to fetch Simon anyway. Jeremy hurried to the Dining House to get Caradoc something to eat. The others helped him to the tower, with Martin and Harriet climbing the winding stair on either side of him to keep him steady. Riva and Ink followed behind.

"Are you all right, Ink?" Riva asked.

He looked at her, stunned, and lied. "I'm fine. Why?"

"I was rattled for days the first time I witnessed an expulsion, and everything that came with it," she said. "And knowing how the Spektors have taken an interest in you and how close they were? You must have been terrified."

"Look, I'd . . . rather not talk about it just now. All right?"

She nodded. "I understand."

Ink shook his head, wearied by yet another mystery. "What happened back there? With everyone helping to heal his wound. Cassrians don't have that kind of power."

"Entrian abilities have always been tied directly to what we carry inside of us," Riva replied. "Our inner strength and compassion. Our hearts, you could say. So whenever we face a task too great or too difficult for a single person, others may join in to offer what they can. Entrians have always helped each other in this way. But it was never done with Cassrians."

"Until now?" Ink said.

Riva nodded. "The first time this happened, I was trying to raise Riverfall from the ground. In a thousand years I could never have done such a thing on my own, but I could feel all the strength I lacked in the others around me, and I was able to harness it. They didn't know what was going on at the time, and even now I don't fully understand how it happens."

"But . . . that's incredible!" Ink said. "Do the other Entrians know about this?"

"No. And I shudder to think what would happen if they ever found out."

"Why?"

"Most Entrians believe that our powers are a special gift, given to us as our divine purpose in this world. We consider the use of our abilities a sacred act. Some say it's like a prayer, in its truest and purest form. The very idea that the 'heathen' Cassrians could possibly have a hand to play in it would overturn one of the most basic convictions of the entire nation. There would be panic in the streets."

They reached the top of the stairs a moment later and followed the others through the door into Caradoc's room.

"I'll get your tonic," Martin said.

After helping Caradoc ease down onto the edge of his bed, he went to a cupboard above a small nightstand and withdrew a decanter of wine, a mixing spoon, a drinking glass, and two tall bottles of colored liquid—one blue, the other amber. As this was being done, Harriet brought the wash basin over and sat next to Caradoc. She unwrapped the bandage from his left hand and began to gently wash the blood from his skin.

"You don't have to do that," he said.

"I don't have to do a lot of things," she answered.

Ink watched as Martin measured out the wine from the decanter and poured it into the glass, then took up the bottle of blue liquid and measured it against the amber one. Ink suddenly remembered he'd seen Caradoc leaving Simon's house with those same bottles the first day he'd been put to work with Jeremy.

"What's in those?" Ink asked Riva.

"The blue one is an herbal mixture," she answered, "to help strengthen him. The Key needs blood to work, like oil for a machine. Draws it straight from the heart. That's why he loses so much through the open wound. We've tried so many different things to help lessen the strain it puts on him, but it only seems to be getting worse."

"Can't you heal him? All together?"

"We've tried. Many times."

Ink furrowed his brow as he watched Harriet wrap a clean

bandage around the golden mark. This is what his granddad wanted him to take for himself? A parasite that would slowly and literally suck the life out of him?

"And the other one?" he said. "The dark-colored stuff?"

"A narcotic, Mr. Featherfield," Caradoc answered, looking paler by the minute. "The strongest we could find. It deadens my mind in sleep so I can't dream. It's a kind of protection against all the things I've had to see and hear. Keeps them from returning to me."

Ink swallowed, remembering the devastation of the destroyed city his granddad had shown him. How many more were there? How many that he needed drugging up every night?

"And even mixed with a strong dose of the best wine in the world," Martin said, handing Caradoc the glass, "it's still utterly revolting."

"'Poison' is the word, I think," Caradoc said, looking down at the dark purple mixture.

"Whatever it is, it's made my eyes water," Martin replied as he brought a hand to them.

Riva went around the room and drew the curtains over the windows. "What we really need is a decent apothecary. Perhaps we'll find one near Mastmarner."

"I still can't believe you found seven Spektors in a place like Burgess Valley," Martin said.

Harriet shook her head. "And that poor woman. Living alone with them all this time. God only knows what that's done to her."

"Did the Spektors say anything about Ink?" Riva asked.

"Only that they knew him. Nothing more," Caradoc said, then looked at Ink. "I have to admit, I was fairly relieved to see you still standing there when it was all over. I'm not sure I could've gotten to you in time if the Spektors had decided to pay you another visit then and there."

Ink gave him the ugliest, dead-panned stare he could muster. Caradoc didn't see it. He was too busy draining the tonic as quickly as possible.

CHAPTER 37

WATCHER'S PASS

In the short time he'd been on his own, Ink had spent many a
restless night lying awake, whether from the gnawing ache of
an empty stomach, trying to sleep on cold, hard ground, or
contending with the ever-present fear of returning to the orphanage. There had never been a shortage of reasons. But these dark
and silent hours following the terrible events of that evening? He
knew they would be the very worst of all.

He glanced over at Evering in the other bed and felt a flicker
of envy. How could he be sleeping so peacefully after what had
happened? It didn't seem possible. Perhaps he'd been brought up
in the manner most children usually were. A lifetime of being told
he was loved, safe, and actually believing it. The time Ink had
spent in his granddad's care had not made him accustomed to
such comforts. There'd been no one to tuck him in at night, no
one to wish him sweet dreams or ease his mind with a soft lullaby.
He'd always been convinced that such foolish things only served
to make children silly and soft-headed. But he wanted them now.
He wished for them with all his heart.

He sat awake for hours. No matter how hard he tried he
couldn't clear his head of all the things he'd witnessed—the Spektors, the Otherworlds, the ruined city of Krymenos, even the

rattle of chains and the sight of Caradoc's blood oozing through the golden mark on his hand. It was almost too much for his nerves to bear. He glanced at his hat sitting atop the bedpost. Its elongated shadow looked identical to the top hat his granddad wore. As he stared, his granddad's voice echoed anew in his mind —a sound he had thought never to hear again. But there it was, alive and well in the shallow recesses of fresh memory, shaded by those old familiar tones of accusation and disappointment. Ink grabbed the hat from the bedpost and flung it out of sight.

He heaved a frustrated sigh and shoved the bedcovers away. Maybe knocking his head against a wall would put him out. Or a healthy dose of a strong narcotic. Whatever the case, he wasn't going to sit around waiting. He had to *do* something. Being careful not to wake Evering, he swung his legs out over the edge of the bed, slipped into his boots and coat, then made for the door. He left his hat on the floor.

It was chilly outside. He could see his breath as he stepped onto the path and glanced up. A multitude of stars glistened in the dark sea overhead. He sighed again. What could he do? Go to the kitchen? The Music House? Down to the pipeworks? At least there would be some noise there. But before he could decide, a glint of light caught his eye in the garden, moving among the dark trees like a glittering fairy. He hesitated, wondering if he should dash back inside the house to avoid being scolded for being out so late. He chose to wait instead, watching as a figure melted out of the shadows and into the moonlight.

It was Caradoc. He noticed Ink at once and paused at the edge of the path. The lantern in his hand trembled. Clearly, the narcotic had failed to do its work. They stood looking at one another for several moments, each understanding the others' trouble. With a small jerk of the head, Caradoc motioned for Ink to go along with him.

They walked in silence on a trail that led beyond the houses to the northernmost edge of the village. For once, Ink did not have to struggle to keep up with Caradoc's long strides. They kept an easy pace as they crossed the meadow. The tall grasses reached up to their shins, making hushed sighs as they brushed past them. Ink glanced up at his quiet companion.

"You don't know who your Protector really is, do you?"

His granddad's question echoed in his mind. It was true. Despite his best efforts to uncover the mysteries surrounding the man beside him, he knew precious little. And of everything he did know about him—pirate, fugitive, capable of tearing holes in Otherworlds—only one thing had the slightest chance of relieving any suspicion.

Caradoc was a man of fierce devotion. It wasn't a trait Ink had ever encountered before. He'd always believed that people lived for themselves, and themselves alone. If ties needed to be cut to avoid any kind of hazard or burden, it would be done. But not with Caradoc. He was different. He'd promised Ink protection, even at a risk to his own safety. And Ink knew he would keep his word, regardless of his motives. What had happened to the inhabitants of Krymenos was unfortunate, but Ink reasoned that even if Caradoc was not a safe man for others, he was safe enough for him. For now. Under no circumstances could the same ever be said of the Spektors.

Their journey ended at a part of the border clear of trees. They drew up to the edge and glanced down at the world below. Ink was astonished to see not a vast expanse of dark ground, as he'd expected, but a small, bright city upon the banks of a river, glittering with light and life. Lanterns hung from the decks and masts of cutters and barges in port, lighting up the water on the occasion of some merry festival. Ink held his breath and listened. He could hear music, people cheering, singing and laughing. Here was a world alive. A place where no one had ever heard of Spektors or Otherworlds. Where people lived blissfully in the knowledge that their world was all there was and ever would be.

Caradoc set his lantern on the ground and sat down with his legs hanging over the drop-off. Ink, not about to show himself a coward, did the same.

Neither spoke a word for the rest of the night. It was enough just to be in the others' company, looking down on the paradise below with all its living beacons of warmth and cheer. Even so, Ink felt an ache in his heart as he swept his gaze across the darkened lands beyond. He'd strayed so far from his mission. All but abandoned it. But what could he do while his life was at risk away from the Colonists? Should he tell them? Ask for their help? Reveal all his pains and problems, as Evering had encouraged? Then again, they couldn't even help themselves without having their numbers cut down. Ink shook it from his mind. No. No more worrying tonight. He would let his mind fill with light and song instead.

It was Evering who found them the next morning. They had fallen asleep at the edge of Riverfall, and he was careful in shaking them awake to avoid startling them over the brim.

"You two looked dead when I first saw you!" he said as they righted themselves up and rubbed their faces. "Do you know you slept right through the tower bell? Twice? What are you doing all the way out here?"

Ink and Caradoc looked at one another, uncertain Evering would understand.

"Sight-seeing," Ink finally replied. "What's it to you?"

"Well, you're late for breakfast. Everyone's going off their nut. We'd better get back."

"Hang on, Evering," Caradoc said, getting to his feet and looking out. "We're heading into Watcher's Pass. You've got to see this."

Ink and Evering followed his gaze. Overnight, the village had come up to the doors of the Lockhorns, the largest mountain range in the country. It was named so for the hardy breed of ram often seen in those parts, and for the way many of the craggy peaks twisted upwards like whetted horns. At that moment, Riverfall was heading straight into a wide gorge that ran on for several miles westward. Almost at once, Ink saw something unusual hanging from the mountain walls on either side. Evering stepped closer to the ledge and squinted.

"What? Are those heads?"

Another few seconds drifting closer proved him right. The great stone heads of a lion and an eagle faced each other at the entrance to the gorge, their expressions at once majestic and terrible. After entering the pass below the massive carvings, they were astonished to find there were dozens more, each the head of a different creature and all keeping watch on the travelers who sojourned between them. Caradoc grinned at Ink and Evering's amazed expressions.

"It's said that a group of Entrians climbed up there and made the carvings," he said. "Hundreds of years ago."

They passed beneath the faces of a boar and a bear, followed by a wolf and a horse. The ravages of time and weather had somewhat diminished the quality of the images, but made them no less impressive. Ink pointed a thumb back towards the tower without taking his eyes away.

"Shouldn't you be up there? Making sure we don't knock into any of 'em?"

Caradoc shook his head. "I've already set the proper course heading. It's a straight shot all the way through. Won't have to move us an inch."

"Look there!" Evering said, pointing to a spot near the stone head of a stag.

Three rams stood on a narrow path which crossed the rocky cliffs between the images. They were fierce-looking creatures with shaggy coats of silver and magnificent beards that twisted down their robust chests. Their great horns looked to be at least four feet long and were each curled into razor sharp points.

"Bet they'd make good eating," Evering said. "Could we get closer and try to catch one?"

"We could try," Caradoc answered, "but 'death by ram' isn't exactly on my agenda for today."

"What's that?" Ink asked. The others looked to where he pointed.

In the far distance, gray clouds swelled beyond the end of the gorge. A shadow of a darker shade hovered just beneath them.

"A stray patch of raincloud," Evering said.

Ink squinted harder. "I don't think so."

They waited as it came nearer, growing more uneasy by the second. It was no cloud. Worse still, it appeared to be traveling through the pass at the same level as Riverfall, just below the stone faces.

"God," Caradoc said, almost to himself. "Don't let that be what I think it is."

Then, as if to answer his plea, a break came in the clouds overhead, flooding the gorge with sunlight and illuminating the mysterious object in the distance. Their breath caught in their throats all at once.

An enormous airship was heading straight for them. Its hull sliced through the air with effortless power, gleaming with adornments of ivory and gold. They counted five decks, each with a row of wide windows. The balloon that carried it along nearly filled up half the pass with its size, boasting directional sails on adjustable beams and a network of ropes which hung down to the deck.

It took mere moments for Caradoc to grasp the situation. The next instant, he turned and raced back through the village towards the tower.

"He'll never make it in time," Evering said in a voice of quiet dread. "We're done for. We're done."

They were close enough now to see the crew at work on the main deck, oblivious to the flying mass of solid ground they were sailing towards. The name of the ship was written along the prow of the hull in huge, gold letters:

It was only a few hundred feet from them now. Evering had gone white as a sheet and balled his hands into fists. They were both too stunned to move, heedless of the possibility that the deck of the airship might soon be embedded in the ground on which they stood.

At last, the village began to move sideways, veering slowly to the left. The ship was now headed for Riverfall's eastern side. The boys shook themselves from their stupor and began to hurry along the edge of the border, keeping their eyes on it all the while. They ran until they came to the easternmost point of the village, in the woods between Delia and Jeremy's houses. This would be the final test. If the airship could get clear of this spot, they would be all right. The boys held their breath as the hull came within inches of the drop-off.

But it was too much to ask. They had turned too slowly. With a low groan and a shrill squeal, the airship scraped along the edge of the village, dislodging clumps of dirt and rock. The deck shuddered, sending many of the crew scattering to take hold of rails and ropes. The helmsman clung to the wheel, holding it as steady as he could.

The moment of initial impact with the airship did nothing to faze the Colonists. The violent shudder that followed, however, threw them all to the ground. A grating sound issued out from the pipeworks deep below, and with a sickening crash, Riverfall came to a halt in mid-air. The boys looked at one another with dread. Though they couldn't see it, they knew what had happened. In the eagerness to avoid a collision, the village had become wedged against the mountain side.

"What was that?" a man shouted, clinging to the railing on the quarterdeck.

"Not sure, Captain!" an airman answered.

"Cut the engines!"

While the crew rushed to do his bidding, the first mate hurried across the deck and looked out over the gunwale.

"Felt like something hit us on the starboard side," he said.

The captain followed him. "What the devil could hit us up here?"

"I don't know, sir."

The two men peered out into the gorge, sweeping their eyes along the length of it. Ink and Evering held their breath for fear of being heard, despite knowing sound would not pass through the shroud enchantment.

"Perhaps it was a rockslide," the captain said.

The first mate stood silent, straining his ears. Evering became so unnerved he had to shut his eyes. Ink's own grew wide. The man was looking right through them.

"No," he said. "I think there's something in the gorge with us."

Ink couldn't stand still any longer. They needed a distraction. And it was now or never. He turned and ran along the edge of the drop-off, coming to a halt near a part of the airship where the gunwale dipped low. He glanced back at Evering, who gaped at him in utter bafflement. Ink put a finger to his lips and took several steps backward. He stood still, waiting for a crewman to pass by the spot he'd chosen. Once clear, he took a deep breath, then ran forward at full speed and leapt into the air. Evering clapped a hand over his mouth, stifling a cry.

Ink had misjudged the distance. Instead of tumbling onto the deck as he'd planned, he slammed straight into the hull with his arms hooked desperately over the side. The noise immediately caught the attention of the men on the quarterdeck.

"Who is that?" the captain said.

The first mate took his eyes at last from the village lying inches from his nose and threw a hand out towards the dangling figure.

"Seize that boy!"

Ink pulled himself over the gunwale and landed on deck. The bewildered airmen barely had time to move towards him before he was off running, dodging them left and right. A spiral staircase caught his eye and he made a break for it, flying down to the lower decks as fast as he could. The crew rushed after him.

~

The interior of the ship was grander than anything Ink had ever seen. The marks of supreme wealth and luxury were everywhere he looked. There were velvet-lined chairs, golden candelabra stands, crystal chandeliers, and a hundred other things that would have been the envy of any mansion in Eriaris. The passengers gave out astonished cries as Ink raced by, slowing his pursuers by leaving a wake of expensive wreckage.

"Beg pardon!" he cried as he overturned a serving cart in a dining room.

Whenever he looked back, the mob giving chase behind him seemed to grow in numbers. He made a few false turns, doubled back to confuse them, then dashed up another stairway, startling a maid as he went. A cry flew from her lips as her armful of laundry scattered to the ground. Upon reaching the top floor, he heard her angrily directing the crew to his position.

He paused for a moment and looked around. He was in a long corridor with doors on either side. The voices behind grew louder. He rushed forward and began to try the knobs, hoping to find an unlocked and unoccupied chamber. But none of the doors would open.

"Oh, come on!" Ink said, jerking the handles desperately. "Don't people trust each other any more?" He looked over his shoulder and cringed. The shadow of the pursuing mob loomed on the wall of the stairwell.

There was only one more door to try, set apart from the others at the far end of the corridor. He ran to it and put a hand to the knob, and to his great relief, found the door swinging inward. He hurried into the room, shut the door behind him as quietly as he could, then pressed his ear against it. The mob had reached the corridor. He listened as their footsteps hurried forward, then stopped. They began to argue over which direction he had gone, most insisting that he must have escaped to a lower deck. He breathed a sigh of relief as he heard their voices fade away.

He'd done it. There was nothing now but to lay low until he could return to the main deck and hope the others on Riverfall would be waiting to help him back over. He leaned his forehead against the door and shut his eyes. As he waited for his breaths to slow, he felt a swell of pride. It had been all too easy putting his old skills back into action.

"Hello," a voice said from behind him.

Every muscle in Ink's body froze. Damn. The room was less unoccupied than he'd hoped. He winced and bit his lip. Well, there was nothing to be done about it now. He would just have to face the situation with all the dignity he could muster. After taking a deep breath, he stood up straight, smoothed down his coat, fixed his face with his best self-confident expression, and turned at last to meet his greeter.

His heart dropped to the floor.

It was her.

CHAPTER 38

ALLIANCE

The Entress Seherene sat at a writing desk, pen in hand. The sunlight from the window behind her lent a luminous glow to her figure—a far cry from the stormy conditions in which Ink had first seen her. He couldn't move. He couldn't speak. He couldn't breathe. He recalled hearing stories about mortals being struck dead upon seeing the face of the divine. Now he knew why.

She looked at him with an air of amusement. "Wrong room?"

Ink thought quickly. He had to play this right. He took in a slow breath, then clasped the lapels of his coat.

"No, miss," he answered. "I'm here to take your breakfast order."

A look of surprise entered her expression. She glanced at the door. "Who are you hiding from? Have you gotten yourself into trouble?"

Ink barely contained a scoff. "Seems I'm always in trouble these days."

"Aren't we all?" she replied, curving an eyebrow. "But it's always best to try and make amends." She returned her attention to her letter. "Go back to your cabin. Have a talk with your parents. I'm sure everything will be fine."

394

Ink's face fell. She had dismissed him. Regarded him as nothing more than a child playing a game. But he wasn't about to be dismissed; and he certainly wasn't about to be thought of as a child. He nodded, hooking his thumbs over his belt.

"Maybe you're right," he said. "But then, I suppose you'd know all about that, wouldn't you? Making amends."

That got her attention. She put down her pen and turned towards him. He nearly buckled under the full strength of her piercing gaze. It was like trying to look into the face of the sun. He wanted to turn away, but didn't dare surrender the foothold he'd just gained.

"Who are you?" she asked. "What's your name?"

Ink perked up again. He raised his chin, a cocksure glint in his eye. "My name is Inkwell Featherfield. The first who's ever been, and the last who'll ever be."

He jolted in surprise when she stood up fast from her chair.

"Inkwell Featherfield?" she repeated, looking hard at him.

Ink grew nervous, wondering what he'd had done to merit such a reaction.

"Good heavens!" she said. "You're him! You're that runaway orphan!"

Ink's remaining pride and confidence died away in an instant, deflating him where he stood. He'd forgotten all about the kidnapping notice.

"The entire country has been looking for you!" she said, moving towards him.

He backed away, afraid to let her any nearer. She stopped.

"You've nothing to fear any longer. You're safe now."

He stayed silent, his eyes pained with anxious fear.

She frowned in concern. "Are you all right? Are you injured at all?"

Still, he did not answer.

"How did you escape them? Are they still near? Are they hiding in the mountains?" She hurried to the window as she spoke and looked out. Ink backed farther into the corner of the room near a large canopied bed.

"It's been a long time since we last searched here," she said. "We thought the terrain too unforgiving for human life." When she heard no reply, she turned to him again. "You must tell me quickly, Inkwell. There may still be time—"

She started towards him again, but he skittered over the bed and backed away to the opposite wall. He shook his head, but still couldn't bring himself to speak.

"Listen to me," she tried again. "No one is going to hurt you. I swear it. You needn't be frightened. You are rescued. And you must help us now, before it's too late."

He shook his head again. "I . . ."

She watched in bewilderment as he wrung his hands, his face rife with distress.

"I . . . I can't be rescued."

"I declare that you are."

"You don't understand," he said. "It's not that I don't believe I am, or could be. And it's not that I don't want to be. It's that I can't be. Not now. Not yet."

The Entress looked at him, stunned. Before another word could be said, a knock came at the cabin door. Ink fell back against the wall, flattening himself against the side of a large wardrobe. He looked back at her, making a desperate plea with his eyes for discretion. She stared at him for another moment before replying. "Come in."

The door swung open. A crewman stepped across the threshold and bowed his head.

"Sorry to disturb, my lady," he said. "The ship's been held up briefly by a bit of commotion regarding a stowaway found onboard. The captain sends his assurance there is no danger and apologizes for the delay."

Ink held his breath. With only the slightest movement he shook his head, knowing she was looking at him from out the corner of her eye.

"Thank you, Mr. Mason," she said with a nod. "I appreciate the notice."

"Not to worry, ma'am," he answered. "We'll soon have the little scamp."

Ink felt his cheeks flush as the door clicked shut. Only once the crewman's footsteps faded away did he dare another glance at the Entress. Her expression had turned deadly serious.

"Well, Mr. Featherfield," she said, "may I ask what you're doing here if you don't mean to be rescued?"

Ink looked away, still flattened against the wall. "Look, I ain't stupid. I know perfectly well who you are and what you can do. And if I can't lie without you knowing . . . then I suppose we don't have much to talk about. So you best let me go."

She moved towards him again.

"Don't come any closer!" he cried. "And don't try working any of your . . . special powers on me, either! I'd rather die than tell you anything!"

She halted in her steps, again regarding him with astonishment. "You mean to return to them?"

The tone of dread in her voice made the prospect sound as grim as a death sentence. He did his best to hide the heaviness it brought to his heart, but he knew it wouldn't go completely unnoticed.

"I don't have a choice," he finally answered.

Her steady gaze did not leave his face. "Well. Then I suppose there is little else to say on the matter."

She turned and crossed the room to a small breakfast table. Ink's eyes couldn't help but follow her. The elegant way she moved reminded him of the dream-like dancers he'd seen in the forest of an Otherworld.

"But you needn't take your leave this very moment," she said, seating herself at the table and taking up a silver teapot. "Will you at least have some refreshment before you go?"

"No," he answered, then corrected himself. "No thank you."

Undaunted, she poured two cups of tea and set one of them in front of the empty seat across from her. She looked back at him with a small curve of her lips.

"Will you at least sit with me? Or do you better prefer the company of the wardrobe?"

This was a crisis. She had called him by name, honored his request for silence, and was now inviting him to tea. She had lingered in his memory all this time like a sweet strain of music, but the very idea of joining her at the table went against all reason. It was far too dangerous. Completely out of the question. But before he had even finished the thought, he found himself crossing the room and taking the empty seat.

She removed the lid from a small tray. "Will you have something to eat?"

"No. Thank you."

Another smile hinted on her lips. "I can only imagine what they must have told you about me. But it isn't poisoned. I promise."

He looked away. She replaced the lid over the tray.

"I daresay you look rather well for a captive. Obviously not starving for food or drink. You are not ill-treated?"

He gave this a moment's thought before answering. "No. Not exactly. At least . . . nothing as bad as what could happen if I wasn't with them."

She set her cup down on the table and watched his face closely. "Because you think he's protecting you?"

He looked at her in surprise, but quickly dropped his gaze again. The effect of being so close to her made the enchantment over his senses much stronger. Her eyes were like ageless dark oceans, and for all he knew he might never find his way out of them again if he stared too long.

"He *is* protecting me," he finally answered.

"He could be lying."

"He's not. I know he's not."

"How do you know?"

"Because I've seen what he can do!" Ink cried, becoming

annoyed at the line of questioning. "I've seen that *thing* on his hand! I've seen what he fights against! Not half a day ago I watched an entire house get turned into a pile of matchsticks and dust!"

"That must have been terrifying."

"It was!" he shot back, aware of the sympathetic tone she was trying to effect. "But what would you know about any of it?"

"A great deal more than you could possibly imagine," she answered.

With this he was silenced, and she was gracious enough to let his impudence go at that. His eyes fell to the table again, and he watched as she spooned a lump of sugar into her cup.

"From the age Entrian children begin to fear the shadows on their bedroom walls, they are told stories of the Spektors. We are brought up on them. Not to frighten into obedience or submission. Not to entertain. But to instruct. To warn." She shook her head as she stirred her cup. "That's one thing I could never understand about the Cassrians. Why frighten children with silly tales of headless ghosts and ridiculous monsters when beings of real terror exist right here in our own world?"

Ink didn't answer. He was too busy watching the way she brought the teacup to her lips.

"The level of harm that may be caused by truth passing into myth is immeasurable," she continued. "Wisdom is bred out of an entire people, one generation after the other, until it becomes all too easy to be taken advantage of."

Ink sat back in his chair and crossed his arms. "I think that's just about the nicest way anyone's ever called me a fool."

"Not a fool," she replied, "a victim. One of countless others. But you can help us put a stop to it. Right now. Once and for all. You carry the look of one burdened by knowledge almost too great and terrible to bear. I've seen it before. But you need not suffer alone."

It was all Ink could do to keep his eyes lowered to the tablecloth. He could hear the compassion in her voice, working to play on his heartstrings, and he knew he'd be lost if he glanced up even once.

"Let us help you, Inkwell," she said.

"And how you gonna do that?" Ink replied, growing anxious over how much the balance of power was shifting in her favor. "You got another one of them Spider Keys somewhere?"

"No."

"Well then you can't help me."

"We can try. There may be other ways—"

"Other ways?" Ink retorted. "Like what? You gonna throw rocks at 'em? Scare 'em with loud noises? I've got *Spektors* hunting me down! All right? And they ain't gonna stop 'til I'm dead! But it just so happens that the one person they fear more than anyone else in the world has promised me protection. I call that a pretty nice offer. And so long as he can make good on that promise, I couldn't care less about being a victim, so long as I stay a live one."

"No matter his reasons?" she replied, both her tone and gaze becoming sharp. "No matter that every Spektor he finds—each one you bring to him by drawing it to you—leads him closer to having them under his control?"

Ink was stunned to hear his granddad's warning again. He had almost put the idea of 'controlling Spektors' out of his head, convinced it was nothing more than a desperate attempt to make him turn against Caradoc. But here it was again, and this time coming from a source he felt more inclined to believe.

"You've heard something of this before," she said.

"I might have," he admitted. "Not that any of it makes much sense."

With expert deftness and speed, the Entress gained her next foothold. "The Key is meant for one purpose, and one purpose alone; to return the Spektors to the Crypt, where they are bound, never to rise again. In the last few hundred years a rumor began to emerge. It said that whoever could find the Crypt containing the expelled souls would be able to release them again and command them to whatever purpose they desired."

"Well, that's good, ain't it? Put 'em to work. Send 'em to the factories, the mines—"

"Spektors are incapable of doing good in any capacity," she said. "They are purely beings of hatred and despair, and it is only to these ends that they can be employed. The Keyholders knew this. So when the rumor persisted, they gathered together and swore an oath never to seek such evil power. The exact location of the Crypt was even erased from all record, and the Keyholders of that age vowed never to pass down that knowledge to their successors. But it seems this has not been a complete discouragement. I believe he is well on his way to breaking that ancient oath. If he has not done so already."

Ink frowned. "What do you mean?"

She fell silent for a moment, thoughtfully running her finger along the delicate handle of her teacup. "We have . . . suspicions . . . that a former Colonist by the name of Iophulis Bash was murdered by Spektors acting under orders."

Ink turned this over in his mind. Caradoc murder Bash? It wasn't possible. He'd watched him toast to Bash's life. He'd seen him carve the old man's name on the Memory Tree.

"But . . . why would he have wanted to kill him? There's no reason for it."

"Perhaps they'd parted ways badly," she replied. "Perhaps Bash's leaving was seen as an act of breaking faith with the rest of them. Disloyalty—rewarded with a death sentence."

Ink felt his stomach turn sour. Had he not just labeled Caradoc as a man of fierce devotion? The Entress sat back in her chair, allowing him time to think. She gazed out the window, scanning the overgrown paths in the mountainside.

"A Keyholder was always seen as a hero in the old stories. A protector." A look of deep melancholy filled her eyes. "Dark is the day you learn that heroes are not all you dreamed they were. That they are the myth."

"What about the others?" Ink asked. "You mentioned there were other Keyholders. If what you say is true, can't they do something to stop him?"

"There are no others anymore," she answered. "He is the last."

Ink frowned, his mind filling with every terrible implication brought on by this fact.

"Perhaps you see it more clearly now," she said. "No one can oppose him. No one can match his power or take him to task for his actions. Not while he is free. And for this, I believe him to be the most dangerous person in the world. And not only this one." She tilted her head. "But I think you know that."

His resolve was crumbling. The hardness in his expression softened. The attitude of tough defiance fell away. She leaned forward and gazed into his face.

"You have said that the Spektors fear him more than anyone else in this world. That is the truth. But know this also . . ." A sudden fierceness in her voice made him look back at her. Storm clouds had gathered behind her eyes. "There is no one in the world he regards with more dread than me. That is also the truth. And you need not fear him once you are by my side."

"Your side?" Ink said. "So that's it. I'm just a servant trading over for a new master."

"I know you must be very confused," she said, "and I know a lot of people have been telling you a lot of different things. But there is no ultimatum here. I do not ask you to pledge your allegiance to anything or anyone. Rather I ask that you consider an alliance. Help us, and we will help you. You have my word."

"Do you even know what you're saying? Asking me to give him over is like . . . asking me to carry out my own death sentence! Those Spektors are watching my every move! They'd be on me in a minute!"

"Then why aren't they here now?"

Ink fell silent. He didn't know the answer. Maybe there was something to be said for her offer after all. With all the powers the Entrians possessed, maybe they really could help him.

But then he remembered his grandfather's words. He knew too much now. He'd seen what he was never meant to see. Nothing could ever change that fact. With another shake of his head, he wrenched himself out of his chair.

"Your promises sound all well and good," he said, backing away towards the cabin door, "but 'til you can actually find a way to see 'em through, I'm sticking with him."

"If you will not give him over, surely you can give us the others."

"Nothing doing," Ink answered. "He'd know it was me in a second. And then I get the same treatment as old Mr. Bash if you're right about him. No. No, thank you."

She rose from her chair, her gaze becoming a fiery stare. He put a hand on the doorknob, eager to be gone before some terrible enchantment could be sent flying his way.

"Look, I'm sorry about everything," he said. "I'm sorry about what was done to your people and all. But this ain't my fight. It never was. I'm just trying to stay out of the way. And stay alive."

Her expression softened. The fire left her eyes. She clasped her hands in front of her, as if acknowledging defeat. "I cannot blame you for that. If you must go . . . then go."

It was her cleverest trap yet. Despite his talk, the last thing Ink wanted was to leave her presence, and her eyes revealed just enough vulnerability—her face drawn with just enough sorrow—that his grip on the doorknob loosened.

"Did you ever think," he said, "that you might have this all wrong? It don't make any sense, you know. Why would he care about controlling the Spektors? He ain't got no reason."

"They're Colonists," she said. "I should think the reason was obvious."

Ink shook his head. "They say they went to that island to stop a massacre, not start one. Caradoc even ran supplies to Entrian ports after his own dad got it outlawed. Why go to such trouble appearing so kind and decent towards your people if they was just wanting to kill 'em all? There's even an Entress right there with them! Riva would be able to tell in a moment if they were lying! Why else would she stay with them unless they were really innocent?"

"Because your protector is a master deceiver," she answered. "He knows what truths to tell in front of her to work to his advantage. What he says about running supplies to the Entrians is true, but there was no honorable intent behind it. It was all part of an elaborate plan to earn the good graces of those he hoped to take advantage of in the future. Gaining trust always proves more effective than brutalizing with threats. It earns allies, and in some cases, friends. That's how he was able to gather the Colonists together in the first place. I don't suppose he told you the reason his father pushed your government into cutting off all trade with us?"

"Well, no," Ink said. "Not really."

She folded her arms. "The Entrians were once no better than clans at war with one another. The fighting got very fierce at times, sometimes spilling over into Cassrian streets crowded with innocent people. One day, a fight between two families broke out in a marketplace where his mother had gone. She was killed by a stray bullet."

Ink's frown deepened in dismay.

"Both father and son sought vengeance," Seherene continued. "One, by destroying the livelihoods of thousands of families. The other . . . by destroying the families themselves."

Ink lapsed into a stunned stupor as a revelation came over him like a thunderclap. "Sweet mercy . . . that's what he did. The bad thing the others won't tell me about, except to say it's the only thing in the stories that ain't a lie." His eyes widened. "Something he *couldn't* lie about! They must have seen him do it, or asked him outright in front of Riva!" He looked at her again. "He killed him. That prophet of yours. Darian. He was the one who pulled the trigger. Shot him in the heart and started the whole thing. Didn't he?"

Seherene stood silent for a moment, then went to the writing desk and opened a small drawer. She turned back and held out a flintlock pistol. Ink stepped up to her and took it. It was a small, simple weapon, with the letters '*A*' and '*S*' entwined and stamped into the grip.

"This is it," she said. "The only material piece of evidence we have for their treachery, found on the island in the midst of the chaos. The mark there is a symbol of his father's merchant company. Senior crewmen were issued one upon obtaining a certain rank. He carried it with him at all times, even after he'd left his father's service. I carry it in remembrance of the two men who stood at either end of it. They both mean—and have meant —more to me than anyone else in this world can claim. For better and for worse."

A curious emotion had crept into her voice. Ink glanced up. Her calm resolve and effortless regality had been subdued by the effect of a memory, sending her heart-stricken eyes into a faraway gaze. But it didn't last long. With a blink, she returned to the present.

"He was special to you?" Ink asked, offering the pistol back to her. "This Darian?"

"Very special," she answered as she took it from him. She turned and placed it carefully inside the writing desk. "I watched the light leave his eyes as he lay in my arms. He was frightened. He was so frightened." She closed her eyes for a moment, as if to block the terrible memories from returning. "Not a day goes by I don't feel the wound in my own heart. The piece of me he took with him. I suppose, in some way, I've been hoping all this time to find it again. But perhaps I am only fooling myself. That part of me is gone forever."

Something stirred in Ink's heart. The dejection in her eyes— the utter heartbreak of loss—was the same look he'd so often seen in the faces of the Colonists. The same feeling brought on his own pain, threatening to make it resurface. He'd fought against it every time. Pushed it away, ignored it, for there was never anything to be done about the hurt. No hope of healing, no matter what Evering claimed.

Unless he was right. Ink glanced back at the Entress in near shock as a thought suddenly struck him. He was standing in the presence of one of the most powerful people in the world, able to do anything and go anywhere she wished at any time. She could help him. She could put an end to his search. He would no longer be lost. No longer alone. And his soul welled with such hope and longing, he finally blurted out the great secret he had struggled for so long to keep hidden.

"My parents are gone."

She looked at him, surprised by the sudden confession.

"Not dead," he continued. "Just gone. Missing. They caught some kind of infection traveling along the southern coast. Doctors said it was highly contagious, so they had to go away for a while. I was sent to live with my granddad 'til they were recovered."

Ink stepped back and hung his head, hardly believing what he was doing. But he couldn't stop now. The words rushed out of him in sheer relief at being unleashed at last.

"We were never allowed to visit. Mum and Dad said it was too dangerous. They wrote to us a few times in the beginning, but that stopped when they got worse. Doctors sent word of their condition every few weeks, but there never was any change for the better."

He shoved his hands into his pockets and snuck a glance at her face. She was listening. Not telling him to be quiet or stop complaining. But actually listening. He took a deep breath.

"Then the doctors' letters stopped coming, without any explanation. We tried to get word, but no one answered us. So we decided to make a trip to the sanatorium in person. When we showed up asking after Samuel and Elizabeth Revore, they looked at us like we were out of our minds. Said there'd never been any patients there by those names. Even tried to convince us we had the wrong infirmary. I never saw Granddad so angry in all my life.

Went so mad he nearly got himself arrested. We tried to get help. Called on the law, the priests. Even the Assembly. But they couldn't help us. Or wouldn't. A few months later, Granddad made me swear on his deathbed to keep looking for 'em." He bit his lip, fighting to push away the image of his dead grandfather in chains. "After he died, they sent me to a boarding school. But things didn't go well. Seems I couldn't 'play nice', as they put it. Kicked me out after two weeks. Didn't want to deal with me."

Seherene looked on in heartbroken silence.

"Then it was Kinsington Orphanage," he continued, "just like the notices say. And after I found out what a bloody miserable place that was I decided no one else was going to have any say over my life. No more being hauled from place to place. I finally realized no one in the world cared two bits about me or my parents. So I hitched it out of there as fast as I could and started on the search. Been looking for 'em in every infirmary in every town I pass through. Least I *was*, until . . . well, you know the rest." He shook his head, fighting the lump in his throat. "I don't know why I told you. I never told anyone. I guess I thought maybe you could . . . help. But that was stupid of me. You got far more important things to deal with. And you're right, you know. What you said about heroes. There ain't none. Not sure there ever were. That's the one thing you can always count on when it comes to people. They'll let you down. Every time."

He finished with a sigh and hurried to wipe a tear from his eye. He was such a fool. He'd gone and opened his bleeding heart all over the place. What would his granddad say to him now? What would *she* say?

But words were not her first response. To his complete astonishment, the Entress went towards him, gathered her skirts around her, and knelt on the floor in front of him. She took him gently by the arms and gazed into his face, her eyes full of tender-heartedness.

"This I swear, by everything that matters in this world," she said. "I will find them. I will find Samuel and Elizabeth Revore. I will spread word of them to every corner of this country. I will take up your mission as one of my own."

Ink looked away, a shadow of dread overtaking his hope. "For a price."

She didn't answer. Ink shut his eyes and felt his heartbeat quicken in his chest.

"But . . . you torture them. They say you torture them."

"That isn't true," she replied. "We know they are not all guilty. Each has their chance to explain their actions. We want them alive. No one is asking you to hurt anyone."

Ink opened his eyes at last and looked out the window.

Within the next few minutes the deal was struck, the contract agreed upon, the terms made clear. He would offer what he could to her cause, and in return, she would begin the search for his parents and find a way to get the Spektors off his tail. He was careful, however, to make it plain that until she held up both ends of her bargain, she would never lay a finger on Caradoc.

"And take down all those kidnapping notices," he said. "I don't want any more of that kind of fame."

"Of course."

"You can call off your bloodhounds, too. Bill Stone, that commissioner, whoever else you've got on the hunt."

"I'm afraid Mr. Stone and the commissioner do not fall under my authority. But I will do what I can."

A strange look came into her eyes, as if she was studying him even closer. She opened her mouth to speak, but then seemed to think better of it.

"What?" he asked. "What is it?"

"Forgive me," she said, "but there is a strange energy coming from you. Very small, but potent. It's almost as though . . . you're carrying an enchantment of some kind."

Ink panicked for a moment. Had she detected the spyglass

around his neck? He put his hands into his pockets, desperate to find anything else he might pawn off as the object in question. His finger hit against something cold and hard. It was the ring he'd swiped from the ruins of Margaret's house. He took it from his pocket and showed it to her.

Her face filled with astonishment. "How did you come by this?"

"I . . . found it," he said. It was true. Technically.

"May I?" she asked.

He held out his hand. She took the ring and began to study it.

"Do you know what this is?"

He attempted an indifferent shrug. "A nice paperweight?"

"An Entrian pact ring," she answered. "No two are ever alike. The power this one holds is very strong but has long been dormant. Where did you find it?"

"Just poking about in an abandoned house. What's it for?"

"They're used as a symbol of good faith between two people. A kind of bond. Sacred to some." She took his right hand in hers and slipped the ring over his finger. "Wear it. As a token of our vows."

Ink blushed harder than he'd ever done in his life. She smiled at him, holding the ring between her thumb and forefinger. Ink watched as the silver band shrank to fit his finger. The emerald vine which twisted around it gleamed in the light.

She rose to her feet. "Would you allow me to escort you back to the deck?"

"No," he said. He knew she only hoped to discover his route of escape. "No one's to see me go. I'll sneak out. And if I see you following, the deal's off."

She stepped back from him and nodded. "You're a shrewd businessman, Mr. Revore."

"Not Revore. I won't go by that name anymore. Not 'til they're found."

"As you wish," she said. "Inkwell Featherfield. How did you come by that name? Is there any meaning behind it?"

"Took it from something my granddad always used to say," he answered. "How people always seem to have too much of one thing, and not enough of another. Like an inkwell in a field of feathers. Seemed to sum me up well enough."

"Are you certain you can do this?" she said. "Certain you can play him at his game? You must be clever. Stay on your toes. You must make him think he's earned your respect."

"That's never been any trouble for me," Ink replied. "I'd call the Devil 'sir' if I thought it would put me in his favor."

She regarded this with amusement. "Well then . . . until we meet again, Mr. Featherfield."

He cast one last glance at her, trying to imprint her image into his memory, then turned and hurried into the corridor.

Ink worked his way back to the top deck of the airship with the greatest caution, taking care to hide himself at the first sign of anyone nearby. He grew increasingly anxious all the while, wondering how he would get back to the village. What if they had already left him?

He made it to the upper deck at the stern and found the area devoid of crewmembers—at least for the time being—then crept along to the rear gunwale, hoping with all his might that Evering was still standing at the eastern edge of the village. He crouched behind a barrel and took the spyglass out from under his shirt. After touching his fingertip to the glass, it began to glow. He held it between his hands to hide the light.

"Mr. Godfrey!" Ink heard the captain's voice call out. "Pass the word to start the engines. We can't let the little shrimp delay us any longer."

"Aye, sir!"

A bell rang out from somewhere mid-deck. Ink's heart began to beat faster in his chest. He was running out of time. The sound of hissing steam issued from the propellers below.

"Pssst!" a voice hissed.

Ink perked up, swiveling his gaze towards the starboard side. A rope with a large loop tied at the end came sailing through the air towards his position. Ink caught it before it fell to the deck.

"Under your arms!" the voice said.

He pulled the makeshift harness over his head and secured it under his armpits. Then he stood, casting a cautious glance across the deck. No one noticed him.

The next moment, he was whisked away.

CHAPTER 39

NAME YOUR ENEMY

Ink tumbled to the ground aboard Riverfall. Simon and Evering helped him to his feet and out of the rope harness.

"Are you all right?" Simon asked.

"Blimey, Ink!" Evering cried. "What on earth were you thinking?"

"They were catching on to us. I had to do something."

Simon shook his head. "That was incredibly brave."

"Or incredibly stupid," Evering replied.

"Leave him be," Simon said. "Come on. We've got to help the others get us loose from the mountainside."

"What about Margaret?" Evering asked. "Who's keeping an eye on her?"

"Riva's sitting with her in case she wakes. Ink, stay here and rest if you want. I think you've earned it." He offered a small smile, then took off for the western edge of the village. Evering shook his head at Ink before following him.

Ink glanced back at the airship. Almost at the same moment, the main cabin door on the top deck burst open and the Entress herself came striding out onto the deck.

"My lady," the captain said in surprise, turning from the helm.

"Captain, I need you to cut the engines. Immediately."

He frowned. "The engines, ma'am?"

"I want scouts sent into the mountains on either side of this pass. And call your officers to my cabin. Quickly."

Though baffled, the captain knew better than to contest her. While he busied himself with carrying out her orders, Seherene threw her sharp gaze in every direction, hoping to catch sight of the retreating stowaway. Ink shivered as her eyes swept across the spot where he stood. Her expression grew troubled. Without another word, she turned and disappeared back into her cabin.

The ground beneath Ink's feet gave out a sudden shudder. He faltered, catching hold of a tree trunk as a groaning sound rumbled from deep below. Riverfall was on the move again, and it seemed the silencing enchantment had done its work, for no one aboard the airship looked their way. As the village began to pull forward, Ink followed along the edge of the drop-off, keeping the *Adrasteia* in sight for as long as he could. The activity on deck was a flurry of action, the air full of shouts and calls. The airship's propellers came to a full stop again, and he watched as the captain and first mate led a small group of officers into the main cabin. He halted at the southern end of the village, unable to go any farther, then glanced down at the ring on his hand.

Why hadn't she threatened him? Why hadn't she used her powers to force him to reveal everything? Why not torture? It would've been all too easy for her to get the information she needed. But then, maybe she already had it. Maybe she'd whispered some enchantment and seen into his mind, learning everything she wanted before sending him on his way without so much as a threat of imprisonment for holding his silence. Bloody hell. What if she'd already won? On the other hand, she had looked worried just now. Not triumphant. Perhaps the enchantment had failed. Or perhaps she'd begun to doubt her own claim that gaining trust from someone was always better than threatening.

Whatever the case, there was one thing he knew for certain. She wasn't evil. She wasn't a blood-thirsty executioner, as the others had painted her. She was wise and intelligent. Benevolent.

Full of grace and honor. He had made her smile. And she had promised to help him. Trust no one and all that, sure. It was still better than no help at all.

While Ink was still deep in these thoughts, someone appeared on the southern border of the village a few steps down from him and began to climb a tree. Moments later, the dreadful sound of a familiar *click* snapped the boy out of his thoughts. He whipped his head towards the sound, and his eyes went wide with horror.

There was Caradoc, standing on a wide tree limb, braced against the trunk with one foot ahead of the other. In his hands was the largest rifle Ink had ever seen, the barrel six inches longer than even those the Assembly guard carried.

It was aimed at the airship. Ink felt his heart jump into his throat. Before he could open his mouth to cry out, Caradoc pulled the trigger.

With a mighty *crack*, the rifle discharged, and a thunderous boom resounded across the gorge as the carved head of a ram blew apart, sending huge chunks of stone hurtling towards the airship below. The crew on deck dove for cover as the fragments struck, taking out entire sections of the gunwale and shattering into pieces on the deck.

Ink had little time to witness what followed, for Caradoc had climbed down the tree and was heading straight for him, rifle still in hand.

"What are you doing?" Ink cried. "They think we're in the mountains!"

"Now they'll know we're in the mountains," Caradoc said, then lunged and grabbed Ink by the collar. With one hand he dragged him to a tree and heaved him up into the air against the trunk. "What the devil were you doing on that ship?"

"They were going to find us out! I had to draw their attention off!"

"Why were you gone so long?"

"I was hiding below decks, waiting 'til it was clear!"

"Who did you talk to?" Caradoc demanded. "What did you tell them?"

"Nothing! I didn't say a word!"

Caradoc shook him hard against the tree. "You're lying!"

"No! I swear! Why would I come back here if I'd given everything away?"

"Listen, Ink," Caradoc said, his voice full of menace, "I've had a lot of wounds over the course of my life. But see this one above my eye? It's special. It's different from all the rest."

Ink glanced at the whitish scar over his left eyebrow, deep and jagged.

"It came from the knifepoint of someone I'd trusted," he continued. "Someone I thought trusted me. But I was grateful for it in the end. It taught me something I'd overlooked. Discernment. Taking nothing and no one for granted. Realizing that a youthful face makes a person no more innocent than the gray in my beard makes me an old man. It was a hard-learned lesson from an unlikely instructor. He was fifteen years old."

Ink raised his chin, still struggling under Caradoc's hand. "So what? You think I'm out to give you another scar?"

"I think you're learning how to get exactly what you want from everyone. And I wouldn't put it past you to turn it against us. You've got us figured as nothing more than players in your little game, no matter how hard we've tried to show you goodwill. But you know what, Ink? That's a dangerous way to live. Especially with me around."

"This is madness!" Ink cried, struggling in vain against his grip.

The fire in Caradoc's eyes blazed hotter. "Prove me wrong. I beg you. I don't want it to be this way. I wish to God it wasn't this way. But I can't afford to deal in hopeful wishing. Not anymore."

Ink glanced down. The bandaged hand holding him up had begun to tremble.

"So what now?" he said. "You gonna shoot me?"

He regretted the words as soon as they left his mouth. Something inhuman rose behind Caradoc's eyes, a shadow of something deeper than rage, darker than madness. His grip on the rifle tightened, and Ink began to fear for his life.

"Ink!" a voice called out.

Caradoc backed away, dropping the terrified boy back to the ground. The others came into sight moments later, hurrying towards them.

"Ink!" Delia cried out, taking him in a quick embrace. "Are you all right?"

"Are you hurt?" Harriet asked.

"Good Lord, you've got a lot of guts, kid," Chester said.

The others surrounded him, asking similar questions about his actions and state of health, all of which he waved away as though they were making too much fuss over him.

"What now, Caradoc?" Martin asked. "Is the ship away?"

Caradoc nodded and wiped away the perspiration trickling into his eyes. "All clear."

"Thank goodness for that," Wendolen said. "That's the closest we've come in a long time to ending the day with a headstone for a pillow."

"Oh, don't be morbid, Wen," Josephina replied.

"Why'd you do it, Ink?" Chester asked. "Why'd you risk your life for us like that?"

"You know why," Evering answered, surprising everyone with a note of contempt in his voice. "He needs Caradoc alive."

Everyone went silent as they turned their eyes to the boy. Ink took a deep breath, then straightened his coat and stood as tall as he could.

"That's true," he answered. "But that wasn't the only reason. I ain't really the type to get all soft and sentimental in front of other people, but . . . if I'm being honest, I've found something here I ain't ever had before. Something you've all given me. A good home."

He waited for the sound of scoffing, but it never came.

"I know you've all got your problems," he went on. "I know

things have been bloody awful for you. But somehow . . . there's something here no one would ever expect to find among you. Love. And not the cheap kind you read about in the serials, or the fake kind you see between people in the streets. But real love. I don't know how you manage to do it. Maybe it's 'cause there's little else to be had up here. Maybe it's 'cause all you've got left in the world is each other."

The Colonists looked at one another.

"I fought against it," Ink continued. "Didn't want any part of it. Acted a fool. But that's all changed. I'm one of you now, and there ain't no going back. So let's finish it out. Let's find the real villains and run 'em into the ground for what they've done to you. And if it has to end some day, let's make sure it ends on our terms. I know I talk a good game, but if I do from now on it's only to save your necks. 'Cause I wouldn't dream of ending it all, in spite of everything." He looked at the faces around him, and brought his gaze to rest on Caradoc. "You're my business now."

A long moment of silence followed. Ink knew what they were thinking. A heartfelt confession of loyalty was the last thing they had ever expected to hear from a boy so well-practiced in the arts of cynicism and suspicion. Was it genuine? Or just another game?

Simon was the first to respond, stepping forward with an incredulous smile. "Inkwell Featherfield. Running for his life one moment, then saving us all the next." He held out his hand. "Thank you."

Ink shook it and nodded. "What are friends for?"

He waited until sunset, after all the work was done, supper finished, the table cleared, and everyone off to their own amusements. Simon returned to their newest guest in the infirmary. Others took a stroll through the meadows or around the stone path. Some went to the Music House. Some went to watch the sun disappear behind the Lockhorns. Caradoc remained in his tower, too weakened by heart pains to even attend dinner. Ink himself retreated to the privacy of his room and locked the door behind him.

He went to the standing wash basin between the two beds and moved it aside. A loose floor tile lay underneath, cracked in one corner. He knelt and pried it up, careful not to break it to pieces in the process. The hole beneath revealed his personal treasure trove. Among the items was a kitchen knife, several cigars, a silver comb, a pearl-encrusted brooch, and the silver-tipped pen he'd taken for himself from Bash's house. He reached in for the topmost object.

"Open, Wickwire."

The etchings lit up with liquid fire and the watch case yawned apart, revealing the image of the fallen sun in the sea of stars. Ink shifted his position until he faced northward. The harbor town came into view, black against the strange red glow in the distance.

"Come on," Ink said in a low voice. "Let's get this over with."

He soon heard the sound of pounding hooves. The mysterious horse and rider came into view, galloping towards him down the coastline. The dark cloak billowing around the slender figure made it difficult to spy anything specific in their features, but Ink could only assume it was the same woman who'd approached him the last time he'd looked into the watch. He also noted—with no small amount of relief—that he neither heard nor saw any evidence of chains. The horse also appeared to have full use of its eyes, unlike those the Spektors rode.

The rider pulled up at the lower edge of the image, spraying sand in every direction. Ink tried his best to hold the watch steady.

"What now, boy?" the woman said. *"Have you finally found your courage?"*

Ink felt his mouth go dry. He licked his lips and took a deep breath. "I was told . . . this watch would tell me the truth. And there's something I need to know. My mum and dad. Where are they?"

"Name your enemy," the figure answered.

Ink raised his chin, trying to keep his voice from shaking. "He said you would tell me. So answer. Where are they? Where's my mum and dad?"

He cursed himself as tears pricked at the corners of his eyes.

"You must name your enemy," the woman said again.

"Does that mean you don't know?" Ink replied, growing angry as a tear slipped down his cheek. He wiped it away. "All right. All right, if I do . . . give you a name . . . what happens then? How's it work?"

"You must discover that for yourself. I can tell you nothing more."

Ink shut his eyes, trying to calm his fear. There was nothing for it now. He wasn't able to look for his parents himself. The Colonists couldn't help. Seherene might take back her promise on a whim if it so pleased her. He needed assurances. He needed to know at least that they still lived, even if that information had to come from a pocket watch full of strange magic.

So who was his enemy? He had no love for Spindler, or the police, or for Mr. Mewes at Kinsington Orphanage, but they were more annoyances than enemies. It was certainly not Seherene. And he was fairly certain the Spektors would no longer openly attack him now that his granddad was watching. No. None of these. It was the person who had last made him fear for his life.

He opened his eyes, looked at the rider, and spoke with a strong, clear voice.

"Isaac Caradoc."

The rider regarded this for a few moments—smiling, he thought—then dismounted and drew a gold dagger from within the folds of her cloak. She knelt on one knee, thrust the knife into the sand, and began to carve a symbol into the ground. Whether it was an image or the words of some strange language, Ink couldn't tell. But as the knife passed through the black granules, traces of gold were left in its wake, glittering like stardust across the night sky.

The task completed, the rider stood and sheathed her dagger.

Ink glanced at the opposite side of the watch. The four rows of gold circles had turned into a series of rune-like shapes, each changing form to the rhythm of their own interval. The rider mounted her horse.

"*Well done,*" she said. "*Your journey to immortality has begun.*"

Without another word, she pulled the reins and spurred the horse back across the sand.

"Wait!" Ink cried. "What journey? You didn't answer my question!"

The horse ran on. The rider did not so much as turn her head. Ink clutched the watch with both hands as if he would break it in two.

"I don't give a toss about immortality! You're supposed to tell me! Where are they? *Where are they?*"

But his cries went unheard, and he could do nothing more than look on as she melted back into the shadows of the dark town. With a roar, he shut the watch and threw it hard against the wall, cursing the day he'd ever found the damned thing. Then he reeled and shut his eyes like a man wounded, wiping a fresh round of tears from his face.

Suddenly, his breath caught in his throat. What was this? He opened his eyes again, feeling his heart thump in his chest. It couldn't be. Slowly, and with no small amount of dread, he closed his eyes again. There it was, the symbol in the sand, glittering gold in the darkness behind his eyelids. A cold tinge of horror raced up his spine. He rushed back to the watch, snatched it up, and dropped it into the hole in the floor. Then he replaced the tile and moved the washstand back into place.

For a long time afterward, he sat on the edge of his bed and stared at the ground, too terrified to close his eyes again. He chewed his lip. He cursed under his breath. He clutched the bedpost until his knuckles turned white. After a while his gaze fell on his hat, still lying near the window where he'd left it the night before. He went over and picked it up, feeling the faded second-hand silk, the tattered ribbon, the torn lining. Falling apart. Like everything else. He glanced out the window.

The sun hung just above the tree line of Riverfall's eastern border, staring back at him like an unblinking eye. He looked down and found himself covered in the blood-red glow of the lowering light.

"Don't you dare," he said, raising his defiant gaze back to the sun. "Don't you dare judge me. Trust no one. People will let you down. These are the rules the world made. Not me. And this ain't no time to go breaking 'em." He returned his hat to his head, fitting it down with the smallest tilt over his left eye.

It was a fine thing to say out loud, full of his usual swagger and self-confidence. But the words his heart whispered to him were quite different, filling him with a deep and lasting dread.

What have you done?

THANKS FOR READING

If you enjoyed *The Wickwire Watch*, please leave a review to help spread the word. It is much appreciated.

To read the next book in *The Riverfall Chronicles*,
THE SPIDER KEY
visit www.jacquelynhagen.com/books.

To receive the latest news about *The Riverfall Chronicles*, view a full-color digital map of Eriaris, or sign up for our mailing list, visit www.jacquelynhagen.com.

ACKNOWLEDGMENTS

This book and its sequels have (thus far) been a thirteen-year labor of love, frustration, joy, and doubt. That the stories have survived to publication at all is nothing short of a miracle, and I can by no means take sole credit for any one part of the process. In any creative work there lies the collective influences of a person's entire life, the inspiration of countless sources, countless individuals. There is power and purpose in every interaction, even the ones that last only moments or prove to be challenging and difficult. Nothing, and no one, is wasted. If we have crossed paths at all on this side of the Veil, I am sincerely thankful for it.

I would now like to specifically thank those who have had a direct impact on the writing of this book, its many drafts and sequels, and the support of my spirit and sanity throughout it all.

To my parents, Gloria and Roger. Thank you for filling our house with stories and music, and for encouraging and/or humoring me in all the various schemes and adventures that have led me here.

To my sisters, Stephanie, Lindsey, and Amy. Thank you for venturing through the wardrobe with me, and for journeying even farther into the world I discovered beyond it. You helped to shape it into the extraordinary place it has become.

To my friends, David Clarke, Omar Durvesh, Maia Earl, Loreal Glenn, and Nathalie Rice. You helped me through one of the toughest and most demanding times of my life, from Lackland to Monterey, to San Angelo and beyond. Life may have sent us on to different paths since then, but I will always be grateful for the bond forged between us, and I will never forget it.

To my lovely beta readers, David Clarke, Courtney Durvesh, Omar Durvesh, Kristen Felger, Cassie Jones, David Alan Jones, Hailey Etzel, Heather Mohan, Donna Weaver, and Jack Wilde. Without your guidance and encouragement, the fire of creativity might well have been quashed when it was still just a flame.

To the wonderful Elizabeth Ward, Stuart Bache, and Luan Bittencourt. Thank you so much for all your hard work, expert guidance, and endless patience in bringing this book to real, pulsating life, and for helping me to make it the very best it could be.

To Gorge Romero, without whom these stories would no doubt still be languishing within the dark depths of my computer. Thank you for spurring them into the light and for cheering me on.

To Michael "Maz" DeMasi. Friend. Teacher. Story wizard. Colonist therapist. Keyholder and Defender. You are as instrumental to these stories as the characters themselves. You have talked me down from metaphorical ledges, slogged with me through the Swamps of Endless Revisions, and helped me to see things I didn't know were there—even in my own self. Your insight, heart, and enthusiasm for these books kept me going when I felt I couldn't take another step. You are my Samwise Gamgee on this struggle up the Mount Doom of writing. I cannot thank you enough.

And finally, to God Almighty. Heart of my own heart. Whatever befall.

WEATHER THE WIND

If they send me 'cross the deepest ocean
Send me 'cross the wildest sea
I won't be afraid, no I will not falter
Give me a sail and I will weather the wind
Give me a sail and I will weather the wind

If they send me down to the Devil's furnace
Send me down to shovel the coal
I won't be afraid, no I will not falter
Give me a fan and I will weather the fire
Give me a fan and I will weather the fire

Down, down, don't look down
Cut across the valley 'til you can't feel the ground
Back, back, don't look back
Let free the mule and throw away the tack
Let free the mule and throw away the tack

If they drag the sun down from the heavens
Drive a spike through the heart of the moon
I won't be afraid, no I will not falter
Give me a light and I will weather the dark
Give me a light and I will weather the dark

Oh I saw the grave of a righteous woman
Saw the bones of a virtuous man
And what can I do but hope to follow?
Show me the way and I will weather the road
Show me the way and I will weather the road

Down, down, don't look down
You can't be a king if you ain't got a crown
Back, back, don't look back
Raise up your voice and signal the attack
Raise up your voice and signal the attack

If I'm bound to see a hundred sorrows
Bound to bear a thousand woes
I won't be afraid, no I will not falter
Give me your love and I will weather the world
Give me your love and I will weather the world

Down, down, don't look down
Even if they break your heart to listen to the sound
Back, back, don't look back
Grind down the millstone 'til you hear it crack
Grind down the millstone 'til you hear it crack

Down, down, don't look down
Nobody wants to see their best intentions run aground
Back, back, don't look back
Shake off the dust and get up off the rack
Shake off the dust and get up off the rack
Shake off the dust and get up off the rack

ABOUT THE AUTHOR

Jacquelyn Hagen is the author of the epic fantasy series *The Riverfall Chronicles*. She currently resides wherever the U.S. Air Force needs her to be. In her free time, she devours stories in every form (usually while hanging out with her two big fluffy dogs), but has also been known to play in folk bands, raise chickens, and try to improve her bread-baking skills.

Visit her website at jacquelynhagen.com.

facebook.com/jacquelynhagenbooks
twitter.com/jacquelyn_hagen
instagram.com/jacquelyn_hagen_books

Printed in Great Britain
by Amazon

51956856R00249